Arabesques

Susan Shwartz was born on New Year's Eve, 1949, in Ohio in the American midwest. She became interested in fantasy and science fiction when she was seven years old, and a cousin gave her Edith Hamilton's *Mythology*; her father, who grew up on *Planet* stories, subsequently introduced her to the works of Robert Heinlein, Andre Norton, and Isaac Asimov's at about the time that Alan Shepard went up in his suborbital flight – and she has been hooked ever since.

She was educated in Massachusetts, at Mount Holyoke College. During that time she spent two summers on exchange, living in Trinity College, Oxford, in a programme sponsored by the University of Massachusetts. She studied Shakespeare, paleography and medieval romance. She went on to take a PhD at Harvard University, and was a specialist in Arthurian romance.

For three years she taught at Ithaca College, in upstate New York. Then, wanting a business career and to be closer to the New York publishing scene, she moved to New York City. After switching jobs too many times, she went to work at BEA Associates, an investment firm. She now works for Donaldson, Lufkin and Jenrette. She daily courts overwork with a heavy writing schedule, too. She has written a good deal of non-fiction for major US papers, and is also active on the circuit of fantasy and SF conventions.

Susan Shwartz has written a mass of short stories (one of which was a finalist for the Nebula Award), numerous articles and essays (including an essay on 'Women in Science Fiction' for the *New York Times Book Review* and an article on Jean Auel for *Vogue*), and several science fiction novels including *White Wing* with Sh............................ndall'.
Susan Shwartz....................... available in

Also available in Pan by Susan Shwartz
The *Heirs to Byzantium* trilogy

ARABESQUES

More Tales of the
Arabian Nights

an original anthology
edited by
Susan Shwartz

Pan Books
London, Sydney and Auckland

First published in tne USA 1988 by Avon Books
First published in Great Britain 1988 by
Pan Books Ltd, Cavaye Place, London SW10 9PG

9 8 7 6 5 4 3 2 1

ISBN 0 330 305069

Photoset by Parker Typesetting Service, Leicester
Printed and bound in Great Britain by
Richard Clay Ltd, Bungay, Suffolk

For
Nikolas Rimsky-Korsakov

Contents

Editor's Note

The Middle Ages liked its legends as neatly organized as they were exotic. Thus in the twelfth century a writer could, and did, categorize groups of myths into three principal Matters: the Matter of Britain, or of Arthur and his knights, described as worldly and pleasant; the Matter of Antiquity, or stories of Caesar and Alexander, known as wise; and the Matter of France, which – since this particular writer was a Frenchman – was considered to be *true*.

And it is in this same Matter of France that we encounter the cycle of stories that our medieval critic did not categorize – the Matter of Araby. It shows up in the Matter of France in the *Song of Roland*, where Charlemagne's paladins fall defending 'sweet France' not against Basques (as actually happened) but against Saracen tyrants, sorcerers and wizards; such works inspired their readers to cries of '*Deus lo vult!*' (God wills it!) and going on Crusade.

So for the Middle Ages, Araby referred to enemies in Iberia, North Africa, and in the Holy Land: an inexplicable culture against which the Crusaders took arms, but which seemed as seductive as it was fierce. Many of the Crusaders who returned from Jerusalem displayed unfamiliar and splendid fabrics and rugs, rare spices and fine swords, and told exotic stories of Saladin – or of men and creatures stranger still, tales which crept into the folklore of Europe and tinged it with brilliant colours and half-understood glimpses of a hitherto unknown world. Many of these tales were adapted from the collection known as *The Thousand and One Nights*, stories full of magic, ribaldry and adventure.

Originating in Indian, Persian and Arabian cultures, these tales often involve sorcerers, jinn, travellers and lovers (likely or unlikely couples). Many of them – usually watered down for children – are familiar to us: Sinbad the Sailor, Aladdin and his Lamp, Ali Baba and the Forty Thieves are the examples that spring to mind. Containing all of them, however, is their frame story, a literary device subsequently borrowed by Boccaccio in his *Decameron* and Geoffrey Chaucer in *The Canterbury Tales*. (He also borrowed the story of the flying horse for his 'Squire's Tale', but that's another story altogether.)

The frame story of *The Thousand and One Nights* is probably the most exotic, colourful and beloved part of the entire collection.

For readers who have escaped it in children's-book, symphonic or ballet form, here is the story in brief: King Shahryar has summoned his brother, King Shahzaman of Samarkand, to his court, only to learn when his brother arrives that he has slain his wife for adultery. Shahryar subsequently learns that *his* wife and his entire harem are equally unfaithful. Embittered and convinced that all women are faithless, he hits on an appalling scheme. Each night, he will marry a virgin. Each dawn, he will have her beheaded.

Since to hear is to obey, his faithful vizier has no choice but to present a new woman each night for his king to marry, then to kill. But the vizier himself has two daughters, one of whom, the wise and courageous Scheherezade, determines to put an end to this horrible custom. She insists that her father present her to the king as his next wife. Though her father is appalled, he agrees to do so. That night, as Scheherezade planned beforehand, her younger sister Dunyazade comes to her bridal chamber and asks for one last story – which Scheherezade tells with such skill that the King is enthralled, and such cunning that the sun rises before she has finished.

So he spares her life to let her finish the story – and so on for a thousand more nights (and the birth of a few sons), until finally Scheherezade is able to plead for mercy and persuade her husband to end his practice of killing his brides. Dunyazade marries his brother, the two men make their father-in-law a king, and everyone lives happily ever after.

This is, of course, pure fantasy. But please remember that Araby, as Europe came to know it in the Middle Ages and subsequently, was and is not so much an historically and anthropologically accurate representation of various cultures, but rather a splendid amalgam of people, creatures and places that never existed, except in storytellers' and readers' imaginations. It is the idea of Bactrian camels swaying through the Central Asian deserts, harness bells jingling to ward off demons, that lingers in the imagination, not whether or not these beasts have one hump or two (Bactrian camels have two).

So, shut your ears to the car horns outside. Pretend that you yourself are dressed in sendal, taffeta or brocade, and that you recline on huge cushions and rugs brighter than stained glass, and that you sip snow-cooled sherbet in a palace that can be found somewhere between Samarkand, China and the Hindu Kush, somewhere synonymous with 'long ago and far away'.

The people of the Middle Ages, who knew a good myth when they read it, loved these tales of Araby. So, I think, will you.

SUSAN SHWARTZ

Tales Told at Ramadan

Kashgar's marketplace was a battlefield for the senses. Scarlets, greens and turquoises clashed against one another. The sheen of silk and the deep pile of dusty rugs set off the painful brightness of polished brass and silver, and the more discreet glimmer of gold in an armlet or from the skin of the rare visitor from Ch'in. Rising above the warring splendours came the clamour of vows, curses, and assurances on the graves of several ancestors all at once that the metal was of honest weight, the steel brought all the way from Damascus, the jade carved in Khotan, or that that rascal of a merchant who bowed and oozed so hopefully inside his rickety stall was a dog of a thief.

Today, the bazaar was doubly frenzied as Kashgar prepared for Ramadan, the month-long fast that Muslims observed. Though travellers need not fast during their journey, many chose to break their journey east in Kashgar, praying by day, and by night, feasting, visiting and telling tales until a white thread might be distinguished from a black, and prayers started once again.

Peter of Wraysbury strode through the market, remembering how, on his first journey east, he had accompanied King Edward and observed Lent in the Holy Land. As a man dependent on the charity of a Muslim merchant for his food, he supposed that he would keep this fast too, heathenish though it was.

He stopped to watch the merchant, who had more courage, apparently, than his looks indicated. For the

1

customer to whom he swore by the beard of the Prophet that his weights were honest had the narrowed eyes, drooping moustaches and arrogant stride of one of the conquering Mongol race that had swept through Asia and out into Europe not long ago – perhaps half a century – but what was half a century to Kashgar? What should Kashgar care for terror that had wasted half a world? Its very location kept it necessary, and therefore safe: to the west were the towering Pamirs, to the east lay deserts swept by goblin storms.

Wraysbury leaned against a stall and stared about himself appreciatively. Mongol warrior; conquered Persian noble (his silks frayed, but his hooked nose in the air); a bronzed Egyptian sporting the single earring that distinguished him as a Hajj, one who had survived the pilgrimage to Mecca that all Muslims must make; even a few women striding free, as Mongol women did not fear to do; while others glided by, veiled and silent, towards the stalls of the jewel merchants: all crowded the bazaar at Kashgar, gateway between the mountains and the desert called the Anvil of Fire. They all had business, and freedom to transact it – all but him.

And by the wounds of Christ, thought Peter of Wraysbury, he was probably the only sober thing in that entire market; but wouldn't you just know that *he* was the spectacle that drew the glances that could be spared from wares, whores or picking pockets?

Silence fell as he slipped by, keenly aware that he no longer had his knight's spurs gleaming at his heels. He had sold them to buy food somewhere between Samarkand – now rising like the proverbial phoenix from the ruins that the Mongols had made of it – and the Pamirs. Though he wore a headcloth as much to protect himself from the ferocious sun as to cover the red hair that made the bazaar urchins class him with the beggars, dwarfs and jugglers as an enjoyable freak, he could not conceal his blue eyes, his height, or the noble carriage that was so at odds with his garments. His robes were drab and worn, but they were the best he might expect – no, they were the best he would

2

accept – from the merchant prince whose caravan had rescued him from an agonizing death by thirst in the desert.

Weeks ago, silver in his purse from signing on as a camel driver, he had left Kashgar for Ch'in to fulfil a vow he had made, a vow far stranger than any promise to free the Holy Sepulchre in Jerusalem. For he had heard rumours of a mysterious priest-king who ruled far to the east, a man whose aid the men of the West sought, and he had immediately vowed not to return to England with his king, but to journey further east to seek out Prester John. Thus he had passed like an open-mouthed child through the fabled cities of Persia – Baghdad and Samarkand, rebuilding now – and then climbed on to the roof of the world itself, where midday shone colder than a winter night in England, and finally to Kashgar, where a caravan master had allowed – allowed! and he a knight – him to sign on to serve the camels.

Accordingly, he set out across the desert, putting his trust in God and the truth of his mission, and disaster had struck.

No sooner had the camels snuffled and buried their noses in the gritty yellow sand than the inexplicable order came to swathe himself in heavy felt. Moments later they were engulfed, stifled and pummelled with driving sand and grit. The sky turned yellow, then black, and the winds howled with the viciousness that lent truth to the belief that such storms were brought by demons. And just when the shrieking died down, and the camels rose to their feet, their long legs straightening at the knees, and the men began to dig themselves out, bandits struck: one of the small bands could race from oasis to oasis while the caravans could only plod.

Used to ambushes, Peter of Wraysbury fought until a blow on the head felled him. The bandits, either because they thought he was dead or did not wish to be burdened even with a man whom they could sell, left him lying among the bodies of men and beasts. He had staggered up and, choosing the oldest and smelliest of the camels,

3

secured its headrope and started forward. It would be a terrible thing to lie and wait for death. He preferred to travel towards his goal as long as he could.

And that, he thought, was a case of heaven helping those who helped themselves, at least to some extent. Or, as the people in these parts (even the heretical Nestorians who called themselves Christians) might say, it was his kismet to be rescued by a caravan that approached Kashgar from the east.

At first he had thought the jingling of the bells on the beasts' harness to be the first sign of the madness that death by thirst brings. Then, hope had struck him even harder than thirst and fear. The men of the caravan had proved to be good Samaritans, whatever their actual race might be. They had brought him back to Kashgar and to their master, a merchant prince who only journeyed now in company with the greatest and richest of caravans. Peter might have thrown himself on his mercy. Instead, he had asked for time, and a messenger who might be sent in search of men of the West, to beg them to ransom a Christian knight.

He hoped that somewhere the messenger would find such men. He had no desire to be sold as a slave, though he supposed that he was not the first Christian, or even the first knight, to face that fate in the bazaar here.

The merchant prince had smiled and granted him both the messenger and a space of a thousand days to obtain a ransom or, he said, from this Ramadan to Ramadan three years hence. Those were better terms than the year and a day with which he was familiar. So he had given his parole and was free – for now – to wander the bazaar at Kashgar. No one expected that he might try to flee. There was nowhere that a man alone could flee to.

Day after day he paced the bazaar like a caged leopard. Even the riot of colour and sound had begun to bore him. He wondered if he would go mad before the messenger returned.

'Hail, friend!'

The call came in Latin. Peter of Wraysbury whirled

4

round to face three men of different ages but similar appearance. All were bearded, dressed in clothes that might have been good once but were now worn with travel and sitting in bazaars, and all had wise, deep eyes. Though none of the men looked anything like the others, a kinship marked them: something in the deep wisdom in the eyes, the set of the mouths, and the mobile, graceful hands. They bore no arms, and thus were not nobles; they had hailed him as 'friend' and wore no priests' robes, so they must not be mullahs. What were they? The scattering of coins, bracelets and the occasional ingot lying on a cloth before them gave him a clue: they were storytellers.

Peter of Wraysbury drew near to them, ignoring the routine mutters that his appearance provoked.

'Even that devil of an infidel comes to hear *these* story-tellers,' marvelled a young man in the harness of a soldier before he threw a silver ring on to the cloth before them.

'Nay, most noble warrior,' said the eldest of the three. 'The stranger does not come to hear stories. The stranger is *himself* a story, which he could tell here with great profit, if he chose. Is that not so, friend?'

Dark eyes turned to Peter again, and he realized that he was on display. He bowed and gestured respect at the storytellers, knowing that in these lands, such men had honour.

'Alas, my masters,' he said in Arabic, which he no longer spoke as vilely as he must, in all politeness, claim, 'I am halt of speech in your most noble tongue. And should the younger and lesser dare to speak before such accomplished masters of the taletellers' art?'

Approval ran murmuring round the circle, then surprise as the merchant prince and master of many caravans who held Peter's parole strode towards the storytellers. He stopped beside Peter, clapped him on the shoulder, then saluted the storytellers.

'Ramadan is the month for fasts and prayers,' he began. 'But it is also the month for feasts and for visits. I beg these noble tellers of tales to guest with me on this night and on any other night as they please, and tell their tales to me and to you, my neighbours. After the call to prayers, my masters, I should be honoured if you will come to my house to break your fast.'

As the storytellers murmured acceptance, and the crowd just murmured, the merchant invited Peter of Wraysbury to join the feast too. Coming from a man of a different faith, a man whose property he might be, this was a princely offer.

'I hear and obey,' he said, borrowing from the high-flown Arabic courtesies he had found so hard to learn.

As the call to prayer wailed out, he stood silently while all in the bazaar turned towards the East, where Mecca lay, and bowed themselves devoutly to the dust. Once they had risen, and had re-rolled their prayer rugs, he walked with them – and well behind the guests of honour – to the merchant's shadowy, thick-walled house. The rooms were cool, and the delicious scents of lamb rich with cardamom, rice golden with saffron, and sweet fruits tantalized the guests until, finally, the sun went down.

Slaves lit finely wrought bronze lamps, each pierced with a thousand holes that allowed light and shadow to dance together on whitewashed walls while the guests drank sherbet, washed their hands in scented water, then lay back, sated for the moment. Now they directed their expectant gazes not towards the kitchens but to the three storytellers who reclined near their host. The eldest of them sipped his sherbet, then smiled and set it aside. Raising one hand for attention, he sat erect and began to speak.

LARRY NIVEN

The Tale of the Jinni and the Sisters

'Tell me a story,' said Scheherezade.

In the dark of the tent she could see the glint of his open eyes, but the king didn't stir. She would have felt that. Shahryar said, 'You are much better at that than I.'

Four years they'd been married; seven years she had been his mate. Three boys and a girl had been left to their nurses during this short journey to his brother's palace. She was coming to believe that the bad times were over. But Shahryar was still a dangerous man, and he'd been wire-tight these past two days. Something had frightened him. Something he couldn't talk about.

Sometimes the danger of him excited her. Not tonight. She moved against him anyway and said, 'What other diversion have we, awake in the night, with all of our entertainers left behind?'

He declined the hint. 'Hah. This travelling-bed and the lumpy ground beneath—'

'—Are the reason we cannot sleep. Tomorrow night will bring us rooms in King Shahzaman's palace.'

'Yes. Well, we left the scribes too.'

'Then tell me a story you will not want studied by the scholars.'

He was quiet for a time. Did he sleep? But something burned in his mind. He'd tried to speak, and then turned away, a dozen times in these two days of travel.

He said, 'We never speak of the time before we met.'

7

'No. My father knows the tale. He warned me of your ... trouble.'

'The vizier is a good man ... Sometimes I think I might forgive myself for the women, and then forget. But who can forget a tale without an ending? You know so many tales, but what do you really know of the jinn?'

'Whimsical. Powerful. Prone to extravagance. Dangerous, the ones who fought the Prophet's law. Why?'

'Ten years ago, my brother Shahzaman told me how he had caught his wife in adultery with a slave cook. He told me he'd seen my own wife betray me. I thought of killing him, but I followed him instead, and watched, and still couldn't believe. Then we swore that we would depart and never return until we knew that someone, somewhere, had suffered a greater misfortune. The vizier must have told you this much.'

'Yes.'

'And we went away from our palace with no gear and no retainers. Do you know how long we travelled?'

'Father didn't tell me that.'

'He never knew. Two hours.'

She laughed before she could stop herself.

'We travelled fast. Sometimes we ran to burn off our rage and sorrow. We were seven or eight leagues from my palace and into a meadow, with no dwellings in sight, and exactly one tree. Then a black whirlwind appeared and began to draw into itself. No monkey could have climbed faster than I, yet Shahzaman beat me into the tree.'

'Dare I laugh?'

'It was a long time ago.' But his muscles were rigid and his arms were too tight around her. 'We were hidden before the jinni became solid. That tree was the only shade anywhere. The jinni set a crystal coffer down in the shade. There was a woman in it.'

'Holes in the casket?' An experienced storyteller would have mentioned those.

'Holes? No, it was sealed like a treasure chest, with seven separate locks, but I could see her through the sides. The jinni got it open and she came out.'

8

'What was she like?'

'Not a girl. Twenty-two or -three years old, and ... lovely. Foreign. Yellow like the moon near moonset. Straight black hair. Something about her eyes. I'd need a scribe's help to describe her.'

'You're doing well.'

'The jinni went in unto her. I ... wondered what I would see of foreign practices, but she only submitted. Then the jinni slept. We were going to be there a long time. I tried to shift my weight, and the woman looked up and saw us. She made us come down.'

'How?'

'She swore she would wake the afrit. We came down. She led us away from the tree, and ordered us to go in unto her.' Shahryar laughed; he made himself laugh, and Scheherezade dared not. 'We are kings, Shahzaman and I. When we desired a woman, we brought her to our beds and we took her. We are not *summoned*. We had a hard time of it—' He laughed again, painfully. 'A soft time of it. We'd moved far from the tree, there was no shade, and we were desperately afraid of making noise. But Shahzaman succeeded in giving her what she willed, and watching them excited me ... Should I be telling it the other way around?'

'Was she good?'

'She wrung us dry. We had trouble walking away ... running when we could. But why not? She claimed five hundred and seventy lovers taken under the nose of the afrit!'

'Incredible.' How could he not feel her tension?

'A disgraceful episode. It put the seal on my opinion of women. If even a jinni's precautions weren't enough to keep her for himself ...'

Scheherezade's mind was racing. She had not thought so fast in many years; and what she chose to say was nothing.

'I was a long time losing that hatred. The Qur'an warns against women; I cannot blame myself too much. But sometimes I wonder. She told us that the jinni had snatched her on her wedding night, while she was still a virgin. He keeps her beneath the sea, where no man can reach. How can he have been careless five hundred and seventy times?'

'Did you ask her age? She may have been older than she looked, by the magic of her jinni lover.'

'You're clever. I never thought of that.'

'Or perhaps the jinni set down near a caravan one night.'

Shahryar laughed long and loud. After a time he said, 'Tomorrow your sister will give us a better bed.'

'Tonight you must sleep in this,' she said. And presently he did; but the night was already turning grey.

Four years ago Shahzaman had returned to live in his brother's kingdom in the Banu Sasan. He had married Scheherezade's sister, Dunyazad. Now they took their turns on the throne. But Shahzaman had ruled Samarkand. Now the old vizier ruled there – Scheherezade's and Dunyazad's father but every three years or so Shahzaman returned to see how the kingdom progressed.

Shahzaman had been gone for nearly a month.

Dunyazad had been told of their coming. She arrived with a retinue almost before they had broken camp. She seemed more reserved than was her wont. Her manner was overly formal. Cosmetics failed to hide dark shadows beneath her eyes.

By noon they had reached the palace. Dunyazad handled practical matters well, showing her sister and brother-in-law to a suite of rooms, introducing servants to add to their own sparse retinue. There was fruit and spiced meat, a pitcher of sherbet, water for washing, and enough bedding to hold a small party.

When the servants were gone, Shahryar told his wife, 'We must go out tonight.'

'Yes, my lord,' said Scheherezade. 'Where? Why?'

'I did not know how much to tell you.'

'You have told me only that it was time to visit your

brother's house, to see that all is in order. Well, all seems in order.'

'But all is not. An accusation has been made. I must see for myself. I want you with me.'

An accusation. If she had been standing she would have fallen, for the blood draining from her head. 'I hear and obey.'

'Then sleep now.'

Dunyazad's dinner conversation was brittle-bright chatter interspersed with silences. Scheherezade and Shahryar retired early, pleading sleeplessness on the trip. And softly dressed themselves, and departed on bare feet.

'We need to enter the harem garden,' Shahryar told her. 'Can you lead me in?'

'Not all harems are alike. I can enter. You would be killed, and I might be held as a harem concubine, if we were discovered. Your rank would not save you.'

'I know that, and it is just, but we must do this.' Shahryar's scimitar was in his hand. 'If I must kill a eunuch or two . . . well.'

Scheherezade led.

The entrance was guarded by two eunuchs. Scheherezade engaged them, asking questions about the doings of the harem, until Shahryar had crept past them. Then she alleged a desire to see inside.

She found a wide corridor with a fountain in the middle. The splashing water would cover minor noises. Someone may have seen them around a corner, and recognized the king, and decided not to meddle in politics; or not. Beyond the large, ornate fountain were wide doors leading to a darkened garden, guarded by a pair of armed eunuchs. To left and right were narrower corridors which must lead into the main body of the harem.

She stood pensively beside the fountain. Shahryar was crouched below its rim. She asked, 'Must we enter?'

Shahryar mulled it. 'Perhaps not, but we must see. Do you hear footsteps?'

'Left, the corridor.'

11

He sprinted. She strolled the long way around the fountain, to distract the guards. But the guards were watching the garden.

Shahryar had snuffed the torch. From the dark they watched Dunyazad pass through the doors. The guards' eyes were on her.

Shahryar had found a window.

'I never wanted to spy on my sister,' Scheherezade whispered. 'Must we do this?'

The garden was small. Dunyazad was in plain sight, walking as if she slept. Scheherezade noticed three low bushes; she jumped when one of them moved. A small sheep, or rather a lamb, got creakily to its feet and came to investigate the faces at the window. Scheherezade fondled its ears and peeked around it.

Dunyazad stopped beneath a wide tree and called softly. 'Sa'ad al-Din Saood.'

A man dropped from the tree. He was big, muscular, black in the moonlight. He landed easily, softly, and took Dunyazad in his arms.

Scheherezade continued to look. The interloper was seated on the grass; Dunyazad was in his lap; they were locked in sexual congress. The sounds she made seemed wrung from her. The man made no sound at all, until Scheherezade heard him chuckle, once. His teeth gleamed, white and regular.

Shahryar turned away. He slid slowly down the wall until he huddled at its base. He wrapped his face in his arms and sobbed.

A quick glance down the hall: the guards were facing away, standing rigidly with their scimitars before them. Their faces were immobile, but sweat set them gleaming. They could hardly avoid hearing.

Dunyazad and the interloper separated. The man chuckled again. They talked; Dunyazad seemed to be pleading. Then the man swarmed up the tree, very quickly and silently. Dunyazad sat huddled for a time. Then she stood, adjusted her clothing, and walked back inside.

'We must be out of here,' Scheherezade whispered.

Shahryar nodded. He stood slowly. She had been afraid he would not move at all.

He reached the fountain in a silent sprint, and crawled backwards behind its cover. Perhaps that was unneeded. The guards were looking out at the garden, now that Dunyazad couldn't see them, and they spoke in furious whispers. This must be agony for them, Scheherezade thought. They knew too much. How could their tale end but with a headsman's axe?

Shahryar sat limp on the pillows. His face was ashen. 'It's like a recurring nightmare. How could this happen to us again? Has Allah decreed this as punishment for me and Shahzaman? Because once we behaved like rabid hyenas after our wives betrayed us—'

'What will you do?'

'I will not kill Dunyazad. I will not kill a woman ever again. Enough is enough!' He looked at her at last. 'A woman came to me, one of your sister's harem retinue. She got past the guards somehow, came to me in the roof garden. She said that Dunyazad was betraying my brother. I should have been enraged. I wasn't. I was scared.'

Scheherezade only nodded.

'I *knew* I should kill the old woman. Lying or not, her mouth must be shut. You agree?'

"I—'

'But I've killed too many women! So I put her in a cell and we set out for Shahzaman's palace. But Shahzaman would kill Dunyazad, I think. And the children, because they might not be legitimate. How *could* she? She must *know* what a risk she takes.'

Scheherezade said, 'Allah is not your enemy.'

'Do I have any enemy besides my own fate?'

'I think so.' For her life, Scheherezade had learned how to be tactful; but this was not a time for tact. 'You must have been thinking of betrayal last night, when you told me the tale of the jinni and the crystal casket. Well, the woman was a jinna too.'

13

He stared at her. 'How can you know that?'

'There were no holes in the casket. A woman would have suffocated. And, really my lord! Five hundred and seventy lovers? And jinni fly, don't they? Yours must have seen you and Shahzaman from leagues away, yet he came straight to you.'

'May Allah take my soul. Now.'

'Not yet, my lord. We have work before us.'

'But this is terrible! I've killed more than fifty women!'

'Far more. I can count, my lord. Three years, one each night—'

'No! I tried to live without a woman. I could not. Your father can count them, for he procured them for me. Each night I took a woman's virginity, and each morning I slew her. But not one each night!

'The first half dozen, it felt like vengeance on all the breed of women. After the sixth I would have stopped. But she was not a virgin, and the tenth and eleventh weren't either, and – I was mad, of course.'

'You were made mad.'

'Scheherezade, I took my revenge on women for three years, for the wrong our wives did to us and the wrong that woman did to her jinni husband despite all of his extravagant precautions. But that was a *lie*, and she wasn't even a woman! – You *knew*?'

'It was obvious. I knew you'd suffer if I told you, but it's gone beyond that. *Now* what?'

For Shahryar had gone rigid. He said, 'I *thought* I knew those grotesque syllables. My wife's lover called out his name when . . . when. "Sa'ad al-Din Saood." It's him. The same jinni. Not a man. Again.'

'It seems that a pair of jinn have chosen our family as exceptionally entertaining playthings. See how it fits. Shahzaman discovered his wife in adultery and slew both. A pair of jinn saw. They wondered if you would do the same. One seduced your wife, which I grant must have been easy enough; the orgies sounded – well, practised. Afterwards they heard you and Shahzaman

14

swear your oath. Everybody likes a good story, my heart. Everyone wants to improve it a little.'

'But *why is Dunyazad—*'

'We'll have to ask.'

'He threatened me,' she said.

Scheherezade wondered what Shahryar would say now. *You chose dishonour over death?* But her husband only sipped his thick, sweet coffee.

'I was in my garden the evening after Shahzaman departed. I heard a laugh from all around me. A whirlwind snatched me into the air, flew after the caravan, circled high over my husband's tent! Then came to earth leagues ahead of the encampment. I was rigid with fear. I kept thinking, *What would my sister do?*'

'Scream.'

'I screamed, I begged, I pissed myself, I vomited into the wind. When I reached the ground I ran. The whirlwind became a man twenty feet tall. He ambled alongside me with a big crystal casket under his arm, until I collapsed with black spots before my eyes. then he set the casket down, and unlocked it, and a woman came out.'

'By Allah, it really is him, and I am not mad!' Shahryar exclaimed. 'Was she slant-eyed, with yellow—'

'She was *me*! Do you know how many mirrors there are in this palace? I've been avoiding them ever since, but I can't avoid *him*. He has my image, my *self*!'

'I think I see,' said Scheherezade. 'Calm down, Dunyazad. Have some coffee. Try to think of it as a tale.'

'They took their pleasure in every position Shahzaman and I have ever tried, and one that I don't think any human shapes could take. Nauseating. They didn't stop till morning. The woman grinned at me and said that they would . . . perform, she said. Perform in my harem, and then in the palace itself, and then in the public square, until all the land knew that Dunyazad is a whore. Or the, the male might take his pleasure with me for one night.'

'He lied, of course,' Scheherezade said.

'Of course he lied. Every night for eight nights now. I—' She stopped. Suddenly her fingernails were digging runnels down her cheeks. Scheherezade quickly snatched her hands away, and held them.

'Why do they do this?' Shahryar wondered. 'My love, in all the tales about jinn, have they ever got a woman with child?'

She thought. 'No. Never.'

'Good.' He might be thinking that at least the succession was safe. 'It's not for that, then. But *why*?'

'Power. Dunyazad, my sister, how does it feel?'

Dunyazad looked at the king.

'No secrets now!' Scheherezade snapped. 'We need to know everything, to fight this thing—'

'We can't fight jinn!'

'The fisherman did. So. How does it feel?'

'He makes me— He makes my body—' She couldn't go on.

'Better than a human lover?'

She nodded.

'He makes your body betray you. My husband, he drove you and your brother to a madness never seen before. Do you remember the tales of Caliph Haroun al-Rashid? The woman in the trunk?'

'Yes. The caliph found a man who had strangled his wife, then chopped her to pieces. She was innocent, but he believed the words of a malicious slave he had never seen before. The caliph freed the man, and found him a wife from among his own courtiers! That bothered me, Scheherezade. I would not have done that. And he freed the slave, and two women who tried to murder their sister and killed her betrothed—'

'He did that to be admired for his mercy, to *feel* his power of life and death. So it is with the jinni. He feels his power over all of us. Even women play games of power in their harems.'

'What can we do?'

'We must learn as much as we can. Dunyazad, what do the sheep have to do with the jinni?'

'What? Nothing. They're Persian lambs. A trader brought them as a gift. Four of them. One disappeared the night before last. The jinni said he ate it. Hooves and wool and bones and all.'

'He's getting bored,' Scheherezade said. 'He gave you one more thing you'll have to lie about. We'll have to do something soon.'

Dunyazad poured more coffee. Her hands shook but nothing spilled. 'Magic rings, lamps, bottles. Sister, have you ever seen one? Are you carrying one?'

'Not I. But jinn can be made drunk, and slain while drunk. Can you procure wine?'

'Wine!' Dunyazad laughed. 'No, there's no wine in this palace. Once Shahzaman allowed wine to be bought for foreign visitors. Once in four years, and after the sheik departed we poured the rest of it out. Sister, it's hopeless!'

'It's not. The afrits don't know that *I* know what they are. Perhaps we can tell them a tale.'

'*What?*'

'Tell them a story. What else have I to fight with? Dunyazad, you must show me through every part of the harem. My husband, you may not come. We shall return in a few hours.'

The harem was small by the standards of the day. Shahzaman's peers might have sneered if they had known how empty it was.

They met a dozen servants, women and eunuchs, including a lean eunuch doctor named Saburin. There were two concubines, virgins, kept ready for visitors. 'Shahzaman had a bad time of it,' Dunyazad said. 'He still doesn't trust any woman except me and possibly you. It means I must do all the supervising myself.'

'Shahryar's the same way.'

She found a large room, windowless, with only one doorway, and a curtain to cover it. There were benches and tables and a small bed. Scheherezade nodded. 'What is it used for?'

'If one of the women becomes ill, we put her here. The

17

night air can be blocked off. One can fill it with poppy fumes or whatever smokes Saburin calls for. It's not near the other quarters, in case she has something contagious.'

'Good! Perfect. Now, does the afrit spend all of his time in the tree?'

'In daylight I see no sign of him, and the guards saw nothing when the lamb disappeared. I must come to him after dark.'

'How soon after dark? Always at the same time?'

Dunyazad sighed. 'I wait until I feel safe. But I've been careless, my sister. It isn't only his threats. It's . . . I'm coming to like it.'

'Ah.'

'He knows me inside and out! How can I—'

'Concentrate, sister. He doesn't know when you will come? Have you ever come as early as sunset?'

'No, never that early. Only after pitch dark. These last two days I came early, to get it *over* with!'

'Or as late as morning?'

'No. Wait. The second night I couldn't make myself move. I came very late. We were still together when I saw that I could tell the colours in my robe. I ran.'

'Well, we must take a risk. Now, quickly, get me workmen and paint and a brazier and a great pot of wax, and wood to make a door! He's never been in the harem itself?'

'No, never.'

'I need the bedclothes from your chamber. Unwashed, I hope. Curtains hung *here* and *here*. And I need something else, but I'll see to that myself.'

'I've thought of something else.'

Scheherezade listened, then nodded. 'You have a gift. See to it that they don't use too much perfume or too little poppy smoke!'

She found her husband pacing their quarters. He smelled of exertion. 'I practised swordplay with one of the men who instruct Shahzaman's sons. He had children by three of his concubines, you know, before the curse fell on us.

But time passed and you were still gone—'

'Yes. I have a plan.' She talked rapidly.

He listened, and mulled it after she had finished, and presently said, 'There are two jinn. You plan to attack *two* jinn, without me?'

'You can't enter a king's harem, my lord.'

'And if everything goes exactly right, you might trap *one*?'

'We'll ransom him. The female will have to agree. All we want is to be left alone, after all.'

'They're known liars, Scheherezade!'

'Then you think of something!'

It was as if he held his rage wriggling in both fists. 'Allah has not made me clever enough!'

'Then help! I need a seal of Solomon, with certain inscriptions. I've drawn a picture. I hope I remembered it right. Find a jeweller. Find the best! Have it for me by sunset.'

'You don't understand money. I'll send servants to hire *six* jewellers. We'll use the best seal.'

'I will be very glad when this is over.'

The garden wasn't large either, but it was a wonderful place, full of colour and fragrances, the colours dimming with the dusk. Sounds of traffic came over the high wall: the last merchants going home. Eunuchs moved about lighting torches, while Dunyazad showed her sister around.

The pair of lambs were curious and friendly. 'In Persia they use the wool from the lambs, not the sheep. Hazad treats them like pets.' She named them. She was trying to seem bright and cheerful, but her voice was brittle.

She seemed to be avoiding the big tree in the centre.

Scheherezade led her to it nonetheless. It was huge and strong; it dominated the enclosure. When Scheherezade peered up into it she saw only textured darkness.

And when she turned to her sister, Dunyazad was gaping, her hands at her throat. She wasn't breathing.

'Sister?'

Dunyazad crumpled gracefully.

19

'Guards! Help!'

The two eunuchs came running. There was foam at the corners of Dunyazad's mouth, and her eyes were rolled up nearly out of sight. Scheherezade wrung her hands. 'Is there a place for the sick? Well inside, away from the night air?'

'Yes, O Queen.'

'Take her there. Then get me cold perfumed water and the doctor.' Doctor Saburin was already running towards them. 'Maybe she only needs rest. Oh, she's looked so tired lately!'

She kept Saburin until midnight, then repeated her final instructions and sent him to his bed.

The shape under the bedclothes was quite covered up, with only black hair showing. The covers moved shallowly and rapidly; the occupant was panting.

Scheherezade sipped a sugar sherbet. Presently she set the empty goblet down and went to sit on the bed. Her hand beneath the blanket felt the heat of neck and shoulder. She said, 'I haven't been so frightened in four years.'

There was only the panting, and a twitch of the quilts.

'Dunyazad is seen to be taken ill. She is carried inside. Guards describe the room. One who finds the room will find Scheherezade nursing the poor creature. I wish you could understand. Never tell a story when you can show it!'

The curtains moved back. A eunuch guard stood in the doorway. She'd seen him before: a pudgy fellow, not too bright. Scheherezade snapped, 'What do you want?'

The guard grinned. Leered. 'Both of you.'

''What? Oh, Allah preserve me!' He was changing shape.

He was taller, leaner. His clothing distorted itself to fit. His skin darkened, his lips and nose filled out. 'Your sister is mine already,' he said. 'I want you too.'

Scheherezade's knife was in her fist, the point at her heart. 'You may have me dead.'

20

'You know what I am?'

'A jinni. Of course. Did you cause my sister's sickness?'

'We'll let her rest.' He brushed past her. 'We'll move her from the bed and—'

'*Leave her alone!*'

'You do not give me orders, Queen Scheherezade. Let me tell you what will happen if you use that knife. First, your corpse will disappear into the desert. But none will know that, because you will be seen to leave this room. Then you will be seen to do dreadful things.'

'Nonsense.'

The jinni was still changing. Now it was like looking into a mirror, even to the clothing. 'You slight the jinn if you doubt me,' said Scheherezade's voice. 'Your husband will find his wife taking her pleasure with some slave in the market at high noon.'

'No slave would dare.'

'The slave would be my companion.'

It was one of the skills of the storyteller: Scheherezade's face showed withering contempt. 'You're really not very convincing. You'd never fool anyone. Did you cozen my poor sister with this tale?'

'I can keep my threats, but let us have done with threats.' Scheherezade moved close; she put her hands on Scheherezade's arms. Scheherezade screamed at once, and Scheherezade released her with a frown of distaste. 'Don't be foolish. I've put them all to sleep.' But she glanced down and saw blood on the tip of Scheherezade's knife.

Scheherezade had known the risk.

'I can be of any shape you like,' the jinni said. 'Man, woman, old or young, human or slightly different or wildly different. Only name your desire.'

'To see you gone. Companion? The jinn don't have companions. How could even you tolerate the company of a jinni?' Her arms were getting tired; she still held the knife poised above her heart.

'You are a highly opinionated fool.' The woman considered. 'Very well. Wait here.'

The jinni had been gone for more than a minute before

Scheherezade gave vent to a shuddering sigh. And drew breath as if there were no air anywhere. And hiccoughed painfully when the curtain was thrown back.

Two Scheherezades entered, identical in every respect. 'Show, don't tell. Isn't that what you were saying, story-teller? So, this is what the whole city will see tomorrow unless you grant my will,' one said. 'But you shall be first.'

That one changed. It become the man she had seen with Dunyazad; and then it was Shahryar. Shahryar and the Scheherezade-shape moved to each other. Their hands moved beneath each other's clothing, then clothing began to fall away. Scheherezade watched as if mesmerized. The blade sagged in her hands.

Robes and undergarments and slippers faded into air as they fell away. Both jinni seemed to have forgotten her until, just once, the woman turned to smile at her. 'We take turns,' she said. 'Oh!' as the man entered her.

The sounds were those of Scheherezade's wedding night. Had they *watched*? She covered her eyes; she turned her back; she staggered from the room, retching. She heard a chuckle behind her. They need hardly fear that she would call guards to see *this*!

Now she moved in frantic haste. The new door was wide open, flat against the wall, behind a second curtain. She'd counted on help for the heavy door; she could see guards sprawled everywhere, snoring. But Dunyazad came running down the hall, struck the door and wrestled it like an enemy.

It slammed shut. The seal of Solomon was painted across it in bright scarlet. A third curtain concealed the pot of wax on its brazier. Dunyazad picked it up in both arms. She poured wax down each side of the door, while Scheherezade stamped the best of four seals (two jewellers had been late) along the congealing wax. The sounds from inside had stopped.

They both lifted the pot and poured along the top of the door, knelt and poured along the bottom. Scheherezade stamped carefully, making each mark perfect. Without turning she asked, 'Are you all right?'

'When they don't come through that door, then I'm all right! Here, I've got the nails—'

A voice spoke through the door. 'Open this door at once, or suffer the agonies of the damned!'

Scheherezade ignored that. The door shuddered, and some large animal squealed in pain. Another thump, another incredulous yelp. Her belly unfolded like a tight fist relaxing.

'They can't touch the door. It burns them,' Dunyazad realized. 'It worked. I can't believe it worked!'

'Why not? It's just a big bottle like the one the fisherman found. Putting Arrow in the bed was brilliant. I was going to just cover up some pillows. He didn't smell at all—'

'We washed him half to death.'

'He panted like you were really sick, and he kicked just enough.'

'Oh, I wish I could get him out of there.'

'The poppy will kill him, sister. Two jinn and a dead lamb in there for ever.'

'She's still sleeping,' Scheherezade told her husband. 'I won't disturb her. She earned it.'

'So did you, my warrior.'

'I can't sleep. I'm still shaking.'

'The harem doctor might have something.'

Scheherezade seemed not to hear. 'We've warned everybody. We've posted warnings on the door. Now they're building another wall outside it. Brick. The seal on each brick. Better not forget to brick the roof up too. Oh, Allah, what can we tell Shahzaman?'

'I've thought about that.' Shahryar sampled a sweet-meat, at leisure. 'My brother is a bit in awe of you. We'll tell him part of the truth. You tricked a pair of jinn in there and walled them up. You had your sister's help, but you never told her any more than what to do. The work-men won't know any different. I'll talk to the garden eunuchs. By the time Shahzaman gets home, you'll have some tale to tell him. Something to sear the hair off his ears.'

'I cherish your faith in me, my love. So it's not over yet, is it?'

'It will never be over. Shahzaman will build a new harem, now that there have been Jinn in it, but we can't keep everyone away forever. Suppose those *things* make promises through the door? One day they'll get loose, whatever we do ...'

'It may not happen until we're all dead.' Scheherezade was beginning to relax, finally. 'A pity I can't ever tell the tale.'

'Living through it was something Allah might have spared us. All of us. All these ten years.'

'Some stories are like that.'

'I wouldn't have minded hearing it some time,' the king said. 'As something that happened to some half-forgotten people, long ago, far away.'

GENE WOLFE

The Tale of the
Rose and the Nightingale
(And what came of it)

'*Tum, tum, tump!*' sang the new storyteller's drum.
'*TUMPTY, tum, tum, tup!*'

And Ali ben Hassan, the beggar boy, who sometimes
claimed his true name was Ali Baksheesh, the boy Ali
who was – it was sometimes reported – more thief than
beggar, turned to look. The new recounter of old tales was
young and handsome, his beard as brown as a chestnut;
there was a pistol of Fez (which is where they make the
best ones) in his sash and a smile on his lips.

Ali ceased to pester a camel driver and dashed past the
potter's stall to squat beside the storyteller and extend
cupped hands. 'Baksheesh!' Ali whined. 'Most noble lord,
sultan of story! Ailaho A'alam! I have nothing – nothing!'

'What!' exclaimed the storyteller, continuing to tap his
little drum with his fingers. 'You say you have nothing,
but first beg the indulgence of Allah for telling lies? You
won't get fat like that.'

'But, prince of parable, I desire to see those gardens of
lasting delight which Allah – the Creator! the Ever Beneficent! – reserves for the faithful. How am I to do so if I
tell lies?'

'By lying to Allah, I suppose.'

'Master of mystery!' protested Ali. 'Master of history!
Far be it from you to say such a thing. I did not hear it.'

25

'Nor did I hear your importunate demand for baksheesh,' the storyteller replied calmly, still tapping his drum.

'Do not all good Muslims give alms?' Ali raised his voice. 'Ailaho A'alam! I have nothing!'

'It is truly written that none shall starve,' replied the storyteller. 'Tell me what it is you have, and possibly I may give you something – though it will not be money.'

'I have three things,' Ali answered eagerly. 'Hearken, o rajah of romance, and I shall enumerate them – no, four! By the Beard! Four! For I have this clout, which conceals my private parts—'

'Which may remain so.'

'My turban, my lice, and you! Is it not written that food meet to each shall be appointed to him? You—'

'No,' interrupted the storyteller. 'It is not.'

'—have surely been appointed by the Most Compassionate to feed me. Are you a scholar? And so young?'

'I had a good master,' the storyteller said. 'Mullah Ibrahim the Wise, that holy man.'

'To teach you to tell stories in the bazaar? What are you going to give me?'

'A story, of course. I've one to give, and you've ears in which to receive it. And perhaps if I tell you a story, others will come to listen as well.'

The Tale of the Rose and the Nightingale

Long, long ago (so the storyteller began) there bloomed in the pasha's garden a lovely white rose, the most beautiful flower ever seen. Her waist was a date palm in the wind, her breasts twin white doves, her lips the saddle of a milk-white dromedary without flaw, her face the moon; the perfume of her limbs filled the whole garden, and her flesh shone like silver.

Ali nodded, knowing that in a story a flower might readily be a woman.

A little brown nightingale wandered into the garden (so the storyteller continued) in search of a mate. He beheld the white rose and fell hopelessly in love with her. He began to build a palace for her in the mulberry tree, and each night he serenaded her from its lowest limb, songs filled with passion and parting, songs sorrowful, and songs that wept with so much joy that the stars bent to listen. '*I love you – you – you!*' he sang. '*Only you! Oh, be my bride!*'

And the rose nodded on her stem, and smiled, and at last sent a message by a moth: '*Come closer, O my dearest love,*' it ran. '*But come not too near.*'

The little nightingale was mad with delight. So beat his heart in his tiny bosom that it seemed it must soon burst. She loves me! he thought; and he sang, '*You love me! You love me! You love me!*' Fools may believe it was but the soft wind that caressed the garden, but the nightingale knew better, and so do I. The rose nodded on her stem, and he fluttered for joy.

A stranger had come into the bazaar, an old man whose eyes were always shut, who felt out his path with a long white stick. The boy, Ali, had been too intent on the story to notice him at first; but he caught sight of him as the storyteller said *joy*, for this old man was feeling his way past the potter's stall, tapping each pot with his stick.

'Here, venerable one,' cried the potter quickly, fearful his wares might be broken. 'Permit a wretched man of clay to guide you.' He took the old man by the elbow. 'Where do you desire to go, venerable one?'

'I heard a story told,' answered the old man. 'Or rather, I heard the speech of a storyteller, for now I hear it no more. Once, O my brother, it was my only pleasure to read that which is sacred, heeding nought else, and I did so till I had learned every verse as no man since. Observing that I had no more need for them, the All Seeing One put out my eyes. Now I mumble his verses in the dark – but I hear storytellers, sometimes.'

'What wisdom!' cried the potter. 'Hear him, O you sons

of the Muslims! Here's the storyteller, venerable one. Please to be seated.'

'Thank you, my brother,' replied the old man. 'Thump your clay gently.'

The nightingale flew to a honeysuckle bush near the rose and sang again, and when he had finished his song, a crystal drop of dew fell from the rose.

'Why do you weep, lovely one?' inquired the nightingale. 'Was my song so sad?'

'Because I am to be uprooted tomorrow,' answered the rose. 'Because I am not red. Today, O my lover, while you slept, I heard the pasha instructing our gardener. A red rose of Isfahan is to take my place, for the pasha does not like white roses.'

At this the little nightingale wept too, and for the rest of the night his songs were the saddest he knew, filled with love unrequited and lovers sundered by death.

As dawn came he said to the rose, 'I would save you if I could; but I no more than you can prevail against the might of the pasha. May I have one kiss? I shall count it most sacred for the remainder of my time upon earth.'

The rose shook her dew-weighed head as she stared at the ground. 'You are certain to tear yourself on my thorns,' she said.

But the nightingale cared not a copper for that. At once he flew to the rose's stem and pressed his lips to hers; and as he drew away, his bright eyes noticed a single fleck of scarlet on one of the rose's outermost petals.

'Oh, look!' he cried. 'See this! My kiss has left a red spot there. If we were to kiss a thousand times, dearest rose, you would be a red rose, and so might live.'

'That dot of scarlet is your own heart's blood,' the rose told him. 'it is there because you tore your wing on my thorns, just as I feared.'

'One drop is nothing,' cried the little nightingale,

for he knew then what he must do. Taking wing and flying to a dizzying height, he plunged into the rosebush, where he was torn like one who suffers the Death of a Thousand Cuts.

Bleeding everywhere, he fluttered above the rose.

'That's a very sad story,' said Ali, who was approaching that age at which young men desire women and so come to ruin. 'But a beautiful one too. I'll remember it for a long time.'

'There's more,' the old man whispered. 'I've heard this tale before – we must discover what became of them both.'

In the hour that follows the morning prayer (continued the storyteller) the gardener came into the garden with his spade; he set its blade to the roof of the rosebush, paying no heed at all to the dead bird lying there. But before he had dug deep, he noticed that one single white rose was splattered and dotted everywhere with scarlet.

'How odd!' he said to himself. And then, 'But how lovely! By the Jannat al-Na'im! For the honour of all gardeners, such a bush must not be destroyed. What am I to do?' And so when he had thought upon the matter for a time, he dug up the rosebush indeed, and planted a red rose of Isfahan in its place as his master had ordered him. But he carried the bush that bore the rose the little nightingale had loved to a part of the garden where few ever came, and dug a goodly hole for its roots there. Into this hole, he cast the body of the dead bird he had found in his garden, and he replanted the rosebush on top of it.

Since that day, most of its blossoms have been crimson – the hue of old blood. But once in each year, always at the full of the last moon of summer, the bush bears a white rose spotted and dotted everywhere with scarlet; and it is said that he who picks that rose may choose any love he wishes for so long as the rose remains unwithered, and hold her for ever.

After this, the storyteller recounted many another strange tale, such as that of Yunus the Scribe and Walid bin Sahl, that of Gharib and his brother Ajib, that of the City of Brass, and that of the Four Accused. Listeners came and went, idlers and porters, sherbet vendors, shopkeepers, soldiers and the boatmen of the Nile. But always Ali and the old man remained where they were, and though they put nothing in the storyteller's bowl, he did not complain of them.

At length the hour drew near when the gates are shut, and there was no one left to listen but Ali and the old man. Then Ali said, 'O master of myth, you have given me far more than I expected. What gold is like your words! I shall ask no more – but if I were to ask more, I would ask that you tell your tale of the Rose and the Nightingale again before we go to our beds.'

The storyteller feigned to make a salaam. 'I will indeed tell it yet again,' he said, 'though upon some other day. And I am happy to hear you liked it so well, for to my own mind it possesses every merit a tale requires, of which fantasy, colour and pathos are the chief.'

The old man combed his white beard with his fingers. 'It has another,' said he, 'one you have not touched upon: that of truth. For it is indeed written that such a bush grows in the pasha's garden.'

'What!' exclaimed the boy Ali. 'Why, I'd give my life to see it!'

The blind old man nodded. 'And so would I, boy. So would I. It does indeed.'

'I wouldn't,' said the storyteller. 'For I have found that I'm able to net loves enough without magic. And as for holding them for ever, who but a madman would wish it? Yet I too would like to see a magic rose if I could.'

Ali shook his head. 'I'm afraid you can't, O lord of long words. They say there's a high wall around the pasha's garden, so his wives and the other ladies of his harem can walk there.'

The old man laid a dry hand upon Ali's thigh. 'Nor can I, ever. Yet you might, boy – for I know a means by which one such as yourself may be admitted to that garden.'

Then the boy Ali's mouth opened wide, for he could scarcely believe his good fortune. And at last he said, 'Might it be, O monarch of muezzins, that the rose blooms tonight?'

And the old man answered, 'That rose opened today, for last night saw the final full moon of summer.'

'Then tell me how I can get into the pasha's garden!'

The old man shook his head. 'That I may not do, boy, for it is a secret that may never be spoken; but if you will guide me there, I will instruct you in the method.'

'This very night, my master, if you can walk so far.'

'I cannot,' the old man told him. 'But a donkey can trot any distance one wishes.'

Then the storyteller exclaimed, 'By the prophet! I must go with you. I'll see the pasha's garden myself, if it be the will of Allah, and I'll hire a donkey too.'

'O my masters,' said the boy Ali, for he knew that though they might ride he must walk, 'if you're both going there's no need. Let's hire a boat instead. I know a rais – a captain, my masters – who has a good one, small, fleet and cheap. A boat does not jolt, and it will be cool tonight upon the river.'

'Wisely spoken, boy,' said the old man, preparing to rise. 'If this storyteller and I combine our purses, it should not be too much. But you must guide me to this boat.'

'And I,' said the storyteller. 'For I'm newly come from Baghdad.'

'Then come,' said Ali, 'and I'll show you everything on the way.' And he took the sleeve of the old man's robe and led them down one crooked street after another.

'Here's the water buffalo that turns the well-pump for the whole quarter. His name's Kubbar. See, he lets me put my hand on his horn. Now go through yonder door, my masters, and we'll save ourselves much walking.'

They did as he bid, entering a high-walled building through a narrow hall that soon opened into a wide court.

31

'This is our slave market. The auction's over for today. Never fear, my masters, there's another door on the other side just like the one we came in through. Over there are the sick slaves – you can get one for next to nothing if you want to feed the crows. Here are the well ones. The dark ones are Nubians – they're the best. The yellow-skins are Abyssinians. People say they're too smart to make good slaves. The women are in those booths.'

A light-skinned Abyssinian girl with a great deal of brass jewellery thrust her head through the curtains of one to smile at the storyteller, then put out her tongue.

'She wants to show you that she's not sick,' Ali explained. 'She thinks you're rich because you're dressed so well. She'd like a rich, handsome young master. Most storytellers dress in rags.'

'As did I. But while I was in Bagdad, I told my tale of the Rose and the Nightingale to the caliph, who filled my mouth with gold.'

'Ah,' said Ali. 'I wondered about that. Then you could buy her, for she could be had for silver. There're Circassians too, and Galla girls – they have cool flesh for the hot nights – and some Franks, I think, but you have to beat the Franks every day, or they'll murder their masters.'

'What's that?' inquired the storyteller as they came out the second door.

'That shaft of stone? The idol of an infidel queen. It ought to be pulled down, only it's so tall it would take the houses of believers with it.'

'Ah!' The old man nodded, smiling to himself. 'That's an obelisk, boy. Cleopatra erected that to the honour of her son by Julius Caesar.'

'And right over there's the Women's Bath, my masters,' Ali announced. 'Our eunuchs used to wash there too, but some young men learned to draw their stones up into their bodies and pass for eunuchs, so now they won't let them.'

Another street, wider but as contorted as the rest, led to the docks, where lounging sailors were jostled by the impatient travellers of half a dozen nations: Bedouins,

Greeks, Armenians and Jews, a proud Turk with a small black boy to carry his pipe, an angry janissary with a cocked fusil in one hand and a letter in the other.

'Way!' shrilled Ali. 'Way for the holy one! Way, make way for the caliph's favourite!'

No one paid him the least attention, and they had to push through the crowd as best they could. At the very end of a long wharf three nearly naked Arabs lounged in a small canjiah. 'Up the river to the palace at once!' Ali called to them. 'And with all speed!'

The rais, whose turban was a trifle larger than the others, yawned and rose. 'You wish us to wait for you, sir?' he asked the storyteller. 'You will return to the city with us? Fifty piastres.'

After some reasoned discussion in which the storyteller and the old man frequently swore they would prefer to walk, and the rais declared that it had been his intention to sink his vessel at once and so escape the tax collectors, thirty-one was agreed upon, fifteen to be paid on the spot, and the remaining sixteen on their return; the storyteller counted out the money, the rais shouted to his crew, the crew climbed the stubby masts and freed the enormous rust-coloured sails for the long, slanting lateen yards, and as quickly as a man lights his chibouque, the little canjiah was cracking up the river with white water boiling at her bow.

'Our Nile is the most wonderful river in the whole world,' Ali explained happily. 'It runs – behold, my masters – to the Great Sea in the north. The wind blows towards the cataracts of the south—'

'Except when it doesn't,' the rais put in softly.

'And so a man may sail up and come down with the current all his life and never wet an oar.'

The old man grunted as he made himself comfortable in the stern. 'It's a long time since I've been on this river. I had my eyes then. You'll have to tell me what we're passing, boy, so I know where we are.'

'Then hear, most holy one,' said Ali, who was even more respectful in the presence of the rais and the crew, 'that on my right hand stand the mighty tombs of the infidel kings, black as pitch against the setting of the sun and peaked like so many tents, though each is loftier than many a mountain. Opposite are mountains indeed, carved by Allah and not by infidels, the Mountains of Moqattam, my master, where your servant has never set his foot. Behind our craft, the great, the beautiful city lights the lamps no man can count, which fade with distance, my master, even as the host of heaven brightens. Before us rise the famous cliffs.' Ali looked about for something with which to cover himself, for the night air was indeed chill upon the Nile.

'You grope for your robe, boy,' said the old man. 'But you're sitting on it.'

At that, the storyteller laughed.

It was so, though the boy Ali had never in his life owned a robe. When he stretched his hand towards the wooden seat, it was not wood his fingers encountered but cotton cloth. He stood and held it up, and it was indeed just such a robe as someone of his size might wear, of white striped with a darker colour.

'Ten thousand blessings, my master!' exclaimed Ali. Then he muttered to himself, 'I wish I had a light.'

The old man said, 'The stripes are brown, boy. Now put it on.'

When the robe was settled in place, so that Ali was covered from his shoulders to his ankles, he said, 'O my master, holiest vizier of all wisdom, I had thought you blind.'

And the old man answered, 'Now that night has come, I see more clearly.'

The storyteller touched Ali's arm and pointed. 'What are those dark openings in the cliffs?'

'Tombs, my master. The tombs of infidels of long ago.'

'Some are lit from within. Their lights are faint, but I see them. Look there.'

'Those are ghûl lights, my master,' Ali told him. 'Ghûls dwell in the tombs.'

The old man said, 'Tell him of them.'

'It is unlucky to speak of them, my master,' Ali said, and he looked to one side.

'Speak nevertheless,' said the storyteller, 'and may your ill luck fall upon me.'

'Have they no ghûls in Baghdad?'

The storyteller nodded. 'Evil things that claw at graves by night and sometimes kill the watchmen.'

'So are they here,' said Ali. 'They devour the sere bodies of infidels long dead, and eat the funeral meats left with them. They don their jewels too, and hold an evil carouse, dancing to a music that would drive a true believer mad. When day comes, they hide the jewels, so that honest men cannot find them.'

The storyteller thought upon this for a time, and at last he said, 'What of the kings' tombs we saw? Are there greater ghûls in those?'

The boy Ali shook his head. 'There's a guardian set there by the kings, with a man's face and a lion's feet. Should any ghûl approach those tombs, he would rise and tear it to pieces. If its face were a lion's, my master, it would flee, for all beasts fear them greatly. If its hands were a man's, it could do nothing, for the hands of men are weak against ghûls. Thus it is as it is, and they fear it and do not come. Now let us speak no more of these evil things.'

'Boy,' said the old man, 'take up my stick.'

Ali picked it up – a long slender rod of heavy wood, topped with a knob of bone.

'I can't see which tombs show a light,' the old man said. 'But you can. Stand up, boy! Are you standing up?'

Ali rose again. 'Yes, my master. I stand.'

'Then point my stick at a tomb that shows a light, boy. At the nearest.'

They were abreast such a tomb as he spoke. A faint blue ghûl-light played about its mouth, at times weakly, at others more strongly. 'I have done so, my master,' whispered Ali.

Slowly, though not feebly, the old man's hand reached for his staff, a dark serpent that tested the distance between one branch and the next. After what seemed to Ali a very long time indeed, the strong brown fingers touched the white wood.

And the radiance at the tomb's entrance brightened, as if a balefire had been kindled within, and a great voice boomed forth from the narrow stone doorway. All the horrors of death were in it: the stench of corpses, and the dust and the dirt that follow that stench. As the hyena gives tongue though its mouth chokes on putrescence, it howled, '*Hail to thee, Mullah Ibrahim! Peace be, between thee and me!*'

Ali returned the old man's stick to the place at his side where it had lain. And thereafter he sat with his head in his hands, and said nothing of cliff or mountain, ruined temple or mosque of faith, or of anything else that the boat passed. For he recalled that the storyteller had told him that his teacher had been the Mullah Ibrahim; and he knew that the two, although they might feign to have met first that day in the bazaar, were in reality pupil and master, and that they had snared him for a purpose he could not guess.

At last the storyteller took him by the shoulder and said, 'Come!'

Ali raised his head and saw they were at the landing of the pasha's palace. He saw too that dawn had come, or nearly, for it was almost the hour at which a man can distinguish between a fine white thread and a black one, which in Ramadan signals the beginning of the fast.

He rose as he was bid and mounted the slippery stone steps, the storyteller following him with his hand still gripping Ali's shoulder, and the old man walking before them, tapping each step with his stick.

Sandalwood gates studded with iron stood at the top of the stair. A janissary dozed before them, his back to a pillar, his hand folded across the muzzle of his long, ivory-inlaid musket.

'Hush,' commanded the old man. 'He will not wake, but should we make too much noise, he may lift his head and speak.' He brushed the grey stones of the wall with one hand and held his stick before him with the other.

Ali nodded, though he wanted to shout.

For a thousand steps and more they crept in the shadow of those grey stones, until the wall curved away from the river. The storyteller said, 'Now we must make haste. Night is nearly flown.'

'Not for me,' the old man told him.

Before them stood a cracked ashlar from which the unholy glyphs of infidel times were almost weathered away, the refuse of the pasha's garden on the other side of the wall. Here the old man seated himself, saying, 'Take off your robe, boy, and cast it at my feet.'

Ali did not wish to do so, but the storyteller cuffed him until he thought it better to obey.

But while they scuffled and Ali wept, the old man paid them no heed. His blind eyes were upturned to the dimming stars, his crooked legs crossed under him, the palms of his hands flattened upon the glyphs. He neither moved nor spoke.

'O my master, what is he doing?' Ali ventured when he had tossed his robe at the base of the rose-hued ashlar.

Fingering his beard, the storyteller said, 'He sends his soul to Jinnistan, the Land of Sorcery.'

'Is it near?' Ali inquired.

'As close as the ground under our feet,' the storyteller told him. 'And as distant as Mount Kaf.'

Then Ali opened his mouth to frame another question; and though he did not speak, it remained thus open for some time after, for he saw his robe stir as though there were a serpent beneath it.

'Now,' said the storyteller, speaking softly and quickly. 'Hear me. I'll instruct you only once, and if you should fail it's your life. In the garden, find the great fountain. From it lead half a dozen paths. Follow the narrowest, the path of pink stones. A woman waits at the end, beside the bush I told you of. She'll indicate the correct rose to you. Bring it to me, and you'll be restored to your proper shape. You'll be well rewarded, and all will be well for you.'

Poor Ali did not nod, nor did he express his understanding in any other way; and although he heard the storyteller's words, he scarcely knew they had been spoken. For the robe the old man had given him danced like a pot on the fire, waved its arms, and lifted into the air, filled out in a fashion that showed plainly that another wore it, though that other was not to be seen.

The storyteller pinned Ali's arms to his sides. 'Cease your squirming,' he hissed. 'move or cry out, and I'll break both your legs and throw you into the river.'

And the robe settled over poor Ali's head, blinding him.

Then he could see once more, though the world appeared to his eyes a larger and a far stranger place than he would ever have believed it could. The storyteller had released him; but the robe held both his arms to his sides still, for they were not in its sleeves. Rather, the empty sleeves now flapped and fluttered as if a gale blew for them alone, though the body of the robe was quiet.

The wall of the pasha's garden rose higher than the sky, and though the grey light of dawn was all the light there was, everything Ali saw seemed brighter and newer than he had ever seen anything before. The stars were amethysts and jacinths, sapphires and hyacinths; the Nile a rich mocha sea, a crocodile on a distant mudbank a living emerald. He wished both to sing and to fly, and very much to his own astonishment he did both at once, rising on wings that seemed to fan the air without effort, and thrilling like such a music box as ears have never heard.

The pasha's wall, which had appeared an impassible barrier, was no more than a rope of stones trailed over the ground. He had crossed it before he could decide whether to cross or not, and a country of silver fish-ponds and gay flower beds stretched beneath him, like the most gorgeous of carpets in the faraway palace of the sultan. In a wink he saw the great fountain and the path of pink stones, which soon vanished, however, beneath stately palms and lush fruit trees.

I'm a bird, he thought; and if I wish to be a boy again I must follow that path. But do I really wish it? What is this thing they call the soul, that flies to Jinnistan or Paradise, but a bird that sleeps in the body until it is time to quit the nest? Thus I have died, very likely, already. Why should I die twice?

Besides, when I was a boy I had to beg my bread. As a bird I can eat bugs – there are more than enough to feed all the birds that Allah's hatched since the beginning of the world. As a boy I had lice, which could not be checked without coppers for the bath. As a bird I have mites, which can be checked with a bath of dust. As a boy I played with my fellow boys. But as a bird, shall I not sing all day with my fellow birds? There passes one now, my comrade in the air.

At this thought, the bird Ali glanced to his right, where a wild duck winged its way towards the marshes of the Faiyum. Just as he looked, a falcon stooped for it like a thunderbolt; the unfortunate duck gave an eerie, despairing cry and plummeted to earth.

As did the bird Ali, diving under the shelter of a friendly orange tree and whizzing down the path of pink stones like an arrow.

Through a grotto it wound, past lesser fountains and over a bridge not much larger than a table. At last it ended in a cul-de-sac closed by a large rosebush. A young woman waited there, unveiled, her dainty feet upon a slab of pink stone; but though any man would have called her lovely, she seemed a giantess to the terrified Ali, with hands that could break his bones as a squirrel cracks nuts. And though she whistled most plaintively to him, he was careful to perch well out of her reach.

'Are you the bird?' she inquired of him.

Her voice was gunfire and thunder to poor Ali, and yet he understood her words. He struggled to speak, but his lips were stiff, and he sang instead.

'Then there's no reason to delay,' said the young woman, 'for that fat Omar will soon discover I'm absent from my bed.' With that, she drew scissors from the waist of her embroidered trousers and cut a dappled rose from the bush.

Ali the bird fluttered to the rosebush and clamped his beak on the rose. But no sooner had it shut than the face of the sun peeped over the garden wall. Its first rays struck the little nightingale in the rosebush; at once his feathers were the brown stripes of a cotton robe, and Ali the boy who wore that robe.

And as he staggered from the rosebush, his robe torn and his arms and cheeks scratched and bleeding, still too dazed to speak, the young woman caught him in such an embrace as he had never felt since the day his mother died.

'I love you!' cried the young woman. 'I love you, I love you, I love no one but you! You and you only are the pearl of the firmament to me, and shall be forever!'

Ali took the rose from his mouth and discovered that the young woman was scarcely taller than he; and now that he was a boy once more (and nearly a man) he learned too how lovely she was, her flesh silver and her face the moon.

'Will you tell me your name?' she asked, suddenly shy.

'I'm Ali,' he told her. 'And you are . . .?'

'Zandra,' she said, and they kissed. As their lips met, the dappled rose she had cut for him withered and dropped from his fingers to the ground.

And though he was a trifle the smaller, Ali knew that he was taller than the sky. What had Rustam, what had Akbar-Khan, that he had not? A horse? A sword? A banner and a thousand ragged rascals to follow it? They were trivialities and would be his as soon as he wanted them.

'You're unlucky, Zandra,' he whispered. 'The spell of the rose has made you love a beggar boy; but though he will not be a boy always, nor a beggar always, he will be your slave always.'

'I am unluckier than you know, O my heart,' she replied. 'For this is the pasha's garden, and I am the pasha's. Should Omar the chief eunuch, or any of the others, find us here, he will slay you and hew my quivering body into four quarters.'

'Then they must not find us. Tell me quickly – why did the storyteller send me for the rose?'

'A storyteller?' inquired Zandra. 'Describe him to me!'

'He's tall and straight, and very fine looking,' said Ali, recalling the man to his mind's eye. 'He has a beautiful brown beard, and a masterful gaze. His turban is silk, his vest is green kid, and he wears a pistol from Fez in a red sash. With him is a blind old man, a little taller even than he but stooped, Mullah Ibrahim the Wise.'

'I know nothing of such an old man,' Zandra told him. 'But the young one is no storyteller but Prince Abdullah al Hazik. A month past, he was my master's guest in this palace. He met me in this garden, where no stranger is to be.'

'And are you the pasha's most favoured wife?'

Sadly, Zandra shook her head. 'Only his concubine. There are more than a hundred of us.'

'How did you come to meet my storyteller here? Was it by chance?'

'No,' she said. She drew away from him by half a step, and her eyes found the pink stone at her feet.

'Tell me!' demanded Ali. 'It might save our lives. Do you think it really matters to me that another has seen my beloved's face? I, who love you, and have worn others' rags all my life?'

'We danced for him,' confessed poor Zandra. 'I and all the youngest of the pasha's concubines. Our elders played for us on their lutes and zithers, and on the flute and the little woman's drum. I had cymbals for my fingers, and gold bells on my wrists and ankles, and I played my tambourine. We had danced like that before, but never for a guest so young and handsome. O my heart, you should have heard the music, as fierce and sweet as the wind from sea!'

She whirled, hands above her head and fingers snappping; and her hips were the tossing billows of the wild Aegean from which she came, and her little feet thumped the path of pink stones in the rhythm of her dance.

And though every fool in the bazaar would have said that there was no music, yet Ali heard it plainly, the shrilling of the shabbäbi and the thudding of the darabukka.

Abruptly, she stopped. 'And he looked at me, beloved, and I at him, and I knew he would meet me in the garden, beneath the moon. We went there to cool ourselves when we had danced, and I hid till all the rest had gone. Since that time old Rashsha has carried many messages for us.' Her eyes filled with tears.

'I understand,' said Ali, who had once or twice assisted in the transmission of such messages himself. 'But why did he want the rose?'

Zandra wiped her eyes. 'Because of the inscription on a certain stone that lies beyond our wall. I've never seen it, and I couldn't read it anyway. But he says it says, 'Here is the treasure of Osiris.' That was a king of the infidels, I think. 'I open to love alone.' Prince Abdullah said it would open to the bearer of the rose. Where is it?'

'I dropped it,' Ali confessed.

'Here it is – on the stone. But how fast it faded!'

Zandra bent to pick it up, and Ali was seized with shame to think that he had made this lovely child weep, and that she, the pasha's concubine, should wait upon him, a pauper and a beggar. 'No, no!' he protested. 'Let me get it for you, my lady!'

Their hands met upon the pink stone. It lifted at once as if hinged, and the rose slid from it to lie at the foot of the bush where it lies still. Before them opened a murky and narrow shaft which a flight of steep stone steps descended, as it seemed, for ever.

'*Caught!*' exclaimed a reedy voice behind them.

They turned as one, and Zandra cried, 'Omar! Omar, please, we—'

'*Silence, I say!*' Twice Ali's height, the eunuch lumbered towards them, penning them in the cul-de-sac; his belly preceded his advance as a battering ram leads a storming party, and he held a heavy scimitar at the ready. 'I fear that you must die, my children. I . . . what is this?'

'The secret road to a great treasure, sir,' said Ali, whose wits had been honed on a dinnerless day. 'Jewels and gold beyond counting. Look here.' Quickly he pointed to the glyphs carved on the underside of the stone: a bent object that might be a whip, a human leg and foot, a shallow cup and a crocodile.

'It's plain enough, surely,' continued Ali, who had heard that eunuchs hunger after money and respect as whole men lust for power and women, though he could not read even plain Arabic. 'The lash and the foot mean that anyone who walks here without permission will be beaten. The cup shows that this is where the drinking vessels are, and the crocodile that they belong to the king of the river.'

Zandra whispered, 'Oh, what a pity you must kill us, Omar! My screams and our blood, still more the hacked limbs of our dismembered bodies, will attract a great deal of attention to this spot. You'll be lucky to get so much as a single goblet before the janissaries take charge of everything.'

'But if you were to spare us,' Ali added quickly, 'we could assist you. And since it would be our lives to reveal a word of this, we would reveal nothing, ever.'

'Never!' confirmed Zandra.

'Hmm,' said the eunuch. With his left hand he stroked his chin, which was smoother than Ali's. He looked from one to the other with the clever little eyes of a pig. 'I could take you elsewhere, however. Indeed it seems a capital idea. You, of course, will flee, young man—' Sudden as a cobra's strike, his left hand seized Ali's arm and clamped it like a vice. 'And I should have the greatest difficulty catching you. I suppose you might even scale the wall – no doubt that's how you got in. It would be best if you did not. Our Zandra may fly if she likes. She won't get over the wall so easily, I think, and I shall hunt her down. Come, my children.'

He swung Ali about, and Zandra followed weeping.

With a crash like a thunderclap, the stone slammed closed behind them. The eunuch spun around to stare at it. 'How did you get that open?'

'We just touched it,' Zandra told him.

Ali cleared his throat. 'There's another pink stone on the other side of the wall, sir. It's all rather complicated—'

The eunuch set his foot upon the stone; nothing happened. 'Why, I've touched this myself a score of times,' he muttered. 'What's this about another stone outside?'

'And into that stone,' Ali continued in his most impressive voice, 'are carved the following words: *I reveal the treasure to true love only.*' There's also a man – a most evil man, sir – a certain Prince Abdullah of Baghdad—'

'I know him well,' put in the eunuch. 'A true son of the prophet and a most generous, nobly spirited gentleman.'

'Who's hot on the trail of this very treasure, sir, aided by his old tutor, Mullah Ibrahim. Prince Abdullah, however—'

'Still your chatter,' ordered the eunuch. 'You two touched it, you say, and it opened?'

Ali and Zandra nodded.

'Then touch it again, at once!'

Zandra said softly, 'Our hands were together, Omar. We touched it together.'

'Then do so again. The boy may use his free hand.'

Ali and Zandra joined hands and looked at each other for a moment before they touched the pink stone, which sprang up as if thrown wide by the jinn.

The eunuch nodded to himself. 'You are quite correct, I must spare you. Serve me well, and by my honour you both shall live. His Excellency will hear nothing of this.'

'We will!' cried Ali, and 'Oh, we will!' echoed Zandra.

'And that scoundrel Prince Abdullah wishes to seize my treasure, you say?'

Ali nodded. 'But he thinks it's underneath the pink stone outside. So did I, until we opened this a moment ago. Mullah Ibrahim must have read the writing on the stone for him, but the mullah's blind. Either he read it by feeling the carvings, or Abdullah described them to him.

He couldn't see the stone; if he had, he probably would have guessed it wasn't where it had been in the days of the infidels. I suppose the masons wanted it to build the wall – but it cracked, and they threw it away.'

'And this unworthy prince is still seeking to discover how it may be opened?'

'Yes, sir.'

'Then I'm far ahead of the rogue. And now, children, we must see what I have found. You will go ahead of me, I think. I wouldn't want that stone to shut with myself inside.'

Ali went first, biting his lips, for the darkness and the dank smell of the place frightened him. Zandra followed close behind him, trembling and gulping down sobs. The eunuch brought up the rear with his big scimitar in his hand and a little smile of complacency on his face.

When the three had descended a hundred steps and were far beneath the ground, the stair ended in mud. Had it been night in the pasha's garden above, or even afternoon, the cavern in which they found themselves would have been as black as the pit. As it was, the morning sun shot its rays down the long straight stair after them, tracing a rectangle of tarnished gold at the bottom that seemed to their eyes almost blinding and lent some faint illumination to the whole.

It was not a very prepossessing whole, and scarcely looked like a treasure house – a wide, low cave in which mud mixed with rock and gravel slopped towards an underground pool of dark water. In places, slabs had fallen from the ceiling and lay level with the mud, forming paths of stepping stones that lead nowhere. In others, long stalactites nearly touched the floor, or touched it to form pillars; and in still others, delicate white curtains of stone had been drawn before small and secret chambers. Poor Ali shivered, feeling he breathed the chill air of a bygone time, of the age that had ended on the day the Nile turned to blood. Its unclean idols gathered invisibly about him, half-human figures having the heads and horns and tusks of beasts.

The eunuch hurried into the cavern to search for treasure, forgetful of his captives. Ali would have fled up the stair if it could have been done without abandoning Zandra, who clung to his arm.

'No cups here,' the eunuch grumbled. 'Mere emptiness – dark – dampness – and nothing more. This tomb was rifled long ago, and miserable grave robbers took everything.'

Zandra whispered, 'I'm not sure it's a tomb at all, or that it ever was.'

'All the worse for us, then,' said the eunuch, returning to them. 'I ought to slay you both on the spot. It's my duty, in fact – one I've neglected too long already.'

'I think the treasure might be under the water, Omar. I saw a gleam of gold there, I think.'

'So did I,' said Ali.

And as he spoke the still water was roiled, boiling and rippling with the movements of something beneath the surface.

'Did you?' muttered the eunuch. 'Well, I'll have a look.'

And the snout of a huge crocodile appeared, but the eunuch seemed not to see it.

'Watch out, Omar!' Zandra called. 'The bubbles!'

He glanced at her over his shoulder. 'Look out? For what?'

Only the eyes and nostrils of the crocodile appeared above the water, but they raced towards him, trailing a sharp wake like a small, swift boat's upon the river.

"Omar!"

'What?' the eunuch asked testily.

Then it was too late. More quickly than any man could run, thrown forward by a tremendous stroke of its tail as it left the water and carrying with it a wave half again as large as itself, the crocodile mounted the bank. It was as long as a tree-trunk, broader than two camels; gold rings set with rubies pierced its armoured head below the ear vents, and bands of pure gold studded with amethysts had been riveted around its forelegs. Its jaws seized the

46

eunuch, who fell with a thud that seemed to shake the entire cavern. Once he groaned; an arm moved, and fell back.

He lay still.

Yet there was no blood, and when the crocodile had dragged the eunuch's swollen body beneath the water, that body lay near the water's edge as before.

'Come!' Ali said, and took Zandra's hand.

Already the time for flight had passed. Again the enormous crocodile rushed from the pool, and before they could mount the first step, its jaws closed about them.

It seemed to Ali then that the darkness grew darker still – darker than he had ever known, darker than he had ever believed darkness and night could ever be; it was a long while, sad hours it seemed, before he understood what had happened, what the dark was and why it had come.

There was no more Allah, not then or ever. He had seldom been in a mosque, scarcely ever recited the prescribed prayers at dawn, midday and evening; yet he had known Allah was there, always present in his life, like air. Now Allah was gone, and nothing remained of life but the savage fight – a fight that he, small and weak, could never win.

The darkness opened. He saw Zandra's face and knew he had been wrong.

'O my heart!' Zandra cried. 'What is the matter?'

'Nothing's the matter,' Ali said, and meant it. He sat up.

'First Omar, then you! There's something evil in this terrible place.'

He was weak, but with her help he was able to get to his feet. 'Did you see the crocodile?' he asked.

'A crocodile? No. A crocodile couldn't live down here, could it?'

'But you saw gold, under the water.'

'I thought I did. Something that gleamed like gold, yes. And the water bubbled. I thought that was strange, and I tried to warn Omar, but he didn't pay any attention.'

Ali nodded.

'It was as if something you couldn't see were coming out of the water – coming for Omar. Do you think he's dead?'

'I don't know,' Ali told her, and they went over to look at the fat eunuch.

He lay upon his back and seemed not to breathe. Ali touched his chest; the skin was as cold as the mud where he lay, but his eyes opened at Ali's touch, and he groaned.

'Omar! Zandra cried. 'Are you all right?'

'No,' the eunuch groaned. 'Oh, decidedly not, my child.' He put his fingers to his temples. 'My head – it throbs most abominably and I've had a horrible dream.'

Ali said, 'Maybe you'd better lie where you are until you feel better. One of us can go for help.'

'Master!' The eunuch's eyes flew wide open. 'Your slave must not rest while you stand!' He struggled to sit up, fell backward, rolled on his side and managed, with Ali and Zandra's help, to rise.

'O my master,' the eunuch said when he stood upon his feet at last. 'It is you alone who must be our pasha, and not that brute up there. I see it now. I beg – I most humbly beg – your pardon for not having done so previously.'

He bowed, and for a moment Ali feared he might fall on his face.

'Where is my sword? I shall hew him to kabobs, master, in the bedchamber. It is yet early, I believe, and he'll be still abed. I can manage the other servants for you, never fear. The janissaries must wait your arrival, master, but I doubt you'll have much difficulty with them. And where the janissaries go the army will surely follow. A few gifts to the Porte should then secure your position.'

The eunuch had been looking about distractedly as he spoke. By using both her hands, Zandra was able to lift the somewhat muddy scimitar and return it to him.

'I dreamed I was a whole man, my child,' the eunuch told her, smiling a little at himself. 'Isn't that odd? I've never been one, to be sure – I was only ten. Yet I dreamed I was a whole man, and standing before the gates of paradise. An angel told me—' He shook his head. 'Excuse my wandering, I beg, my master, my lady. I'm still not

48

quite myself. And so terribly cold. I shall return to the surface and do as you have bid at once. No doubt the exercise will warm me.'

Ali raised his hand to stop the eunuch, but Zandra pulled it down again. When he was gone, Ali asked her 'Do you think he'll really do that? Kill the pasha?'

Zandra shrugged. 'As Allah wills it, O my lover.'

Together they climbed the stair. They climbed slowly, with Ali's hand reaching back to grasp Zandra's, and the eunuch had reached the top and vanished before Ali had mounted the twelfth step. When they stepped out into the sunshine, the sun was only a bit higher than it had been when its first rays had struck the little nightingale. The dew of heaven still lay heavy on grass and bush, and a lark was singing as it flew.

The pink stone shut behind them; and although they have spoken of it now and then, they have never tried to open it again.

'All will be well now, my lover,' Zandra said. 'I feel it. And yet it might be wise for you to climb over this wall before someone who doesn't know it finds you here.'

Ali nodded, and at that very instant Prince Abdullah al Hazik of Baghdad seized him from behind.

'So here you are, guttersnipe! Here you are at last. And you, you little slut.'

He struck Zandra across the face, and Ali, with his free hand, jerked the pistol of Fez from the Prince's sash and shot him through the heart.

Next day, smoking his pipe upon the divan, Pasha Ali ben Hassan ordered that Mullah Ibrahim the Wise be brought before him. The captain of the janissaries did as he was bid, and when the old man stood in the audience chamber in his chains, cast his broken staff at his feet.

'O Mullah,' said Ali, 'I am informed that there is known to you a certain stone, known also to me, inscribed, "Here is the magic of Osiris".'

The old man nodded without speaking.

'And who was this Osiris?'

'The first king of this country, Great Pasha,' the old man mumbled.

'In the infidel times?'

'In any times, Great Pasha.' Calling thus upon his wisdom seemed to strengthen the old man. He stood straighter and spoke with something of his earlier, proud manner. 'The first of the pharaohs, learned and good, beloved of all his people and loving them. Or so it was written long ago.'

'I take it then that he is dead,' remarked Ali, and all his courtiers laughed.

'Long since,' the old man told him.

'I have myself discovered a stone bearing certain infidel signs,' Ali murmured. He described them. 'Tell me – and if you wish to keep your life you had better tell me truly – what they read.'

'They form the name of the god Sobek.'

'And nothing more, boy,' the old man said.

The captain of the janissaries raised his whip, but Ali shook his head. 'Tell me his legend.'

'After a lifetime of study, I know but little,' the old man confessed. 'Sobek was pictured as a man having the head of a crocodile. He was the patron of the throne, and the protector and counsellor of the pharaohs. His sacred crocodile was kept in a lake not far from here, where one who sees may see the ruins of Sobek's temple. I know no more.'

'If this Sobek was the protector of the pharaohs,' hazarded Ali, 'he must have been the protector of Osiris.'

'That is so, boy.'

'And what befell Osiris?'

'He had an enemy,' the old man said slowly. 'Sutekh. It was well known in those times that crocodiles could steal magic, seizing the magician's power and dragging it into the river. Sutekh took the shape of such a crocodile – some say of Sobek's own sacred beast – and stole the powers of Osiris. Thus were his human foes enabled to take his life.'

Ali stroked his chin, feeling the beard beginning to

sprout there. 'If this Sobek was an infidel god, surely he would take Sutekh's life for such a crime.'

'Sutekh also was a god,' the old man said. 'None but Allah himself could encompass Sutekh's destruction.'

'Yet he might be imprisoned?'

'As you say, boy.'

From behind the screen behind the divan, Zandra whispered, 'Ask him whether our love might destroy Sutekh, Ali.'

'O Mullah,' said Ali, 'if Allah *were* to desire the death of this Sutekh, might he not act through love?'

The old man nodded. 'It is by that means and no other that Allah acts. Yet what is that, but to say he acts with his own hand? For love is Allah himself, and thus poisonous to those who do evil.'

The captain of the janissaries called, 'Hear the wisdom of our pasha, O Muslims!'

Ali asked, 'And if Sutekh were to seek to devour love?'

The old man answered, 'Sutekh would surely die, boy. Can a small god devour a greater? It was for that reason Sutekh could take only the magic of Osiris. The life of the king fell to the daggers of men.'

'And if Sutekh were to die, the magic of Osiris would pass to another?'

The old man bowed his head. 'So once I dared to hope, boy, that I might have eyes once more.'

Ali nodded, though he knew that the old man could not see it. 'Mullah, you could have done me evil; yet you did not, and I will not revenge myself upon a holy man, old and blind.'

From behind the screen, Zandra whispered, 'Ask him—'

Ali shook his head. 'Captain, find Mullah Ibrahim a boat. He is to be freed and returned in safety to the city.'

The captain touched his forehead. 'I hear and obey.'

On the day before the great wedding of the Pasha of All Egypt to the Lady Zandra, the rais of that boat was carried before him. The poor man salaamed again and again, kissing the tiles in his terror.

51

'Flower of Islam!' he cried. 'Your meanest servant grovels at your feet. Spare his wretched life! He is your slave.'

'The mullah is gone, Great Pasha,' explained the captain of the janissaries drily. 'Dead, unless Allah wills that he live.' He fingered the edge of his scimitar.

'We passed the cliffs at evening,' the unfortunate rais wailed. 'A darkness fell upon my miserable craft. When the darkness lifted—'

'Peace,' said Ali. 'We will speak no more of these evil things.'

TANITH LEE

Foolish, Wicked, Clever and Kind

Death, the Unmaker of Men, came one sunrise to visit a nobleman in the city of Baghdad. The nobleman's fine house stood on the east bank of the Tigris, set round with rose gardens and groves of pomegranate trees, but this did not hinder Death, who passed by the pools and over the lawns and in at the portals without a second glance. Death was much-travelled and had seen many things and, besides, was not inclined to dawdle, having several appointments in the city before midday prayers.

The nobleman lay unsleeping on his pillows. Two slaves, who had tended him through the night, for their part slumbered exhaustedly at the bed's foot. The nobleman did not rouse them. He turned his eyes towards the doorway and beheld, unsurprised, the figure standing there.

'Is it you?'

'It is I,' said Death.

'I am not sorry to see you,' replied the nobleman. 'But for a single item I should be ready to depart.'

'There is always something,' remarked Death.

'I have vast wealth, and three sons,' said the nobleman.

'Not all men are so fortunate,' answered Death severely.

'This is true. But I have a presentiment now. With my passing, there will be discord and quarreling. Disaster hovers over the roof like a vulture.'

'Just so,' said Death, not unkindly, 'did your own father whisper to me, on the evening I called upon him.'

The nobleman sighed. 'You are wise. It is a fact. There is no hope nor help save in Allah. My sons must take their chance, as do all men, in the shadow of Fate. Therefore, I am ready. Let us be going.'

It had happened that Khassim, the nobleman's eldest son, was hunting on the plains beyond the city. Though messengers sought his camp, they could not find him. Thus, after some days, when he returned home, it was to discover the house in mourning and his father already buried.

Khassim rent his clothes and flung away his turban. He told his servants to burn the skins of the beasts he had killed, two of which were the coats of lion. He called the barber to shave his face, saying, 'It is not fit I should wear the aspect of a man, seeing I was not here at my father's end.'

When he had been shaved, Khassim shut himself up and wept guiltily. To the second brother, Shireef, who – in the eldest son's absence – had carried out the funerary duties, Khassim had barely been able to bring himself to speak. (Although to the youngest son, Ahmed, he paid no heed, for it was the habit of both elder brothers to discount him always.)

At last Khassim came from his chamber with a cloud, if not a beard, about his face. Calling two or three of his servants, he vowed to ride that moment to the tomb of his father, and on the uncanny spot to keep a vigil through the night, praying to God, and expressing his sorrow and respect.

Shireef, watching him depart in the hour of evening prayers, murmured, 'It is the cock who crows at the sun's rise, and the donkey who brays after it.'

Then Shireef, handsome as bronze, smiled and went to walk among the roses.

The night sky was clear and dyed with darkest blue, and

all the stars burned in it, when Khassim entered the cemetery and approached his father's tomb. He was alone, for his servants he had permitted to remain outside the graveyard gate.

Standing before the great mausoleum, the eldest son bowed his head and began his devotions, and the stars slowly wheeled across the canopy of heaven.

Presently Khassim yawned. A mighty weariness had overcome him. He glanced at the sky. The moon was only just now rising and it was many hours yet till dawn.

'O my father,' said Khassim, 'my misery has worn me out. Allow me to lie down on the ground and sleep awhile. These stones will make only a comfortless couch, of which I am most deserving. And soon I shall be somewhat refreshed and may continue my vigil.'

This declaration delivered, Khassim stretched himself on the earth at the tomb's foot, with his sash for a pillow. He fell immediately asleep.

When he waked it was with a dreadful start.

Nothing seemed stirring, however, save for a melancholy night bird which sat nearby in a bush and occasionally called. But the sky was growing pale, and among the stars the unseen Hand of God was discernible, snuffing their lights one by one.

'There is no strength save in Allah,' said Khassim. And standing up he resumed his sash, and would hastily have commenced praying once more, when his attention was diverted. Between the graves close by, some persons were slowly walking, carrying lit tapers in their hands. Arriving before a large white tomb, this procession halted, and there stood forth the figure of a woman.

She was dressed in some splendour, and veiled, and when she raised her slender hands, jewels gleamed on them.

'My dear lord,' she cried, in the direction of the white tomb, 'as usual I have fasted and prayed, and watched all night under the wall. Now I approach to rain upon the ground the water of sorrow. Three full years I have mourned you, nor wed another, nor found any other man

55

indeed who might replace you in my heart, so perfect were your virtues and accomplishments. Alas, alas, the sight of this burial place is now the only sweet I have.'

Now here is true devotion, thought Khassim with sullen admiration.

And at that moment the woman cast aside her veil that she might kiss the surface of the tomb. Even in the dimness it was evident that she was beautiful, and, when the glow of the tapers covered her, that she was also young.

Seeing her loveliness and her grief in the loneliness of morning twilight, Khassim was impelled to step forward.

As he appeared the young woman uttered a low cry and stared at him with her large, wild eyes.

'Pardon me, lady,' said Khassim, 'and do not tremble. I am no afrit that haunts the cemetery, but a human man, who like yourself is here to mourn among the graves.'

The young woman in her turn took a step towards him, and then another, her eyes still fixed upon his face. As for her attendants, they made no move at all.

'Tell me your name,' said she.

Khassim told her his name and, for good measure, his lineage.

Then she wept again, most beautifully, the tear-drops spilling from her eyes like oval crystals.

'Although it is a sin, I had wished you a ghost,' she said. 'For you are the image of him that I lost, my dead husband, dearer to me than all the world.'

Then she turned from him, and summoning her maids, she leaned on them, and went with a halting, graceful tread away.

But Khassim apprehended one of the male servants.

'Tell me your lady's name, by the Faith!'

The man was not loath.

'This is the Lady Nadina, a widow known throughout Baghdad for her misfortune, charm and wealth. She was wife but three days. Yet, since her loss, for three years – thrice in every month save Ramadan – she fasts and keeps watch, then comes near dawn to embrace her dead lord's tomb.'

'But had he no kindred to care for her?' asked Khassim.

'None. And as for offers of marriage, she would have spurned and fled from them, so precious is the one memory to her.'

'And is it a fact,' began Khassim, 'that I—'

'You are his living likeness, sir,' announced the servant, bowing low. 'Such is Fate, and only Allah is God.'

Just as the man was proceeding after his mistress, Khassim once more caught up to him, and offered him a generous sum of money.

'Although she is famed in Baghdad, I have never before heard of her. Where is her house?'

'Upon the west bank of the river, in the Street of Happiness, beside the Fountain of the Ivory Pigeons.'

Such absolute directions even Khassim was unlikely to mislay.

'What is amiss with you, elder brother?' inquired Shireef of Khassim in the late afternoon of that following day.

'Nothing at all. Everything is well.'

'You have been closeted in the library, next in the bath and with the barber. Surely, after your vigil at our father's tomb, you are in need of slumber and rest?'

'No, rather invigorated.'

'And where are you going now, in such glory?'

'To pray and to give alms to the poor.'

He is not generally so pious, thought Shireef to himself. *Allah grant he has not gone mad and is about to squander all our inheritance.*

Then Shireef called one of his own slaves, a mute Circassian pale as lime, and instructed him to follow Khassim and his retinue, and observe where they went and what they did.

Sunset came and rushed away, and night, and the evening prayers, and the moon stood high above Baghdad, staring upon the palaces and gardens of men as if to say: What passing foolishness is this?

Not until the hours of earliest morning did the

Circassian return, and entering the apartments of Shireef, tell him in a language of signs known only to themselves what had gone on.

Reaching the Street of Happiness, Khassim had halted at the Fountain of the Ivory Pigeons, where his retainers erected a costly awning. All sat down upon cushions of silk. Musicians made music, and incenses were burned.

'Who is this fellow blocking up the street?' demanded the passers-by. They approached, and Khassim's servants informed them that here was a doctor, versed in mathematics, medicine and philosophy, who might be consulted upon any matter, but especially in ways of alleviating great grief of the heart.

However, when the traffic of the street sought to consult this learned man, his servants pushed them aside. 'What? You have lost all your gold in a night? Your only son has been bitten by an asp? Tush! These are items too trivial to trouble our master with them.'

Presently an old woman came pushing through the crowd. Going up to Khassim's servants she exclaimed, 'My mistress lives in that fine house there. Her first grief is famous throughout Baghdad. Now a second grief has been added. Can your master do anything for her?'

'Why certainly,' said Khassim's steward, 'if it happens the lady's name is Nadina.'

'Such perspicacity,' remarked the old woman.

They conducted her to Khassim, who, muffled in a false beard, and trembling from beard to foot, affected nonchalance and questioned her.

'My mistress lost her husband to Death's long sleep after three days and nights, but such was their quality that she has mourned him three years. Last night, at his graveside, she met with a young man who so resembled the dead lord, she has gone into a fit of sorrow sufficiently dreadful that we despair of her life.'

'I know the very cure,' said Khassim. 'Find some means that I may come to her.'

'Only allow me,' said the old woman eagerly, leering

58

and pinching his arm, 'space to get back in the house. I will leave a little side-door ajar. Within waits a porter. You cannot mistake him, he is coal black. He will take you to my mistress.'

Khassim gave the old woman some money, and ordered his servants to disperse the crowd.

It was by now sunset, and there came the call to prayer. In a short while, when the street had grown quiet, Khassim rose from his cushions and hastened to the side-door of the house. Sure enough, it stood ajar. Khassim hesitated, looking for the porter. Suddenly there sounded the flap of wings. On a golden perch was a falcon, black as a coal. This, having fixed Khassim with a glittering eye, flew up and away into the house. Khassim followed, and the door swung shut.

Now it may be supposed the Circassian slave of Shireef would be baulked by this shutting of the door. But that was not the case. Limber as a snake, the pale slave found a means to climb the house-wall by a vine which flourished there. Coming on to the roof, he next detected a lighted window, and wriggling like a serpent got a purchase to peer in at the lattice. What should be in the room but a veiled young woman reclining on a couch. Next moment in ran Khassim.

He had no more than stammered a beneficence, when the young woman threw off her veil, and raising her lovely face and hands, entreated him.

'My sadness is insupportable – help me, learned doctor!'

Khassim, who had perused ancient scrolls to ascertain the best and most proper form in which to deceive and have his way, was now overcome by compunction.

'Lady, I am modest in the profession—'

'The seat of my pain is here,' cried the lady, touching her heart. 'Since you are a philosopher, and plainly an aged man – to have grown such a great grey beard – there can be no wrong in revealing myself to you. Pray examine me, for I must be cured, or die.' And so saying she threw off every stitch of clothing and stood before Khassim naked as the young moon. Her skin was fragrant and supple, her contours rounded and her waist slender. At her wrists and ankles sparkled brilliant jewels, and her black hair flowed about her to her knees.

Khassim dropped at her feet.

As he did so, the hideous beard was dislodged and fell from his shaven face.

Nadina gave a cry.

'Alas! How I am shamed. What wicked trick has Satan put into your head, dishonourable man? Woe to me that ever I loved you, or mistook you for another, whose virtues and honesty were beyond all question.'

Khassim commenced kissing her toes.

'Lady,' bleated he, 'I will wed you. There will be no shame. I will marry you in the sight of the city. Only appease me now.'

Nadina made a move towards him, then seemed to recollect herself. 'You must repeat your promise before my witnesses.'

'Yes, yes, gladly. Be it only swift.'

The woman clapped her hands and in came some of her servants, one of whom was bundled in the mantle of the old woman who had first got Khassim access to the house – and yet who now seemed ill fitted by her garment. In his haste, Khassim took small note of this, and boldly made his vows once more. Nadina then dismissed the retainers and took Khassim to her bosom, enjoining him to have his way. Which, with much energy and outcry, he did.

Near morning, appeased and exhausted, the young man sank into a profound sleep. No sooner had he done so than his bedmate left the couch and gave him a box on the ear. It did not wake him. She then left the room and passed into an adjoining chamber.

Now this chamber had no windows, and was unlit. Thus the watchful Circassian who, until this instant had not once lost sight either of Khassim or the woman, now did lose sight at least of the latter. Nevertheless he made out faint whispers and a low and bitter laugh. Presently, back into the lighted rooms stepped the widow, clad and combed, and bearing the black falcon on her wrist. Apprehending she might come to the window, the Circassian prudently hid himself.

Nadina spoke to the falcon.

'Go now to our lord the magician,' said she, 'and tell him, "this fish is hooked".'

Then the falcon came darting straight out of the window.

The bird winged away across the city sky, where night was waning, until, far off in the pearl-pale height above the river, it vanished, a black speck, in at the top of a tall black tower.

And with this news, the Circassian returned to Shireef.

The wedding of Khassim and Nadina lasted many days and nights. What quantities of precious gums were burned, and firecrackers exploded and filled the dark with jewellery rain. Music and song, feasting and delight, made loud the mansion.

The moon waned, and began again to wax, the guests departed, and there came an evening when Khassim called his brothers to a private dinner. Or, he called Shireef. To the youngest brother, Ahmed, it was made apparent that, although invited, he need not bother to present himself.

Khassim's wedding had not, for a wonder, depleted the kitchens. Many sumptuous dishes were served, while musicians plucked melody from the gunibry and the Nubian kissar, and maidens danced with bells at their waists and ankles.

At length, Khassim turned to Shireef and embraced him fondly, having tears in his eyes.

'Dearest brother Shireef! How I shall miss your company when you are no longer in my house.'

Shireef smiled. 'Am I then due to be elsewhere?'

'Certainly. You know tradition recommends it.'

'That the younger brothers be ousted once the eldest is wed?'

61

Khassim sighed. His beard was now of natural luxuriance, but the role of bridegroom had but increased his girth and balconied his eyes. 'Dearest brother Shireef,' said this smug bolster, 'you shall be given your portion – which though small is as lavish as I may spare. I stand as father to you now, and believe me, it is not good to be idle. What better work could you have than the management of your estates?'

Shireef mused upon his estates, reduced by his neglect to some slight areas of dust disdained even by locust and jackal.

'Or,' postulated Khassim, 'undertake the holiest of all journeys – travel to Mecca. Though I cannot afford to finance the enterprise, be sure my sincerest wishes would go with you. Indeed, I should envy you your days of fasting and prayer, your proximity to the sacred shrine . . . all that you would learn from hardship on the road.'

Shireef mused upon Mecca and hardship.

'Yes, Khassim,' he answered. 'You are as sage as you are generous.'

A nightingale sang in the gardens, her song so beautiful that men no longer could make out the words: Blessed is God, who created the seven heavens. His work is faultless. Turn your eyes upward to the sky: Can you detect a single flaw?

But the veiled and mantled form which approached Shireef under an almond tree said only:

'I represent my mistress. What is it, lord, you would say to her?'

'Oh,' said Shireef, 'can it be that you are that old hag who attends her, the one who claims herself to be named *Nadina*? She who has taken to impertinent grinning at me as if she is privy to some secret about me. She whom I would have whipped?'

'I do not believe I am the hag you refer to, lord. But I ask again, what you would say to my mistress.'

'I would not say much. Only that I have put a watch on her comings and goings, and on the venturings of her slaves. And so have learned a thing or two.'

'What things can these be?'

'Why, that she serves a magician in a black tower. That Khassim is her dupe. But mostly,' amended Shireef, eyeing the figure narrowly, 'I have learned that her beauty intoxicates me, and my life is worthless to me unless I make her my own.'

The mantled one let slip a fold of the silk, and the liquid eyes of Nadina the widow-wife looked coldly on Shireef.

'You have gathered your bricks,' said she. 'What house would you build?'

'Rather than aid the stupid Khassim, I would myself take on the luscious lady, and myself serve her mage-master. *I* am no fool, but I have thoughts of power. Let us be rid of the idiot and ally together, fairest love.

Then Nadina discarded the silk from her face entirely, and stared at Shireef as if she measured metal on a scales.

'It is a fact,' said Nadina, 'I have no liking for Khassim. But do you mean I should, by my arts, kill him?'

'Let us not incur the full wrath of Allah,' said Shireef. 'Let us only anger God a little. It would be amusing, would it not, if you are able – to turn Khassim into the likeness of what he is: a fat, saddled donkey.'

Nadina, catching the smile of Shireef as if by contagion, curved her lovely mouth as the sickle moon is curved, or the sword.

'A donkey. And thereafter?'

'He shall be reported dead on a journey to Mecca. I shall wed you. Your wealth and status you shall keep, and I practice at your side your master-magician's will. Between whiles, we shall extravagantly couple.'

Finding her yet smiling, Shireef leaned to bring their smiling mouths together. But Nadina slowly drew back.

'Say that I agree. First, at the feet of my master, you must be proved.'

'I am ready.'

Nadina clapped her hands. From the boughs of the almond tree shot downwards the black falcon. As it came it screeched once, and the nightingale fell silent, and all the garden hushed.

But the falcon dropped upon Shireef's arm and gashed his hand with its beak so the blood flowed and he cursed it.

'Be wary, beloved, to whom you offer oaths,' said Nadina. Going up to him, she showed him a feather no bigger than a rose petal. 'Put this beneath your tongue instead. Take care when you loose it out again.'

Shireef now frowned, but he put the feather into his mouth.

Next second he was changed. His body compressed itself, he was bereft of arms, and reins of fire sprang from his heart through his backbone. His vision was cleft. Then he leapt upwards, and he was a falcon, dark as bronze in the light of the stars, his wings outflung and his beak firmly clasped to hold in the talisman as he flew over the mansion's top.

Two others sped before him, one black, one grey, but they went westward, and he followed them.

Below rushed the roofs and walls of Baghdad, the river like a belt of fluted Basra steel, fretted with sleeping ships. But on the west bank there ran up in the air to meet them a black needle with an eye of cold yellow.

Towards the needle's eye they were pulled in like a triple thread. And through the eye they pierced, one, two, three, and Shireef was the third, and they cast themselves down in the precincts of the magician.

Immediately a huge voice like a brass bell boomed through the chamber. The words were of an unintelligible language. But no sooner had the voice pronounced than the feather fell out of Shireef's mouth. And at once he was a man again, and beside him was the woman, his brother's wife. (Although the black falcon did not alter itself, but only perched in the window embrasure like a thing of jet.)

Then a pair of doors at the chamber's other end burst open, and the mage entered the room.

He was tall, and clad in robes both fabulous and curious, many jewels, and rings flashed on the fingers of his left hand, sulphurous, bloody, white and blue. His face was itself like that of a bird of prey, but with gluttonous lips.

'I have brought this one, lord,' murmured the woman Nadina, on her knees, 'as you foretold me I should.'

The magician glared on Shireef, and Shireef's cool heart quailed. But he said, 'I am at your disposal, mighty one. If you judged I would come to you, you will know what wishes I have carried here in my soul.'

'Never doubt I do,' replied the mage. 'You are a child of the planet Marikh, of the fellowship of envy, war and murder.'

Once these sentences had been spoken, Shireef felt the floor of the tower give under him. He was whirled away before he could so much as cry aloud.

When the tumult settled, Shireef found himself on a great bare plain, and above stormed a sky like fire, where copper-coloured eagles fought and tore at each other. Near at hand grew a solitary plant, with flowers of scarlet. But no sooner had Shireef observed it than the stony soil under the plant cracked open and there heaved up from the earth beneath an enormous scorpion, which turned instantly and began to move towards him.

Shireef stood his ground. He stared into the red eyes of the beast, the sting of which surged high above him.

The scorpion spoke.

'Get upon my carapace, little man.'

And Shireef noted that between its eye-stalks there was the mark of King Suleiman, which had bound it to the magician's will. So Shireef got himself up on the scorpion's back, and it scuttled off with him, over the desert plain under the sky of fire, until they arrived at a deep well, the bottom of which was not to be seen.

'Unwind your turban, little man,' said the scorpion, 'and tie the end to my foreclaw. Then lower yourself into the pit.'

Shireef did not waste words, but obeyed the scorpion,

though he doubted there was enough silk in one man's turban to support him all the distance into the well's depths.

The scorpion crouched over the well-head, as Shireef, hand under hand, climbed down into the sightless gloom below. After a time even the shrieks of the battling eagles grew dim, but still there was enough of the turban left to bear him. And when Shireef suddenly reached the end of the silk, lowering his feet, he touched a floor with their tips.

Another voice spoke out of the dark.

'Come here and embrace me.'

Shireef had no more than looked about when the dark became manifest. An enormous serpent had upreared itself, and next coiled him round. And he saw it plainly for it was itself luminous. But he did not struggle when the scaly mask approached him and the blood-red eyes beamed on him. On its brow was the mage's mark.

'Thus you have passed, without flinching, all the tests but one,' said the serpent. 'Now you have only to answer the riddle I will pose you. But if you cannot, you shall be slain.'

'I await the riddle,' said Shireef (though he shuddered once).

'I am subtle,' said the serpent, 'I am cruel. Put into me pure gold and you will get back dross. Feed me and I will shrivel. Starve me and my poison will swell and increase. I am to all men a hollow coffer to be filled and a shut door that will not be opened. What is my name?'

The nobleman's second son smiled once more, there in the dark, in the serpent's clutch.

'Your name,' said he, 'is Shireef.'

The serpent sighed. 'There is no stronger for good or ill than he that knows himself.' But its words and breath became then the whirlwind, which tossed up Shireef the subtle, the cruel, the hollow coffer, the closed door, through toils of pitch and flame, and out into the magician's tower.

As the eyes of Shireef cleared, he beheld this mighty

sorcerer standing before him touching his forehead with the point of a strangely shining sword. It burnt Shireef, but he made no complaint.

'Now you are my slave,' said the mage. 'But to other men, a prince you will be, and a tyrant. Only if you fail me, you will fall, and then the tiniest beetle, crushed beneath a beggar's heel, even that will pity you.'

'So be it,' said Shireef.

The porters of the dawn uplifted and bore off the silver-studded lid of night. From the minarets there poured out over the city the call to prayer, and in the stables of the mansion above the Tigris, one raised himself and bethought him of offering worship to God. But such was not possible.

'Allah is merciful! Now what is this?' gasped the unfortunate one. But from his mouth issued other sounds entirely.

Presently grooms came to the stall, and leading out the fat, ungainly donkey, which heaved forth unusual moans, and stumbled over its four hoofs continuously, they took it off to be sold in the market.

However, as the donkey was led away, one of its sideways eyes glimpsed, behind a high window, two round smooth arms (upon which familiar bracelets sparkled) encircling the neck of a man whose name was not Khassim. And then the donkey lamented indeed, but what it got for its pains was a kick.

All this while, it may be remembered, there had existed a third son, the nobleman's youngest, Ahmed. Since his elder brothers quite discounted him, he had not much figured in their lives. He had, nevertheless, attended his dying father, and mourned him, observed Khassim's courtship of a young widow, and the wedding, and at length received his order to quit the household with no vast astonishment, nor any demur.

It was true that Ahmed, of all his kin, had the least in the way of resources. And it might be said he had been

67

careless of what he had. For he had spent much of his slight riches on entertainments and gifts for his friends, and given most of the rest away in alms.

This very day, indeed, on a street of the city, Ahmed might be perceived handing his last coins to a beggar, who blessed him. But another person, coming on the scene, upbraided Ahmed. 'Young fellow, I know your situation. What do you mean by it, leaving yourself with nothing in this feckless manner?'

'Only three things are sure,' remarked Ahmed pleasantly. (He was in all forms very pleasant, not least to the eye and the ear.) 'God is above us, Fate surrounds us, and one day, every man must die.'

'That does not justify the prodigal,' chid the other.

'Perhaps you are right,' conceded Ahmed with grace. 'But it seems to me that I will put my trust in Allah the All-Wise. Being human, I am, at my best, liable to fault. But God is perfect. A man has only to be patient, to be shown his path.'

Now the one who had been questioning and chiding Ahmed was a stranger, very tall and clad in white, and the hood of his mantle hid his face. Yet as they talked, the white of him seemed to become ever brighter, until Ahmed could hardly keep his eyes on it. Moreover, the tones of the stranger, which at the start had been irritated, now turned musical, kingly and profound.

'Perhaps,' said this interesting man, 'you should go to the houses of your friends. When you were wealthy, you were unceasingly kind to them, and no doubt they would be glad to help you at this hour.'

'It is considerate of you to advise me,' said Ahmed, 'but I would rather my friends were left in peace. None of them is rich, and all have burdens of their own. For myself, I am light-hearted, and besides, consider this an adventure. Who knows what God may put in my way? For if a child asks his father for bread or a fish, will that father give him a stone?'

'There are many fish,' said the stranger, then, 'in the river.'

And that said, he turned aside into a walk between the walls of two buildings, and there his white brilliance faded abruptly, so he was not to be seen.

But Ahmed thought to himself. *That is as good a path as another*.

And so he went down through Baghdad, that great and enterprising city, to the rim of the brown river Tigris.

On the banks, at a spot where the fishermen were setting to work with their nets, Ahmed paused. After a time, seeing a handsome and well-dressed youth gazing at them attentively, some of the fishermen left off their toil and came to ask his desire.

Ahmed replied that he was of a mind to learn the trade of fisher.

The fishermen scoffed.

'Do not mock us, high-born boy. This life is not for you.'

So then he asked their permission merely to observe them and what they did. To that they agreed, and resumed their labours, now and then jesting at his expense.

But Ahmed did watch very closely, and after midday prayers he went on along the shore, and finding a fisherman sleeping beneath an awning, roused him and acquired from him his mended net in exchange for a silver ring. (This fisherman, not believing his luck and thinking Ahmed to be addled, went scampering off in haste.)

Ahmed waited a space, until the time of day and state of the water seemed propitious, then wading out, he cast the net.

At the first try, nothing came up but some weed from the mud; and at the second try, a rotted piece of timber. But Ahmed only laughed and said, 'The river is joking with me. I can hardly blame her. How many thousands of years she has taken her way here, but I shall come and go like a gnat across the surface.'

All day he cast, but with no results, though never losing heart.

Then, well into the afternoon, the upper air grew thick with birds. This seemed to augur well, and he cast the net a final time.

Almost at once it turned heavy, but from the movement of the cord in his hands, he could tell something live had been snared.

Ahmed hauled on the net, and his catch resisted him. The sun had come down low over the river, glowing between the walls on the farther bank and making on the water a spill of gold. And up out of this molten gold there suddenly burst the net. Its captive was a large fish, gleaming like nacre, with a crest of golden filigree and emerald upon its head. And this fish lay in its cage in the sunset, staring at Ahmed sorrowfully from the most beautiful eyes.

'Why,' said Ahmed, 'though I have hoped all day for a catch, you I cannot keep. Surely you are the queen of fishes? Trust me. I will cut the net and let you go.'

And without another thought, he drew his knife and cut the net. Out swam the remarkable fish, but it did not at once dive down under the river. Instead it circled Ahmed, round and round, lifting its face from the water and gazing up at him, and then, taking the edge of his coat in its lips, it began to tug and pull at him in turn.

'Dear fish,' said he, perplexed, 'be wary of those circling birds above.' And, when it did not heed them, 'Where is it you would take me?'

The fish vanished under the surface, but still keeping the edge of his garment in its mouth. Ahmed was amazed. The fish reappeared, and stared at him once more with imploring eyes.

'If I follow, I shall surely drown,' said Ahmed.

The fish loosed his coat and spoke to him with the voice of a girl.

'Do you believe you hear me speak?'

Ahmed, startled, answered: 'Yes!'

'Believe then also that, through my friendship, you will not drown under the river.'

And that said, she again pulled at his garment. Ahmed,

bowing to the east, murmured, 'Most wonderful is God, who has made all things, and of such variety!' And then he dived after the fish into the depths of the Tigris, leaving only the broken ripples of gold to mark their going down.

Under the river was darkness, but the magical fish gave off a light of her own, and moved like a swift lamp before him. As she had promised, Ahmed found that he could breathe without difficulty, although he had no inkling by what means.

Shortly, the fish led him amongst a forest or town of ancient, foundered ships, merchantmen and fishing-craft both, anchored where the flow of the river had left them, and plastered over with black slime. Beyond this place lay a valley like a cauldron of pale sand, lit by a faint luminescence the source of which was not to be seen. And here rested one last ship, a magnificent vessel, as it looked only newly sunk. Her sails were reefed, and the carving and paint on her sides stayed vivid.

To this ship the fish hurried, and, darting up, disappeared over the rail. Ahmed swam after, and no sooner had he gained the deck than he met a sight which halted him.

Three maidens of great loveliness, clad like princesses, prostrated themselves to him, their draperies and veils blowing softly at the motions of the water. Then one, rising up like a flower opening in the dawn, conducted him along the deck, to the cabin, the inlaid doors of which stood wide.

Within the cabin, gilded lamps set with carbuncles burned with sorcerous fire, and carpets of Samarkand hung, dyes unimpaired, upon the walls. And in the splendour there waited a maiden whose loveliness was, to the loveliness of her servants, that of a peerless rose amid jasmine. She was dressed in clothing of nacre silk, and wore a headdress of golden filigree adorned with chains of emeralds. And the eyes of the maiden were like a world of midnight skies, so lustrous they were, and so heavenly.

'Behold me, as I really am,' invited the maiden. 'But

know, that only here, sheltered by the contrivance of my father on this sunken ship, may I take my proper form.'

Then Ahmed said to her, 'Lady, even in the guise of the fish, it seems I knew you. Did I not call you a queen of your kind?'

'So you did, and set me free. Woe had been your lot if you had dealt otherwise, for even in the shape of a fish, my father left for me some protection.'

'If I had harmed you, I should have deserved nothing better than woe.'

Then the lady bade him be seated, and the charming maids entered and served for them a feast of rare delicacies from the earth's four corners.

And while they feasted, they spoke of trivial and gentle things, but when they had finished with the feast, the maidens brought perfumes and honey and sweet-meats, and the juices of fruits, and crystalline water, all of which was miraculously possible in the river's depths, nor did the river in any way taint anything. Then, on tortoiseshell harps, the maidens made silvery music. And to the sound of it, in a voice also of silver, the lady recounted to Ahmed her story.

Her name, she said, was Jehaneh. Her father, a rich man, a scholar, and something of a mage, had also been a traveller through inclination. And in his maturer years he had settled on the city of Baghdad for a domicile, and even on the wife he would take there. Accordingly he set out, with all his household and his only daughter (the child of a previous union which Death himself had dissolved). Many months of exotic travel ensued, until they entered the mouth of the mighty Tigris.

Now the ship was a possession of the scholar, and the captain a former servant of his. The voyage had been of the pleasantest, and perhaps, entering the homeward stretch, they had grown too trustful of Fate, seeing it had been good to them.

Some miles below the City, where the arid shores came down lion-like to drink at the river, the ship's watch spied a floating raft and a man lying on it who feebly hailed them.

The flotsam was grappled and the unfortunate brought on board.

Being revived, he explained that he was a journeying noble from a distant land, who had fallen prey to the plot of enemies. His slaves, corrupted by these men, had turned on him, robbed and abused him, and left him for a corpse in the desert. He had struggled to the riverbank nevertheless, and fashioned the flimsy raft, but his strength then giving way, he abandoned himself to the will of God.

Jehaneh's father, finding the man to be like himself a traveller, and erudite, soon took to him. But not so Jehaneh herself, who had been privy to some of their talk behind a screen. Her father, however, fondly put by her doubts and would hear no word against the man.

It happened that the father of Jehaneh, in his youth, had gained possession of a very extraordinary ring. It contained a perfect sapphire, the gem of the planet Mushtar, ruler of justice and strength, and it had, besides keeping the wearer in fortune and health, certain sorcerous properties. The scholar for a fact never, since getting hold of it, removed the jewel from his finger, and by now flesh and metal had all but become one.

In the midst of the night, as the ship lay at anchor, and each save the watch might be supposed asleep, Jehaneh woke from an anxious doze, thinking she heard her father call to her. Her maids still slumbered, and the whole ship seemed doused in a velvet gloom, unleavened by stars or lamps.

Proceeding to the curtain and screen that marked off the scholar's portion of the cabin, Jehaneh called to him in turn. 'It is nothing of any import,' replied the scholar. 'Only that I was having a peculiar dream.'

'Pray tell it me, my father.'

Then the scholar ruefully recounted that in the dream he had felt something plucking urgently at the sapphire ring, but starting up awake he found matters otherwise.

'And surely no one,' he added, 'could take the ring from me unless they have the finger with it.'

At his words Jehaneh was filled with terror, but she did not speak. Being courageous, she drew a dagger which she kept for her own protection, and sat all the remainder of the night by the screen, listening and alert, in vigil over her father's slumber. But not a sight nor another sound, nor any disturbance, occurred throughout the last hours of darkness.

Then the dawn began to bloom on sky and river, and in the first soft moments of the light, a loud fearful cry galvanized the ship.

All who might rushed out on to the deck, and there they came on the ship's watchman, gibbering with fright. When once he could bring himself to utter, he declared that, just as the darkness was fading, he had perceived a slender stream of mist curling out from the passengers' cabin. This, swirling upright, put on a shape so awful that it had almost deprived the observer of reason. Questioned as to the nature of this shape, the man answered that it had been a giant thing, somewhat resembling a man, but three times at least man's height, tusked like an elephant, and with the claws of a lion.

'It is a jinni!' exclaimed the crew, virtually as one.

'Truly, I think it may be so,' said Jehaneh's father, and she saw that he had turned deadly pale. Motioning her to follow him, he went back instantly to the cabin. Seating her before him there, he spoke thus: 'I have been stubborn in not heeding your instincts when earlier you warned me. See now what has befallen.' And he showed her his hand. Jehaneh was struck by horror. There was not a mark on the flesh, but the finger which had worn the sapphire had shrunk down and wasted away until it was no bigger than the digit of a three-day infant. The ring itself was gone.

Even at that moment a shadow seemed to cover the ship, as if the dark of night were returning.

'That one is a powerful and evil sorcerer, there can be no doubt,' continued the scholar. 'Perhaps some misfortune did indeed chance upon him, so he requires the virtue of the ring, or perhaps he is only greedy and a player of games. Whatever, we are in much danger still. Dearest daughter, he can intend only wickedness, and I possess one method alone by which to protect you and the innocent maidens who are yours. There are spells I know of transformation, and this ship being mine, I have also long since fitted it with uncanny means and benefits, for one can be sure of nothing save the omniscience of God.'

Then the father told his child that, if she would suffer it, he would transform her and her maidens into fishes, and send the ship to the bottom of the river. For the captain and crew another remedy should be found. The scholar alone would brave, as best he might, the schemes and rage of the magician. Should he survive, he would seek and free Jehaneh – and he would have said more to her, but that second the door rushed open and there stood the wretch they had succoured, grinning at them, with the stolen sapphire on his hand. Behind him the sky was as black as in eclipse, and inky cloud had enveloped the ship, and the sailors might be heard calling on Allah.

'See where your generosity had delivered you,' said this evil man. 'Now you are my slaves and your treasure and goods shall be at my service too, and this dear daughter I will have for my pleasure.'

But the scholar rose to his feet and shouted aloud a spell of such substance that the river boiled and the black sky seemed to crack.

Immediately all the crew of the ship, and the captain, were flung up in the air, and there they found themselves a flock of birds, mewing and soaring. For Jehaneh and her maidens, their peerless skin and silken garments turned to the sheerest scales, and they were cast away into the water like four pearls beyond price.

The evil magician stood in anger, cursing all things, until he was moved to take the scholar by the throat. Even as he did so, with a colossal shudder the great ship sprang a hundred vents, took water and began to go down.

'So all escape but you! Then you must pay for all.'

'For that reason I have remained,' responded the scholar.

And these were the last words and sight Jehaneh had of her father as the spell dashed her away into the river's depths.

'Therefore you see me, most unhappy of women,' said Jehaneh at her tale's conclusion. 'Bereft of the father whom I loved, and held safe from the vengeance of his foe solely by a form which, save here, I am unable to relinquish. The ability of speech too I have retained, though I have learned that few can hear me. For most, being convinced fish cannot talk in the tongue of men, cry out to them as I may, they stay deaf to me. Other safeguards my wise father placed on me also, for once or twice I or my maidens have been trapped in the net of a fisher who could not free us. But before we came ashore, the strands of the net would part and change to serpents and strike at him, and the man would run away screaming with pain and fear. But such things are small consolation. As you will have noted, my father's own powers are such that he must certainly have escaped himself, had he not deemed it needful that one linger to deflect the sorcerer's spite, and in itself this argues ill for his survival. Three years have passed since that black dawning. Yet always I have hoped that I should some day come on a man who is both clever and kind, who would have the wit to hear and to credit me. (For the ability I possess to breathe beneath the water in woman's shape is extended to any who keep me company, whether I am woman or fish.) Tell me, therefore, if in you, as I pray I have, I discover a champion?'

Ahmed, who was bemused, though not at all displeasingly so, replied, 'If you wish it, it shall be my wish also. What would you have me do?'

'Against all wisdom, my heart tells me my father is living yet – though, lacking the ring, in thrall to the sorcerer. I am not able, but you if you would might search for him and, if it is written, effect his release.'

'For that, I must overcome the magician.'

76

'It is undeniable. I must not ask you to put yourself into such peril.'

'There is no need to ask me,' said Ahmed, 'for it is my only desire in the world to bring you happiness.'

For some months then, Ahmed was in the service of the fish-maiden.

By day and by night he hunted the city, going here and there, and falling into chat with whomsoever he could, but learning nothing much. For his purpose, and also having generally sparse funds, he assumed the attire of a beggar. That fraternity, many of whom recalled his charity in better days, were considerate of him, and often enough he shared the edible titbits of their profession, or slept under their protection beneath the walls and wells of Baghdad the bountiful. But now and again Ahmed might have a piece of silver or a goblet of ribbed glass, and these things he would sell, and distribute the money, keeping for himself what was necessary and no more. And such items were the gifts of Jehaneh.

Rising from the river on the nights of the new and the full moon, a shimmering fish, she would greet Ahmed with tender looks and gracious thanks, for all that he had no news to return her. (Sometimes a flock of birds overhung their meetings, black on the moon, and so high up their likeness was not to be discerned. Ahmed presumed these birds must represent the crew of the sunken ship, transformed by the scholar's protective spell.) But whatever the magical atmosphere of their meetings, the young man would not go down again with Jehaneh into the river, to feast with her on the ship or to review once more her human beauty, saying he had not yet earned this reward.

One dusk, just after the call to prayer, the figure of a tall man stepped into the path of Ahmed, who was hastening to the mosque. The ethereal summons was dying like dim music in an ember sky, but Ahmed courteously stopped and asked his interrupter how he could serve him. To that the man replied: 'Do not go by this road, but rather take that alley, there.'

Now Ahmed could not but notice that the alley was a less convenient route to the mosque, and some idea of the robbers of the west bank went over his mind. Yet the tall one, clad in white, had so commanding and benign a presence that Ahmed merely thanked him and obeyed. And in those instants Ahmed recollected the stranger of the white mantle who had sent him to the river to fish, and in that way brought him together with the exquisite Jehaneh. A minute more and such reveries were swept from his brain by an appalling din which was going on in the alley behind a pot-seller's shop. From the yard there burst oaths and the thud of blows, the smash of pots, and frantic braying. Ahmed looked into the yard.

'Shaitan take the beast!' cried the potter, as he wrestled with a donkey among the breakages. 'The creature is possessed, I am sure of it.'

'How can you think it?' inquired Ahmed.

'Because, having no business to, it inclines to worship Allah. And that is very well, but I am not a rich man, and I have lost a great many pots through the predilection of this animal for throwing itself down on the ground, with its hairy nose towards Mecca, at every cry to prayer. I have had the beast for seven days and it has already cost me a fortune. I got it from a seller of gourds who, I now realize, had had the same trouble but spared me the information, saying his fruit had been bruised by camels.' And that revealed, the potter laid about the donkey again with his stick. 'What is more,' affirmed the potter, between smitings, 'at sunset tonight a lord and his retinue rode by on horses, going to a banquet, and this spawn of the Devil began to roar and prance, and ran after them along the street to the very gates of a mansion there, and more of my wares perished in this excursion. A thousand ills drop on the beast!'

'Stay your hand,' said Ahmed, helping the potter to do so. 'Here are some silver coins. Will you accept them in exchange for your donkey?'

'In exchange for such a curse I can accept nothing. How can I cheat you as I was cheated? It is a worthless animal inhabited by afrits.'

'Nevertheless,' said Ahmed, 'pray take the dirhams and rest your stick.'

So the potter agreed, thinking privately that the handsome youth was touched, and gave the donkey's rope into his hand.

Out into the dark street they went then, Ahmed and the donkey, both demure and silent. But when Ahmed set his hand on the donkey's head, it shook him off peevishly. Ahmed murmured, 'Since you wish to pray, I will take you to the gate of the mosque. There you may feel free to worship as you require.'

This Ahmed did, going to the mosque and halting the donkey at the gate. Sure enough, the donkey instantly prostrated itself and mumbled the softest and most pious of brays. Ahmed prayed beside the donkey, seeing nothing wrong in that, for it seemed to him that a creature which had the wit to praise God was a better companion than many of his fellow men.

When they had finished their prayers, Ahmed, turning to the donkey, saw that it was weeping. The round tears coursed down its face and fell like heavy rain into the dust.

'Be comforted, O donkey,' said Ahmed. 'No man shall beat you ever again, or deny you your religion, or force you to bear a load. While I live I will care for you and feed you and if I cannot we will go hungry together. Come, God made you and holds the world in His arms. Fear nothing. You shall be my brother.'

At these words, the donkey came up to Ahmed and hung its head, like one ashamed. But no sooner had Ahmed stretched out his hand again, than the animal was off, running along the street, but looking back constantly, sometimes pausing and stamping with its hoofs, until Ahmed hastened after. And while this was happening, Ahmed bethought him of Jehaneh once again, and wondered if here too was one enchanted out of human shape.

Where the street ended, there stood the high walls of a

mansion, the boughs of whose scented garden trees seemed to lift the moon in their branches. But above the trees, and higher at this hour even than the moon, there arose a straight black tower with a solitary cold light ablaze in it.

Having reached the mansion's wall, the donkey slunk into the shadow of an archway.

'Whose house is this?' asked Ahmed of the donkey's ear. 'Someone who has wronged you, it seems to me.'

He was consumed by curiosity, and securing the donkey, Ahmed pulled his ragged beggar's garb about him, and went around the wall until he arrived at a great door, which was of ebony studded with grotesque faces of brass.

Ahmed rapped on this door.

Presently it was opened by a Nubian porter clothed in a leopard's pelt. But the eyes of the Nubian were like milky fires – which not every man would have seen, but Ahmed saw them.

'Who knocks?' asked the jinni, and the teeth of it were all pointed.

'A poor beggar,' grovelled Ahmed. 'Alms, for the love of Allah.'

At that, the jinni grimaced, and reaching into a bag tied at its waist, threw down a loaf before Ahmed.

'Blessing and honour stifle and smother you, lordly one,' said Ahmed. 'And who is your master, that I may bless him also?'

The jinni needlessly showed yet more its fangs, and pointed away into the house.

'Look there. That is my master.'

And Ahmed, gazing through the lamplit vestibule, saw a feast going on in an inner court. But though he perceived the dancing of girls like roses on amber stalks, and the thrill of fountains gushing wine, and golden stuffs that glowed, and over all heard loud laughter and the clash of cymbals, he could not be certain of any face, or catch any voice or name.

'Well then, said Ahmed, 'I will bless him as the Lord of the Black Tower.'

'Do so,' said the jinni playfully, picking its teeth with a

large dagger. 'By that title he comes to be known in your city. Or else they call him the Mage of the Birds. Or, the Master of the Four Rings.'

Ahmed hesitated. Then he said merrily, 'Yes, I have heard of him. The rings are all great diamonds, are they not?'

'Tush! said the jinni. 'What could you know? One is a diamond. And one a topaz and another a ruby. These three are old friends of his.'

'That is only three rings,' said Ahmed. 'You misnamed him then, since he masters only those.'

'Recently he has acquired a fourth ring,' said the jinni. 'A sapphire, if the likes of you know even what such a thing can be. Now get off with you, or you shall be bitten!'

Ahmed removed himself from the portal and the door was slammed. Ahmed returned to share the loaf with the donkey, saying to it only, 'Brother, your enemy is also mine.'

But near midnight, when the feast began to end in the mansion of the black tower, Ahmed and the donkey went down to another place of shadows to see who left the house.

And in that fashion, after some watching, they beheld, both of them, he who had ridden past the potter's shop formerly, arrayed like a king and mounted on a horse of snow: brother Shireef.

'Welcome, matchless husband,' said Nadina, bowing like the lily.

'It is late,' said he.

'Wisdom glitters in your every word.'

'My meaning is: it being late, why then are you here, paragon of wives?'

'Only to salute you, and promote your health and vigour with this herbal drink I have prepared.'

Shireef regarded the cup which had just been borne in by Nadina's old servant woman. (This crone had become something of a trial to him, as she was constantly peeking and leering at him. And this very minute, having set the cup by the window, she gave him such a ribald look and wink that Shireef was moved to strike her – but before he could do it she had waddled out.) For the drink, it was jewel-clear and delicious-smelling.

'I may not yet seek my bed,' announced Shireef. 'Our master has bidden me back, in the guise we use, one hour from this.'

'He tries you sorely,' said Nadina. 'Nevertheless, drink, dear husband. It will increase your mental capacity.'

Saying this, Nadina went to the table and took up the cup, which she brought to Shireef. But as her back was to the window, there suddenly appeared there a pale, ghostly apparition, which dolefully shook its head. This was the Circassian mute, Shireef's slave, who being bidden ever to spy on any of his mistress's mixings and fermentations, had proved this one to be a narcotic of unusual potence.

Something in Shireef's demeanour caused his wife to glance behind her at the window, but the Circassian was already gone into the branches of a benighted tree.

Shireef accepted the cup, but said, 'Why will you try these tricks? Is it to make a fool of me before the magician, or to make me seem disobedient to him? Or is the drug slower, that it should seize on me in flight, and opening my mouth in a yawn, the talisman be lost, and I tumble to oblivion?'

'You mistake me,' said Nadina.

'Then swallow the syrup yourself.' And with one hand he offered her the goblet, while with the other he drew the dagger from his sash.

Nadina's eyes flashed like swords, but she sheathed them with her lids. She took the cup and sipped at it. It fell from her grip and she after it, to lie still as marble that breathed.

'Witch,' said Shireef, 'I have informed your master several times of the pest you become to me. I shall be rid of you soon enough, when once he too is bored with you.'

Striding to the table, he picked up a small feather which lay there. Placing this under his tongue, he was transformed at once into a bronze-brown falcon. Exactly then, in through the window came bounding a tattered beggar who, with a whoop, caught the falcon in a snare of rags and, gasping the bird by the neck, forced open its beak. Out dropped the magical feather of the metamorphosis, and there lay Shireef upon the ground, with his younger brother Ahmed kneeling upon him.

'Here is my own knife, freshly sharpened,' said Ahmed, 'and by you, the spillage of the drugged drink. I offer you the same choice as you offered your wife. Lap the one or endure the steel of the other.'

'What crankiness is this?' rasped Shireef, half-choked and greatly discommoded.

'Nor will your albino servant come to your aid,' confided Ahmed, 'since, finding him occupying the tree I had climbed as I listened to your connubial conversation, I have tied him there that he may enjoy it better. Come now, no more delay, for I gather your mage-master is expecting you.'

Shireef lay snarling, but the knife now pressed on his windpipe. He turned away and sucked up some of the opiate from the floor. Ahmed encouraged him to take more.

'The sun rose,' said Shireef, when he had done drinking, 'and the sun declared, "It is day." But later the night returned. Be thou warned.'

'Hush, go to sleep, my brother,' said Ahmed.

And Shireef discovered he must.

Ahmed threw off his beggar's trim and, stripping his brother, put on instead Shireef's glories of the banquet. Clad in this raiment, Ahmed much resembled Shireef, for they were close kin. Next, taking the feather, Ahmed put it under his tongue. Another second and he was in the air, and up and out through the window he went, across the gardens, and west over the city towards the sorcerer's tower.

As the falcon-Ahmed approached the tower, he saw, flying about it, another of falcon-kind, blacker than the night. But this bird, having circled him once, gave a thin cry and winged away.

One more slave of the mage's, no doubt, thought Ahmed, and he went in at the window of the sorcerous chamber.

Here lamps yet burned, and even as he flew among them a huge voice of brass boomed out in some unknown language. The feather fell from Ahmed's mouth and he was a man again, albeit in the likeness of his brother.

A pair of doors opened and the magician entered, in his occult robes. Ahmed bowed to the floor. But as he did it, he heeded the four great rings on the mage's left hand, a topaz, a ruby, a diamond, and a sapphire.

'You return promptly, Shireef,' said the magician. 'And you have cause. Every day my influence in the city expands, and such as yourself have value for me, but not of a bottomless sort. Be ever diligent, or I will slough you. There are those that you sat at dinner with tonight in my hall, who – waxing careless – shortly shall be cast down, where worms and flies shall pity them.'

'Master and lord,' said Ahmed coolly, and in the tones of Shireef, 'almost I was prevented from attending you. That daughter of sheep, the woman Nadina, this very night would have drugged me and kept me from your service.'

'Yes, she grows stupid,' said the mage, seeming to ponder. 'But as I have intimated, she has her grievance.'

Ahmed prudently forebore to comment. The mage toyed with an ebony wand, and the huge jewels flamed and snapped on his fingers.

Presently Ahmed, lowering his voice into an icier vein, inquired, 'Will you not grant me leave to slay the woman?' And going nearer the magician, he drew out his own knife mildly, as if to display the weapon's sharpness. 'See, I have whetted the edge of this for her throat.'

'Stay your annoyance a season more,' said the sorcerer. 'There is other commerce to be seen to first. But perchance I will give you the gift before too long.'

At that Ahmed clasped the sorcerer's hand, with its garland of rings, and pressed on it his kiss. Then, raising both his head and his knife, with all his strength he dealt the mage a terrible blow. The whetted metal sheared through the sorcerer's wrist. The blood flushed forth and stained the robes of both, and the floor of the chamber and its furnishings. But Ahmed sprang away, the severed hand held fast in his.

'What have you done?' screamed the sorcerer.

'Do you not know, lord?' asked Ahmed. 'Why, I believe I have removed your powers from you. For they are in these jewels, are they not? Each one renders you facility in something, and the sapphire here completes the whole.'

The magician foamed at the lips. Lightnings whipped about the chamber, and the lamps went out.

'Not all my powers, not all!' raged he. And pointing at Ahmed he thundered like the storm: 'Go you to the outer heaven of your planet, ascendant at your birth, and be imprisoned there.'

And then he added words in the unknown language of his sorcery.

At that Ahmed was in the midst of a whirling, as if the earth erupted and the sky fell. He was plunged away, holding yet the dripping knife and the severed hand.

Once the tumult ceased, Ahmed uncovered his face, got up and looked about him. He stood upon turf smooth as that of his father's lawns, but of a violet hue, and with blue flowers breaking. Close by was a lake of opalescent water whose muted ripples came constantly to shore among the gem-like pebbles lying there. Above hung a sky of hyacinth and rose, over which, sometimes, white doves went drifting.

Ahmed was sustained by amazement. So serene was the environment that any fear left him.

(The sorcerer, thinking his assailant to be Shireef, had condemned him to the outer heaven of his birth planet, Marikh, pictured formerly. But as it was Ahmed that he hexed in this way, he had sent him to another spot, that of his personal planet, Aspiroz, the ruler of beauty and healing.)

The young man wandered dreamily a while along the shore of the translucent lake, until at length he came to a pasture where milk-white bulls were grazing on the flowers. One of these animals came walking over to Ahmed, and addressed him in the mortal tongue.

'Throw down your knife,' said the white bull. And on its forehead he saw there was the mark of a balance.

So Ahmed, charmed by the gracious creature, threw down the knife, which changed immediately into a flowering bush.

'For that other loathsome thing you hold, regard the jewels that are on it, then throw it down also.'

Ahmed again did as the bull suggested. The severed hand, when it struck the earth, shattered into a hundred fragments, and these became smooth opaline pebbles that rolled away towards the hem of the water. But the rings flamed on in the grass.

'The topaz,' said the bull, 'you must rub to make warm. The ruby, spit on, to make moist. The diamond turn three times eastward. The sapphire you must admonish by its secret name, which few men know, but if you wish, I will tell it you.'

'I thank you for these clues to power,' said Ahmed. 'But it is not my destiny to become a sorcerer. There is one I have been told of, in whose possession such baubles might be well and virtuously utilized. For myself, I wish only to win home to my city, be rid of an enemy there, and finally to set free the father of her I mean to make my bride.'

'Both last intentions will be a simple matter,' said the white bull. 'The second is even now being seen to. But for the first, you must after all rub the topaz. Only remain courageous and speak boldly, and you will have your way.'

Ahmed thanked the bull, which galloped off so weightlessly that the young man perceived at last that it was winged.

Then, bracing himself, he gathered up the four rings and rubbed the topaz.

Soon it grew hot to the touch and began to coruscate like burning sulphur. Next, out of the rosy air there tore

86

seven fearsome beings, palpably jinn, each one towering up higher than three elephants together. One had tusks and claws and the mane of a lion, another was like a Nubian, but with pointed fangs and a leopard's tail, a third had blotched skin of black and white, like a goat's, a fourth had four pairs of arms, and the three others were of such an aspect they were actually indescribable. But each had also the mark of Suleiman on his forehead. And as it appeared, each grovelled and moaned at Ahmed, calling him *Master*, and asking what he craved.

'Return me instantly to the sorcerer's black tower in Baghdad!'

And no sooner said – than done.

In the tower chamber a single lamp had been lit. By its radiance, stretched upon the ground was visible the body of the magician. He had been slaughtered, stabbed, and his eyes plucked from his head. On his breast a black falcon perched, fanning with its wings and mewing shrilly. Before the lamp stood a woman, a dagger lying at her feet. It was Nadina. As Ahmed was whirled into the chamber, with the seven jinn in attendance upon him, she fell to her knees and hid her face in her veil.

Ahmed dismissed the jinn, which vanished. But he had pushed the rings on to his fingers, and these he showed Nadina. 'Know I have at my beck a strong army.'

'Lord,' said Nadina, 'will you not reckon how I adore the mage, by my act on him with that dagger? And will you grant me room to tell my story?'

Ahmed assented.

Then Nadina told him this, as follows:

Some years before, her own father, having glimpsed Death idling at his gate and practising his knock, arranged for Nadina a marriage. The man was a friend of her father's youth, not young, therefore, but hale and wise, and possessed of wealth, and very learned. Nadina had, besides, seen him when she was but a child, and always kept for him a great partiality. At that time he was situated in a distant country, where previously he had wed

87

and buried a wife, who had borne him one daughter.

The bridegroom was already making towards the city and his new union, when Nadina's father happened on Death in the garden, and Death, as is his wont, would not take no for an answer. Left unprotected in her sorrow, Nadina prayed that her husband would quickly reach her side. It was not to be. Even as he sailed the river towards Baghdad, an evil sorcerer was in pursuit of him and of a magical ring in his keeping. And this one succeeded in his malign plans, had the ring, and enslaved the scholar.

Now Nadina would have learned no detail of this, if it had not been for the scholar's former servant, the captain of the ship. The scholar had turned him into a black falcon to save him from the magician's spleen. And the bird, having earlier been told the road to Nadina's house, flew there. Being herself something versed in occult art, Nadina was able to decipher some of what he would relay to her. All in all, the plight of her betrothed.

Nadina was overwhelmed by distress, but taking no measure of her own danger, she sought out the abode of the sorcerer and went there to beg for the liberation of the scholar and his daughter – whom she also supposed the mage's prisoner.

'Young woman, I will enlighten you. Her, the stingy father altered into a fish, and hid her in the river, where she may waste her fishy, chilly life as she desires. But in the case of the scholar, maybe I will let him go, if you will permit me, with proper compliance, your favours.'

'And if I do that, lord,' had answered Nadina, 'I will be ruined.'

'It is all one to me,' said the mage, licking his fat lips. 'Either way, you will not have your wedding. But if you please me, then the scholar shall live.'

So then Nadina said she would do what he wanted, and arranged to visit the tower during the secrecy of night. Returning to her house, she summoned an old woman servant, who had been with her all her life, and who indeed had nursed her as a child. To this crone, Nadina made a proposal. By her own sorcerous skill, Nadina would throw over the old woman an image of Nadina's self, a form young and fair, exact in every point. The hag would then go into the mage, who would enjoy her, supposing it was Nadina he violated, while Nadina would be at some distance secure in her virginity and honour. The old servant cackled with glee at the plot, and said she was not averse to this bargain for, though the magician was wicked, she had heard he was lusty enough, and it was some while since she had had a chance at such sport.

The exchange settled, the crone (to every appearance and sense Nadina, equipped even with her dulcet voice) betook herself to the magician's tower, and spent there a night of many adventures. So she at least was no loser. But when the true Nadina presently sued again for the freedom of her husband-to-be, the magician had this to say to her: 'Because of the satisfaction you gave me, I will spare his life. But since you are so winsome, I am not yet done with you, and you will, besides, be of use to me as a snare. Therefore, I shall keep your scholar secure, and so he shall remain unless you go against me. Then I will send him head over heels out of the world.'

And to that end he showed her the scholar, where he had shut him up, and Nadina grieved, for looking on the man she loved him freshly, as she had not known how to love when a child. But the mage continued, 'You shall be a widow, though never were you a wife.' And next he sent the scholar into a deathly sleep, and incarcerated him in a large white tomb in a cemetery of the city. 'Go mourn him there with extravagance. And when men marvel and make eyes at you, lead them on and say they resemble your mortified lord.'

In that way Nadina and her household were coerced into the practice of wrong-doing, even the same which she exercised on Khassim, in order that the magician might tangle the rich and the eminent in his web. But Khassim was too foolish, and it had come to wicked Shireef to take his place. Until, growing quite desperate, Nadina had vowed she would kill her tormenter the mage. She prepared a narcotic to see Shireef from her way. He learning of the ruse, she only pretended to drink the drug and to swoon, and next seeing Ahmed also intent upon the sorcerer's overthrow, she had put on the falcon-form the mage loaned her, and hurried after.

When she reached the tower, what should she find but that Ahmed had completed half the task before his exile. Weakened by the loss of the rings and by his wound, the sorcerer was outmatched. For there came at him a black falcon that had only feigned subservience that it might await just such an opportunity, and a young woman armed with a dagger and all the ferocity of outrage.

'If you do not accept my words,' said Nadina now, kneeling at Ahmed's feet, 'then slay and be done with me. But go you after to the white tomb, hard by your father's resting-place, and break in. The sapphire ring, put on my bridegroom's finger, will restore him. Of his chaste and noble daughter, alas, I have no news.'

Ahmed laughed. 'Trust me, lady, but I do. Come, get up and be at peace. What the law has seen to cannot be undone, but you shall be to me my honoured sister, my brother Khassim's wife.'

'Never,' cried Nadina, rising angrily. 'That donkey? It is the one bad thing I have done without excuse, yet do not regret. For the rest, my old servant woman has taken on my offices with each of those lechers, the fool and the cruel. And it is she, not I – though it is a fact she bears the name Nadina as I do – who is wed to each of your brothers. I am yet as God made me, and have known no man, nor will do so, save the man for whom I was meant, whose graces are to all others the sun above dying lamps.'

'I congratulate you,' said Ahmed. 'But which donkey is it you refer to?'

As if in answer, a miserable but insistent braying clamoured over the mansion's walls.

Thus, in the earliest waking of day, there was much going up and down and to and fro about the west and east banks of the Tigris. In the cemetery there came the ill-omened sound of mallets and picks ringing on mortar, a trespass inside a tomb, and at last a man emerging into the light, giving thanks to God and his rescuers, and on his hand a sapphire ring, and three others to neighbour it, of topaz, ruby and diamond. And thereafter a black falcon was transformed into a ship's captain, and a whole flock of birds, swooping down, into a shouting and gesticulating crew. While from the deep of the brown river, a splendid vessel was brought up solely by the means of words, and on the deck were seen some pretty maidens, and one other whose beauty and joy outshone the day.

Following on these things, one wicked brother was removed where harsh punishment might complement harsh crimes. And one sillier brother emerged from the hide of a pack-beast. And he, seeing his prayers had been heard even over the potter's blows and breakages, went swiftly seeking the sacred city of Mecca, there to circle seven times the shrine, to touch the holy stone – and left behind him a wife old enough to be his grandmother, who yet hoped he might gain some wisdom on his road.

While for marriages, there were two more of them. The nights were made into pure gold by the blaze of torches and firecrackers, and the songs were so sweet and the sighs so profound, who could hear the nightingale now as she sang on her branch in the nobleman's garden?

But sing she did, and this was her message: Behold how the desert is reborn when Allah sends to it the rain. He that gives life will give back life again even to the dead.

But Death himself did hear this, as he was passing, on other business, the mansion's gate.

And Death nodded resignedly, for he had seen a second passer by at the garden's edge among the roses, an angel in blinding white, who was not beyong nurturing the happiness of men.

But nevertheless, thought Death, *the resurrection is far off*. To this house, as to all houses, he would return, some other evening.

SUSAN SHWARTZ

The Caravan's Tales

Ramadan ended and the storytellers departed, though they promised to return . . . if not next Ramadan, then the one thereafter, or the one after that: it was all kismet, they said.

'We shall return,' said one of the taletellers to the knight-prisoner, 'if only to hear how your own tale ends.'

'I fear, my masters,' said Peter of Wraysbury, 'that you will hear no happy tale. For if no ransom comes, I must surely be sold as a slave.'

'You have been as a guest, a son, in that merchant's house. Do you truly think, even though you be of a different faith – but it is all in the hands of God,' said the storyteller, and broke off.

'For mine own honour, how may I eat a man's bread, wear a man's robe, live in his house, yet make no repayment? And of what other repayment would I be considered capable?' he asked. 'I would not be the first to pay my debts with service.'

In Outremer, it had been the lot of many knights. His grandfather had taken a laming wound at the battle at the Horns of Hattin, where Saladin had crushed the Franks, and had told him how many wounded were taken up, doubtless to be sold.

The storyteller stared at him as if he were a freak of nature: well enough; he had got used to that gaze. Then the man shrugged. '*Ma'alesh*,' he said, using the wonderful Arabic word that means that things will go as they will go, and that no man can do aught to change them. It was practically the first word of Arabic Peter had learned. 'The game will play itself out. And are we not all in the hands of Allah? Let his blessing shine upon you too, foreign brother.' And then he was gone, headed for Khotan, perhaps, and points south into the kingdoms of Hind.

Once again Peter of Wraysbury paced into the bazaar and through it. For the first time, he turned to Kashgar's western gate, where he stared longingly at the high Pamirs, the mountains from whence his help must come, if it came at all. Perhaps his messenger had perished in a rockfall or in one of the snowslides which were a curse on the *bam i dunya*, the roof of the world, as the Pamirs were called. Or perhaps he had crossed the mountains and now wandered through Persia. Perhaps – and this was Peter's hope – he had met one of the parties of priests and knights whom His Holiness had sent to seek out the Great Khan in Karakoram, good men who would listen to the tale of an English knight and succour him.

As the storyteller said, he was in the hands of God. *In manuas tuas, Domine*, he whispered, bowing his head in a brief prayer. Then he blinked furiously at his tears. The guards here, he knew, would not despise him for weeping; they might only think that he had done that for which he must repent and, God knows, he had.

But as he blinked, he saw scores of tiny black figures like ants staggering down against the gold of the great dunes. In the clash of sunlight upon the anvil of the sand, their bodies shimmered, and Peter blinked a third time. He had seen oases that were no more than the sun on sand and mind and eyes. Surely this caravan might be another such illusion.

But when the dots did *not* vanish, even after he scrubbed his fists across his eyes three times, he shouted hoarsely and alerted the guards. Thus it was that Peter of Wraysbury, exile and captive, was first in Kashgar to see the caravan approaching the city from the west. The merchant who persisted in calling him 'guest' arrived panting at the gate. He too stared for a moment, then drew himself into his usual portly solemnity and waited as the caravan approached.

Wise in the ways of caravans, he pointed out the men who travelled in this one long before it reached the gates: a rug merchant, his camels laden with long, drab cylinders that would unroll into carpets the brilliance of which would rival the windows in the great cathedrals of Canterbury or York; a silk merchant bearing the heavy brocades of Persia for sale in the East, or in exchange for the gauzy silks of Hind. The files of armed men surrounding several beasts meant that sellers of fine gems, gold and silver travelled in the caravan.

Peter of Wraysbury caught his breath. He was a knight, which meant that he walked only when he could not ride. And there, approaching Kashgar in the caravan's train, were horses to gladden the heart of any man, and delight those who judged themselves judges of horseflesh: arched of neck, curved and sturdy of back, strong yet fleet, each with a lineage far longer than their silken manes or tails.

His heart leapt, and he turned eagerly towards the caravan master, forgetting his resolve to consider himself the man's property and do as he was bid. He begged to be one of the men chosen to ride out to welcome the caravan and bring it in triumph to the city. And, to his surprise, the merchant agreed.

'Seek out the men of note,' he commanded, 'and greet them fairly. Bid them come to my house. For surely, it will be some weeks until they are ready to set out once more; and they must be my guests until then. They will have tales to tell, and to hear. I myself may tell one. And you, my guest? Perhaps you will hear word of your far-off home, or share stories with us.'

To Peter's astonishment, the merchant grinned at him, then gestured at him to be gone. Why should the man care? No bonds of blood or religion bound them: as he saw it, he was dependent on the merchant's charity.

Or was he?

'I can ride and fight,' he assured the merchant. 'I

beseech you to employ me, lest I grow fat and idle.'

'Yet you claim noble birth. Shall such a man labour as one of my drovers?'

'Our Lord was a carpenter,' retorted the knight. 'And was not your Prophet himself a driver of camels? I count no honest work beneath me.'

'Then ride out now, oh honest knight, and do your honest work. At sunset, though, you must return to my house to feast and hear the new tales.'

JANE YOLEN

Memoirs of a Bottle Jinni

The sea was as dark as old blood, not the wine colour poets sing of. In the early evening it seemed to stain the sand. As usual at this time of the year the air was heavy, ill-omened.

I walked out on to the beach below my master's house whenever I could slip away unnoticed, though it was a dangerous practice. Still, it was one necessary to my wellbeing. I had been a sailor for many more years than I had been a slave and the smell of the salt air was not a luxury for me but a necessity.

If a seabird had washed up dead at my feet, its belly would have contained black worms and other evil auguries, so dark and lowering was the sky. So I wondered little at the bottle that the sea had deposited before me, certain it contained noxious fumes at best, the legacy of its long cradling in such a salty womb.

In my country poets sing the praises of wine and gift its colour to the water along the shores of Hellas, and I can think of no finer hymn. But in this land they believe their Prophet forbade them strong drink. They are a sober race who reward themselves in heaven even as they deny themselves on earth. It is a system of which I do not approve, but then I am a Greek by birth and a heathen by inclination, despite my master's long importuning. It is only by chance that I have not yet lost an eye, an ear or a hand to my master's unforgiving code. He finds me amusing but it has been seven years since I have had a drink.

I stared at the bottle. If I had any luck at all, the bottle

96

had fallen from a foreign ship and its contents would still be potable. But then, if I had any luck at all, I would not be a slave in Araby, a Greek sailor washed up on these shores the same as the bottle at my feet. My father, who was a cynic like his father before him, left me with a cynic's name – Antithias – a wry heart and an acid tongue, none proper legacies for a slave. But as blind Homer wrote, 'Few sons are like their father; many are worse.' I guessed that the wine, if drinkable, would come from an inferior year. And with that thought, I bent to pick it up.

The glass was a cloudy green, like the sea after a violent storm. Like the storm that had wrecked my ship and cast me on to a slaver's shore. There were darker flecks along the bottom, a sediment that surely foretold an undrinkable wine. I let the bottle warm between my palms.

Since the glass was too dark to let me see more. I waited past my first desire and was well into my second, letting it rise up in me like the heart of passion. The body has its own memories, though I must be frank: passion, like wine, was simply a fragrance remembered. Slaves are not lent the services of houris, nor was one my age and race useful for breeding. It had only been by feigning impotence that I had kept that part of my anatomy intact – another of my master's unforgiving laws. Even in the dark of night, alone on my own pallet, I forewent the pleasures of the hand for there were spies everywhere in his house and the eunuchs were a notably gossipy lot. Little but a slave's tongue lauding morality stood between gossip and scandal, stood between me and the knife. Besides, the woman of Araby tempted me little. They were like the bottle in my hand – beautiful and empty. A wind blowing across the mouth of each could make them sing but the tunes were worth little. I liked my women like my wine – full-bodied and tanged with history, bringing a man into poetry. So I had put my passion into work these past seven years, slave's work though it was. Blind Homer had it right, as usual: 'Labour conquers all things.' Even old lusts for women and wine.

Philosophy did not conquer movement, however, and

my hand found the cork of the bottle before I could stay it. With one swift movement I had plucked the stopper out. A thin strand of smoke rose into the air. A very bad year indeed, I thought, as the cork crumbled in my hand.

Up and up and up the smoky rope ascended and I, bottle in hand, could not move, such was my disappointment. Even my father's cynicism and his father's before him had not prepared me for such a sudden loss of all hope. My mind, a moment before full of anticipation and philosophy, was now in blackest despair. I found myself without will, reliving in my mind the moment of my capture and the first bleak days of my enslavement.

That is why it was several minutes before I realized that the smoke had begun to assume a recognizable shape above the bottle's gaping mouth: long, sensuous legs glimpsed through diaphanous trousers; a waist my hands could easily span; breasts as round as ripe pomegranates beneath a short embroidered cotton vest; and a face ... the face was smoke and air. I remembered suddenly a girl in the port of Alexandria who sold fruit from a basket and gave me a smile. She was the last girl who had smiled upon me when I was a free man and I, not knowing the future, had ignored her, so intent was I on my work. My eyes clouded over at the memory, and when they were clear again, I saw that same smile imprinted upon the face of the jinni.

'I am what you would have me be, master,' her low voice called down to me.

I reached up a hand to help her step to earth, but my hand went through hers, mortal flesh through smoky air. It was then, I think, that I really believed she was what I guessed her to be.

She smiled. 'What is your wish, master?'

I took the time to smile back. 'How many wishes do I get?'

She shook her head but still she smiled, that Alexandrian smile, all lips without a hint of teeth. But there was a dimple in her left cheek. 'One, my master, for you drew the cork but once.'

And if I draw it again?'

'The cork is gone.' This time her teeth showed as did a second dimple, on the right.

I sighed and looked at the crumbled mess in my hand, then sprinkled the cork like seed upon the sand. 'Just one.'

'Does a slave need more?' she asked in that same low voice.

'You mean that I should ask for my freedom?' I laughed and sat down on the strand. The little waves that outrun the big ones tickled my feet for I had come out barefoot. I looked across the water. 'Free to be a sailor again at my age? Free to let the sun peel the skin from my back, free to heave my guts over the stern in a blinding rain, free to wreck once more upon a slaver's shore?'

She drifted down beside me and though her smoky hand could not hold mine, I felt a breeze across my palm that could have been her touch. I could see through her to the cockleshells and white stones pocking the sand.

'Free to make love to Alexandrian women,' she said. 'Free to drink strong wine.'

'Free to have regrets in the morning either way,' I replied. Then I laughed.

She laughed back. 'What about the freedom to indulge in a dinner of roast partridge in lemons and eggplant? What about hard-boiled eggs sprinkled with vermilion? What about cinnamon tripes?' It was the meal my master had just had.

'Rich food, like rich women, gives me heartburn,' I said.

'The freedom to fill your pockets with coins?'

Looking away from her, over the clotted sea, I whispered to myself, '"Accursed thirst for gold! What dost thou not compel mortals to do,"' a line from the *Aeneid*.

'Virgil was a wise man,' she said quietly. 'For a Roman!' Then she laughed.

I turned to look at her closely for the first time. A woman who knows Virgil, be she jinni or mortal, was a woman to behold. Though her body was still composed of that shifting, smoky air, the features on her face now held steady. She no longer looked like the Alexandrian girl, but had a far more sophisticated beauty. Lined with kohl, her eyes were grey as smoke and her hair the same colour. There were shadows along her cheeks that emphasised the bone and faint smile-lines crinkling the skin at each corner of her generous mouth. She was not as young as she had first appeared, but then I am not so young myself.

'Ah, Antithias,' she said, smiling at me, 'even jinn age, though being corked up in a bottle slows down the process immeasurably.'

I spoke Homer's words to her then: 'In youth and beauty, wisdom is but rare.' I added in my own cynic's way, 'If ever.'

'You think me wise, then?' she asked, then laughed and her laughter was like the tinkling of camel bells. 'But a gaudy parrot is surely as wise, reciting another's words as his own.'

'I know no parrots who hold Virgil and Homer in their mouths,' I said, gazing at her, not with longing but with a kind of wonder. 'No jinn either.'

'You know many?'

'Parrots yes, jinn no. You are my first.'

'Then you are lucky, indeed, Greek, that you called up one of the worshippers of Allah and not one of the followers of Iblis.'

I nodded. 'Lucky indeed.'

'So to your wish, master,' she said.

'You call me master, I who am a slave,' I said. 'Do *you* not want the freedom you keep offering me? Freedom from the confining green bottle, freedom from granting wishes to any *master* who draws the cork?'

She brushed her silvery hair back from her forehead with a delicate hand. 'You do not understand the nature of the jinn,' she said. 'You do not understand the nature of the bottle.'

'I understand rank,' I said. 'On the sea I was between the captain and the rowers. In that house,' and I gestured with my head to the palace behind me, 'I am below my master and above the kitchen staff. Where are you?'

Her brow furrowed as she thought. 'If I work my wonders for centuries, I might at last attain a higher position within the jinn,' she said.

It was my turn to smile. 'Rank is a game,' I said. 'It may be conferred by birth, by accident, or by design. But rank does not honour the man. The man honours the rank.'

'You are a philosopher,' she said, her eyes lightening.

'I am a Greek,' I answered. 'It is the same thing.'

She laughed again, holding her palm over her mouth coquettishly. I could no longer see straight through her, though an occasional piece of driftwood appeared like a delicate tattoo on her skin.

'Perhaps we both need a wish,' I said, shifting my weight. One of my feet touched hers and I could feel a slight jolt, as if lightning had run between us. Such things happen occasionally on the open sea.

'Alas, I cannot wish myself,' she said in a whisper. 'I can only grant wishes.'

I looked at her lovely face washed with its sudden sadness and whispered back, 'Then I give my wish to you.'

She looked directly into my eyes and I could see her eyes turn golden in the dusky light. I could at the same time somehow see beyond them, not into the sand or water, but to a different place, a place of whirlwinds and smokeless fire.

'Then, Antithias, you will have wasted a wish,' she said. Shifting her gaze slightly, she looked behind me, her eyes opening wide in warning. As she spoke, her body seemed to melt into the air and suddenly there was a great white bird before me, beating its feathered pinions against my body before taking off towards the sky.

'Where are you going?' I cried.

'To the Valley of Abqar,' the bird called. 'To the home of my people. I will wait there for your wish, Greek. But hurry. I see both your past and your future closing in behind you.'

I turned, and pouring down the stone steps of my master's house were a half dozen guards and one shrilling

101

eunuch, pointing his flabby hand in my direction. They came towards me screaming, though what they were saying I was never to know for their scimitars were raised and my Arabic deserts me in moments of sheer terror.

I think I screamed; I am not sure. But I spun around again towards the sea and saw the bird winging away in a halo of light.

'Take me with you,' I cried. 'I desire no freedom but by your side.'

The bird shuddered as it flew, then banked sharply and headed back towards me, calling, 'Is that your wish, master?'

A scimitar descended.

'That is my wish,' I cried, as the blade bit into my throat.

We have lived now for centuries within the green bottle and Zarifa was right, I had not understood its nature. Inside is an entire world, infinite and ever-changing. The smell of the salt air blows through that world and we dwell in a house that sometimes overlooks the ocean and sometimes overlooks the desert sands.

Zarifa, my love, is as mutable, neither young nor old, neither soft nor hard. She knows the songs of blind Homer and the poet Virgil as well as the poems of the warlords of Ayyām Al-'Arab. She can sing in languages that are long dead.

And she loves me beyond my wishing, or so she says, and I must believe it, for she would not lie to me. She loves me though I have no great beauty, my body bearing a sailor's scars and a slave's scars and this curious blood necklace where the scimitar left its mark. She loves me, she says, for my cynic's wit and my noble heart, that I would have given my wish to her.

So we live together in our ever-changing world. I read now in six tongues besides Greek and Arabic, and learned to paint and sew. My paintings are in the Persian style, but I embroider like a Norman queen. We learn from the centuries, you see, and we taste the world anew each time the cork is drawn.

So there, my master, I have fulfilled your curious wish, speaking my story to you alone. It seems a queer waste of your one piece of luck, but then most men waste their wishes. And if you are a poet and a storyteller, as you say, of the lineage of blind Homer and the rest, but one who has been blocked from telling more tales, then perhaps my history can speed you on your way again. I shall pick up one of your old books, my master, now that we have a day and a night in this new world. Do you have a favourite I should try – or should I just go to a bookseller and trust my luck? In the last few centuries it has been remarkably good, you see.

ESTHER FRIESNER

An Eye for the Ladies

'My bride is *what*?' The rosy plumes of the prince's turban trembled.'

'Raped, Lord of a Thousand Graces,' the Vizier replied, head bent, hands folded on his bosom. 'In the less drastic sense of the word. That is, she has been stolen away, purloined, absconded with, carried off against her will. In brief, she is no longer here.'

The prince's younger brother took a step back and nearly fell off the dais. A tumble would have been small price to pay to escape the scene he knew was coming, and Jaffar hated scenes; especially scenes staged by Prince Hussein. They tended to end so messily.

Jaffar had first witnessed one such at the age of five, when the then seven-year-old Hussein had been deprived of the innocent pleasure of whipping a clumsy slave to death. The tutor of the royal princes of Kairwan, being a philosopher, had pointed out quite rationally that it would take a seven-year-old lad far too long to gain the desired effect of a whipping death. The slave in question would sooner perish of old age. He superseded Hussein's demand and had the slave's head chopped off instead.

Whereat Hussein complained to his adoring mother, who had the tutor trussed and presented to her beloved boy for his birthday, along with an imported Muscovy knout. The tutor lived to experience the refutation of his theory concerning determined seven year olds.

'How have you let this happen?' Hussein now screamed, fetching the Vizier a pair of clouts to the head that made that august person stagger. No one dared make a move to correct Hussein's breach of etiquette. The Sultan of Ishkan might have taken the Kairwanese prince to task had he been there, but the sultan was absent. Even so, it is doubtful he would have done more than make muted clucking sounds.

Ishkan was a principality of the smallest size, a sultanate suburb of Damascus allowed to maintain its independence from reign to reign according to the sense of humour of its more powerful neighbour. Kairwan needed no such concessions, and the princes had come accompanied by a thousand heavily armed reasons for their city's self-sufficiency, as opposed to Ishkan's eternal state of multilateral universal placation. A company of them were with the princes now, in the Vizier's famous Peacock Chamber.

Clucking sounds; extremely muted clucking sounds at most. If that.

The Vizier bowed before necessity, and also to avoid a second assault. 'O Beloved of Beauty and Spoiled Child of Good Fortune, there are some things beyond the powers of mortal men to understand. Our princess, the incomparable Laila-gul, was one day steel – preparing herself to welcome you as her lord, and the next . . . gone.'

Prince Hussein turned the colour of a ripe fig. 'Gone? Women do not just *go*! In Kairwan we keep our women well sealed behind stone walls, bars of wrought iron, the swords of a hundred Nubian eunuchs! Also, my mother keeps an eye on them. It is not cheap, but it gets the job done. Are you fools so lazy or so stupid that you cannot keep one princess secure? Or is the slut so clever in her wantonness that she has eluded you? Truly, my precious gem of a mother had told me that there are wicked women in this world who may outwit a hundred greybeard sages with what they conceal beneath a beard not quite so grey.' Hussein frowned. 'I have often pondered the mysterious meaning of her words. Oh well, it is of little moment now.' He shrugged and turned to his golden-haired captain of the Crown Prince's Comrades. 'Kill everyone you can catch.'

The captain bowed low, hand on the pommel of his sword. 'Will my lord require heads?'

Hussein threw one arm around the captain's broad shoulders. 'Ears will do. Or what you will.' He gave his captain a hug.

A heart-rending wail went up from the massed sycophants, toadies and other hangers-on at the Vizier's court. Already the air was filled with the whistling of keen blades. The Vizier stood transfixed by the horror of it all. The first five courtiers to fall to the captain's sword had been deeply in his debt. His thoughts flew to higher things, however, when Prince Hussein drew a heavily jewelled dagger and bawled:

'Since it was from your lips I heard of my bride's fate, I will kill you myself, Bird of Ill Omen!'

'Mercy, Great One, I am unarmed!'

'What? Would you dare *contemplate* defending yourself against my just wrath? I will kill you for that alone!' Prince Hussein leaped for the Vizier's throat. It was a lovely leap, despite the prince's pendulous belly, and so graceful that he seemed to freeze in midflight.

Seeming is often being. The wide silk sash around Hussein's waist tautened like a mastiff's choke-chain and the prince, brought up short, crashed to the floor. With a curse he turned to see Jaffar still holding the other end of the sash.

'I will kill you for that, Jaffar!' he shouted as he picked himself up.

Jaffar wore the look of a child surprised by his own misdeed. 'I just thought you ought to find out a bit more about what happened to your bride, that's all,' he said. 'He can't tell you much if he's dead. It's only a suggestion, of course, my lord and my brother.'

Jaffar was the meekest of men, to all appearances. Soon after the incident with the tutor and the whip, he had done his best to avoid all confrontation when his elder brother's interests were at stake. He was wise, for five. The blood they shared was their father's only, and Jaffar had been quick to note the high mortality rate among his other half-siblings whenever one of them showed too much backbone.

Hussein's adoring mother had her little hobbies.

'What good will it do to learn more?' Hussein demanded. 'If the wench is gone, she's gone!'

Jaffar spread his hands. Like the rest of him, they were slim, dark and handsomely formed, needing no adornment to enhance the gift of the Omnipotent. 'But where is she gone? How is she gone? These remain unanswered.'

'What?' Hussein cupped his ear. 'I can't hear you over all these screams. Captain! Postpone the killing a moment. My brainless brother has something to say.'

'So does a monkey.' The captain grinned. Hussein called him naughty and spanked him once for old times' sake.

Prince Jaffar sighed. He was an Aristotelian at heart, a lover of the rational, whereas his brother appeared to be a devotee of the more popular misinterpretations of Plato.

'Well?' Hussein was impatient. 'Speak! Why should I care where and how she has gone?'

'Because, my brother and my lord, her dowry has gone with her.'

'Alas,' said the Vizier, 'this is true, and I wish that the princess's father were here to tell you so himself.' Dourly he eyed the carnage spattering the Peacock Chamber. 'You have no idea of how dearly I wish that.'

'Where is your lord, then? Hiding himself for shame?'

'Nay, Master of Soft Words. His Majesty is even now in pursuit of the fiend that has carried off his stainless daughter.'

Hussein had but one eyebrow, which ran bristly and unbroken from temple to temple. Thus he might not bring his brows together when stricken by incredulity, yet still he gave that effect. 'A fiend? What fiend is this?'

'Woe!' cried the Vizier. 'I had hoped to spare you the pain of hearing this. Of all the treasures of Ishkan, our princess was the crown. The peerless Laila-gul is a lady whose virtue is but a step removed from her beauty, and whose intelligence outshines beauty and virtue both as the sun outshines the moon and stars.'

'We had heard of the princess's beauty in Kairwan.' Hussein waved away the Vizier's information as old news. 'That is what caused us to ask for her hand. My adoring mother thought that a beautiful wife was just what I deserved. We did not know that she was intelligent, too. You may inform your master that her dowry will have to be doubled to make up for this sorry flaw in the girl.'

'Lord, you may speak of doubling dowries when you have a bride again. I shall forever recall the hour of our sorrow. It was midnight. A fearsome howling arose out of the south-eastern sky. A black whirlwind devoured the stars. Sand torn from the bosom of the desert lashed our walls. Men wept like women, for very fear, and women were silent, no doubt too frightened to cry out. Some were so astounded by the fury of the blast that on the morrow they claimed they could not even recall there having a been a storm, for they had slept right through it.

'But there had been a storm. Oh yes, and such a one as we had seldom seen! For with the dawn came news that the princess was no longer in her bed. Her windows were flung wide, the curtains tattered and sand everywhere. We searched for her, but did not find her. Her father, my lord, was distracted with worry.'

'Well he should have been,' Hussein said smugly. 'He knew I'd be displeased to hear he'd misplaced my intended.'

A sigh shuddered the Vizier's crabbed shoulders. 'As we searched the palace precincts, we discovered the gardener's chief assistant crouching beneath the princess's window. A fine lad, hair black as soot, he was now hoarier than I, and gibbered. Between gibbers, we gleaned the awful truth. He had been in the gardens tending the artichokes, he said. (This was later confirmed by the princess's chief handmaid, who shared his fondness for the prickly fruit, and would often lend him a hand in straightening the stems.) When the storm struck, he alone was in a position to look up and see the horror at the tempest's heart: A jinni! A monster, gigantic, one-eyed, and supremely ugly, who clasped the tender white body of our princess in his taloned paws!'

'Pah! You insult my intelligence. Such creatures are legends, no more. The jinn are for frightening children.'

'Do not be too quick to dismiss legends, my brother,' Jaffar put in softly. 'Remember what happened to your adoring mother's brother?'

Hussein snorted. 'He should never have let the boy near that accursed lamp in the first place. He should have known the brat would rub it! Boys are forever fidgeting with things. The trouble with wicked magicians is they're so busy being wicked they never stop to think things through. Well, maybe you have a point, Jaffar. Don't make a habit of it.'

Jaffar subsided into a welter of self-protective self-abasement.

Hussein returned his attention to the Vizier. 'So. A jinni carried off Laila-gul, is that it?'

'Regrettable but true. He bore her off into the wastes of the Arabian desert where the serpent and the scorpion hold sway. Her father has set out in pursuit with his finest troops, but he has also left word behind that if any man find and return his child, that man shall have his weight in gold and his hands filled with jewels.'

'Hmm . . .' Hussein stroked his moustache. Then he patted his belly. Then he studied the size of his hands. He arose from the dais.

'Put up your swords!' he commanded his men. 'We have acted in haste. Our bride is gone, but we shall have her back, and when we do . . .' He rubbed his fingers together as if already counting out the doubled dowry plus the reward. 'To me, my men! We march after the unholy jinni!'

The trumpeters raised their horns to their lips and blew a blast that rattled the hanging of the Peacock Chamber. The drummers beat upon their massive leopardskin-draped kettles until it sounded as if the thunder itself had come to nest in the rafters. The Crown Prince's Comrades raised their voices in a shout of loyalty and eagerness to do their master's bidding. The surviving courtiers keened.

'I'm afraid you can't all go,' said the Vizier. The Peacock Chamber fell still.

'What? Why not?' Hussein's voice lost some of its imperious tone. He was starting to whine.

'My lord, for a troop of this size to march into the Arabian desert requires a baggage train of at least double measure. Nay, triple, for you have no idea of where you are going. Be counselled by me. Go alone, or with one companion; two at most. You will have a better chance.'

'A better chance to die in the desert!'

'Commander of Several Obedient Camels, not so. For if you swear upon the holy book that you will undertake this quest, I shall place at your disposal the last – the very last – of the enchanted carpets of Ishkan.'

Hussein's face remained blank as new-washed linen, but Jaffar's ears perked up amazingly at the Vizier's words. 'By the Thousand Virgins of Paradise! I thought that the enchanted carpets of Ishkan were but a legend.'

'Do not be too quick to dismiss legends, my lord.' The Vizier smiled kindly on Jaffar. 'Some have the audacity to be true.'

'But I have heard that these carpets have the power of flight!'

'And so they do. Each is woven by a nubile royal virgin of Ishkan. Each step is done entirely by the lady, unassisted, from procuring the wool, to dyeing it, to spinning the yarn, to weaving the pattern. A princess may weave only one such carpet in her lifetime, and several of our more unfortunate ladies met untimely ends during the creative process.' The Vizier gazed at the ceiling. '"Never try to shear a ram in rut", I told her, but would she listen?'

'Old man, you babble,' Hussein snapped. 'If you do possess so wondrous a carpet, why did the princess's father himself not take it to seek his child?'

The Vizier coughed into his hand. He blushed becomingly. He cleared his throat and said, 'His Majesty was not

. . . qualified. Even as a virgin must weave them, so the enchanted carpets of Ishkan may only be flown by—'

Prince Hussein pointed his nose at the ceiling and howled.

While the captain of the Crown Prince's Comrades did what he could to calm his lord, Prince Jaffar drew the Vizier aside. 'Only a virgin may fly the carpet?' Receiving an affirmative, he inquired further, 'You mean that after the fair Laila-gul was stolen away, her father could find *no one* in all the palace fit to fly the wondrous carpet?' The Vizier shook his head. 'Nor in the city?' Another denial. 'Nor in all the *sultanate*?'

'It has been a very rainy summer. Besides, you have not been listening. A *nubile, royal* virgin, I said. So long as there is at least one such aboard the carpet, it will fly. But to find that one— Ha!'

Jaffar coughed into his hand. He blushed becomingly. He cleared his throat and said . . .

'Is that it?' Jaffar leaned well over the edge of the flying carpet and pointed at a pile of grey stone far below. 'Do you think that could be the jinni's castle?'

Hussein dug his fingers more deeply into the pile of the rug and moaned. Had he been barefoot, he would have held on with his toes too. Face down, he made no move to confirm or deny his brother's discovery. 'Why couldn't the wench have woven a bigger carpet?' he complained pitifully. 'Everywhere I look . . . the edge and the abyss!'

Jaffar could not fathom Hussein's fear of heights. He was enjoying the flight, and would have done so more if not for the highly embarrassing decoration of his vehicle. The edge and the abyss were far less upsetting for him to gaze at than the undulating surface beneath his royal haunches. This lovingly loomed pattern represented many couples – human, animal and undecided – entwined in what could only be described as suggestive postures. No, not suggestive. Their intent was plain as a market whore's wink. Jaffar found the carpet quite large enough, and shuddered to think what further permutations of anatomy the weaver might have wrought given a larger canvas.

Jaffar recalled how agitated he had become when the Vizier first unrolled the unholy thing in the Courtyard of the Bears. He felt his cheeks crimson and he affected a great interest in the topmost turret of the Ishkan palace. Anything rather then look at the writhing mob of leering figures at his feet.

Hussein, for his part, fell to his knees on the rug and studied it with the zeal a scholar reserves for the holiest of books. 'Now if I had *this* for a prayer rug,' he said, passing a trembling hand across damp lips, 'there'd be no need to guess what I was praying for! To me, Captain. There's a new idea here I want you to note down for later.'

The Vizier interposed himself between Hussein and his captain. 'That can wait. You must leave, O Most Gracious in All Your Departures. Even now the princess may be suffering unspeakable affront at the hands of the godless jinni.'

'Never mind the princess. Fetch me the wench who wove this!'

The Vizier suppressed a look of justifiable pride. 'Find our matchless lady and you will have the weaver.'

So it was that Prince Hussein was suddenly in a great hurry to reclaim his bride. Jaffar never could get over his elder brother's mercurial nature.

Now their quest was upon the point of completion. 'I am certain that must be the jinni's fortress, my brother,' Jaffar said. 'Even from this height, it is monstrously huge, and there is no sign of man's habitation for leagues about. Who else would build so great a monument in the heart of the Arabian desert?'

'The Egyptians are notoriously unreliable in that respect,' Hussein managed to utter. 'But let us land – please God, let us land! – and we can see whether you are right, for once.'

Jaffar spoke the words the Vizier had taught him for commanding the carpet. It swooped down in slowly diminishing spirals like a falling leaf, bringing the brothers ever nearer to the mysterious pile of stone. As they descended Jaffar noted that what looked like random tumbles of masonry from above were really sturdily mortared towers and battlements. They lacked the grace of the fortresses and palaces with which he was acquainted, but no one could deny that they were at least as resistant to attack, and twice as formidable to behold.

The carpet touched earth in a broad courtyard within the walls. Pearly gravel crunched beneath it. Hussein scooped up fistfuls and pressed them to his lips in gratitude.

Then he gave his brother a hearty buffet on the shoulder. 'Dolt! You have landed us at the jinni's doorstep! Couldn't you have picked out a safer point of entry, one more sheltered than this? Behold!' His hands swept upward to encompass the triple rows of ogive windows ringing the courtyard on all sides. 'Even a one-eyed jinni will find it hard to miss us now.'

'You mistake, sir,' came a high, sweet voice from the air. 'Either that, or you are vain enough to believe yourself worth notice by my master.'

Hussein gave a little squeak, jumped, and wormed himself under the carpet. Jaffar looked up, seeking the source of those admonishing words.

'Over here, sir. Third window from the left on the eastern wall, middle row.'

Jaffar felt his heart do all the painful things of which the poets sang with so much masochistic glee. His eyes were flooded by a dream of beauty too perfect to be real, a maiden of ebony and ivory, of coral and obsidian and gold. Parts of her looked as if they might be velvet too, or at least good quality cotton gauze.

'Close your mouth, sir,' the lady said. 'You look like the fish we had for dinner.' She ducked from sight an instant, then reappeared with a rope ladder which she let fall from her niche. 'Come up, if you will.'

With some difficulty, Jaffar persuaded Hussein to come out from underneath the carpet. He was finally forced to jerk it off his trembling brother and roll it into a bundle which he stowed under one arm before climbing the lady's ladder. Rather than be left alone in the courtyard, Hussein followed.

They stepped over the sill into an apartment whose luxury laughed at the outward sternness of the fortress housing it. Beside a perfumed, plashing fountain, the lady from the window reclined naked upon damask pillows, a lute in her hands. Fans of ostrich and bird-of-paradise plumes stirred the air, waved by unseen hands.

Hussein collapsed to the floor and gibbered like the gardener's assistant.

'I take it you are my bridegroom and *that* is the God-touched village idiot they made you take along for luck?' the lady inquired. She was not pleased when Jaffar told her the truth of things.

'Marry *him*? You're bad enough, from the meatless look of you, but *him*? I knew I was right not to put up too much of a fuss when the jinni carried me away. I was rather hoping something like that might happen. Every time I dropped a perfume flask or struck a servant I made sure to shout, "May the jinn of the Arabian desert take me if I must endure such clumsiness again!" Foolish oaths always bring trouble in the market tales, but I never dreamed they'd work so dependably in real life.'

Since the lady seemed to have no immediate wish to be rescued, Jaffar decided not to press the point. Moreover, he was now by no means eager for her rescue himself; not when it meant the eventual disposal of so much loveliness into his brother's bed. Wise from the age of five, he knew when to change the subject.

He flicked the carpet open and sat on it beside her. 'I trust, my lady, your captivity has been everything you'd hoped? Seeing as how you desired it in the first place.'

'Oh yes, quite nice. The jinni is stuffed with all the arcane knowledge of the ages. He's been giving me algebra lessons on my day off. Did you know there's more to life than integers? The things they don't teach a girl!'

'Shameful.' His dark gaze burned over her body.

Laila-gul sighed and set aside her lute. 'If only the princess were more tractable.'

'Princess? But I thought that you—'

'What rank has a princess from the world of men in the realm of the jinn? That is like expecting the empress of Byzantium to bow before the daughter of some mud-hut Afric chieftain. Here I am a servant, no more, and my chief duty is to be companion and lady-in-waiting to the Royal Lady Shakana Izritak Nurgolias ha-Kaf bat-Afriti.'

Before Jaffar might ask about the lady who bowed beneath such a devilish burden of syllables, the perfumed chamber shook to the tolling of a deep-throated bronze bell. Laila-gul sprang to her feet, a sight which raptured the breath from Jaffar's body. 'Oh! My lady summons me. What a pity. I had hoped to hold on to you for a little while longer. You may be meatless, but you have very nice eyes and you seem like a good listener. My master always lectures and his sister whines a lot, but neither likes to listen.'

Jaffar did not like that way she spoke of holding on to him, as if he were a toy. 'What have I to do with it? You are the one summoned,' he said coldly.

'And commanded to bring you with me. There is nothing my master does not know. The art that commands unseen hands to wiggle ostrich fans may also command unseen eyes to spy and unseen lips to report every dust mote's passage through this palace. From the moment you landed, you were discovered. Now Lady Shakana demands that we come to her.'

From his heap on the floor Hussein wailed, 'I do not want to be eaten! My adoring mother always told me tales of fine young men devoured whole by the evil jinn.'

Laila-gul spared him a contemptuous glance. 'Were I you, I wouldn't worry. Even a hyena draws the line at eating some things. Besides, the summons was not for you.'

Hussein covered his face and wept wildly for joy. He only paused long enough to look up briefly at his brother and say, 'Thus does Fortune spin her wheel. Farewell, Jaffar. May we meet again in Paradise. Oh, before you go, why don't you toss me that emerald aigrette from your turban? No sense filling the jinni's crop with such costly grit.'

Laila-gul made a noise of disgust, linked her arm with Jaffar's, and dragged him away before he could obey his brother's directive. On second thought, she snagged the carpet too.

In the corridor beyond her room, Laila-gul spread the carpet, sat upon it with Jaffar, and spoke the words of power that made it fly. The prince gave his fair conductress many a sidelong glance of bold speculation, knowing as he did the requirements for flying the rug. He attempted to touch upon the subject casually.

'What do you mean, you didn't think I was still a virgin!' The lady was so indignant, she slapped him.

'I— That is— The pattern . . .'

'A lady may use her imagination, may she not?'

'Also, Paragon of Noble Beauty, everyone at your father's court rather assumed – jinn having the reputation they do for lechery – that by now you had been . . .'

The princess guffawed. 'Fellow, have you ever *seen* a jinni? Have you no idea of the creature's *size*? In all respects. My master's race may be lecherous, but they do know the laws of physics.'

The carpet winged through titanic halls, crossed courtyards of unmatched splendour, sailed along beneath jewelled porticos whose most rachitic-looking pillar might have purchased the royal houses of Ishkan and Kairwan combined. By and by it coasted to a stop in the chambers of the Lady Shakana.

The jinni's sister was clad more modestly than the Princess Laila-gul, which was immediate evidence of the mercy of the Almighty. What there was exposed of her face and flesh was enough to turn a camel's stomach or set the heart of a royal tax-collector to beating in human time. Jaffar noted that her single eye was bloodshot where it was not yellow, black and the green of cistern mould. It was circled with blue kohl, the lashes dyed orange to match the lady's tusks. Two spots of rouge stood in high relief against her dewlapped cheeks, and one fastidious

116

claw was dipping carmine from a pot to her warty lips when Laila-gul knelt before her.

'IS THIS THE MAN?' The jinna's voice put Jaffar in mind of a pool of slowly congealing beef drippings.

'Yes, my lady. He has come to rescue me.'

With the bellow of a wounded hippopotamus, the Lady Shakana collapsed weeping into her cushions. Jaffar saw waves of flesh like miniature mountains slide back and forth beneath her robes as she sobbed. 'AND YOU WILL GO WITH HIM! YOU WILL GO, AND LEAVE ME ALONE, BEREFT, BORED PAST BEARING! OH, WHERE IS THAT CURSED BROTHER OF MINE WHEN I NEED HIM?'

Laila-gul nudged Jaffar in the ribs. 'Go to that chest in the corner and fetch a fresh shroud,' she hissed.

'A— shroud?'

'With a nose that size, a good shroud is the only fitting handkerchief for my mistress. Fortunately, my master finds shrouds very easy to obtain from a ghoul of his acquaintance. We often discuss the works of Pythagoras together. Hurry, bring it! Or would you rather see what happens when her nose runs?'

Jaffar did as he was bid. He even passed up the go-between and presented the cloth to Shakana himself. Her single eye blinked slowly when she saw him waiting on her.

'WHY ARE YOU MEN SO CRUEL?' she asked.

'Royal lady, how can one of your race speak of cruelty to one of mine? *I* didn't come here to eat *you*.'

'EAT . . .? UGH! WHAT MANNER OF GUT-TERSNIPE JINNA DO YOU TAKE ME FOR? WE HIGHBORN FEMALES NEVER ANTHRO-POPHAGIZE OUT OF WEDLOCK.' She tried to look down her nose at him, but it was difficult to accomplish with one eye. She abandoned pride for misery. 'NO, YOU HAVE NOT COME TO DEVOUR ME, BUT TO DESTROY ALL THE HAPPINESS I SHALL EVER KNOW. YOU HAVE COME TO RESCUE MY ONLY FRIEND.'

The creature's grief was so sincere that Jaffar found his heart moved by her despair. He even sought out a dry corner of the now sopping shroud and dabbed at a stray tear the size of a pomegranate.

'Please don't cry, my lady. The princess doesn't want to be rescued. Besides, I'm sure your honoured brother will be back any moment and he'll eat us right up.'

'MY HONOURED BROTHER ...' It was a snarl Jaffar prayed would never be directed at him. 'MAY IBLIS CURSE MY BROTHER FOR WHAT HIS WORM-CHOKED HONOUR HAS DONE TO ME!'

The jinna sat up straight and poked Jaffar in the stomach to emphasize her words. He sprang aside nimbly at each thrust, narrowly avoiding being skewered on the point of a hennaed talon. 'DO YOU KNOW HOW OLD I AM, MAN? TWENTY-NINE CENTURIES OLD, AND NEVER ONCE KISSED! ALL MY FRIENDS ARE ALREADY MATED MOTHERS, BUT I LANGUISH HERE, UNTOUCHED, SECLUDED, LONELY. AND WHY? BECAUSE MY BROTHER WILL NOT HAVE ME DO LESS THAN MARRY, AND MARRY WELL! TWENTY-NINE CENTURIES OF VIRGINITY ON MY HANDS, AND NOTHING TO SHOW FOR IT!'

Jaffar swore inwardly nevermore to feel diminished by his mere nineteen years of a similar state. He tried to console the jinna. 'Your marriage will be all the more brilliant when it comes. All your friends will envy you.'

'HA! WE ARE THE LOWEST BRANCH OF ROYAL BLOOD. THE TRUE KINGS OF OUR RACE MAY CHOOSE FROM FAR TENDERER GAME THAN I. YET STILL MY BROTHER PERSISTS IN HIS ILLUSION, STILL HE GUARDS MY VIRGINITY AS IF IT WERE WORTH SOMETHING.'

'Your brother, my lady, is a very wise being,' Laila-gul said primly. 'He knows best. You might do more to fill the hours of your waiting than eat dates and read the more overwrought Persian poets. You could improve your mind, as I do.'

'SPOKEN AS ONE VIRGIN TO ANOTHER,'
Shakana said bitterly. 'YOUR MIND IS FULL OF ALL
KNOWLEDGE BUT WHAT IS WORTH KNOWING.
YOU GORGE ON BOOKS AND STARVE FOR
EXPERIENCE.'

'I do not!'

'*I* HAVE READ THE POETS YOU SCORN. *I*
KNOW WHAT I'M MISSING, AND BELIEVE ME, I
WANT IT! I WANT TO ESCAPE MY PRISON, AND
SOON! I HAVE HEARD THAT MEN ARE
CLEVERER THAN WOMEN.' She returned her atten-
tion to Jaffar. 'THIS HAD BEST BE SO. IT IS WHY I
SENT FOR YOU. I WANT A WAY TO LEAVE THIS
PALACE, THIS PRISON. I WANT A LIFE OF MY
OWN, JUST A SMALL ENCHANTED LAMP OR
RING SOMEWHERE THAT I CAN CALL HOME,
AND THE FREEDOM TO ENJOY IT. WELL?
SPEAK, MANLING, AND BE SHARP ABOUT IT!'

'I . . . You . . . Uh . . . Why don't you just fly away in a
sandstorm?'

'*THAT* IS ALL YOU CAN COME UP WITH?' The
single eye narrowed. 'AND TELL ME, WISE ONE,
WHAT'S TO KEEP MY BROTHER FROM CATCH-
ING THE NEXT SANDSTORM OUT AND BRING-
ING ME BACK?'

'Oh.'

'ALAS, AS I FEARED, THERE IS NO ESCAPE
FOR ME BUT MARRIAGE, AND A WORTHY
MATCH WILL NEVER COME. GO AWAY. YOU
ANNOY ME. I THINK I SHALL ASK MY BROTHER
TO EAT YOU WHEN HE COMES BACK.'

Laila-gul gave Jaffar's hand a compassionate squeeze.

'YOU TOO, LAILA-GUL. I'M SICK OF HEARING
YOU GO ON ABOUT HOW WONDERFUL MY
BROTHER IS.'

Jaffar yipped as the princess's grip tightened. As
Shakana sank back amid her scrolls and sweetmeats, the
two humans fled the room. Both were so flustered by the
jinna's threats that they had run a goodly distance before

they remembered they had the enchanted carpet with them.

'Why, of all the foolish—!' Laila-gul stopped short when she remembered and stamped her tiny foot. She crushed a border of pinks, for their flight had conveyed them into one of the numerous palace gardens. She unfurled the carpet on the grass. 'Get on,' she told him, once seated herself.

Jaffar did not obey. He looked very thoughtful. So preoccupied was he that for once he let drop the mask of meek subservience he had worn for fourteen years. Contemplation made him more comely, as Laila-gul was quick to notice. 'The jinn are a singular breed,' he observed at length.

'Nothing like them on the face of the earth,' Laila-gul agreed. She could not recall why she had ever thought of him as meatless.

'Ah, there you are wrong, Princess, and there the jinna was right. You lack experience, though you have imagination.' He toed the carpet cautiously. Its design no longer seemed so frightful; fascinating, rather. 'In truth, the jinn have their like in a most numerous creature: human children.'

'You are mad! It must be the fear of being eaten that has unbalanced you. I confess I am upset by the prospect myself. One moment my mistress calls me her only friend, the next she plans my consumption.'

'Precisely. Changeable as a child, fickle, wilful, selfish, destructive, gullible—'

'My master knows all things! He is wiser than any mortal! How can you call him childlike?'

'The only difference between the gullible wise man and the gullible fool is that the wise man keeps silence better afterwards. And children can be very wise. I recall myself at the age of five when—'

Laila-gul smacked the carpet. 'You are an impossible man! If the jinn are like children, what of it? We shall still be devoured by these "children"!'

'No, we shall not, my lady, for we are grown folk, you and I.' His tone brooked no argument.

Hope touched the princess' face. 'And grown folk can command children, do you mean?'

'Command them? You speak from books again.'

'Rule them, then?'

Jaffar only laughed. 'Ah, you really must let me rescue you, Princess. There is so much I want to teach you of the real world.' His delight in that prospect shone in his face.

'The real world for me must end where the walls of your brother's *haremlik* begin. Do not taunt me with promises.'

Jaffar knelt beside Laila-gul on the soft bosom of the carpet. He framed her startled face gently with his hands. 'Your world shall never touch my brother's. This I do not promise; this I swear. Having met you, I know you to be . . . unworthy of Hussein. He deserves a larger prize. Much larger.'

Laila-gul's luminous eyes twinkled with amusement as they lingered on the prince's handsome face. Soon something more than amusement shone in her glance. She laid her hands over Jaffar's, welcoming his caress. 'I think I read your meaning. Are we not wise, we grown folk?'

Jaffar's hands strayed from the princess's face. She drew a shuddering breath of pleasure. 'We are wise,' he whispered in her ear, 'but wisdom will not make these children mind, my lady. We must use the one magical force that forever sets grown folk apart from children and allows them to direct the little terrors where they will.'

Laila-gul stretched full length upon the carpet and twined her arms around the prince's neck, bringing him down with her. 'And what is that, my lord?' she breathed, slim fingers busy with the fastenings of his robes.

'Deceit,' said the prince, 'and the ability to follow directions. Would you mind moving over a bit? I wanted to see one part of the carpet for referen— Ah!'

'Where have you been so long?' Hussein demanded. His earlier fears of immediate consumption had left him once and for all the moment he saw Jaffar and Laila-gul return uneaten. Now all his thoughts were bent on instant departure. 'Answer me!'

121

'Picking flowers,' Laila-gul replied. 'What is that to you?'

'When I get you home, you will learn to keep a civil tongue to your husband,' he growled. 'Come, Jaffar, spread the carpet and let us fly far from this place!'

Jaffar did as he was told, but when the three were settled on the rug and the words of power spoken, nothing happened. 'Alas.' Jaffar shrugged expressively. 'I know we acted in haste, my princess. I had hoped the magic might be more flexible in its demands, but . . .' Another shrug.

'Why won't it fly?' Hussein's eyes were wide. He drummed his heels on the carpet as he would kick a stubborn horse. 'Lift up! Lift up!' He jerked at the fringes. 'What's wrong with it?'

'Oh dear.' The princess laid her fingers to her lips. 'We should have thought of this before, Jaffar.'

'Definitely, my lady. But we were so affrighted by what the jinna told us—'

'—about how her brother, whom she hates, will be back *any moment* to eat us all—' Laila-gul supplied.

'—that in our fear we clung to each other . . . and we clung a little too closely, that's all.'

'You— You— with *my* bride? I will have my adoring mother deal with you when we get home, Jaffar!'

Jaffar bowed humbly before his enraged brother. 'I am yours to command, as always. But as neither the princess nor myself now qualifies to fly this carpet—'

'—and as the jinni will be back *any moment*—'

'—whether we get home at all is a moot point.'

Jaffar and Laila-gul allowed Hussein a nice long bout of hysterical sobs and screams before the princess raised one finger in the accepted gesture of inward revelation and exclaimed, 'Praise the Omnipotent, there is still one person left nearby who *might* be able to fly you to safety, Prince Hussein.'

'You are a fool,' Hussein snuffled, wiping his nose on his sleeve. 'Where do you expect to find a nubile royal virgin in this wasteland?'

*

'NO!' cried the Lady Shakana, pulling away from Hussein in revulsion. 'NOT UNLESS WE'RE MARRIED FIRST.'

'MARRIED?' Hussein's shout almost equalled Shakana's dulcet tones. 'To THAT?'

'She is a princess,' Laila-gul said demurely.

'A great princess,' Jaffar amended, 'and virgin.'

'And just as eager as you to escape this place.'

Hussein clapped his hands over his eyes and gave himself up to anguish.

'Hush, my brother. The Lady Shakana will hear and take offence,' Jaffar whispered in the crown prince's ear.

'And what of that? Must I choose between fire and flood? To be wed to this abomination or ingested by her nightmare next-of-kin?'

Jaffar put a companionable arm around Hussein's shoulders and walked a little apart with him. 'Your choice is far simpler and not at all that horrible. That jinna is your only way out of here – apart from via her brother's digestive system – yet she will not run off with you unless you are wed. She has said so herself. They are great believers in personal honour, the jinn. But why shouldn't you give into her wishes, if marriage is all she wants? My brother and my lord, surely a man of your high intelligence recognizes what an opportunity is here.'

'I do?'

'Do not try to deceive me. You were always the brighter of us in studying the sacred law.'

'I was?'

'Did not your adoring mother say so repeatedly? And our law provides a man with an easy escape from the bonds of undesired matrimony. Behold, you have but to wed the jinna, have her convey the carpet home, and once you are there, you need only say 'I divorce thee' thrice to be rid of her!'

Hussein brightened. 'That's right, isn't it!'

By the time the brothers returned to where the ladies sat in similar conference, Prince Hussein was more than ready to plead his suit with eloquence and fervour. The

123

Lady Shakana heard him out in silence, then said:

'I SEE YOU READ ALL THE WRONG LIT-ERATURE TOO. AT LEAST WE HAVE THAT MUCH IN COMMON. AND YOU ARE ROYAL. YOU UNDERSTAND MATTERS OF HONOUR. YOU SHALL BE A KING – THOUGH MERELY A MORTAL ONE – WHICH OUGHT TO KEEP MY FOOL BROTHER CONTENT ENOUGH TO LET ME BE. VERY WELL. LET US BE WED AND GONE WITHOUT FURTHER DELAY.'

'Hearkening and obedience, Gem of Ten Thousand Pit-Mines,' said Hussein.

Jaffar and Laila-gul witnessed the bonding of the fortunes of man and jinna in a ceremony under the open sky where haste displaced formality. No sooner were the happy pair united by mutual pledge than Hussein cried, 'Now, my wife, let us away!'

The jinna bowed to her wedded lord and without ado grabbed the enchanted carpet from Jaffar. Before he or Laila-gul could protest, she had spread it on the ground and stood on it. But her feet were too big, and so she was obliged to balance on one, which covered the entire area of the rug. Wobbling like an ungainly stork, she seized Hussein in her talons and uttered the words of power. The carpet rose straight into the air until it was not more than a black dot against the sky.

Still on the ground, Jaffar and Laila-gul gaped after it.

'Oops,' said Jaffar.

'SO MUCH FOR YOUR PLAN, MANLING. WE JINN MAY NOT BE AS CLEVER AS YOU, BUT AT LEAST WE ALWAYS CONSIDER THE LAWS OF PHYSICS. TWO BODIES MAY NOT OCCUPY THE SAME SPACE AT THE SAME TIME. NOT ON A RUG THAT SIZE.'

Jaffar wheeled. A shadow out of nowhere had fallen across the whole courtyard. Laila-gul gave a small cry and threw herself into his arms. 'Alas, it is my master!'

'YOUR MASTER NO MORE,' the jinni boomed. 'I ONLY BROUGHT YOU HERE TO KEEP SHAKANA

COMPANY, SO I MIGHT HAVE A LITTLE RESPITE FROM HER CONSTANT CARPING.'

Jaffar nearly sprained his neck trying to see all of the jinni. He was less ugly than his sister, perhaps because he had not tampered with Nature's handiwork, nor attempted to gild the dunghill. There was even an air of good humour about him, though Jaffar's rapidly beating heart ascribed the jinni's warm smile to rising healthy appetite.

Jaffar put Laila-gul from his arms and shielded her behind him. 'She is blameless, my lord. If you crave vengeance, punish me.'

'FOR WHAT? FOR GETTING RID OF MY SISTER?' The jinni's lone eye closed as he roared with merry laughter. 'THE ALL-HIGH BLESS YOU, MANLING. YOU HAVE DONE IN A DAY WHAT I HAVE FAILED TO DO THESE MANY CENTURIES. YOU HAVE MARRIED OFF THE SNIVELLING CREATURE, AND ROYALLY, NO LESS!'

'Yes, but . . . to a mortal, my lord. I know you wanted to wed her to a king of your own kind.'

'A RUSE. MUCH AS I CANNOT STAND MY SISTER, I HAD NO HEART TO TELL HER THAT NONE OF OUR RACE, KING OR COMMONER, WOULD HAVE HER. THEREFORE I MADE PRETENCE OF KEEPING HER PRISONER HERE. NO ONE ASKS WHY THE FRUIT ON THE TOPMOST BRANCH REMAINS UNPLUCKED; THUS NONE EVER COMES CLOSE ENOUGH TO SEE THAT IT IS ROTTEN.'

'Your sister cannot help her looks.' Full of self-righteousness, Laila-gul came forward. 'Perhaps one eye is not enough to look behind poor Lady Shakana's unfortunate face.'

The jinni crouched down and peered at the two mortals. The slow blink of his eyelid was like the lowering of a heavy fringed curtain. 'CHILD, AN UGLY FACE IS NOT ALWAYS THE SIGN OF A BEAUTIFUL SOUL. AND I HAVE TWO GOOD EARS, WHICH WERE

ALWAYS FILLED WITH MY SISTER'S COM-
PLAINTS. WHOEVER HER HUSBAND IS, I PRAY
HE IS A MAN OF GREAT PATIENCE AND FOR-
BEARANCE.'

'He is my brother,' said Jaffar, 'and he is not.'

The jinni shook his great head slowly. 'POOR MEAT
FOR MARRIAGE, THEN. THE SECRET OF
PAIRED HAPPINESS IS TO ALWAYS KEEP ONE
EYE PARTWAYS CLOSED TO THE FOIBLES OF
YOUR MATE. YES, EVEN IF ONE EYE IS ALL
YOU HAPPEN TO POSSESS. THINK YOU TO BE
CAPABLE OF THAT MUCH, MANLING?'

Jaffar looked at the Princess Laila-gul and smiled like a
moron. She returned his adoring gaze with equal idiocy.
Their hands joined, their arms linked, their thighs pressed
one against the other as if skin were an inconveniently
random barricade to two souls that long to occupy only
one body. The jinni stroked his upper lip reflectively.

'SO MUCH FOR PHYSICS. AH YES, I THINK YOU
BOTH WILL HAVE THE PROPER EYE FOR
MARRIAGE.'

He cupped his hands above them. Sand began to sift
through the monster's gnarled fingers. The golden rain fell
more swiftly. It swirled around the pair, a chrysalis spun
of wind and dune and magic, turning ever faster and faster
until the jinni's sandstorm-spindle flew up with them into
the sky and raced the clouds for Ishkan.

'Without dowry, you say?' The Vizier could not believe
his ears.

'If she will have me,' Prince Jaffar replied.

'But— But— If you have treated your royal brother as
you claim, you can never go back to Kairwan. He will kill
you! And what use is a penniless prince?'

'The same use a princess in my condition is as a
marriage-pawn,' Laila-gul whispered mischievously to
Jaffar.

'I suppose I could always become a philosophy tutor,'
Jaffar suggested. 'But not to royalty.'

The Vizier threw his hands up in despair. Long questioning had extracted no sensible answer out of either the smitten prince or the beauteous – and now properly clothed – princess. Messengers had been dispatched into the desert to fetch back her father. All the Vizier could do now was wait. From the courtyard without came the roistering sounds of the Crown Prince's Comrades. They were drunker than usual and were singing a song about what they would do to the old Vizier when good Prince Hussein came back at last.

The singing stopped abruptly, as if cut off by a sword. All heads within the Peacock Chamber turned sharply at the sudden silence outside. Hoofbeats clattered across cobbles. A murmuring like the rush of the sea built slowly from below. As it grew, a man in the travel-worn garb of a royal messenger of Kairwan staggered into the Peacock Chamber and prostrated himself before Prince Jaffar.

'Hail, Child of Beneficent Stars! Hail, Crown Prince of Kairwan!'

'Me? But my brother—'

'—is dead.'

'Of what cause?'

'Of divorce, Highness.' It seems that his new bride belongs to a people who recognize but one way out of marriage. A matter of family honour, as she said before she ate Prince Hussein. Take comfort at least in the fact that his adoring mother was the appetizer. Your father begs you to return. His freshly widowed daughter-in-law has made mincemeat of the succession and departed for parts unknown.'

'And so I will return as my father commands.' Jaffar renewed his grasp of Laila-gul's dainty hand. 'But not alone.'

The messenger cocked his head to one side. 'This one doesn't eat people too, does she?'

'Not indiscriminately.'

The room filled with the Crown Prince's Comrades. Their swords flashed as they acclaimed their new lord. Loudest among them in their homage, presenting himself

127

to best advantage, was the golden-haired captain. He did not seem to have mourned his late lord overlong.

Prince Jaffar believed he caught the tail-end of an appreciative smile upon the lips of Laila-gul as she stared at the captain. The captain was muscular and handsome and young, and he did have experience in serving royalty. Perhaps Laila-gul was merely an idealistic admirer of the Beautiful through the Thing of Beauty.

Perhaps not.

Philosophically, Jaffar partways closed one eye.

Somewhere the Arabian desert sky filled with laughter.

NANCY SPRINGER

Truthseeker

She had been named Karida, 'the virgin', for the virgin daughter of an emir could be advantageously wed. In due time, when she came of marriageable age, the poets of her father's court declared her fair as the trumpet-flowers of morning and graceful as the gazelle. Graceful they could see she was by the swaying of her silks as she walked, but fair they could only surmise from what they had been told. No man but her father had ever seen her face. As was the custom, she went swathed to the eyes when not cloistered in the confines of his harem.

In fact, the poets spoke truth. Karida was very fair. What more might be true of her, no one inquired or cared.

Her father's name was Kansbar Ben Kasil, Emir of Nard, and from time to time he mused with pleasure on his possession of a chaste and beautiful daughter. 'Play the lute,' he would command her sometimes of a tedious evening, and she would answer in softest accents, as was required of her, 'I hear and obey.' And she would play. For she knew her situation, and if her father said to her, 'Sing', she sang; and if he then said to her, 'Be silent', she would be still. For she had no choice in any of these things, or in most others. Only her thoughts, behind her veil, were her own.

She was one who tried to think the truth. Truthseeker, she should have been named. Her eyes, through the slit between the veil that covered her face and the cowl that covered her head and hair, her amber-coloured eyes looked out and saw the world while she sat silent.

Truth is, she said to herself within her mind, I am little better than a slave, for all that I clothe myself in perfumed silks.

And she looked on her father the emir and knew him to be a petty tyrant and a boor.

Now Emir Baghel of Zel, the neighbouring emirate, was Kansbar ben Kasil's bitter rival for wealth and power and the favour of the caliph. And this Baghel sent his chief vizier to Emir Kansbar with a decree that Kansbar ben Kasil and all his household should be Baghel's guests for a fortnight – even though it was customary that the women should have stayed at home. Nor could this vaunting and overweening hospitality be denied. It bore the strength of command, for Baghel had more slaves, both white and Black, and more dinars of red gold in his treasury, and more officers and attendants and cresset-bearers, and both he and Emir Kansbar knew well that of the two, Baghel was the more powerful. And Baghel's emirate squatted at the verge of Kansbar's.

Therefore Kansbar ben Kasil went, with all his household, and for two weeks ate sweetmeats and drank fine wine made bitter by innuendo and hidden insult. And Karida, as was seemly, kept herself veiled and spoke not.

She knew her peril, and every morning and evening she thanked Allah that her father liked Baghel no better than she did, though for different reasons: hers being that, beneath his huge turban of white silk, he was a gross-bodied old man with a long nose, pendulous lips like those of a camel, bristles coarse as a boar pig's, and fierce, burning black eyes like those of a jinni. She knew that if her father had chosen to wed her to Baghel, she would have been wed. And Baghel turned his burning eyes on her often, praising her silence and beauty and virtue.

Likely even before he had seen her he had planned what he would do. On the last day of the fortnight he decreed to Kansbar ben Kasil, with many pleasant words and teeth bared in the grin of a snarling dog, that he would have Karida to wife. And his mamelukes, well armed, stood all around to guarantee that he was not likely to suffer refusal.

But Kansbar ben Kasil opened his mouth wide in seeming delight. 'Thus shall our own houses be joined!' he exclaimed. 'O my lord, I tell you, you shall have not only the fair Karida herself but twenty others, the fairest virgins of my emirate, to come with her as her handmaids, for your pleasure. This to repay your hospitality. Nay,' as Emir Baghel's jaw sagged, 'do not demur, for you are deserving of whatever poor offering I can vouchsafe you.'

'You shall send but the maiden herself and her retinue,' decreed Baghel suspiciously. 'There is no need for you to come yourself with any others of your household, for already I have borrowed too much on your span of life.'

Kansbar ben Kasil nodded cheerfully. 'I am a busy servant of Allah,' he agreed, and then he fell to stroking his beard and reckoning up the time he would need for his preparations. And the maiden Karida, sitting by, bit her lip beneath her veil while her silent eyes watched all that passed.

The next morning, Emir Kansbar and all his household departed homeward, and all that ten days' journey he said nothing to his daughter Karida of what had transpired. But as she looked at him her heart eased, for once out of Baghel's sight Kansbar flushed hot all over with rage. He cared for Karida little more than he did for his best racing dogs, but he would not willingly have given a dog to Baghel. Even less willingly would he thus bestow a valuable daughter.

Therefore, as his first command on returning to his own emirate of Nard, Kansbar ben Kasil sent out his viziers to bring to him fair, slender, beardless youths who were skilled in the use of arms, all such youths that they could find.

In good time his viziers brought comely youths before him, and Kansbar had them contest against each other to show him their skill in arms. Out of them he chose twenty who were fair of face and graceful of body, yet fierce fighters. Then he looked over them all and chose one youth who had made for himself but a poor showing in the fighting, yet all heads turned towards him for the sake of his beauty, his skin like silver and his amber eyes. For his skin was like Karida's skin, his eyes like hers. This youth's name was Azim.

And the other youths the emir sent away, but the twenty-plus-one remained before him. And he ordered that they should be taken into his harem, under guard of eunuchs, and there be bathed and dressed and adorned in the garb the women had prepared for them. For these youths were the damsels Kansbar proposed to send to Baghel; and Azim would take the place of Karida.

Nor had the preparations gone unnoticed by the maiden herself, for her clear eyes saw all.

Great was the hubbub in the harem when the youths were brought in to be arrayed as damsels and schooled in the manners of maidens. Wives and concubines giggled and shrieked as they took charge of their wards, and the older women, the guarders of virtue, scolded at the young virgins and warned them away. But Karida had a thought, that she would see the one who was to take her place. And she had a half-formed determination, because of what she had lately learned of truth. She obeyed the old duenna who drove her to her private chamber, but then she came out again, and eluded her guardians, and sought out the young man Azim.

She found him in his bath, and he had driven the others from him, even the eunuchs, so that he might be alone, for he was melancholy, as showed in the inclination of his comely head. Karida peeped at him through a doorway, and saw that he was fair, very fair, and her heart pounded. There was cause for fear. If caught in what she was about to do, she could be beaten and turned out at the gate, a prostitute. But it was not for fear that her heart beat hard.

She straightened her shoulder, drew tight her veil and went in to speak with the youth, and Azim gasped and flushed and snatched at a napkin to cover himself, though Karida's steady gaze stayed all on his face.

'It is the full moon at rising,' he stammered in courtly compliment.

Karida felt a small demon moving in her, such as she had often felt while enduring the flatteries of court poets. But this time she spoke her thought, her own boldness making her bold. 'What do you mean?' she retorted. 'Say you my face is round like a plate, and flat, and fishy white?'

'Nay! Lady Karida, your countenance is as fair as the sun in a cloudless sky,' Azim tried again, 'and your speech softer than the gentle zephyr.'

'I am keeping my voice down,' Karida told him between clenched teeth, 'so that no one hears us.'

'Your forehead,' whispered Azim. 'It is as white as the lily flower, and your brows like bent bows that send arrows of devotion winging to my heart.'

Karida sighed, though not with devotion, and wished she could send a real weapon winging to his head. But without reply she reached up and undid from its place on her neck a small pendant hanging on a thin chain of gold, a modest brown gem that she had bought once from a Frankish merchant, at a price no one else would pay. Stooping, she placed it so that the chain adorned Azim's head and the stone came to rest on the centre of his forehead.

'You'll look well thus,' she teased, 'once you're arrayed as a woman.' But her reason for placing it on him was other than it seemed, for the jewel was the quirin, the stone of truth, from the nest of the lapwing, a strange bird far to the northward, and Karida had given much gold for the small brown gem, and not because its clear colour was the same as that of her eyes.

Azim met her mocking gaze, opened his mouth and spoke. 'Cruel one,' he said, 'heavy is my heart that ever you were born to look like me. For because of your fair skin and amber eyes I must go forth to be slain at the hands of Emir Baghel and his guards and mamelukes.'

Karida's face sobered. 'It is you damsels who are supposed to take Baghel unawares,' she put the case to him, though gently, 'and slay him.'

'Ah, lady, it is fitting that I should go forth in the cowl

and veil of a timid damsel, for truly I have no courage, not so much as a scampering mouse. Alas that I ever learned to fight, for I have no heart for it. I wish only to play the lute and live in safety and comfort.'

'Then you should stay in this harem,' said Karida, 'for it is safe, and comfortable, and full of lute music. And I should leave it, for it is my prison.'

She took the quirin off his head and placed it again around her own neck, and above her veil her eyes smiled as she looked into his.

'When you are arrayed,' she told him, 'I will change places with you.' Then she turned away and left him before he could speak again.

Thus it happened that when Azim stood awkwardly with the twenty others, dressed as a damsel and veiled, with his brows plucked to thin them, with embroidered slippers on his feet and bracelets tinkling on his ankles, with voluminous trousers of silk swaddling his legs and a silken gown girdled around his hips by gold and jewels, with a red fez on his head whereon were sewn the coins of Karida's dowry, with bangles of gold jingling on his wrists and rings of gold glinting on his fingers – as he stood thus ill at ease, a hand reached from behind a curtain and pulled him swiftly away, and hurried him along a passage-way, and it was Karida herself, leading him to her private apartment, for she trusted no other to bring him there.

She stood beside him and quickly compared, her eyes keen. The two of them stood of much the same height, and clothed much the same. Only a few outer garments would need to be exchanged. She snatched the fez from his head and settled it on her own, along with the yards of veiling that cascaded from its crown. 'Give me your weapons,' she ordered Azim. 'Quickly!'

'But—' Even as he protested he handed over the knife and short sword hidden in the folds of his gown of Egyptian silk. She girded them on and managed the other changes herself, deftly. 'But what is to become of me?' Azim was saying. 'Surely your servants will discover me. My life will be the forfeit.'

'You must indulge in languor and melancholy,' Karida told him. 'Go forth not, bathe not, speak not. Go into a maidenly decline. Play the lute all you like. If my father asks you to sing for him, weep. He dislikes weeping and will send you away. So long as you wear your veil and do not speak, no one will trouble you.' A life of melancholy, she thought sourly, ought to suit him well. Without further speech she turned away from him and left him in her chamber, running to join her twenty warrior lads.

The next morning's rising sun saw the one and twenty of them bound towards Zel in caravan. The damsels swayed in camel litters, and a hundred eunuchs rode white mules to either side.

Now it seemed to Karida that the leadership of these 'damsels' must belong to her if Baghel was to be fooled. And she took it unto herself, and let her orders ring out loud and clear, no longer troubling herself to keep her voice softer than the morning zephyr, and none of the lads travelling with her suspected that she was a maid, for never had they known a maid so forthcoming. But they thought she was Azim, and grumbled, for Azim had earned no such leadership.

Therefore the boldest among them took counsel and named their own leader. He was Hazad, 'the free', and his skin was fair as moonlight, his eyes like dark pools in moonlight, his hair shone black as a raven's folded wings. With the others at his back he came during the noonday halt to the place where Karida lay on the ground sleeping, and he roused her with the jingling of his anklets and the toe of his slippered foot. On his body he wore a woman's trousers of pleated silk, but in his hand he held his sword. 'Up, Azim,' he ordered.

'Fool,' snapped Karida, 'you will discover us all to any eyes that might happen by.' For he wore his veil and cowl unfastened, thrown back on his shoulders, as Karida had given orders that none of them should do, though the veils fretted the youths sorely.

'Stand up, craven,' Hazad taunted. 'Never fear, I will not wound your pretty face. I intend but to thrash you

135

with the flat of this blade, for overweening.'

Karida stood up very quickly, far more quickly than he expected, and in such wise that her head caught him hard under the chin and sent him sprawling, unconscious. She took the sword out of his limp hand. 'Anyone else?' she inquired, hefting it and peering around.

There was not. Those others present backed away, for their champion had been vanquished in one blow.

'Take him away,' Karida ordered, and she resumed her place on the ground. The next day she gave the sword back to Hazad privately, and conversed with him, and afterwards thought to herself that he was fair, with his cheeks (what she could see of them above the veil) colouring like crimson windflowers under the dark flesh of his eyes, and she wondered if the rest of him was as fair as Azim had been in his bath with his bare shoulders moving in the light, for she had never seen the bared shoulders of a man before that time. But she did not let Hazad see this wonder in her eyes, for he would have thought her a catamite, and she had just made a faithful damsel of him.

He and the others obeyed her more willingly each day of the journey, for her eyes saw truth and her commands rang fair, and by the time they reached Zel, she felt sure of the loyalty of their hearts.

At the city gates they were stopped by the guards. Only the damsels were to be allowed within the walls, by Baghel's behest. The retainers were to remain without, where provision would be brought to them, and then they were to return to their master Kansbar.

'This is no more than we expected,' Karida told her assembled damsels, and once more her voice was as soft as the zephyr at dawn, for many were the ears that might listen. 'Our lord Baghel is suspicious of treachery. We must be brave and go on by ourselves.'

She could say no more, for Baghel's city guards stood by. With hearts pounding beneath their rustling silks and eyes darting above their veils, on foot the twenty hand-maids entered the city, carrying their mistress with them, as was fitting to her station. And they made their way to the emir's palace, and within, where, in the audience hall on his chair of estate and carpet of sanctuary, Baghel awaited them.

Baghel waited, coarse bodied, his thick lips drawn back to show teeth like the tusks of the jinni. Baghel waited until Karida stood before him with her dowry on her head and her twenty handmaids at her back, and then his eyes between their fatty pouches burned like coals, and to the number of a hundred his mamelukes and armed attendants closed round. For he knew all of Kansbar's plan, as Karida had surmised he might.

'Fools,' he jeered. 'Foolish youths! Foolish Kansbar, to send you thus! Think you not that I have my spies?'

Hazad looked around him wildly and felt for the hilt of his weapon, hidden beneath his jewelled girdle. But before he would draw it and lose his life in glorious defeat, Karida spoke.

'You think we are *youths*?' she cried, and her cry was as sweet and piercing as the voice of the nightingale in spring. 'Have you not eyes to see, o my lord the Emir? You insult us, for I aver there is not a maiden here who walks not with the grace of the gazelle, the radiance of the cloudless moon! We have come here, flowered gardens for your delight, most daintily arrayed and modestly veiled, and you call us youths!'

Baghel's porcine eyes had widened, for the voice was the voice of a passionate maiden. But still he might have doubted (for a voice can easily mislead) had not Karida continued to lament.

'O my lord who was to be my husband, I am dishonoured! I and all my handmaids have met but with dishonour in your presence! I cannot be your wife, nay, not even your concubine, if you think that this is the face of a youth—' And as if half maddened by despair she wrenched the veil from her face, and Baghel gasped, even the mamelukes gasped and some of them hid their eyes, for the face thus shamefully revealed was that of the most lovely of maidens. And Hazad and his cohorts (though Karida hoped they showed not half of what they felt)

137

stood as stupefied as any in that audience chamber, for it was assuredly not the face of Azim.

'And is this,' Karida cried, 'the bosom of a youth?' And she rent her garments to her waist, and with her hands spread them wide.

Then all was hubbub and utter confusion, for the mamelukes shouted, dropping their weapons and hiding their eyes with their hands, and some of them ran away lest they be cursed. And Baghel did not hide his eyes, but stared in stupefaction; likely he could not have moved had a dervish with a scimitar risen up before him at that very moment. And Karida's 'damsels' rushed to surround her, concealing her with their bodies so that Baghel could gaze no longer on her nakedness.

'Fools,' she hissed at them, 'slay him!'

But the moment had passed. The uproar in the audience hall had brought servants running from every direction. And Baghel had closed his gaping mouth, and his small eyes glittered as thoughts of Karida's bosom which she had revealed to him drove out his thoughts of treachery.

'Show them to quarters,' he ordered the women and eunuchs among the crowd, 'the finest my harem has to offer, for it appears that these are indeed damsels of gentle estate.'

Therefore his servants carried them through his palace, past columns of topaz and chalcedony, through halls perfumed with incense and sandalwood, past fountains that plashed into a broad, tile-lined lake beneath a dome made of gold and sapphires.

Karida gazed about her in haughty silence, her lips pressed tight. Once in the sumptuous apartment that had been appointed for her, she ordered the servants of Baghel imperiously out of the chamber and away from her. They were glad enough to obey, for a rich glint of madness showed in her amber eyes. Then she stood with her arms folded across her chest, gathering her sundered clothing around her, and her twenty 'handmaids' cowered before her glance. With a tilt of her head she ordered one of them to the door, to warn if they might be overheard.

'Fools!' she raged at them all, though she kept her voice low. 'Flatfoot, lackwit fools! I gave you plentiful opportunity to kill him!'

Hazad had removed his veil, offering it to her, though she would not take it from his hand; and his comely face, thus exposed, was as dumbfounded as Baghel's had been. His lips faltered for speech. 'You – you are she,' he stammered. 'Truly, I mean. The Lady Karida!'

'Of course I am Karida!' She did not allow her voice to rise, but vexation flooded her cheeks with red. 'Stop looking at me like a bawling calf! Who else should I be? – Do not answer.' With a visible effort she calmed herself. 'We must think what to do. He will send for me tonight, and order me to play the lute and fondle him, and I want no part of him.'

'You must take the reins and invite him here, my lady,' said Hazad more collectedly, 'where we of your retinue can be around you.'

Karida looked at him, measuring him with her gaze, then nodded. 'Show me the ways of these weapons I wear,' she ordered.

'You will have us here to help you,' Hazad said.

'Show me nevertheless, for I have no fighter's skill except to butt with my head.' Karida gifted him with a small smile, watching the colour rise in his clear cheeks. Truly, he was fair, and, she deemed, utterly faithful to her.

'It is nothing, my lady,' he stammered. 'It is but to plunge the knife hard, with all your strength, and aim it between the ribs.'

'Truly? I had thought there was some secret to it.' Karida shrugged. 'Leave me, then, to prepare myself.'

Thus it was that, after evening prayer, Karida lay on her couch, calm, elaborately robed, perfumed with musk, unveiled, lay with her hair twisted and looped in strands of pearls and her fairest damsels (including Hazad) standing by, to welcome her new lord, whom she knew would not be unwilling to attend her.

And Baghel came in to her as if strolling into a pleasure garden that he owned.

Nor did he say to her verses, or tell her that her face was like that fair, full, rising moon, or take time for the usual preliminaries of sweetmeat feasting and lute music and sherbets. He pulled the turban from his head and commanded Karida's handmaidens, 'Leave us.'

And to her consternation, they did so, their eyes over their veils wide, white-flashing and fearful.

Then, when she looked into Baghel's burning eyes, she saw why. That coal-black gaze held her in thrall, as the eyes of the cobra held the bird victim. He was immensely powerful – how she knew it, Karida could not have said, but this man was puissant in no ordinary way, more so than any emir. And Allah knew, the power of emirs was fearsome enough.

Karida lay as if carved from alabaster as Baghel stripped to his bulky waist. And even when he began to pull open her clothing, she felt that she could not oppose him, that she could not move her hand to seize the knife that lay hidden between the cushions of her couch. Though truth was— truth was—

As Baghel pulled silks apart with a meaty hand—

The chamber door burst open, and Hazad stumbled in, staggering, as if fighting his way against some mighty force, his fair face unveiled, and in his hand a short sword. Just within the entry he fell to the floor.

Small assistance – but Baghel's burning eyes turned away from Karida for a moment, and her heart blazed with wrath and fear for Hazad's sake, and her hand shot to the hilt of her own weapon. Truth was, she could move, though she might be killed for it. She cried aloud, and with the strength of both her arms she plunged the knife into Baghel's side.

No blood flowed. Nor did the emir so much as flinch, though the knife stood driven to the haft between his ribs.

Baghel jerked erect with rage, and with a roar he turned on her. And Karida gave herself up for dead, for it seemed to her that the fire of his glare would turn her to

140

ashes where she lay, even before his hand descended, wielding a blow that would slay her or knock her unconscious.

But before that heavy hand could fall, another blade flashed, and behind Baghel Karida saw, veiled to the eyes – herself? Azim! But how—

There was no time to question how. Azim struck Baghel once with the short sword, and it glanced off the emir's shoulderblade, to no good effect, and then the burning eyes had turned on him, the emir's roar shook the chamber, and Karida saw how horror had taken Azim in its freezing grip, rendering him all but helpless – though he stood his ground – and she knew he would be killed in the next breathspan, and she as quickly after. She rose up on her couch, lifting knife to aid him—

Her stroke never fell. Black-haired Hazad stood at the centre of the chamber, only slightly swaying, and with a voice as compelling as a trumpet call he shouted, 'Marid!'

And Baghel did not roar, but turned to face Hazad and stood still.

Marid. An evil jinni of the most potent sort, a mighty lord among the jinn. Karida felt her blood chill as she fingered the haft of her weapon. Small wonder the knives did Baghel no harm, if he was what Hazad said he was.

Hazad spoke on with panting passion. 'Marid,' he repeated, 'I know you.' I see the fire that burns in your belly. I see the lava stone that is your heart. I see the dead murderer's skull within your head. Above your eyes there sprout horns. Around your belt grow seven serpents' heads. Between your buttocks grows an ass's tail. Your soul gibbers, sooty black.'

Karida stared at Hazad, seeking truth: for only a woman, the virgin daughter of a sorceress, herself skilled in the arts of conjuring, could see and know these things he claimed to know. But before she could think longer on it, Baghel roared and took the shape of a lion, and leaped at Hazad with outstretched claws.

But Hazad was gone.

So it seemed at first. But the lion circled and bit at

himself, growling; Hazad had become a flea, and had leaped to the middle of the lion's back, where the beast could not reach him with its teeth and paws, and clung there, biting him. The lion changed to a serpent and coiled to attack the flea. But on the instant Hazad was an eagle standing atop the serpent, gripping it with sharp talons, lifting into the air on great wings. It flew no farther than an arm's length above the floor when it found that it was clutching a snarling jackal. Hazad let go and became a hummingbird, speeding away.

'Hazad, flee!' Karida shouted, full of terror for him, before she thought what Baghel would do to herself and to Azim, should Hazad leave them to him.

But Hazad flew only as far as the high ceiling of the room, then turned to an adamantine stone, falling straight at the skull of the jackal. Before it struck, Baghel was a fly, speeding away, and within an eyeblink Hazad was a kingbird, diving at him with gaping beak. Then Baghel was a raven, and the two birds met in mid air, driving at each other with beaks and clawed feet, and Karida found that Azim stood by her with his hand holding hard on to her arm, whether to protect her or take comfort from her she could not tell.

The raven that was Baghel bulked three times Hazad's size. Karida saw blood on Hazad's breast, gemming the white feathers there like small rubies. Her lips began to move, whispering a petition to Allah. But Hazad, though small, attacked Baghel so fiercely that the raven let out a wrathful, croaking cry and turned to a fireball flaming in mid air, swiftly growing – it would consume Hazad, Karida, Azim, the chamber, the palace and everyone in it! It would consume the countryside. It might well consume the world.

'Hazad!' Karida shouted in most unmaidenly wise, though what she wanted of him she could not tell.

And Hazad changed form to that of a whirlwind which encompassed the fireball, a whirlwind of such ferocity that it knocked Karida and Azim to the floor; the walls of the chamber fell away. Karida hid her head with her hands.

And all was a blur of wind and fire: then water. For outside the bounds of the chamber lay the tile-lined lake where fountains plashed, and Hazad took Baghel there. Nor could he escape the force of the whirlwind's spinning, or gather himself and change shape. Whirlwind became a waterspout, and the fire expired. Then the wind fell away to a calm, and all grew very still.

Karida got up and ran to the fountain pool, with Azim close behind her, and there, face down on the water, unmoving, floated Hazad.

Karida plunged in, but Azim reached the conjurer first, turning her over and taking her in his arms. 'Does she breathe?' Karida demanded.

Azim stood where he was, up to his waist in water, dumbfounded. 'She is a woman,' he whispered. For through tattered clothing Hazad's breasts showed, inflicted with bloody wounds.

'Of course she is a woman!' Karida stormed. 'Unless she is a demon, which I think not. Does she breathe?'

'Yes.'

'Carry her to yonder chamber, then.' Karida pointed out one that was whole. 'Place her on the bed. Quickly!'

Karida tended Hazad herself, for all the servants in the palace had fled their master's great wrath. Even those 'damsels' who had come to Zel with Karida had fled, out of shame that their courage had failed them. Only Karida and Azim and the young maiden who called herself Hazad remained.

Her wounds were many, but none of them mortal. Karida bathed them and anointed them, gave Hazad palm spirits to drink, and Hazad opened her eyes a moment, looked at Karida, looked at Azim, who stood behind the lady, then lidded her eyes again and slept. Karida sat beside her, and Azim went out and brought back a glowing lamp of scented oil, as he had brought Karida unguents and bandaging and all other things she needed.

Karida looked up at him. He had taken off his wet clothing, his gown, his veil, and put on a youth's clothing, and his golden hair in the lamplight shone very fair, and she remembered how fair his shoulders had been, watersheened from his bath, moving in morning light. In order to gaze no longer at him, she spoke, asking, 'How did you come here?'

He shrugged. 'I followed.'

'You are not entirely a coward,' Karida told him.

'In truth, my lady, the old hags who rule your father's harem frightened me worse than men armed for combat.'

Karida did not smile. 'You came at my time of worst need,' she said. 'I was not expecting to beard a jinni.'

'For all the good that I did,' said Azim.

'You turned Baghel away from me. You gave Hazad time to gather her powers. It was inestimable good.'

Azim set down the lamp and knelt, so that his head would be lower than hers. He faced her across Hazad's sleeping body. 'I deemed you were going into danger, more than you knew,' he said in a low voice. 'And in truth, fair one, the words I first spoke to you were not all courtly courtesy.'

Karida looked down and did not answer him, and grew conscious for the first time that her face was unveiled and her clothing unkept, her bosom as nearly revealed as Hazad's had been. And she said to the ground, 'Go, Azim, find yourself a place to sleep. Leave me.'

He obeyed.

The lady sat by Hazad, and Hazad stirred and murmured in her sleep. Azim was very comely, Karida mused. There were many thoughts in her mind, and one of them was that she wanted him. She would have liked to keep him for her own. But she thought also of Hazad, what little she knew of the maiden, and of what had glimmered in Hazad's dark eyes, looking at Azim.

Then Karida lifted from around her neck the quirin stone on its golden chain, and she laid the stone on Hazad's forehead, between the parting of Hazad's wings of raven-black hair. 'Speak, sister,' Karida urged gently.

Hazad opened her lips and spoke in her sleep.

'He is so beautiful,' she said softly, 'the curls of his hair like the sun rising over fair, deep lakes that are his eyes, and his skin like a clear sunlit sky. But he is ill-named, Azim, 'the defender', for he is useless but to be a pleasure and an ornament. He cannot defend me.'

Karida waited. In a moment Hazad went on.

'I hate him. He is such a craven. I – I love him. I have loved him since the first time I saw him. But he cannot defend me, and he will never be mine, for I am a runaway, a fugitive, and should the sultan, my father, ever discover me I will be locked in chains for ever. I would not be a woman, to wait on men's pleasure and serve them. I dare not be a woman ever again.'

Hazad suddenly became restless and rolled her head from side to side, throwing off the quirin. Karida picked up the small brown stone in her hand, and Hazad opened her eyes. 'I thought I sensed something of magic,' said the maiden, her stare hard on Karida. 'You have placed that on me as a frontlet.'

Karida reached up and positioned the quirin on her own forehead, then opened her mouth and spoke to Hazad. 'When I thought you were a youth,' she said, 'I desired you.'

Hazad smiled, her eyes suddenly merry. 'Just now I deemed you desired Azim,' she said.

'I desire some such comely youth for my own, some day. I dare not return to my father's house, for he will first punish me with starving and imprisonment, then wed me to some ugly old grandee who holds the caliph's favour. Yet what at all is there for a woman in this world, but to be at the will of some man?'

'That is why I became a youth,' said Hazad.

'Sleep again, my soul sister,' Karida told her. 'Rest. Know me as a friend. I must think.' Then she removed the quirin from her own forehead and placed it around her neck again. Hazad slept, and Karida roamed to the top-most tower of the empty palace to watch the dawn. Two faces drifted before her inner eye, one as fair as the other: Hazad's, and Azim's.

'Before I knew she was maid, I deemed I would have one or the other for my lover,' Karida muttered to the brightening sky. 'What, am I to have neither, now?'

And a small while later she grumbled to the dawn, 'Hazad has the courage and warrior prowess of seven soldiers.'

And later, again, she said to the rising sun, 'Hazad saved my life.'

Footfalls sounded on the steps of polished tile behind her. Azim had sought her out. He wore better clothing this morning, a young lord's clothing: a turban of red silk and, over his shirt and trousers of heavy silk, a pelisse of sable, with a dagger at the girdle. Karida turned, schooling her expression to indifference.

'One sunrise greets another,' he said, his eyes intent on her.

'Have you slept well, Azim?' She spoke to him with simple courtesy, nothing more. From her eyes downward her veil covered her face.

'How could I sleep?'

He would have said more of how her beauty had ravished his senses and left him sleepless, but Karida chose not to understand him. 'Yes,' she agreed, 'it was an unsettling evening. Azim, you should go to Hazad. When she awakens, she will want you.'

'I!'

'Assuredly. Could you not tell by the one glance she gave you yestere'en? Yon maiden is utterly devoted to you.'

'To me!' Azim's astonishment straightened him and took away the melancholy from his face. 'But she – when I knew her for a youth, I mean – never did she give me any favour but scorn and drubbings!'

'Azim.' Karida allowed her eyes to smile at him. 'Know you nothing of a woman's ways?'

He gawked at her a moment longer, then turned and went down to Hazad, and Karida loitered on the lookout's tower, smiling into the face of the rising sun and considering how certain desires might be brought to pass.

She stood with the quirin in the palm of her hand, and

her eyes looked out on truth. 'I am a woman,' she said, 'and few enough are my choices.'

So it was that, a few days later, when the dust of Emir Kansbar's armies darkened the horizon (for he had his spies, also, and had marched to take hold of his long-time rival's properties, and expected he might find his missing daughter among them); three young people on foot left Zel, bound for distant places. One was a comely black-haired youth with the clothing and bearing of a seasoned traveller, wearing a short sword girded at his waist. One was a lissom damsel in cowl and veil; she walked at the side of the first, and he protected her with the strength of his arm. And the third, who went his own way, was a handsome, beardless, turbaned youth with skin like silver and amber-shining eyes.

The first was Hazad. The second was Hazad's lover, Azim, veiled from the sight of all eyes but hers. And the third was Karida.

SUSAN SHWARTZ

Towards the Realm of Jade

'Jinn,' said the goldsmith. 'I mislike them. They are shifty, treacherous things: never the same for a moment.'

The merchant who led this caravan to Khotan to buy jade only smiled. His had been the tale of a loving, faithful jinna; the rug merchant who told of the troll-like one in silk, the jewel dealer who spoke of the stone of truth and the lecherous jinni had parted ways at Kashgar. They were bound, they said, for Turfan. Bound, Peter thought, closer to the cathedral and palace of Prester John. *I wish I might have gone with them, but it is already much that the merchant lets me ride with him to Khotan.*

Riding with them were the silk merchant, bound to trade his wares in a realm where silk and jade were common currency, the dealer in fine horses, and the goldsmith, plus many, many more men, their horses, and their camels. The horses were fair; at night he had begged leave to curry them: bays with coats like ruddy fire and dappled whites with ancestries longer than their manes and as noble as their carriage. And then there were the camels, with their groaning and their whims and their vile dispositions.

They reminded Peter of the weather: changeable as a jinni and foul as a camel's breath. He ought to know about that. Last night his own mount had tried to bite him, and the rest of the men had stood about laughing as he dodged and struck out. Bad enough that the beast's swaying had made him as sick as ever he had been on the boat from Kent to Calais: he could not bear to be ridiculous now, among strangers, until, 'We all have dodged the daughters of Iblis!' shouted the merchant. 'Now it is your turn!'

He had been able to laugh at that. And, miraculously, that seemed to have contented the beast he rode.

The air prickled, and his camel moaned yet again. Despite the heat and the stillness of the air, Peter shivered . . . *remembering that day, but a week or two out of Kashgar, when his camel had put her head down then hidden it in the sand, and all the drovers had snatched for heavy felt in which to wrap themselves against the driving grit and the shrieking wind of the black storms . . . and then, sweet Christ, and then the bandits had come . . .*

He leapt down from his camel, seized the nearest roll of felt and, just as the merchant shouted for a halt, was racing towards the herd of horses to help their owner shelter them. The grit rose in stinging whorls, the sky turned yellow and the storm was upon them. Men and beasts huddled beneath the stifling felt and prayed for the storm to be over, or for one more bead of sweat to drip from their brows and cool them for a brief instant.

And then, with the same speed as it had attacked, the storm subsided.

Slowly men and beasts unwound themselves, while the merchants checked their food, water and packs.

Now comes the ambush, Peter thought, and shivered once again.

The merchant glanced up at the sky, where banners more brilliant and more sheer than the silk merchant's wares glowed across the vault of heaven, then at his exhausted companions.

'We go no further today,' he decreed. 'Make camp, and tonight we shall mount guard. But you,' he beckoned at Peter, 'you come here.'

Obediently, Peter approached.

'You too will stand watch tonight: against the same kind of bandits who left you for dead.'

Peter nodded his assent. *Well enough*, he gestured with one hand at his sash, which bore no scabbard, *but how shall I defend us*?

149

The merchant smiled at him. Turning towards his pack-train, he rifled through one roll and from it drew a sword in a richly tooled scabbard, which he stripped from the fine Damascus with the gleam and chime of superb metal, then handed blade and scabbard to his hostage.

He had been but eighteen, recently knighted by his father's lord; he had knelt to receive his sword and have the lady gird it round him . . . yet before ke knew what he did, he had knelt again in the grit of Heathendom to receive this new blade, finer than any he had ever borne.

All that night he stood watch, clutching the blade as a drowning man might clutch a rope, staring out into the desert. As he watched, it sang to him as wind stirred the sand – of jinn, magicians, riches and dreams.

Behind him rose the voices of the other men, in prayer or in story. If Peter shut his eyes and pretended that the men spoke French or English, he could almost believe himself back in the Holy Land with his lord. The fantasy brought tears, then anger at the men who, for so he thought, refused to answer his pleas, and anger even at the honour that held him here, stupidly faithful.

And then, sweeter than any attar of roses or water after a long thirst, came the song of a veiled woman who swayed before him, beckoning, promising him heaven and earth, his freedom and all the riches of the East, if he would but leave his post and come with her . . . delights such as Solomon had known, or Lancelot with Guinevere, if he would but grant her a single kiss . . . fame and honour, and strength surpassing that of all the Nine Worthies . . . and Peter shook his head.

You deserve a king, lady, or no man at all. But his rejection grew increasingly wistful; and the veiled figure danced closer and closer until he could feel her heat and smell the sweetness of her breath beneath her veils. He felt himself swaying too, and in the last conscious gesture of which he was master he drew up the pagan sword and sketched a cross in the night air.

She shrieked and shrank back. A moment later no lady stood on the sands, but a ball of fire, which flashed up into the sky then disappeared with a growl of thunder.

From behind him came men armed with swords and torches, half angry, half afraid, and wholly surprised to see Peter standing there, still holding his post.

All except the merchant who was his master. 'The desert, says the heathen, is haunted by goblins. At night, sometimes, they sing to you. Did you hear one?'

Peter jerked his head *aye*.

The elder man sighed. 'So too have I. Let Khalil take your post now, and come back to the camp. Eat, listen to the stories, and after a time, perhaps you can sleep.'

The Englishman nodded, glad to turn his back on the treacherous desert. Perhaps the men would speak of Khotan, the fabulous source of all the jade in the kingdoms of the Mongols, towards which they rode. Or perhaps they would not. But they were men, not goblins, and he would be glad of their company.

He stumbled once, and was abashed when the merchant put out an arm to catch him.

'I but tripped over . . . what is this?' Peter breathed in wonder.

'Yet another ruin swept clear by this storm, only to be buried by the next,' said the merchant who urged him on. 'Spars of wood . . .'

'No,' breathed the other, and knelt in the sand to retrieve the object over which he had stumbled. It was a lamp of antique design, wrought of metal so heavily tarnished that there was no telling if it were silver, bronze – or gold. Stamped on to it was a star of six points; and it was heavily sealed.

Still kneeling, Peter offered the merchant the lamp, and the man recoiled. 'It might be gold, a great treasure,' Peter said. 'Who knows what lies beneath the grime of centuries? Shall I polish it clean?'

'*No!*' cried the merchant. 'It is the home of that creature who enticed you. I beg you, hurl it from us!'

Heathenish superstition, thought Peter. And yet . . . and yet . . . the singing sand swirled up, and its song swirled with him. A cat's paw of wind sent tendrils of the sand floating towards him with the grace of a dancer, swaying like a woman veiled in love and mystery . . .

And he seized the lamp in both hands and threw it far out into the desert.

Gradually, the wind subsided, and so did the singing. Peter and the merchant turned towards a camp where the men had started a fire from the dried-out wood of the ruins nearby. And after a time, the silk merchant held up his hand for silence, and began his story.

ANDRE NORTON

The Dowry of the Rag Picker's Daughter

The Way of The Limping Camel was six houses long and
one wide – if mounds of tumbled earthen bricks could still
be termed houses. Yet they were indeed inhabited by the
very least and lowest of those who vowed allegiance to
Caliph Ras el Fada, whose own dwelling at the other side
of the city proudly showed a blazing watchtower striped
with gold leaf.

The least of the houses on the Way had been claimed by
the rag picker Muledowa. He was always careful to thank
the Great One of the Many Names for his great luck in
finding it when his former roof had near landed on his
head and had put an end to two ragged hens which were
the care of his daughter Zoradeh. Well had he used his
cane on her, too, for not foreseeing such a catastrophe
and being prepared against it.

He sighed as he slip-slapped along in his worn sandals,
for no one looking upon Zoradeh's unveiled face would
ever come brideseeking— Nor could he even put her up
for sale in the market of slaves either. For again her
jinn-given face would put an end to any hope of sale.

Deliberately he pushed Zoradeh out of his mind as he
wished he could push the whole of her misbegotten face
and skinny body out of his life as well. At least this day the
Compassionate, and All-Powerful, had smiled in his direction. His grip about the edge of the collection bag tightened as he trudged along.

*

Caliph Ras el Fada might be the ruler of Nid and at least ten surrounding territories. But he was not the ruler of his own harem; and he frowned blackly every time he thought about that. He too had a daughter, the veriest rose of a daughter, in whose person and face no man could find fault. The trouble was no longer hidden – and it was one often found among women – love of power and a hot temper. Better she be bagged and left in the waste to trouble mankind no more than introduced into the company of any foolish man. For Jalnar had a strong will and a sharp mind of her own. All smiling eyes and cooing lips could she be until she got her will – then, like some warrior female of the jinn, she became a force with whom no man could deal. Willing indeed was Caliph Ras to get rid of her. However, gossip was gossip and spread from harem even into the marketplace. Since rumour had near a thousand tongues he could not cut out every one of them.

Also there was the matter of the future rule of his town. Though he had taken four wives, and been served by a variety of eager and willing concubines, he had unaccountably no other child who had lived past the fifth year save Jalnar. So he could not leave any heir save her husband – and he had yet to find one willing to accept, no matter how large a dowry he might offer. None for three years, at least until now. He ran his fingers through his beard, trying to put out of mind all else about this self-styled wizard Kamar save the fact that he had not only made an offer for Jalnar but had already gifted her with one of the dresses for her bridal viewing – all of silvery stuff so sewn with pearls as to be worth a fortune.

The caliph clapped hands and summoned his favourite mameluke sending him to the harem with a message for the head eunuch. But still he was too ill at ease to retire to his gold-embroidered cushions, and his hand gave such a hard tug to his beard that the tweak brought smarting tears to his eyes and words to his lips which were hardly those of a sublime ruler and respected Commander of the Faithful.

Down the Way of the Weeping Camel came Muledowa.

Zoradeh moved closer to the wall, waited to feel his digging stick hard laid about her shoulders, though she could remember no recent fault which would arouse her father's ire. To her great surprise he squirmed past the tall pile of broken mud bricks which served as a door without any great cursing. To her even greater astonishment, he stooped to gather up the chunk of crumbling masonry which sealed the door and thumped it home, keeping his gathering bag still tight-pressed to him under his other arm. For the first time she could recall, there was an upturn to his lips within the thick beard which might be almost taken for a smile.

The shadow smile still lingered as he looked to her.

'Fortune sometimes aids the worthy man after all.' With great care he placed the bag on the pavement between them. 'I am at a turning of the road now, and soon I shall mount a fine she-mule and have a slave to run before me. Nor shall I grub among foul things for bread to fill the mouth.'

She eyed him warily, afraid to ask any questions for fear he might well slide back into that other whom she had always known. But he had gone down on his knees and was tugging at the fastening of the bag. Still paying her no attention, he brought forth something which caused her to cry out when she saw it.

Creased and possessing a ragged tear down the front, as if its last wearer had ripped it, or had it torn from her body, was such a dress as she could not believe ever existed except in some tale. It was silver, shimmering, and seeming to reflect the light here and there, and there were small and large pearls cunningly sewn into the pattern of it. It was such a garment as only a houri would wear.

Her father was holding it up to the light, turning it carefully. He lifted the torn portion and held it in its place. Then, for the first time he spoke to her. 'Loathly thou art, but still there is some use for you. Bring out your needle and the rightful kind of thread and make this as perfect as can be done. And –' he looked to the bucket of water she had brought within the hour from the well in the street, 'wash your hands twice – thrice – before you lay hand on this. A princess's ransom might be in your hold.'

Zoradeh reached out a hand to the shimmering pile of beauty. Then she leaned far forward and kissed the dusty pavement at her father's feet.

'On my head and hands be this done,' she said as she gathered the bag around the treasure. In her were a myriad of questions but she dared voice none of them. She could only fear in silence that her father had in some manner stolen the robe.

'Aye, on your head, your hands and your eyes.' He went back to the broken door before he turned, with infinite malice in both the look he directed at her and in his voice as he answered, 'Good fortune seldom pays two visits to a man, and this is mine!'

He looked back at the shimmering heap and then went out. Zoradeh listened to the slap of his worn sandals. He was going down the street towards the small inn where he would drink minted tea and strive to outlie his two rivals for the rest of the afternoon.

She followed orders and washed her hands three times, daring to put in the rinse water of the last immersion a bit of well-shaved cinnamon bark, so that its fragrance warred against all the other and fouler odours in the small courtyard. Then taking up the bag which was still half wrapped about the wonder her father had brought home, she scrambled up to the part of the house which she had made her own, her father not choosing to follow her over the loose bricks which often started sliding underfoot. Once this must have been the harem of a noble house, for there were still fading pictures painted in flaring designs on the wall. But now it was Zoradeh's own place of hiding. She spread out the bag as far as she could and stood up to shake free the robe.

Carefully the girl examined the tear across the front of the robe. It was a jagged opening apparently made by a knife and, as she moved, pearls dripped from broken threads. Hastily she folded it tear-side up and explored the bag and the floor about until she had near a full palm

156

of the gleaming gems. How many had been lost along the way her father had followed or still laid near to where he had found it? Find it he must have done, for Muledowa was the last man in the city to put his right hand into jeopardy for thievery.

Oftimes before she had mended thrown-away things her father had found in the trash, and done so so well that he was able to sell such to a dealer in old clothes in the market. But she had never set fingers to such as this before. Bringing forth her packet of needles, she chose the smallest, and using ravellings of the material itself she set to work.

In the tree-shadowed court of the harem which formed nearly a third of the caliph's palace, Jalnar lay soft and at ease on a pile of silken rugs while a slave rubbed her feet and ankles with sweet-smelling cream. She held up her silver hand-mirror and studied her reflection in the polished surface critically. Nor did she turn her head as she spoke to the blowsy bundle of shawls and face veil which squatted a few feet away.

'They say that there be only two lots for a woman – marriage or the grave. To me it seems that these be equal choices and there should be a third – a hidden rule within the hour. You did as was told to you, Mirza? The thing will never see the light of day again?'

'Hearing was doing, flower of all flowers. It was thrust deep among the foul refuse of the city – no one would go delving for profit there.'

'In a way, old one, it is a pity. For I have never seen its like. But then I have never been courted by a wizard before and who knows what tricks of magic he bound around it – what tricks he might use against me when I went among his womenfolk. Wizards claim great powers, and they may be right. Better not yield to such a one.

'It is the duty of the caliph to provide me with at least seven bride dresses so that when I am shown to my lord, he sees me in full beauty. Why should this Kamar present one, thus breaking custom? Perhaps he would

157

so bind me to some afrit who would be ever with me that I may not in anything have my will.'

The bundle of shawls shook. 'Precious as water in the desert, speak not of such horrors. It is said that some may be summoned up merely by thinking of them. It could well be that the wizard wishes only to do you honour, and that such affairs are arranged differently in his country. I have heard it ever said that foreigners have queer customs.'

Jalnar slapped down the fan on her knee and kicked out at one of the girls who were soothing her feet. 'Be gone, it is done as well as your awkward hands can do so. And you, Mirza, forget such foolishness. Has not the mighty Orban himself laid upon this castle and all it contains a protecting shell? All have heard of Orban. Who has raised a voice to cry aloud the deeds of Kamar? Only by his own words do we know that he claims to be a wizard at all.

'If he is one and has striven to burden me with some fate of his own devising – well, we have taken care of that, have we not, old one?'

'Hearing and obeying, great lady,' came her servant's answer, so softly that Jalnar had to strain to hear it, and her ears were the keenest ever known in Nid.

'Go now, all of you, I would sleep away the heat hours that I may appear at my best at the second showing—'

There was a grunt from the shawls and Jalnar laughed.

'So it has been said that Kamar wanted his gift shown tonight. Now *you* will whisper in the halls and kitchen that he misjudged my size – that my workers of needlecraft need to make some changes in it. Since he cannot come into the harem to search and ask, he needs must accept my word for that if he ask outright. You may tell all your old gossips that I shall wear it on the seventh night, when the contract is to be signed which will make me one to answer his slightest whim. That will bring us time and we can plan—' her voice slid down into a hissing whisper as she waved all those with her away.

Zoradeh had feared the task her father had set her, for the stuff of its making was so fragile she thought that even handling might bring more destruction. Yet her needle slipped through the gauzy material as if there were holes, there already awaiting it. She made fast each pearl with interweaving. It would seem that the rent was less than it looked at first and she finished well before sundown. Standing up on the scrap of wall left to the house she allowed the faint breeze to tug it out to the full. Truly a robe for a princess. How had her father come upon such a thing?

She held it close to her and wondered how it would feel to go so bravely clad through the days with maids a plenty, eunuchs and mamelukes to obey and guard her. Now she looked carefully down along the street and then it was but a moment's work to undo her trousers, which were patch upon patch, and her faded, much-mended shirt. Over her head went the robe and it settled down about her, seeming to cling to her as might another, fairer skin. Zoradeh drew a deep breath and brought forward the water pail, waiting for the slopping of its contents to end so that she could use it as a mirror. Then she whipped the end of the head veil, worn modestly, about the lower part of her jinni-given face and looked.

Ah! with her face thus covered she looked like someone out of a fair dream and she straightened her back, aching from many hours of being bent above a task, giving her head a proud little toss ... Princess! So did clothes make the woman. Were she to venture forth with some guards and a bevy of maids, would her passage not have them talking about a princess very quickly indeed?

'Pearl among pearls!' The voice startled her so that she nearly lost her precarious footing and fell forward into the courtyard. There was a man in the outer lane, mounted on a fine black horse which seemed to dance with eagerness under his hand. And he wore the red scarf of the caliph's own guard looped about the rim of his helm.

'Fortune's own daughter!' He smiled gayly and raised his spear in salute. 'Foolish is your lord to allow such a treasure to be seen. How came you here to glow like a lily under the full moon, but set in a marsh of muck so hard to reach and pluck forth—'

She must rid herself of this stranger before the return of her father, and what better way to do so than to prove to him what ugliness could be seen as a woman's face? Deliberately she jerked the wedge of the shawl from the veiling of her face, and waited for him to show distaste and dislike of the tooth-gorging, wrinkled mask as all the rest had done. Yet he did not turn away his head, spit out some charm against afrit or demon. Instead he brought his horse closer to the crumbling wall and called up to her.

'Are you wed, pearl of great price? If this be so I shall search out your husband and ask him to try blade against blade with me – and I am counted a mighty swordsman. If the Uniter of Souls has decreed that you are not so tied to another, tell me then your name and that of your father that I may make him an offer—'

She had backed away from the edge of the wall, now sure that she spoke with a man whose wits were awry. She answered:

'Master, why do you make me the butt of your cruel pleasure? You see me clearly – and so seeing you view what no man would bargain for.' Then she scrambled down the rude inner stairway of her perch, not listening to aught he called after her, rubbing the tears from her eyes. So she stayed in hiding until she heard him ride away and was able to reach for her own clothing, and fold away the mended pearl dress in the bag.

She could hope that he might forget his foolishness and that he would not indeed set forth a hunt for Muledowa, for the latter would indeed deem the guard mad – as would any in this quarter hearing him speak so of the rag picker's daughter, easily the most foul of countenance of any who drew water from the public well, and went openly unveiled, for who would do *her* any dishonour? She wrapped the dress carefully in her father's collection bag and hid it under his sleep mat, hoping he would take it away soon. For within her, long hope awakened, and she would not be so hurt again.

*

In the palace of the caliph there was much to do, for the seventh-day bride feast had yet three nights to go. Jalnar bathed and then had her smooth, pale skin anointed with a scent made of many herbs, so that it would seem a whole garden had broken into the bathing chamber. Her dark hair was brushed until there was the look of fine satin to its length, and the maid had just finished with that when Mirza scurried into the room and bent her shoulder, the more so that she might kiss the ground before her mistress's feet.

There was such a look on her much-wrinkled face as made Jalnar wave her attendants away and lean towards her with a whisper for a voice.

'Old one, what trouble does Fate or afrit lay upon us? You look like one on the way to the beheading block, no chance of any mercy at the end of that journey.'

'Well, my lady, do you choose such a description.' Plainly there was both fear and anger to make her voice like the croak of a carrion crow. 'Our caliph, the great lord, the Prophet-descended one, has given an order – already he must be close to the guarded doorway – and he said with all men hearing him that this night you shall do proper honour to Kamar after the fashion of his own people and wear for his viewing the robe which he brought—'

'It is too tight, too small, it was damaged in the chest in which it came to me – I would do him greater honour if I wear it on the final night after it is repaired.'

Mirza began to shake her head – first slowly and then with greater vigour, 'Lady, the companion of jinn will see through such excuses and would even if it is you who speak them.'

Jalnar caught a lock of her hair and held it between her teeth. The plan she had thought was so simple – how could she have hoped to use it against a wizard?

'What shall I do then, mother of maids?'

'You have the robe brought forth and then perhaps it may be repaired in time. For those at the banquet sit long over such delicacies as your honoured father has set before him. He is, thank the Compassionate, one who is not easily disturbed from any meal.'

'There is wisdom in your speech, old one. Go and have out that rag and my best sewing maid, to whom the All-Seeing has given a great gift of needle, shall see what she can do. It might be well that I wear the robe from the far eastern nation which was gifted to me three years ago, and then have the wizard's rag brought in to show and say that I would keep the honour of its wearing to the last night of all, when my father gives me to this hunter of stars and teller of strange tales despite all his present urging.'

To hear is to obey,' mumbled Mirza.

She once more padded away. But when she sought the hole into which she had thrust the robe there was nothing of it there – save a number of date seeds and the rind of melon. For a moment or two she looked about her wildly, thinking surely she must have been mistaken. Only she remembered so well other points of reference to that hidey-hole and they were still about.

'Grub you for the kitchen leavings, old one?' A boy who wore only a ragged loin cloth, and who was grey with the grime of the dump, looked down upon her from a neighbouring mound of refuse. 'There will be naught worth the having there, for old Muledowa has already been here. Though his bones may be old so he cannot scramble around well, he has never lost what may bring him any sort of a bargain. Even the afrit would welcome such skill as he has.'

'Muledowa?' Mirza raised her voice a little. 'He is known to you, quick one, and he has been here today?'

'As the sun weighs upon us with its heat, so it is true. Also his find here must have been a fine one, for he turned and went towards his home, looking no more this day. I strove to see what he held, but he rolled it so quickly into his collecting bag that I got no sight of it and when I asked him a question he spat at me as if we were strange cats a-foe over a choice morsel of baked camel.'

Jalnar twisted the lock of hair fiercely between her hands upon Mirza's return as she said:

'Go you to Raschman of the guard and say to him that one of my maids stole out at night and buried something among the rubbish where it was later found by this Muledowa and taken away – that it must be a plot between the two of them and—' She hesitated a moment and then added, 'Say that it was Dalikah who did this – for all know that I have had her beaten for breaking my bottle of scent and she has good reason so to play, having ill thoughts against me. Tell the guardsman that you have heard of this rag picker who lives in the refuse of the town and to send there to obtain the bag. Only warn him not to open it or look upon its contents for it is doubtless true that it has been overlooked and magicked by the jinn.'

'And Muledowa and those who live under his roof who may have already seen what lies within that bag, my lady, what do we with them?'

'I do not think,' Jalnar replied with a small cruel smile, 'that he will have shared such a secret with many – they would be on him as a hawk upon a desert snake if he had. But if he does have other of his own blood – let that one or all others be brought also.'

Mirza struck her head three times against the floor at the princess's feet. 'Hearing is doing, lady.'

So she left Jalnar to be swathed in the green gown of her choice and slipped away through the gates, for all the guards knew her well and she often ran errands for this or that of the ladies of the inner rooms.

Though she had never invaded this before, she went to the outer place where she huddled by the door of the guards' room, trying to catch the eye of the man who was making swooping motions in the air and talking loudly.

'—fair as the moon in full glory, she moves like swallows awing, her skin like the softest satin such as those in the Forbidden Palace lie upon for sleeping. Ah, I have seen beauties a-many in my day—'

Two of the listeners laughed and the man's hand went to his sword hilt, his face frowned in warning.

'Brother by the sword,' one of the listeners spoke. 'Is it not that many times you have seen maids of surpassing beauty, only later to find some irredeemable flaw in them? Let us all go then to the ruin by the outer wall and test whether your story be right or whether some jinni has ensorcelled your eyes—'

But the young man had already seen Mirza, and now he came to her with some relief in his expression. 'Why do you seek us out, mother?' he asked with some respect and a tone of courtesy.

'My lady has been grievously despoiled of a treasure.' She told her story quickly. 'One of the slave girls took ill her punishment for a fault and stole a robe of great price. She hid this in the mound of refuse beyond the palace and there it was picked up by one Muledowa, a picker of rags, and carried home. My lady would have back her belongings and with them the rag picker and all else under his roof who might have seen this thing – for she fears it all be a piece of sport by those afrits who dislike all mankind. Of this she wishes to be sure before she tells her father of it – lest she, too, be drawn into some devilish sorcery.'

He touched his turban-wreathed helm with both hands and said:

'Having heard, it is as done.'

Zoradeh was kneeling in the ruined courtyard of her home, washing her father's feet and listening with growing fear to his mumbling speech, for he was talking, if not to her, then to some jinni who had accompanied him.

'Orbasan will pay me much for this treasure,' he stretched out an arm so he could finger the bag which held the robe. 'Then I shall buy a donkey and, with the aid of that creature, be able to carry twice as much from the refuse heaps. For I am an old man and now it hurts my back to stretch and strain, to kneel and stand erect again all for some bit I may take. There is much greater profit to be had with things I cannot carry. Eh, girl,' for the first time he looked directly at her with a cruel snarl twisting his lips, 'how then has the work gone? Let me look upon, your handiwork. If you have erred then you shall taste of my stick until each breath shall cost you sore—'

164

Zoradeh brought the bag quickly and spread it out before him, taking care that she did not touch the wondrous thing with her own hands, damp and dusty as they were. For a long moment her father stared down at the fine silk and moon-like pearls. His hand went out as if to touch and then he drew it back quickly with a deep-drawn breath.

'Aye, worth a vizier's ransom at least, must that be. We shall get but a third, a fifth, an eighth portion of its price in gain. Yet I know no one else—' His hand went to his beard as he ran his nails through the crisp years' sullied grey of it. 'No,' he added as one who had just made a decision of great import, 'not yet shall I go to Orbasan with this. We shall put it away in secret and think more of the matter—'

But even as he spoke they heard the clatter of horse hooves on the uneven pavement without, and Zoradeh clasped the robe tightly while her father lost all his sly, cunning look in a rush of fear – for no one rode horses within the city save the guard of the caliph or that protector of the city himself. Her father got swiftly to his feet and hissed at her:

'Get you inside with that and put it upon you, they will think it is some foreign trash discarded by a trader. Best stay in open sight and not try to conceal it lest it shows that we believe ourselves at fault!'

She hurried into the single of the lower rooms which was walled and ceilinged and so might be considered a home. There she tore hurriedly out of her own rags, wondering the while if her father had lost his wits – or was he pulled into some jinni's plot and did as his master bade him? The robe slid easily across her body, and she had just given the last fastening of a breast buckle when her father's voice raised high reached her ears.

'Come, my daughter, and show this brave rider what matter of luck I did have this morning—'

She pulled the throat scarf up about her chin, though that was nothing but to hide better her devil-face, and made herself walk out into the half courtyard of the building. There her father stood in company with three of the

guard – one of those being the young officer who had so
teased her earlier in the day. All three stood silent facing
her as if she were some evil afrit ready to suck the flesh
from their bones.

'Lady – where got you this robe of great beauty?' The
captain found his tongue first and she, believing only the
truth might save them from whatever vengeance might
strike now, dared to say in return:

'Lord, my father brought it and it was torn and of no
value to any. See – do you see here the stitches I, myself,
set to make it whole again?'

Hurriedly she gathered up a portion of the skirt and
held it out – though so perfect had been her repairs that
none might see the work and would swear an oath that it
was indeed second goods, that which was thrown away
because it was damaged.

'That is my lady's robe,' grated a sour voice from the
door as Mirza pushed through the opening to join them.
She was panting and red-faced from her effort to join
them. 'These are thieves which that misbegotten she-mule
of my lady's following got to come to her aid.'

Muledowa had fallen to his knees and now he gathered
up a palmful of sand to throw over his dirty headcloth.

'Lord of many, commander of archers, I have made no
pact with any – woman or afrit or jinni. It is my way of life,
sifting out that which others have thrown away – things
which can be resold in the second market which our great
lord, the caliph himself, has decreed established for those
of lean purses. This I found torn asunder and thrust into
the pile of refuse before the Gate of the Nine-Headed
Naga at the palace.'

Mirza came forward a step or two, thrusting her face
close to Muledowa, and spat forth her words as might a
cat who finds another within its hunting place. 'Find it you
did, provider of filth and evil. But first you had notice of
the place from Dalikah, who has already tasted of my
lady's justice.' She turned to the guardsmen. 'Take you
this fool of a thief and also his ugly daughter to the left
wing of the palace where lies the screen through which my

peerless lady views the world. Since this crime was committed against her she would have the judging of it.'

Thus with a rope around his throat, fastened to the saddle of a guardsman, Muledowa was pulled at a pace hard for his old bones to make. While Mirza took off the topmost of her swathing of grimy and too-well-worn shawls which she tugged around Zoradeh, forcing the girl's arms against her body as tightly as if they were bound and keeping the headveil well over her head.

So they set off across the city, while behind them gathered a crowd of idlers and lesser merchants and craftsmen who were all agog to see and hear what must be the story behind such a sight.

They came into the courtyard that Mirza had described, but to Mirza's discomfort she found there the caliph himself and the wizard Kamar who had come to see the fair white pigeons which were one of the joys of the caliph's heart.

Seeing the caliph and thinking that perhaps one fate might be better than another, for the Lord of Many Towers was reputed to hear either truth or lies when spoken before him, the ragpicker jerked on the rope about his neck and fell upon his knees, giving forth that wail with which the honest meet with misfortune. The caliph made a gesture with his hand so that the guards left Muledowa alone.

'Wretched man,' he said, 'what misfortune or ill wish by an afrit brought you to this place, and in such a sorry state?'

'Only the lawful enterprise of my business, great one.' Muledowa upon his knees reached forward to touch the pavement before the caliph three times with his dust-covered lips. 'I have no evil within me which wishes danger to you or any under this roof. It was this way—' and with one word tumbling over the other in his eagerness he told his story.

'Now that be a marvellous tale,' the caliph commented when he was done. 'Child,' he beckoned to Zoradeh, 'stand forth and let us see this treasure which your father found.'

Trembling, and with shaking hands, Zoradeh dropped the shawl from her shoulders and stood in the bright sunlight of the courtyard, her head hanging and her hands knotted together before her.

'Where is this tear over which so much has been made?' asked the caliph.

Timidly she passed her hand over that part which she had so laboriously stitched and rewoven. Then Kamar, who had stood silent all the while, looking first to those gathered in the courtyard and then at the pierced marble screen as if he knew who sheltered behind that, spoke:

'You have a deft needle, girl,' he commented. 'She who is to wear this will thank you. My lord,' he turned to the caliph then and said: 'My lord, as you know this robe was gifted to me by the Fira Flowers. Let her who lightens this city now put it on and I shall pronounce on both robe and the enhanced beauty of she who rightly wears it such a spell as will never more part them.'

The caliph considered for a moment and then answered: 'Let it be as you will, Kamar. It seems that by odd chance alone it has been returned to us. You,' he pointed to Mirza, 'do you take this maiden behind the screen and let her change garments again – this time with that flower of my house – Jalnar.'

The tall lady wearing the shimmering green was not the only one waiting behind the screen. There was also a gaggle of maids reaching into the shadow behind her and it seemed to Zoradeh that every time one of those moved, if only for so little, there followed a breeze of the finest scent set wandering. She gasped but Mirza had already dragged the face veil from her and now she waited to see the disgust of the princess and the loathing of her maidens rise. Yet, and she marvelled at that, they had gathered around her at a distance and none of them showed the old loathing her jinni-like face had always roused in all she met.

Two of the maids hurried to disrobe the princess while Mirza's dry and leathery hands were busied about her own body. The shimmering robe of the moon-like pearls was handled by the old hag while in turn she took a grey, dulled slave robe and threw it to Zoradeh, leaving her to fasten it about her as best she could.

But the princess—!

Zoradeh gasped and heard a cry of fright from one of the maids, while another knelt before the princess holding up a mirror of burnished silver so that she might look at herself. The robe covered her skin as tightly as it had Zoradeh's, but she had not yet raised the face veil. And—

'Jinni-face – now she bears such – the teeth which are tusks – the skin of old leather,' whispered Zoradeh under her breath, glancing quickly about to make sure none had heard her. For if Jalnar was in truth not a jinna, her features were twisted in the same ugliness that Zoradeh's had shown all her life long.

The princess screamed, and putting her hands to her face, rubbed hard as if to tear loose a close-fitting mask. At the sound of her cry two armed eunuchs burst in upon them, but seeing the princess they both shivered and drew back, like wise men not daring to question those who had other powers.

But that cry not only brought the eunuchs. For the first time there were visitors to the inner harem which custom and law denied them. The caliph, his curved sword in his hands, was well at the fore part of that invasion, but close indeed to his very heels came the guardsmen, one of them still dragging Muledowa on his restraining rope. And they halted too, even as the eunuch guards had done.

For the princess stood a little apart from them all shaking her misshapen head from side to side and moaning piteously.

'My daughter!' The caliph looked to Kamar who was the only one who had not drawn weapon. 'Wizard – what has happened to my daughter who was as the full moon in all its glory and now wears the face of a jinni – even of an afrit. There is weighty magic here, and to my eyes it is evil.' Without warning he swung his sword at the wizard, but before the blade touched Kamar it seemed to melt, as

169

if it had passed through some fire and the blade dripped down to form a hook.

'My lord,' Kamar wore no armament which could be seen, yet he appeared totally unaware of the swords now pointed at him. Zoradeh thought that for sure they would attack him, yet he had no fear at all. 'My lord, this robe was my gift and it has powers of its own. It draws the inner soul into the light.' He came a little more forward then and looked to the princess instead of the men who stood ready to deliver his death.

'What,' Kamar asked then as if speaking to all of them, 'What does a man wish the most in a bride? Fairness of face sometimes fades quickly and also it makes its owner proud, vain and thoughtless of those who serve her. You—' he made a pounce forward and caught at the mirror which the maid had left on the floor. Turning, he held that before Zoradeh and she cried out a plea to save herself from looking at what hung here.

Only she did not see a jinna's twisted face above the grey garment they had given her. Instead – she drew a deep breath of wonder and glanced shyly at the wizard for some answer to this.

'You are also a maid marriageable by age, but none came to seek you out. Is that not so?'

'I was – I had the face of a jinna,' she said in a voice hardly above a whisper. 'My father is too poor to find me a dowry – thus even a humpbacked beggar does not desire me under his roof. But—' she rubbed her hands down the smooth flesh of her face, 'what has happened to me, lord?'

'You have met with truth and it has set you free. Lord of Many Towers,' he spoke to the caliph now, 'I came hither to have me a wife. I have found the one that Fate, which is the great weapon of the All-Compassionate, intended should rule my inner household—'

He held out his hand to Zoradeh, and she, greatly daring for the first time in her life, allowed her fingers to lie on the rein-calloused palm of a man.

'But, my daughter—' The caliph looked at Jalnar.

'In time,' answered Kamar, 'the Compassionate may

bring to her her will and desire, but they must be by her earning and not because she dwelt before her own mirror in admiration for what she saw therein.'

Jalnar let out a wail as deep with feeling as that of a newly made widow, and then, her hands covering her face, she rushed from the room of the screen, her maids following in disorder.

Kamar went now to Muledowa who sat staring as if he did not believe what he had seen. Kamar took a heavy purse from his sash and dropped it before the bound man.

'Let this one go free, lord of many mercies,' he said to the caliph. 'For he shall live under my protection from this day forth and what troubles him also troubles me. Now, my lady, we shall go—'

She flung her neck scarf over her head and shoulders, veiling a face which even now she could not believe was hers, and followed Kamar from the room.

It is said among the tellers of tales that they lived long past the lifetimes of others. And that the Divider of Souls and the Archer of the Dark did not come to them in any of the years that those living have tale of. But of Jalnar – ah, there lies another tale.

JUDITH TARR

Kehailan

In the Name of Allah, the Merciful, the Compassionate!

There was once in the land of Egypt a most wise and learned vizier, as renowned for his mercy as for his justice, whom even his enemies honoured with the name of 'incorruptible'. Egypt, it was said, was blessed in its sultan; the sultan was blessed in his vizier; and the vizier was blessed in his wives and in his servants, and in a son who was the light of his eyes.

This son, the only child of his old age, was much loved and much indulged, and he was most appealing to look at, a fact of which he was all too well aware. Between his father's love and his own great beauty, he had managed to elude all but the most ineluctable of duties, and even those had not excessively troubled his peace. For he had a mameluke, a slave taken from among the most beautiful youths of the Franks and raised in all the ways of the True Faith, who was his age to a day, and who was closer to him than any brother in blood. In one respect only did they differ: the mameluke, whose name was Khalid, was a slave as much of duty as of the vizier's son. What his master could not or would not do, he inevitably accomplished, always with competence, and often with brilliance. The vizier's son, it was said, was the most fortunate of men. His conscience was his slave; when it troubled him, he had but to dismiss it from his presence.

Aside from his own face, the vizier's son gave his heart's love to three things only: women, song and the horses which his father had bred, which were the best in all of

Egypt. A doe-eyed darling, a new song in a new mode, a foal begotten of the dawn wind – these were all his desire. For his love of the last, he had won the name *al-Kehailan*, which signifies the pure strain of the horses of Arabia.

On the day on which al-Kehailan began his twentieth year, he should have been as joyous as any young man could be who had all the world at his feet. He rode on a hunt in the wilds outside Cairo. His companions were picked men of his father's own guard, and the fairest youths of the sultan's court; and he was the fairest and the most accomplished of them all. He bestrode the most exquisite of his mares, the Pearl of the East, who had run against the wind and left it gasping in her dust. His mameluke's bags were bursting with the fruits of his archery; his newest slave awaited him in the seclusion of the harem, a Circassian virgin of surpassing beauty, the enjoyment of whom would crown his night as the hunt had crowned his day.

And yet, as he rode, his brows were one black line of discontent. 'Duty,' he said to his mameluke. 'Duty. Always duty. Do you know no other word?'

'I know one other,' said Khalid. They were, for the moment, alone; as always in such circumstances, he had forsaken the submission of the slave for the directness of a brother. 'Love. Your father loves you, Kehailan. And how do you repay him? You squander his riches in your debaucheries. You mock his wisdom with your folly. When your presence in the diwan would gladden his heart, you abandon him for the pleasures of the hunt.'

'He will feast on those pleasures tonight.'

'Surely. And will you feast with him? A Circassian maiden holds your heart, a Saklawi colt your mind. When you have ridden them both, you will sleep, with never a thought for your father's sadness. He never sees you but when you would have another mount or another woman; when you have won his consent to either, you leave him, with a scant word of gratitude to ease his loneliness.'

'Loneliness?' Kehailan was not, yet, angry. He was very proud of his self-restraint. 'He has all of Egypt to bear him company.'

'All of Egypt,' said Khalid, 'is not his son.'

It was nothing new, this litany of Khalid's. It was the mameluke's besetting flaw. Not only did he do his duty, and Kehailan's besides. He did his utmost to impress it on his master. But that the slave should dare it on this day of all days, when nothing should have marred the purity of his master's joy, came very close to the edge of the unforgivable.

The Pearl of the East fretted gently, eager to rejoin the chase. For once he had no thought for her. 'My father takes joy with me in my youth. When I am older I will be as drably dutiful as ever you can desire.'

'Will your father be alive to see it?'

Kehailan was still. Even the wind had paused to marvel, so motionless did he sit. With utmost softness he said, 'You are my slave. My hand holds your life and your death. Speak again of my father's passing, and you die.'

He spoke the purest truth. Khalid bowed to it. But he said, 'You hasten that passing with your profligacy.'

Kehailan swept out his sword. Khalid bowed his neck and waited, entrusting his soul to Allah; but keeping his eyes steady on his brother and his master.

With a cry of despair, Kehailan clapped spurs to the white mare's sides. Never in her life had she known such pain. She gasped with the shock of it, stretched to her full length, and fled.

Kehailan let the mare choose her own wild path. Tears – of rage, he could hope – had blinded his eyes. He cared little where she bore him, and less what he might find there.

He heard it first: a roaring like wind, but deep as the voices of dragons. It was laughter; but laughter such as he had never heard.

The mare wheeled and shied. Kehailan battled her into trembling immobility. His eyes had cleared, and gone wide.

He had come to the heart of the wilderness. It was a wild place, a place of ruins and of greenery, such as the creatures of the air are said to love. In its centre upon a shattered pavement roiled a madness of wings and horns and claws, from which rolled the laughter. It reared up, and it was an Afrit of truly miraculous hideousness, and beneath it, struggling, a woman as white as the moon. She was bound with silk and steel, her body all one great cry.

Kehailan abandoned the saddle. The Afrit's tail lashed; its wings fanned the stench of the nether pit. It rose over the woman. Its fangs gleamed as it laughed, fondling her with one great taloned hand so that she writhed and tossed.

It was, most emphatically, *he*. Kehailan checked at the sight of that shaft which would have shamed an elephant. Surely the demon would not, could not accomplish what so plainly it had begun.

Most certainly it meant to try. Kehailan leaped high in the air and smote with all his strength.

The fine Damascus steel, child of nine forgings, treasure of his house, rebounded as if from adamant. Its edge was sorely notched. The Afrit's hide twitched as at a stinging fly. Kehailan struck again at the base of the great bull-neck, seeing Khalid in it, gaining force from his wrath. The blade broke at the hilt. The Afrit, distracted, turned its horrible head.

'Allah,' whispered Kehailan, alone and unarmed and beginning to suspect that he should be afraid. 'Ya Allah.' The Afrit stiffened at the Holy Name. Kehailan, inspired with terror, raised his voice to something very like its wonted clarity. 'In the Name of Allah, the Merciful, the All-Knowing, and by the Seal of Suleiman, upon whose memory be prayer and peace, I command thee, be gone!'

The Afrit towered against the sky. Kehailan stood straight and composed himself for death. The demon clapped its mighty wings and roared. It swelled; it smouldered; it burst in an appalling stench.

The silence was thunderous. Kehailan's hand stung. He

gripped the broken hilt of his sword, and it was as hot as if he had held it in a fire. He dropped it with an exclamation.

The woman, bound still, beseeched him with her eyes. She was even more beautiful than he. He would have fallen upon her as she was and had his will of her, but the splendour of her gaze made him pause. He bent to unbind her. If his hand escaped his will and ventured a caress, it was no fault of his; nor did she seem to take it amiss.

As the last cruel shackle fell away, her arms rose and coiled about his neck. Her lips seized his. Her eyes laughed and beckoned and were irresistible. She drew him down into her garden of delights.

Kehailan left it late and reluctantly, with many a backward glance. But the gate had closed against him. His flesh, feeble creature, was glad of it. It lay all spent, and sang of sleep. Only her fingers held him back from it, wandering in the downy thickets of his beard. 'My heart,' she said, and her voice was musk and honey, 'and my conqueror. I owe you more than my life.'

He stared at her, dazed and blinking. He was in love, he knew it surely. He had forgotten every graceful word he ever knew. 'Come,' he stammered. 'Come with me. I love you. I must have you.'

Her finger silenced him, a mothwing brush upon his lips, more potent than any blow. Her eyes were dark with regret. 'Alas,' she mourned, 'I may not.'

'Who? Who is he? I will kill him!'

His passion made her smile. 'You are my heart's beloved. It is only . . .' She broke off as if she would veil a secret. She kissed him until his every muscle had loosed, and withdrew, holding him down with one slender hennaed hand. 'No, my dear lord. Truly I cannot. And yet, for the horror from which you freed me, and for the delights with which you have bound me, I would give you one small gift.'

Hope sang in his heart. 'You?'

She shook her head, all sadness. 'I am not my own to give. But of the rest that the world may offer, I grant you your heart's desire.'

'You are my heart's desire.'

He drowned in the sweet sorrow of her smile. When he had come to life again, she was gone. He stood in a green solitude upon a broken pavement, and in his hand a hilt without a blade. Her voice filled his ears. 'Utter the words of Faith, and it is yours, whatever you wish most to possess or to be.'

And even her voice was gone, and he was alone.

The silence shattered. Horns rang, hounds bayed, men shouted aloud, hot upon a scent. The hunt burst out of the wood, his own guards foremost, and leading them all, crying his name, Khalid.

A great rage surged up in him. That she was gone, and they were not. That he could never be free of them. Free as the beast of his name: child of wind and fire, swiftness made flesh, unvexed, untrammelled, untormented.

His head tossed. His heart swelled, bursting, crying aloud its deepest desire. To escape them all. To be free. 'There is no god but God,' cried Kehailan, 'and Muhammad is His Prophet!'

The hunt parted to swirl about him. None of it vanished. Khalid sprang down, unslain and untransformed, even his pricking tongue intact; reaching to embrace, and to bind, and to beg pardon in his fashion that had ever been too haughty for a slave. Kehailan thrust away from him, cursing the falsity of women. He had nothing that he wanted, and least of all the freedom he had prayed for. From Khalid, from guilt, and from the iron bonds of duty.

Something was strange. Like an itch, but an itch deep within. Like pain, but pain that was close to pleasure. His eyes were growing dim. But his ears unfolded wonders. And his nose . . .

'Allah!' Khalid's shock was sharp in his nostrils. 'Kehailan. *Kehailan*!'

Kehailan threw up his head. His blood had turned all to fire. But it was not pain. It was a wonder and a splendour. He stamped: the pavement rang. He shouted his exultation: it was a stallion's scream. He wheeled, tossing his mane. The hunt stood stock-still. He laughed at them.

Some of them were wondrous sweet. Mares with languid eyes, slender necks, rumps rich and full and brimming with blessed madness.

But freedom was sweeter. He gathered his wonderful new body, leaped a wall of hounds, drank deep of the wind's wine. Already he was drunken with it. He laughed and spun and sprang into flight.

Khalid lay on his face at the vizier's feet. His garments were rent and torn; his turban was lost; his head was heaped with the ashes of his grief, that he must break the heart of the man who had been a father to him. Even before he could gather breath to speak, the vizier knew what he would say. 'My son?' the old man asked, calm with the immensity of grief.

'Alive.' Khalid gasped it. 'But—'

The vizier breathed a prayer of thanks, but darkened again all too swiftly. 'But? He is ill? He is hurt?'

'No,' Khalid said, 'O my father. But—'

'He is taken? He has fled?'

'*My lord!*' Khalid's desperation silenced the litany of disaster. 'Oh, my lord, I cannot speak of it. Come with me and see what you must see.'

They had lured him with his own Pearl of the East, bridled him and bound him and compelled him to return to his father's house. In the end, for weariness, he had submitted. He stood in the court in a wary circle of men, sweating and trembling, but snorting defiance.

The vizier saw him, but only when he saw in none of the circling faces the lineaments of his son's. He approached the stallion with respect but without fear. A more hangdog creature had seldom come to face him. Its head dropped almost to the ground; its ears flattened. It backed as far as its bonds would allow, and tried to crouch, as a hound when it is whipped, or a son when at last he has passed the limits of his father's forbearance.

The vizier gentled him, speaking softly. 'Peace, be still, O son of the wind, O dancer in the dawn, O brave in battle, great-eyed, white as the moon, thy mane a fall of sweet water, o beautiful, be still.' And he was still but quivering, as hands learned the shape of him, his strength and his soundness, and the silk that was its covering. '*Al-ashab al-marshoush*,' the vizier named the colour of him, a whisper, calming him: the grey that was best beloved of kings, rose-dappled, flecked with ruddy darkness, mark of the strongest and fairest of horses.

'A *kehailan*,' said the vizier, 'of remarkable perfection. Come out now, my son; have no fear of my danger. Whatever you have paid, such beauty is well worth the price.'

The stallion gasped like a man. His body, driven to extremity, reared up. The vizier caught the bridle. His servants had begun to melt away.

Khalid prostrated himself again at the old man's feet. 'A *kehailan*,' he said to the stones beneath him, 'and al-Kehailan. This is your son, O my lord.' And he told as much of it as he could know, and more that he could guess; nor was he so very far from the truth. 'And thus after a hard chase we caught him, and we brought him back to you, my lord; but of the sorcerer who wrought this, we have found no sign. If I may have your leave, I will go, I will search—'

'You will do nothing.' Khalid shrank in upon himself. He ventured a single glance upward; that sufficed. The vizier's face, so placid in respose, so noble even in deepest grief, had stilled into a mask more deadly than any snarl of rage. His voice was terrible in its gentleness. 'You have never loved him. You have always lusted after what is his. You drove him to this, you, with your serpent's tongue, your net of truth that, woven, shaped a lie.'

Khalid shrank more tightly still. He did not venture to sift the truth from falsehood wrought of grief. His guilt loomed larger in him than any threat of death. His intemperate tongue had driven his master away, full into the sorcerous trap.

'I am called merciful,' said the vizier, 'and I cannot be otherwise. I do not take your life. Ill as you have served my son, you remain his servant. If he chooses, he will slay you. It is no matter to me. I have forgotten your name.'

Khalid lay down and wept. The vizier went away. They all went away, taking Kehailan, leaving the mameluke to his sorrow.

Once the first shock of his father's grief was past, Kehailan found again his first delight in his ensorcellment. He had all that man or beast could wish for. A stable of his own, silken-walled, deep in straw; a manger of marble and gold filled with the golden barley of Yemen, scented with spices and made rich with a leavening of mutton; a wide garden to run in, and cool water to drink, and sweet singers to beguile his ears; and the loveliest mares in Egypt to be his wives and concubines. No one spoke to him of duty. No one vexed him with cares of state. No one compelled him to any will but his own.

Not even Khalid. Khalid had learned the virtue of silence. He served his master with mute obedience, fed him, tended him, made him beautiful for his mares and for his own pleasure.

The vizier he seldom saw. He was rather shamefully glad of it. The old man's sorrow cut too close to the bone. It made him wish, however briefly, to be a man again. It made him remember that he had been the most credulous of fools. Khalid had told no more than the truth; Kehailan had brought all the rest upon himself.

His tale spread as all such tales must. His father's guards kept the importunate at bay; when one or two enterprising persons breached the wall of the garden and began to conduct the curious therein for a high price, their quartered bodies appeared without for the education of their imitators.

But some, the vizier himself admitted. The priests intoned the Qur'an over Kehailan, and invoked the Holy Name, and prayed day and night about his stable. The Khalifah himself sent his personal saint; the emirs of Alexandria sent a sibyl in a bottle; the syndics of Cairo dispatched three mullahs and three masters of the art of magic. Kehailan received the prayers with proper devotion and the incantations with proper awe, but with no slightest alteration of his enchanted shape.

The magi cast endless horoscopes. The rabbis droned over their Kabbalah. Even a Christian exorcist wheedled and grovelled his way into Kehailan's garden, fouled its sweetness with his unspeakable incense, wailed his backward prayers and danced his twisted dances and cast out not even the shadow of an imp. But a demon came at the climax of his rite, and bore him gibbering away.

The philosophers fared no better. The Platonists informed him that his form was a shadow of the true Form, and that he must reconcile the two through the exercise of his will. The Pythagoreans reminded him that he had fallen down the ladder of creation; he must restore himself, or he would be reborn as a creature lower still: a dog, or an ape, or worse. He was appropriately horrified, but he remained a man in a stallion's body. The Aristotelians endeavoured to disenchant him with invocations of purest logic; the Epicureans intrigued him with the doctrine of life as the simple pursuit of pleasure; the Stoics instructed him to suffer in silence. He learned that he was an illusion; that the world was a dance of atoms in the void; that all was nothing and nothing was all, and philosophy was merely another name for windy nonsense. When the rival schools began to come to blows in his garden, he watched the spectacle until it palled; then he drove them out.

Scarcely had he recovered his equanimity when the doctors fell upon him. They stabbed him with needles. They bled him and purged him and dosed him with potions. Milk of the nightmare. Mares' nests powdered and steeped in hippocras. Water from the Hippocrene; coltsfoot, horsetails, horse chestnuts, leaves of bay; herbs distilled in arrak and kumiss and concoctions viler yet. He went mad on hippomanes, and might have died, but for the mercy of Allah and the swiftness of Khalid's hand. The mameluke struck down the poisoner and cast out all the man's cohorts; and he did battle with the maddened beast, sang to him, stroked him, nursed him back to trembling sanity.

The women were, Kehailan conceded, more pleasant to look at than the pack of learned tormentors. Sweeter to the ear and to the nose, and much gentler upon his body. They pleased him as a brisk brushing pleased him, and no more. They did not shatter his spell with human lust. Not with his mares dropping great-eyed foals who would be grey when they were grown, and coming into the foal-heat, and casting him into perfect paroxysms of desire.

And yet, Kehailan had begun to think, stallionhood was rather less than bliss. It was not the vexation of all the attempts to restore him to humanity. Beyond and about them lay vast expanses of sheer and deadly boredom. No one would presume to ride him. He could not converse; his speech was stallion speech, and sorely limited. Music was only half of itself when he could do no more than listen; and what was fair to human ears, all too often was a torment to his more-than-human senses. Even his mares were losing their power to beguile him. They were not like human women. Unless it was their season, they had no care for love; and they were most emphatic in expressing it.

Humanity began almost to seem appealing. He wondered what had transpired in the court. He found himself remembering what little of the diwan he had ever harkened to, and running through passages of the *hadith*, and pondering obscure points of law.

All of that lost to him; and perhaps, he told himself until he was certain that he believed it, well lost. He had a cure for memory: to mount a willing mare, or to race the wind in his garden, or to linger by the pool to marvel at his own moon-bright beauty.

A year to the day after Kehailan's ensorcellment began, Khalid approached Kehailan in his garden. The mameluke bowed down and kissed the earth between his master's hoofs. Kehailan left off his desultory grazing. 'O my master,' said Khalid. Kehailan waited prick-eared, knowing that tone from of old, and bearing in mind the power of hoofs and teeth. 'O my master, it is now a year since you fell under this deplorable enchantment. Many have begun to despair of your walking again as a man. Even your father—' Khalid's voice wavered. 'Even your honoured father has forgotten the sweetness of hope.'

Abruptly and most astonishingly, the slave gave way to tears. Kehailan nipped his arm to make him stop. He raised his head. His face was as Kehailan had never seen it, raw and ravaged with grief. 'Yes, O master. Your father is dying. Little as it matters to you, whose only care has ever been your own comfort. He has provided for you and for your get. You need suffer nothing for his passing.'

Kehailan tossed his head. He was too shocked for anger. Of course his father was not dying. Why, only yesterday . . .

The day before? A fortnight ago? A month? Or perhaps, a season?

The old man could not bear to see him. That was all. He understood it. He was magnanimous: he forgave it.

'He has taken to his bed,' said Khalid. 'He has arranged for the disposition of his property; he has laid aside his office and composed himself for death. Because,' said Khalid, 'without you to be the comfort of his old age, he sees no profit in living.'

Kehailan raised his voice to its utmost, a great ringing scream of rage and denial. Khalid fell back, hands clapped to his ears. Kehailan beat down the gate of his garden.

His hoofs clattered on tiled floors. Servants fluttered, squawked and fled. One bold soul with a halter leaped aside from his headlong assault. 'Make way!' Khalid called out behind him. 'Let him pass!'

The last door fell open before him. Carpets eased his passage. He was nearly blind in the dimness. Voices were praying. The air was heavy; it choked him.

The man in the bed bore his father's scent, but could not be his father. Not this feeble creature, wasted to a shadow, too weak even to whisper a greeting. His father was the wisest and strongest of men. His father would live for ever.

For the first time he yearned truly for hands. For arms to embrace that body, and throat and tongue and lips to utter human words. He could not bow down in prayer as a good Mussulman must do. He could not even weep.

He wanted to be a man. He wanted it at last, with all that was in him.

His body mocked him: *kehailan* of perfect beauty, and perfect heedlessness, and perfect idiocy. He had fled humanity, with all the troubles that beset it. Now he had nowhere to flee. Wherever he turned was death's bloodless grin, and the black shadow that was his own impenetrable folly.

Khalid left the son beside his father's bed. Out of all the gathered futilities of doctors and sorcerers and philosophers, he had distilled one dram of wisdom. Someone had laid the spell; that someone had not come forward to lift it; and Kehailan's will alone could not set him free.

Khalid had not been idle, knowing what he knew. His searches had discovered nothing. His spies had revealed that the vizier's enemies rejoiced in their rival's pain, but that they had had no part in it. This plot ran deeper, if plot it was, and was not the caprice of some prankster of the jinn.

While Kehailan faced himself and saw a mortal fool, Khalid slipped out of the palace and the city. A guard or two was richer for his passing; one honest man slept and would wake, Khalid hoped, with no more than an aching head.

The creatures of the night made revel under the moon. Khalid passed among them in the armour of his Faith. He was not without fear. His bowels had loosened with it; more than once he halted to grant them their sovereignty. But love drove him on; the Name of Allah preserved him from harm. The wings of Afarit did no more than brush the summit of his turban. The imps of the empty places mocked him and danced about him and wove knots in his mare's mane, but laid no hand upon his body.

Cold, shaking, his mare near collapse with terror, Khalid came to the heart of the wilderness. The moon had cast upon it a mighty enchantment. Upon the fallen stones floated a palace of air with walls of light, a vision of beauty without mortal substance. Khalid's hand, brushing a column, passed through it, sensing only a breath of coolness, a memory of fire.

The Sultan of the Afarit held high court within the walls of light, seated on a throne of air and fire, hearing the pleas of his subjects and receiving their tribute. Khalid gasped at the riches which the spirits of the air laid at their master's feet. The barest tithe of them would have rivalled the wealth of Suleiman; the full court passed the bounds of mere mortal comprehension.

Amid such shining splendour, the court of the Afarit was appalling in its ugliness. Demon forms flapped and writhed and screeched. The bodies of beautiful women bore the heads of snarling beasts. Faces of surpassing comeliness shone above the shapes of nightmare. Monsters out of blackest dreams promenaded in silk and jewels, chattering the airy chatter of courtiers.

Most hideous of them all was the Sultan of the Afarit. It dawned slowly upon Khalid that the expression of the demon's face, which in a man would have been a grimace of most horrible rage, was a smile of purest contentment. When he smote his hands together in delight, thunder rolled. The dance of lightning was a tribute to his joy.

Khalid tethered his mare in shadowed safety and crept closer to the palace of air. The demons' clamour came clear to him, telling in many guises the tale of their sultan's gladness. The worst of his enemies and the greatest rival for his throne, Muammar of the line of Iblis, had fallen into the depths of the nether realm. 'In the very act of ravishing our lord's daughter, he fell,' said an Afritah close by Khalid. 'Aye, our own dear Princess Subhiyah, whom the Queen of the Indies bore to our lord, and whom he loves as his dearest self. A mortal man came upon the monster at his labours, and felled him with the Name of Allah, Who wrought both men and jinn. Great is his honour who freed us of that scourge, human creature though he be.'

'Surely,' said the Afrit beside her, 'our princess gave him fair recompense.'

She laughed and tossed her snaky hair. 'More than fair! He had his heart's desire. But he could not have our princess. *She* is meant for the son of the Sultan of the Jinn that dwell under the earth.'

'But I hear tell,' said another Afritah, whose closest kin seemed to be the wild boar, 'that she gave her saviour somewhat more than her intended might be pleased to know of.'

'Mortal blood *will* call to mortal blood,' sighed her scaly sister, not entirely in scorn. 'Puny creatures as they are, with scarce a drop of magic in them, still they have a certain . . . something. When they are good to look on, they are very good indeed.'

'And quite accomplished, in their way.' The tusked Afritah smiled and tweaked the Afrit's mighty yard, turning his scowl to an expression of sheerest outrage. He roared and snatched. The two females laughed and let him seize them, and together bore him down, making amends for their presumption in every way they knew.

An Afrit, it is said, is terrible in copulation. Khalid crawled away, bruised and buffeted and most astonishingly enlightened.

From another and less lascivious assemblage he learned that the Princess Subhiyah was present, and that her father intended that very night to proclaim her betrothal to the Prince of the Jinn. His emissaries bowed even now before the sultan, offering gifts that as far outshone the rest as the sun outshines the moon. Khalid turned his face away lest he be blinded, and his mind lest he forget why he had come.

It was written that he must come here on this night of all nights. Surely also it was written that this princess was the one whom he sought. His heart raised a prayer to the

All-Seeing; his eyes cast among that unearthly throng for a female as appalling as the sultan himself. Each seemed more ghastly than the last, but none was as ghastly as he.

And yet, he reflected, as despair rose to darken his eyes, rumour had joined her in congress with her saviour. Kehailan had been a mighty warrior of the bedchamber, but he had been and remained the most fastidious of stallions. He would not have sullied his white body with a tusked and taloned horror.

Close by the sultan stood a figure which Khalid had taken for a slave: a handmaiden, perhaps, of no more than mortal stature, demurely and modestly veiled. Now that Khalid paused to examine her, she was not so ill to look on. Her garments were of surpassing richness, even in this realm of supernal wealth. Her jewels were dazzling in their profusion. Yet they paled before the splendour of her eyes. The hand that held her veil before her face was slender, and graceful, and white as milk. One midnight curl had escaped to kiss the satin of her forehead, where between her brows' black arches burned a ruby like an eye of fire.

Khalid's manhood rose to sing her praises. His heart sang the descant. *It is she. It must be she!*

Before his mind could rouse to counsel prudence, Khalid had flung himself at the sultan's feet. The clamour of the court was stilled. Demon eyes burned wide; demon talons stretched. The Grand Vizier of the Jinn swept out a sword as long as a man, with an edge of adamant.

'In the Name of Allah!' gasped Khalid. 'Sultan of sultans, prince of the princes of the air, have mercy upon my humanity!'

There was a mighty silence. Khalid could not still his trembling. Great as his terror had been, it was nothing to what racked him now.

The sultan spoke. His voice was as deep as thunder in the mountains of the moon. 'In the Name of Allah,' he said, 'and of Muhammad His Prophet, upon whom be prayer and peace. What madness brings you here, O mortal man, where no mortal may trespass and live?'

'A madness, O sultan,' Khalid replied, 'of love and loyalty.' Khalid's back tightened, awaiting the rending of talons.

'Love?' The sultan seemed bemused. 'What knows your kind of love?'

'You know it also?' Khalid bit back too late his burst of insolence. No blade struck off his head; he mustered courage to continue. 'O sultan, love is the creation of Allah; its expression is His creation through mankind. I have a master whom I love, who is more than a brother to me. He has a father whom I love, who is more than a father to me. For their sakes I come to you, O lord of lords of the line of Iblis.'

'Men do not lie within my dominion,' said the sultan.

Khalid stole a glance under his turban. The demon king was inscrutable in his hideousness. 'O sultan, hear my tale and judge whether your mightiness may deign to end it.'

'I hear,' said the sultan.

Khalid nearly forsook his wits, so mighty was his relief, so immeasurable his fear. He bent all his will to the telling of the tale, omitting only the speculation of the court that Kehailan had had more than his heart's desire in recompense for his banishment of the Afrit.

When he ended, he was weeping; and many of the court wept with him, moved to deepest compassion by his tale of the vizier's decline. Through that storm of wailing and sobbing, he barely heard the voice that spoke above him. It was not the sultan's. It was musk and honey; it was as beautiful as the princess herself. 'Rise, O most valiant of servants. Let us look upon your face.'

Khalid could not do other than obey. He dared not raise his eyes. Her feet, he perceived, were of enchanting smallness.

'A fair face,' said the princess, 'and an honest face, and a face that cannot choose between the lily and the rose. Surely, O my father, he should live, if only to complete his choosing.'

'He is much too lovely to die.' It was a demons' chorus, woman-shrill. The sounds of grief had faded. They were all about him, marvelling, abandoning sorrow in the beauty of his face. Hands stroked him; some were soft as sleep, and some were wicked with claws. They searched out his every secret. They knew nothing of sacred shame.

'Roses!' they cried in high delight. 'Roses win the victory!'

Khalid would happily have died. But the mercy of Allah is imponderable. He lived, and suffered, and could not even swoon.

The princess of the Afarit took his burning face in hands as light and cool as wind. Only she could have done such a thing, and done it without sacrifice of modesty. He had to look at her; he could not help himself. Her beauty weakened his knees. Her smile all but slew him.

'O my father,' she said, 'such bravery demands its tribute. For love and loyalty he dared even your wrath that shakes the sky. Surely you will condescend to give him what he seeks?'

'The spell is not mine to break,' said the sultan.

'But,' she said, 'it is mine, and it is his upon whom I laid it. Together we may end it. If, O my father, you grant me leave to go to him.'

The Grand Vizier of the Jinn whirled his great sword about his head. 'Outrage!' he roared. 'Conspiracy! She seeks a mortal lover. She spurns our mighty prince.'

The princess knelt in supplication at her father's feet. 'O lord of air and fire, your will has ever been my own. Yet in this I cry you mercy. I spoke no word against this marriage, for that I dared not; and when I was abducted by Muammar your enemy, I learned the name of fate, and I saw a new face of love. He was beautiful, my saviour, but of flaws he had sufficient; he did not sate me with perfection. I took him, O my father, I chose him for my husband.'

The Jinn drew together, snarling in their throats. Afarit closed in about them.

'Peace!' cried the princess, flinging wide her arms. 'Hear me out, I beg of you. I am a halfling, of mortal woman born. My arts are potent, but they are not the arts

189

of the Afarit. I am a woman and a sorceress; my substance is mortal substance, partaking but little of the subtlety of air. Am I a fit mate for the prince of the spirits of the earth? His blood is unimpeachable in its purity. His form is a terrible beauty. His virility is a legend among the insatiable Jinn. How may I hope to be worthy of him?'

'No mortal man is worthy of you,' said the sultan. 'And a mortal man whose heart's desire resides in the mounting of mares—'

'His heart chose that shape, O my father, than which there is no fairer. Is not the horse blessed of Allah? Did not Suleiman, upon whom be prayer and peace, neglect the hours of prayer from noon until sunset, so rapt was he in contemplation of his horses? Do not the Bedawi of the desert grant their greatest joy to three things: the birth of a boy, the emergence of a poet among them, and the foaling of a mare? Did not the Prophet himself, upon whom be prayer and peace, say unto His mares, "Blessed be ye, O daughters of the wind"? What shame therefore need stain my lover's name, that he dwells for a space in the body of a stallion? The spell was a testing, and a teaching and a waking of his wisdom. If truly he has learned to be wise, he will stand again upon the feet of a man.'

'And if he has not?' The sultan's voice was terrible to hear. 'If you go to him, you cannot return. So was it written in the hour of your birth. Will you accept the full burden of mortality, if your chosen mate remains a brute beast?'

'Whatever shape he bears,' the princess said, 'I love him.'

'And we?' thundered the Grand Vizier of the Jinn. 'Are we to endure this mockery?'

Khalid knew the scent of war as it smoulders into flame. 'O sultan!' he called out with reckless daring. 'O lords of the Jinn. O pearl of beauty. Is there no recourse? Is there no princess of the Afarit, save this one alone? Surely, had she a sister of the pure blood, that

190

sister would rejoice to be united with so splendid a husband as the prince of the Jinn.'

The mameluke stood quivering in an awful silence. If in his ignorance he had erred, then he had erred unpardonably.

'I have,' said the sultan, 'nine hundred daughters.' He stroked his tusks, pondering.

Only the Princess Subhiyah ventured to disturb his reflection. 'Aishah, O my father, is as beautiful as the moon. She wept when I was chosen for the prince; she loves the very rumour of him. She would be transported with joy, were you to summon her now and confirm her betrothal. And,' said the princess, 'her blood is the purest blood of the children of Iblis. She is altogether worthy of so puissant a prince.'

The Jinn had begun to be mollified: the more so when the maiden herself was brought, and she was wondrous fair. Her wings were silk; her skin was cream; her talons were finest ivory.

But the sultan did not speak the word that would set the halfling princess free. He looked at her, and from those terrible eyes, great tears began to fall.

She wept with him, but she said, 'O my father, it is written. Will you deny the will of Allah?'

'*Allahu akbar*,' said the sultan. 'He is great; He is ever merciful. I am the slave of His slaves.' He rose, and he was as tall as the sky. His wings veiled the night. 'Go,' he commanded in the roar of the thunder. 'Go in His Name.' His arms swept up. His hands smote together; lightnings leaped into the heavens. In a roaring of wings, the Afarit rose up.

Khalid lay on the cold earth, with the dawn swelling grey about him. Painfully he stood. The palace was empty and broken, its walls vanished with the moon. His own black mare stood by him, and with her a fine blood bay, and on its back a figure wrapped in veils. Khalid mounted without a word, with scarcely a glance. He dared none, or he would break. The bay led the black towards the walls of Cairo.

The vizier was sinking into the stillness of death. Kehailan looked fain to die with him, lying prostrate by his bed, given up to grief. At the coming of the Princess Subhiyah he scarcely stirred. His sisters had come and gone; this, surely, was another of them, veiled before the doctors and the imams. He took notice only of her silence, which was a blessing after so many choruses of lamentation.

She bent over him and laid her hand upon his brow. She gave him no greeting. Her scent was – almost – intoxicating. 'Would you be a man again?' she asked of him.

He surged up in startlement. He knew that voice. But what he knew, he could not remember.

'Follow me,' she said.

He heard, and he obeyed.

In his garden Khalid waited all white and worn, as if he had fought a bitter battle and won, as yet, no victory. The Pearl of the East stood beside him, with her foal dancing about her, and a splendour on her that comes only to a mare who is ripe for her stallion's taking.

Kehailan gathered to leap upon her, but a light small hand held him fast. 'Would you be a man?' the stranger asked again.

He turned his head. Even her eyes were hidden in veils. She was a voice and a perfume, and a hand upon his neck.

'You must choose,' said Khalid. 'The mare or the woman. Your choice is your fate. You have only the one; once it is made, you cannot change it.'

That was the voice of his conscience, soft and level and implacable. Kehailan shivered; snorted, stamped, tossed his head. Khalid said nothing. The veiled woman waited in silence.

The mare called softly. She was his love and his delight, his queen, the mother of his son. She yearned to bear him another.

The hand left his neck. He was free. The mare beckoned with all her body.

A flicker of movement caught his eye. He glanced at it, and held. The veils lay fallen on the grass. The moon had risen in the clear daylight, and overcome it. He knew her, the richness of her, slender where she must be slender, deep-curved where beauty willed it, and all her secrets open at last to his memory. She smiled, shy and bold together. 'Yes,' she said, 'O my heart's delight. It is I. What heretofore I could not give, I have won for you, if still you wish to take it.'

His nostrils flared. The sight of her would wake desire in a stone. Khalid had hidden his face from it. But he said, 'Your father, my lord and my brother. Remember.'

Kehailan bucked, protesting. The Pearl of the East nipped his flank. Her eyes were pools to drown in. Her body was moonlit madness. She offered fire and peace, simplicity, the forgetfulness of the beast.

His body knew what it would have. It was a stallion. It took no delight in human flesh.

The woman stroked his neck. Her hands were silken pleasure. Her eyes were a gazelle's; her lips were honeyed roses; her breasts were great goblets brimful of sweetness.

His hoofs would batter her flower-softness; his great stallion maleness would rend her human fraility. He turned from her to the one who could endure the full and thunderous force of his passion.

The woman clasped her arms about his neck. Her limbs were serpent-supple. Her voice whispered in his ear, words of love, tantalizing, promising all Paradise. 'A man,' she said to him. 'Be a man, O beautiful, my love and my lord.'

He stumbled back. He could not. He was bound in this shape; he could not will to be free of it.

'For me,' said the princess of the Afarit. 'For your father whom you love. For your brother who dared death and worse than death to win this choice for you. Be a man.'

He lunged towards the Pearl of the East; he wheeled away. Khalid huddled on the grass. The lady stood shining in the morning. She held out her arms.

A shudder racked him. In one eye shone the mare; in the other, the woman. They blurred, and drifted, and melded together. They were all one image of sweetest madness. Man, stallion, both and neither, he flung himself

193

upon them. He mounted a white mare. He mounted a white woman. He paused and poised and knew, in that instant of choiceless choosing, that one alone would walk the long road back with him from the garden of desire. And if it was the mare, Kehailan the man would die with all his dreads and doubts and dullnesses. But if it was the woman . . .

He opened his eyes on a splendour he had forgotten. He breathed in musk and honey, muted, dulled, yet intoxicatingly sweet. He wept with purely human grief, and purely human joy, and purely human terror.

His son's voice brought the vizier back from the gates of death; his son's face healed him more swiftly than any physic. He rose from his deathbed to take up all that he had laid down, but first, to weep upon his son's blessedly human neck.

With his father's joyous consent, Kehailan took to wife the Princess Subhiyah, who had given up her immortality for the sake of his perfect imperfection. If his ensorcellment had not made a wise man of him, it had taught him at least the beginnings of wisdom. With his father and his wife to guide him, and with his own will marred only on occasion by a lapse into his old folly, he rose high among the sultan's most valued servants. When at length and at a great age the vizier passed into the embrace of Allah, al-Kehailan took up his office, and held it in as great honour as had his father before him. It was said of him that he never failed to temper justice with mercy; that he could scent a lie as unerringly as a stallion scents a jackal among his mares; and that whenever he was tempted to fall short of his duty, he betook himself to his stables, where the children of his hoofed children grew strong and wise and beautiful under his watchful care. Their blood lives yet among the horses of Egypt. There is none fairer nor more valiant, nor more intolerant of human arrogance.

As for Khalid, whose tongue began it all and whose spur of wisdom had earned for him the name of his master's conscience, when the vizier had come to himself again, he forgave the mameluke with all his heart, and set him free. In reparation for his sufferings he gained the fairest of the vizier's daughters for his wife, whom he had loved since they were children together; and the vizier made him brother to Kehailan in name and in law as he had always been in heart and deed. That the brothers lived in perfect amity is, perhaps, too simple an ending for their tale. They lived in love, and for the most part in peace. And if Kehailan had learned to be the wiser in pursuit of his duty, Khalid in his turn had learned to curb his tongue in the curbing of his brother's folly. When Kehailan rose to his father's vizierate, Khalid rose with him, to stand at his right hand and to be, as ever, the better half of his self. And thus they lived in wealth and in gladness until the book of their lives was written, and as they had passed in the same hour into the wilderness of the world, so did they pass together into the hands of Allah. Praise be to Him, Lord of the Worlds, the Beneficent, the Merciful, in Whom are the beginning and the end of all tales!

ELIZABETH SCARBOROUGH

The Elephant In-law

Umm Malak trembled in the doorway, her seamed face
shining with tears, 'Even as you commanded, my son, so
has it been done, alas!' she said, her voice hoarse with the
continual monologue of lamentation that had marked her
passage from the harem gate of the emperor's palace to
the humble dwelling she shared with her one, her only,
her cherished son.

'As you insisted, though very much against my counsel,
I sold all we own to buy the gold – though why the silver
we had wasn't perfectly good enough is beyond me. The
Empress Dildar is fond of silver. *She* looked very nice in it
the few times I saw her, very dignified, very regal. Silver is
the moon's metal and fine enough for anyone, I should
think. But no, I risked all we own, knowing as only your
mother can know, O my son, that your excellence more
than matches your arrogance, a trait you surely have
inherited from your late father, may Allah the All-
Merciful, the All-Compassionate preserve him, for my
side of the family has always been humble enough. So,
though I knew full well we would be cast into the streets
from the home where you were born and I have lived, lo,
this quarter of a century, I did as you wished. Though I
knew that, with no goods and no home and no materials
for you to ply your trade, no family would give you their
daughter. Though I knew in my heart that because of this,
I would never have grandchildren. Even so-knowing, I did
as my brilliant son asked. For am I not a loving and
obedient mother in all things? And now, poor unworthy

196

woman that I am, I have presented myself to the emperor's harem so that your gift could be entered in the competition. Just so that some women who are no better than they should be wouldn't be bored, just so that the emperor's new lady, whose arms are already stretched like an ape's from the weight of her bracelets, should see if the artistry of my son was worthy of her attention. Ah, the strain on my digestion! I did not sleep for weeks in anticipation. My feet are worn off to the ankles from the walk, but I would be so happy if only they had fallen off before I did this thing. If only my tongue could have shrivelled and fallen from my head first.'

'Mother, please,' Malak said wearily. 'If the empress preferred another bauble to mine, surely she, in her wisdom and mercy, returned it and we can sell it to some other rich person and pay our mortgage and regain our goods and still retain a handsome profit.'

'How well my wise son understands the ways of the mighty and powerful! For you are correct, my boy. The Empress Dildar would have done even as you have said, *if* only you had lost the competition,' and she struck her head against the door frame in despair.

'If only? But, Mother, are you jesting? If so, this is an odd time of life, I must say, for you to suddenly develop a sense of humour. If only I had lost? There is but one other alternative.' His voice rose with eagerness. 'The rich prize promised, the—'

A shower of thatch rained on his head, carrying with it several lizards and a small snake which promptly scuttled into cracks in the baked mud walls. A crunching, rustling sound emanated from above, and suddenly daylight dazzled through a hole in the roof through which a sheep could have been thrown.

'The rich prize,' his mother said heavily. 'Arise, my son, and claim it before it pulls the house down around us. Aiyee! We are doomed!' and she turned, her abayah flying, as she smacked at something with all her might. 'Do not eat this house, you nasty creature! It is not even ours to feed to you.'

Malak leaped up and all but knocked his mother over, thrusting through the doorway to view this alarming prize. He saw parts of it even before he was outside; the rocking grey columns of wrinkles, skin like the beds of streams dried into curling cracks after the spring floods, the massive ears, the domelike head swaying slowly back and forth, the moist trunk lifting casually upward for another bite of roof to feed the pink triangular mouth.

'An elephant?' he asked.

'An elephant indeed, alas,' she said. 'A hungry elephant. A *large* hungry elephant. Oh, my son, surely your enemies put word of this contest into your ears that you should sell all we had in the world to win such a prize!'

'Actually, Mother, it was you who urged me to compete, if you'll remember,' Malak said, extending a wondering hand to rub over the elephant's leg. But the elephant stepped backwards when his hand would have touched her and the tiny reddened eye nearest him glittered menacingly. 'But all is not lost. If we hire out this elephant at once, we can still hope to win back our home and perhaps a bit of silver for me to work, a morsel of food to keep us going while we find a buyer for her. If not,' he said, mindful of his rumbling stomach, 'I have heard it said that elephant meat, though tough when from an old cow such as this, and not too tasty, is very filling.'

The elephant glared at him with a baleful eye. This time it was he who stepped backwards and looked for something with which to defend himself, finally seizing upon a stone. The cow trumpeted at him, her challenge shrill and her trunk lowered as she planted one earthquaking foot in front of the other.

'Aiyee! You have angered her, and she surely will crush this house and we will be beggars as well as debtors!'

'She will crush *me* and I will be with Allah, leaving you to meditate on the evil you've brought upon your poor son. Why would the good Empress Dildar play her people so foul a trick? She knows of our poverty – Mother?' Hope raised his voice an octave. 'Mother, are you sure you did not forget something? Jewelled raiment, perhaps, for this elephant? *All* royal elephants have it. Quantities of gold braid and silver bells and jewelled silken hangings. Admittedly a poor reward for such a masterpiece as my creation, but from such trappings I could perhaps fashion something else. Something more marketable than this large devourer of roofs. I am so hungry I could eat her raw right now!'

From behind the great grey hindquarters a thin and rasping voice cried, 'No!' and a street urchin (or that was what she seemed) ran forward and fell upon her face between the elephant's forelegs. The hump on the urchin's back was evident even as she knocked her brow three times upon the hot and stony earth. When she lifted her face, Malak turned away.

Only some terrible tragedy, a fire perhaps, could produce such deformity, or so he would have thought, but the girl's face bore no scars, only the ugly drag on one eye pulled down and one pulled up almost to the hairline, of a mouth with the right corner in a permanent snarl of teeth and gum and the left nostril spread wide and slitted. Her whole person was befouled with grime, dung and straw.

The threat of beggary was new to the house of Malak. Though never as prosperous as an artist of his calibre should be, he had had plenty of work since his father died. And although his mother complained that she had handled the funds well enough before his father's death and saw no reason why he should take away the management of the household funds from her, he had done so and had at least seen to it that they had enough to eat and a roof over their heads.

But whereas his father had done simple jewellery – the transformation of coins into necklaces and earrings, et cetera, he aspired to greater things, bought finer materials, and took longer to make each piece. His plan was to sell his work for higher prices to wealthier customers. These clients were kind enough to send servants who condescended to take his work on approval, with the promise that their masters would pay him when they decided whether or not they had a use for such trinkets.

They never did seem to decide, unfortunately, and humble people such as himself did not dun the mighty.

So such a sight as the girl before him was not one he had seen every day of his life, and, indeed, was one he wished never to see again.

'Who are you to tell my son what to do with his elephant, er – girl?' his mother asked, the countenance of the poor creature robbing Umm Malak of some of her customary eloquence.

'I am Maham,' the creature said, and mother and son both grimaced, for Maham meant moon-faced or beautiful, and was a royal-sounding name for such an abomination of womanhood. 'And if it please you, master, the Agata Aghacha has sent me to be the keeper of this elephant.'

'So we are to feed you too?' Umm Malak wailed.

'Wait,' Malak said, 'the Agata Aghacha, magic lady, is she not the princess the emperor brought back from his last campaign in Syria? She who is called the Syrian sorceress?'

The urchin inclined her head, 'Even so, master.'

'But what has she to say in the matter of who keeps and does not keep my elephant, the prize awarded to me from the Empress Dildar herself?' He found himself growing possessive of his massive trophy when he thought of her that way, for no recognition from the well-loved empress was wholly to be despised. He thought that before he sold or ate the beast he might ride her around the village for a while and enjoy being looked up to for perhaps the last time in his life.

'Everything, alas, for it was the Agata Aghacha, not the Empress Dildar, who bestowed the elephant, O jewel of my loins,' his mother said, and then jerked him aside to whisper fiercely, 'she it was also who sent this spy to us, so watch your tongue else it has no head to wag in.'

Whatever else the girl's deformities, her hearing was excellent. She bridled and opened her misshapen mouth, her voice like the cawing of a choir of crows. 'No spy, my lord, but helper – interpreter if you like, for this elephant is a mother to me and I alone can tell you her will.'

'I have no interest in the will of elephants. On the contrary, it is the elephant's business to interest herself in my will. And the least part of my will is that you take yourself off and trouble us no more, for I can feed you no better than I can feed your grey, scabrous, oversized mother.'

Unaccountably, the red inner lid of the girl's distorted eye moistened. 'Oh, sir, do not taunt her so, for she cannot help being thus.'

'And I cannot help being paupered. Begone. I cannot feed you. I cannot!' His voice escalated in anguish at the injustice of his situation while his mother wrung her hands and wailed in harmony.

Abruptly, both were cut off by their prize's angry 'Ahrrreeeeryha!'

The crippled girl clasped herself close to the elephant's mouth and the beast calmed, mumbling and grunting.

'My mother has heard your problems,' the girl told them when they took their arms away from their heads, 'and she says that if you will meet her conditions, she will show you how you can survive a little longer and feed us all. If you succeed, you may aspire to greater things.'

'Young person, I do not know what manner of superstitious fools you think you are addressing, but my son and I do not believe in the jinn. We are modern, pious folk who seek to do Allah's will. What makes you think that my son, the finest jeweller in all the realms of the Mughul, would permit himself to be dictated to by an elephant, even if she could talk, which she cannot. Which means that he is in fact being dictated to by a beggar, a cripple, and probably a leper for all we know. I mean no offence, you understand, my child, and had we charity to extend to you, naturally we would do so, for we value the laws of hospitality. You simply have caught us at an extraordinarily bad moment.'

'Why should you listen to me, woman?' the girl demanded with such an imperious tone that she temporarily gave the illusion of having a back straight as a wand. 'Because my mother has offered you a solution to your ills as a sign of good will and as a test. You should therefore listen to me because it is sensible and,' she said with a nod to the elephant's bulk, 'because she said so.'

'Were it not for you we would have no problems,' the son growled.

'Were it not for the Syrian sorceress, you mean,' the beggar amended, again humble. 'Now, are you or are you not willing to meet the mighty one's conditions?'

Malak looked at Umm Malak, who looked back at him and shrugged.

'What are they?' both asked.

'Firstly, that no hand be laid upon my great mother or myself without express permission.'

'I would not,' the young man said drily, 'dream of it.'

'Secondly, you must not sell us either singly or together, at least until you have seen the sun set on this day. Agreed?'

'Ah well, what is one day, after all? Agreed,' he said.

'Good. Now you, mother of my master, must borrow an abayah of good quality for me that I may cover my shame. It is not fitting that my face be seen abroad.'

As much for the sake of others as for your own modesty, the mother thought, but agreed, and soon borrowed a suitable garment from her friend Umm Mustapha, the second wife of the ironsmith, who was a prosperous man.

When the girl had masked her ugliness, the elephant knelt gently and allowed her to mount its great grey head. Just as gently, the girl placed both bare feet behind one giant ear flap.

The beast remained poised upon her front knees.

'My mother gives you both permission to ride upon her back, but warns that you must take no untoward liberties,' the girl said.

The young man started forward but the elephant raised her trunk warningly.

'But you said she said . . .'

202

'She would remind you of your filial obligations. Your mother is old and has journeyed from the inner city without food today for your sake.'

Umm Malak gave her son a smug look, 'Perhaps there is more to this prize than there at first appeared, my son. Wisdom certainly,' and only after he had helped her mount did he do likewise.

'Now then,' the girl said, 'who is your greatest debtor?'

'Actually, it is between Abdul Hamid, who bought silver nose rings for his twelve wives with a drop of garnet for the chief wife and a toe ring for his youngest daughter, and Hamid Abdul, who bought twelve silver toe rings for his twelve daughters with a garnet nose stud for the mother of the eldest.'

'Abdul Hamid, then,' Maham said after a brief consultation with the head of their mounted procession. 'It is not seemly to demonstrate our power over a poor man who has twelve daughters and is still kind enough to buy them presents, so says my mother.'

'Aiyee,' said Umm Malak. 'She is wise indeed, this elephant.'

'She shows an unusual grasp of logic for an elephant,' Malak agreed grudgingly, 'and a female elephant at that.'

Thus they journeyed in relative state to the home of Abdul Hamid.

The servant of Abdul Hamid met them at the gate. 'Who are you and why come you to my master's home?'

But before Malak could answer, the elephant emitted a short trumpet, and glided her ponderous way through the gate and into the garden, where she cooled herself by spraying her sides with water from the fountains.

'We are emissaries of the Empress Dildar,' said Maham.

'She has come down in the world, to send such emissaries, may Allah defend her,' the servant said.

'Even so,' said the girl. 'And yet, the emissaries of a very great lady may travel incognito. It is in all of the stories that such things may be done. It would behoove you, therefore, to entreat Allah's protection for yourself,

203

if you fail within the blinking of an eye to summon your master.'

The elephant sprinkled him with a delicate spray of water for good measure.

When Abdul Hamid saw them and heard their business, he was sceptical, not to say sneering. 'I will have my servant punished for allowing such rabble to disarray my gardens. I am an honest merchant and need no such—'

'Not so honest if a wealthy man like yourself refuses to pay a poor jeweller for the fruits of his labour,' Umm Malak scolded.

'Who *are* you? You have not the appearance of an empress's emissary to *me*,' he said.

'But so we are,' the beggar lied so steadily as to gain Malak's reluctant admiration. 'For think you, man, how could peasants so poor-seeming as we afford to ride so fine an elephant as this? A man of wealth such as yourself will recognize the quality of this creature, for it is clearly one of the rare breed of imported beasts the great Babur Khan himself coddles in his stables and to whom he feeds bushels of nightingale tongues daily. Why, people such as we outwardly appear would never be able to afford to feed even a common riding elephant, much less so elegant a beast as this – especially if people like you took advantage of us and did not pay us for our goods and services. No, indeed, no commoners could own an elephant like this. Even if they could, it would avail them nothing, for this is a fighting elephant trained to sack and pillage. She would be of no use in domestic service. Too dangerous.'

And the elephant uprooted a small shrubbery and threw it into the fountain by way of demonstration.

'Ah – I see what you mean,' said Abdul Hamid. 'And also I see that fine people such as yourselves riding a fine beast such as this are sullied by visiting such a modest garden as mine. I will not be so discourteous as to detain you longer, but beg you to give my regards to your mistress and, as you have such magnificent transportation, perhaps you would be kind enough to give this purse of gold to that little jeweller, whatsisname – there's enough in there to cover the trinkets plus a little interest as compensation for my faulty memory – no, no, please tell your beast, not my roses! The – uh – the thorns will prick your fine beast's elegant hide and uh – yes, well then, good day.'

And the party departed in triumph.

'To the marketplace!' cried Umm Malak when they were well away.

'To Hamid Abdul's,' cried Malak. 'This works most wonderfully well.'

'I thought we were not going to trouble him,' Maham said.

'I did not know what you were going to do. Since it is only to get the money I'm owed, I see no reason to spare him. After all, what sort of consideration is he showing his daughters to give them presents he has not paid for?'

The elephant agreed, Maham said, that this showed an unusual grasp of logic for a peasant – and a man at that. 'She agrees,' Maham told him, 'but only so that you may purchase fine hay for her bed and the choicest imported bamboo shoots for her repast.'

'Anything,' he said airily.

The second transaction went much as the first except that Hamid Abdul saw the implications of the situation without as much persuasion and expressed his admiration for both elephant and mahout. 'I don't suppose the empress would part with such a beast? I would be prepeared to offer a thousand dinars, cash up front, of course.'

'A thousand dinars?' Malak scratched his chin.

'Two thousand!' Hamid Abdul said. 'Other than my occasional fits of absent-mindedness I am a generous man and a retired veteran elephant skilled in sackage and pillage . . .' his eyes glittered with the possibilities.

'Are you quite sure, Maham, that your mother would not be more comfortable in such rich surroundings as these with twelve happy bouncing girls to keep her company?' Malak inquired solicitously.

For an answer the elephant, having obtained the delinquent payment and interest, stalked from the garden, crushing the sack of dinars the merchant had laid at her feet to tempt them.

That night there was much rejoicing in the house of Malak. The elephant reclined upon her bed of fine hay and supped upon succulent bamboo shoots while Malak and his mother dined on pistachios and roast duck and kumquats and oranges and rice, of course, but what rice! Rice seasoned with coriander and honey and little slices of dates and garbanzo beans. Afterwards everyone felt full except Maham, though the skinny creature had eaten as heartily as her mother, though not of bamboo shoots.

'You were very hungry,' Malak observed, feeling rather ashamed that he had considered himself to be starving when by comparison with her he had truly been only a trifle peckish.

'When last I was allowed to eat, I ate little for fear of poison,' she said matter-of-factly, and curled up to sleep beside her charge.

But while the others slept, he could not, for he had one more task to perform. When she awoke, he drew the girl aside and handed her a jingling bundle. 'Mother will have to return Umm Mustapha's abayah, but here is one for you. I took the liberty of adding a veil trim of coins – the ones with the empress's insignia upon them were going for a quarter of their value for some reason, and seemed most appropriate to our new undertaking. You will look much more like the empress's emissary in this.'

For a moment the twisted face seemed alight with inner pleasure, but then the elephant grumbled sleepily.

'She asks, what work is that?' the girl said.

'Why, visiting the houses of the rich—'

'Do others owe you money?'

'A few, but even those who do not, with the aid of the elephant—'

She handed him back the robe. 'Do not even think of it. Justice is one thing, extortion another.' Her knotted wrist poked from the overlarge and borrowed abayah at a pitiful angle. Her eyes were proud in their ruined settings.

Maham hung his head for a moment. 'I only thought to—' he shoved her hand away. 'No, no, keep the garment, for now at least. You have earned it. But you understand, our prosperity has no permanence. There is not enough left to buy back our house and with the elephant to feed we will soon be back where we started.'

Malak was a good prophet. By noon the next day his stomach was rumbling again, and the last date had mysteriously disapppeared from the tray by the door. Umm Malak licked her forefinger and picked up the last three grains of rice, moistening them again with her tears. When she had savoured their meagre goodness, she began to weep again, and the weeping rose predictably to a wail, 'What good did it do us to face the great ones? What good did it do us to eat well one night? For we shall still starve and lose our home and be on the streets and—'

The elephant mumbled again. Maham cleared her throat and interpreted, 'Mother says she has considered that, and in order to prevent things from being the way they were formerly, or worse, you must meet another condition.'

'Anything,' Malak said eagerly, for the first such promise had worked out well enough, if a bit modestly, and anyway, even if the elephant's new ploy did not work, it would give him some respite from the sound of his mother's despair.

But now he saw that it was Maham who appeared distressed. 'No!' she said to the elephant. 'No, you cannot ask that – ah, well, if it must be—'

'What?' he asked. 'What does she ask?'

'It is necessary that you marry me,' the girl said, cringing slightly, as if expecting a blow.

'It – is?' he asked, but his question could barely be heard for his mother's weeping.

'It is,' the girl's whisper was rasping as a cat's tongue, 'so that no more shame than necessary shall befall us and no punishment upon you later for taking advantage of poor defenceless – of a girl and her elephant.'

At that moment Kakur Daoud, the holder of their mortgage, and his wife arrived at the door, having stepped with much awe and comment around the elephant, Umm Maham. 'Greetings and Allah's blessing on you, Malak, Umm Malak,' Kakur Daoud said with a polite bow and an acquisatory gleam. 'We are pleased to see evidence of your new affluence of which we have heard so much. Last might in the marketplace talk of your purchases rivalled even the news that a messenger arrived yesterday with the head of Babur Khan's enemy for the empress, and that Babur Khan himself, thanks be to Allah the Compassionate and Compassioning, will soon be restored to the bosom of his prayerful people.'

'Allah be praised,' chorused Malak, Umm Malak and Maham, Maham most feelingly of all, and most sadly.

'I am pleased to hear this news, Kakur Daoud, for my family and I were occupied with business all the day and had no time to inform ourselves.'

'Indeed. It is with the knowledge that you have become a man of affairs that my wife and I have come to see you, rather than indisposing you to come to us, regarding the payment of the mortgage. Seeing that you have acquired – er – livestock and have here the remains of a fine dinner, I can tell that my patience and prayers on your behalf have been rewarded and affluence at last attends you.'

Umm Malak began to wail again.

The wife of Kakur Daoud was a wise and holy woman, her knowledge widely respected, her tongue widely feared. She smelled frailty in others as a raven smells death, and the tears of Umm Malak fairly sent her into a frenzy of spurious concern.

'Umm Malak, do you weep at your son's good fortune?' she asked ingenuously.

'No!'

'Then why?'

The elephant grumbled and stood, extending her trunk

208

towards the roof again. Malak gestured frantically to Maham to stop the beast. 'My mother, uh, weeps because she is happy. That is, we were coming to consult you, wife of Kakur Daoud, on a possible matter of matrimony. My fine work won us this splendid elephant from the emperor's harem, and with her came this young woman.'

'It is this girl's duty to be always with this elephant and to live with us but, you understand, she is a good girl with an – er – influential mother – and it is desirable that all propriety be observed and shame avoided. Can you think of a solution?'

'You are a single man?'

He gulped and nodded.

'Well then!'

Homelessness was staved off another three days by the wedding, which was a much simplified and extremely cut-rate version with a potluck feast and borrowed finery. The neighbours were not, in truth, anxious to bring their best dishes or to loan their nicest clothes to the bride, for even though she remained veiled all the time, her hunched back and ruined eyes could not be hidden. Only the wife of Kakur Daoud regarded the girl warily, for deformity was often connected with the supernatural, the one afflicted being either the victim of the evil eye or with the power of it at her command. The girl was obviously one of the latter. And even if she wasn't, the small reddened eyes of the fretful elephant were evil enough to convince anyone that respect was definitely in order. Everyone in the area had houses with thatched roofs, after all.

All through the festivities the elephant rocked and mourned and made small cries (small for an elephant) like a crying infant (whose cries are not so small, as any mother could say). But at last it was done and man and wife were alone in the little house, with the other merrymakers still making merry without.

Umm Malak started to enter, whispering, 'My son, though once more the elephant was correct and this was a good measure to stave off starvation, there is no need to go to extremes. If you do not consummate this wedding,

209

when our fortunes are reversed you may at least—' but she did not finish for a broad grey band coiled around her middle and carried her away from the house and a broad grey rump blocked the entrance, even before Malak shut the door.

He was not as practical as his mother but he knew enough to make the best of a bad situation. The girl had bathed and smelled sweet with borrowed perfumes, and her neck was still kissable. To his surprise, she drew forth from her own rags a silken sheet and laid it beneath them. In the morning it bore the stain of consummation.

However, by that time no one was there to witness it, nor indeed could they have seen anything if they had wished to witness it, for thousands of thundering hoofs had created a veritable sandstorm, and nobody could see further than an arm's length in front of them, nor hear a world that was said.

The elephant bellowed as if in pain, and rocked like a ship on a stormy sea.

Umm Malak returned to the house and shut the door behind her, panting, coughing, blowing sand from her nose and mouth. 'The emperor returns,' she said.

'Aiyee. Perhaps Kakur Daoud will forget us a day or two longer.'

'Yes, now you are a married man with a wife and an elephant mother-in-law who will not work and will not provide for her own unruly appetite, but seems to expect your own aged mother to beg in the streets to support her.'

A section of roof tore away and a long trunk dangled down, the eastern well crumbling dangerously as flat grey feet poised upon its upper edge and a broad face and palm frond ears poked inside.

'She's gone mad! She'll destroy this house!'

'She grieves deeply, does my mother,' the girl apologized, and tried to quiet the elephant.

'*She* grieves, hah!' Umm Malak said, ready to match her wail for trumpet.

The elephant silenced her with a snort, then conferred with the girl, who interpreted.

'Kismet has linked our fate with your own, as matrimony has linked our families. Now, if you dare, all must be risked on one final gamble. Together we must mount upon my mother's back and enter the palace harem and seek Babur Khan.'

'B-But, wife, my er – light of my life, in a manner of speaking, Babur Khan owes me nothing that we should so approach him. Also, be so good as to remind your esteemed charge that Babur Khan has many other elephants as mighty as she.'

'She says you are not the only one to whom something may be owed. Also she says that there are *no* other elephants as mighty as she, which certain people will by Allah find out to their everlasting regret when she is through with them.'

Thus it was that Malak, Umm Malak and Maham rode through the dust storm in the wake of the thundering hoofs, right past the guard at the palace gate, who, if he saw the elephant, mistook her for one of the returning hero's more substantial steeds. She strode right through three archways, through tree dust-veiled gardens, and turned left at a wall full of morning-glory vines which concealed the entrance into a broad windowless passageway.

Umm Malak had to gag herself with her veil to keep from crying out with fear. Malak was nearly faint with admiration as well as fear, for never had he seen such beautiful workmanship, such fine materials, such costly application, and this was only a secret passageway! He wished that before the emperor had him tortured to death for his impertinence, he could have a tour of the rest of the palace.

But Umm Maham trudged on, each footfall like the knell of doom, until at last she came to a little door too small for her to enter. Here she knelt and her passengers slid from her back.

From the other side of the door, a mighty voice boomed.

'Greetings, my pretty pomegranate, from the lord of

your heart, the king of your mountain, the snake in your bed. It is I, your Babur, returned safe and sound. Did you get my grisly present?'

'Yes, lord and master, I certainly did and I must say he did not look too happy about the outcome of your contest. I trust that in *our* little contest of the night to come, we shall both emerge blissful.'

'Ah, my Dildar, you have grown randy in my absence. Have you been asking those slave girls for naughty things to say to me when I returned? I – Dildar, I thought your voice sounded rather lower than usual but took it that you must have a cold. Have you been ailing, my love? You seem to have lost a great deal of weight.'

Malak glued his eye to the peephole Maham had just uncovered. A lissome form upon the cushion-strewn divan lifted a veil assuredly meant for seduction rather than concealment, for the rest of her was scarcely concealed at all. He grimaced. He could have his eyes burned out just for seeing this, but he wouldn't need them if he was going to be disembowelled and dismembered anyway. He wondered idly just how painful castration *really* was.

'Why, Agata, my sweet, what do you in the bed of my wife?'

'I hoped to fulfil her duty to you, my lord, since she spurns to do it. I think, you know, that she was upset about never having given you a son. She took off the day your message arrived. I hadn't the heart to tell the messenger when you had been fighting so hard and gone so long. I wanted to break it to you gently when I could be here to – console you.'

'And my daughter?'

'Oh, she left too. There is a rumour that they fell in love with two Moorish pirates, who have no doubt robbed and killed them now.' It was a story that made no sense to either Malak or his mother. The Empress Dildar was a lady of two score of years and twenty stone of weight and did not readily flit about, even with Moorish pirates. Besides, she had been the reigning empress for many years, despite having failed to provide a male heir.

Nevertheless, Babur Khan looked into Agata's eyes, accented by the jewelled baubles that dangled above her brow, and stood and swayed and sank to his knees beside her, seemingly as convinced as he needed to be.

'Come, my love, that wilful old cow would never provide you with your heart's delight and your realm's necessity. I will do so and thereby, through my son, recoup the victory my father's warriors lost to you.' But this last she said to a man entranced. As she raised her arm, Malak saw that she wore the beautiful bracelet he had made and for which she had repaid him with only misfortune.

'By the beard of the Prophet, why does he not heed her words and smite her?' he demanded of Maham.

'He is ensorcelled and only you can break the spell.'

'I?'

'Yes. If either Mother or I are seen before the spell is broken, all is lost—'

'What all? I am a simple man. I know nothing of politics.'

'I know sufficient, my son, to know that if we are caught here, it will be most inauspicious,' his mother said. 'So far you have listened to this elephant's daughter instead of to your own dear mother, and see where it has got us? Why not—'

The clanking of swords and the pounding of footsteps echoed in the distance. 'An elephant, do you say? How can that be? The captain of the guard himself was not five feet from the entrance—'

'I distinctly saw an elephant disappear through that wall. Already you have seen that the wall held the door, why can you not believe that the door held an elephant?' asked the other voice, a soldier's from its clipped and precise tones.

'Aiyee,' Umm Malak cried, but softly.

'What am I to do?' Malak asked.

His wife handed him the silken sheet, still bearing its stain. 'Rush in, throw this over the face of the sorceress and say unto her, "Here is the blood of your victim and the seed of your outrage cast back on your face to be seen by all; and by it may you be undone."''

Precious time was lost while he tried to remember it. The soldiers could be seen down the hall, small as ants, but they were ants who saw the elephant ahead of them and broke into a run. 'Now or never, my love,' Maham said, and her husband, his eyes wide and stunned, plunged through the door to confront the nearly naked sorceress and the vaguely enchanted emperor, who regarded his new mistress with the expression of a cobra watching a flute player.

'Here is the outrage of your undone – here is the face of your blood—' he began and in the hallway his mother screamed. The emperor temporarily snapped out of his enchanted reverie and leapt to his feet. Malak knew he could never get his tongue untangled in time. Then Maham shrieked a shriek of despair and a soft, moist something nuzzled his ear and within his mind he heard the correct words and spoke them, flinging the sheet over the face of the astonished sorceress, who was desperately trying to improvise another spell against him. But the direct aid of the elephant in-law was stronger, 'Here is the blood of your victim and the seed of your outrage cast back on your face to be seen by all; and by it may you be undone,' he cried as the sheet writhed over the woman's face. She clawed it off almost immediately, screaming for the harem guards, and the emperor pinned Malak to the wall with his arm, his scimitar being with his pants, which were in the anteroom.

But when the Syrian sorceress was free of the sheet, her once beautiful features had been warped into the same conformation as Maham's.

'What?' cried the emperor, beholding this, and paused in his programme of strangulation.

Outside, the heads of the two guards banged against the tile as they flung themselves to the floor in front of a large imposing lady. 'Oh great Empress, forgive us, but have you seen an elephant anywhere nearby? Perhaps this crone who accompanies you and the Princess Maham may—'

The Empress Dildar, clothed in the pyjamas she had worn the night Agata Aghacha transformed her, veiled in a hastily torn piece of Umm Malak's abayah, did not deign to answer them, saying instead, 'Beloved husband, if you do not unhand our son-in-law this moment, surely he will die, and you will have ill repaid the man who saved your family from disgrace and your empire from usurpation and ruin.'

'Yes, dear,' said Babur Khan. 'Guards, will you please remove this hideous woman,' he indicated the sorceress, who was screaming into her mirror, 'to some suitable dungeon.'

'And for the love of Allah, gag and blindfold her and bind her in chains of iron so that she may work no more ensorcellment,' the empress said, efficient as ever.

'Very unlike you to let an upstart of a concubine get the best of you, my dear,' the emperor said when they were all later settled on silk-tasselled cushions around a golden tray filled with fricassée of hummingbird parts.

'She was exhausted from attending me, father,' the Princess Maham, whose beauty indeed put the moon to shame, defended her mother.

'Even so,' said Dildar, whose presence was still massive and awesome, though the only bit of grey about her now was a distinguished silver thread running through her onyx locks. 'The woman bragged to see me, when she had transformed me, of how she induced my poor daughter's fever to ruin her beauty, and of the insultingly impossible way she had devised that we could be restored – only by the marriage blood of a Maham so hideous that no man (so thought the Syrian, believing face and form and riches a woman's only wealth) would wed her.

'Why should she do such a thing? My own daughter was no rival to her,' the emperor said.

'She would have no one her equal or set above her for any reason. Once Maham and I were out of the way, she

215

laid a spell over the harem so that no one should question her right to my place within it. When you returned, my love, she was going to gain power over you as well, even as she was doing when we arrived.'

'You cannot believe I was actually falling for that?' Babur Khan said. 'No, of course not. I saw through her right away. I only wanted to see what she would do.'

The empress nodded an acknowledgement, smiled and continued as if he had not spoken. 'But we were still a threat while within the harem, since her magic would not allow her to kill us directly, so when the time came for the competition I had formerly announced to support the local artisans, she chose the finest object for herself and gave me to the artist as the prize.'

'She would have restrained me, but I hid from her and watched and followed,' said Maham, 'for only the loving heart of her daughter could understand my mother in her transformed state.'

'But, your pardon, exalted wife, if I may be so bold as to interrupt, unworthy person that I am,' Malak said, 'why did you not simply tell us your identity so we could have—'

'Could have what?' the empress asked softly, her brow arching like the wing of a raven. 'Denounced the sorceress? But how? She allowed no one to know we were missing. When I appeared as an elephant, she told the astonished eunuch she couldn't think how I had wandered into the harem and had me removed to the garden, where she could gloat over me. When she had ruined my poor daughter and reduced her to rags, no one recognized her any more than they recognized me as an elephant. And she made sure that only impoverished artists in the poorest of circumstances had their work admitted, so that I would be humiliated and starved, and he who won me would be ruined and angry and would presumably vent his wrath upon me. To break the spell, we needed a special man, one of refined sensibilities who would have the open-mindedness to heed even a beggar and her beast if they could show him the merit of their counsel. And who would then listen to their advice even if they suggested that he tie himself in matrimony to a hideously deformed, impoverished woman just as he himself was about to be ruined.'

'She meant she needed a fool,' Umm Malak mumbled to herself.

'What was that, mother of my husband?' the princess asked pleasantly.

'I said how nice and cool it is here within the harem, your highness, how soothing after the heat and dust outside.'

'Poor my ladies!' Babur Khan cried, and caressed the knuckle of his senior wife, his kadin, his empress of twenty years. 'For her perfidy, no punishment is too great for the sorceress. It is up to you to say how she is to be dealt with. The oil is at a mere simmer right now, but I'm sure it could be heated to boiling in no time—'

The empress's eyes narrowed to slits, then she shook her head. 'The wrong was not done solely to me. Daughter, you also were grievously harmed by the accursed Agata. What say you?'

The Princess Maham looked shyly at her husband, 'I say, we would not have been saved had my clever and courteous Malak not listened to me, no matter how crazy or how ugly he thought I might be. So now I think I would listen to him. Tell us, Malak, the woman who almost ruined us would have callously ruined you too, merely for making her a beautiful ornament. What punishment shall we inflict?'

Malak hesitated. 'I have heeded well the praise and rewards that Allah has heaped upon my head for listening to my lovely wife, and through her her mother, and that lesson in this matter is not lost on me. It is necessary to the survival and joy of us all to have our words and thoughts and hearts heeded, even as my esteemed wife acknowledges by according me the singular honour of this decision. But before I pronounce sentence, I must know, this witch, her sorcerous powers can be neutralized?'

'Indeed. When our imperial enchanter finds out she's

been witching without a licence, she will not be able to turn water into tea.'

'Very good. In that case, I know just the thing. She shall remain unharmed and unchanged from her present state and be awarded to my mother as her personal servant.'

And as he said it, so was it done; and all lived happily ever after – save one person who was never allowed an uncontradicted opinion or an uncriticized remark or deed for all the remainder of her short, unhappy life.

SUSAN SHWARTZ

Tales of
The Mongol's Guards

The days and weeks sped by. For months, perhaps, there
might come no caravans; and then, suddenly, the tiny
serpents would writhe over the dunes, become blacker
and larger until, finally, one could be certain that a caravan approached, and no demon-spawned illusion. And
when that happened, Peter of Wraysbury would be one of
the men to ride out and bring the caravan to a resting
place. For he was a part of the work now, trusted to bear
steel and ride a spirited horse. He had even been sent on
one caravan himself, south to Khotan where he listened as
the traders chaffered for jade, silk and polished brass
brought up from the south.

There he had seen a statue, its body swaying gracefully,
its face carved like a Greek hero, and wondered why the
merchant would not covet that too. 'An idol,' scoffed the
caravan master.

Had he silver to spare, he might have succumbed to that
lovely little figure of a piper.

What he gained, though, was knowledge. The dancer
had a name – Krishna – and a story, unseemly though
holy, as were many of the stories from the south. His
Arabic improved, though, out of all measure, and he
learned enough of Farsi and one of the tongues of Hind to
listen in the marketplace and understand more than curses
and the cost of rice. Now he could even read the swirls
that passed for letters hereabouts, and he discovered the

219

Persian Book of Kings, or *Shah Namah*, as thrilling a collection of deeds as any story of Arthur and his knights.

And other tales there were besides . . . it was a wonder, in this land that cloistered away women, chaste and unchaste alike, that so many of the tales he most enjoyed were said to be the work of a queen, the very queen of whom the first storyteller had spoken.

Definitely, a man could love a woman like that. Out under the stars, on the way back to Kashgar, Peter dreamed of her – black-eyed, red-lipped, silken of hair and of touch. Then he dreamed of another woman, the far more earthy and fairly attainable dancer who had shown him quite definitely that his fair hair and blue eyes did not make him repulsive to her. Such women made an art of lust, the other men in the caravan told him, chuckling. They had been right.

He had been happy while on the march. But returning to Kashgar made him feel like a falcon that had flown free, then been forced to submit once again to the tyranny of hood, jesses and imprisonment in the mews until the next order came to hunt. God alone knew when that might be.

But when he returned to Kashgar, he found that another caravan had arrived, bringing new faces and a wealth of stories – all fascinating, but none the story that Peter longed most to hear: that of a messenger returned with the ransom that would free him. Surely, somewhere between Acre and Samarkand, there must be some Christian soul with will and funds enough to pity him and release him? Despair was a sin, but day by day he found himself inclining to it. He would never see his home – nor fulfil his vow of finding Prester John.

Nevertheless, as he walked through the bazaar he had not seen for some months, he made his greetings cheerful to one and all. They should not know how he feared to be sold on the block; he forced himself to turn and stare at it, marking with his eyes the place where, one day, he might find himself standing. He strode past the stalls he most liked to visit, seeing how crowded they were.

Several of the caravan master's other drivers saw and hailed him. He had travelled with them, worked with them, eaten with them, all but the rare Hindu up from the south, who could not eat with those not of his race. He had been to their homes, had even, at times, caught tantalizing glimpses of veiled swaying forms and heard their laughter when they looked at his blue eyes through the screens of the women's quarters.

It did not occur to him to wonder at the freedom the caravan master allowed him: perhaps, he thought, the one time that the thought brushed into his head, the man simply wanted a more valuable slave. Or perhaps he wanted a return on the money he had spent feeding Peter; his work was one way to gain that.

An instant later, he found himself, like everyone else in the narrow passageways, flattened up against the stalls as a troop of men strode by. Though all wore Mongol harness, they were an odd group of companions; but then the very notion of 'Mongol' had changed less than half a century after the conquest. Many had converted to Islam, though others kept still to their own ways and the harsh but fair laws called the Yasa.

Fierce as the Mongols were, however, those laws apparently permitted them to tolerate all types of men and creeds. *Better than we of Europe do*, Peter thought. A group of companions in that troop was proof of the Mongol talent for coping with all types of people. One was a man who looked like a scholar of Ch'in; in his face, despite the arms he bore, was the gentleness of the healer-born. Another had the high-bridged and haughty nose of the Persian aristocrats whom the Arabs had dispossessed and who were by no means totally sorry that Arab rule had given way to Mongol. *An exile like myself*. The third man bore the features and muscles of the Mongol-born. They strode as arrogantly as they must have ridden, crossing the desert: masters of the world.

That hurt to watch, Peter thought. For a moment, he struggled with a disgraceful urge to flee and hide, to try to smuggle himself into a caravan (not that all in Kashgar would not instantly know of his master's pet foreign devil) and escape any way he could.

It was the wheel of fortune, he thought, which had exalted him into his knighthood and now cast him down. It might spin again: who knew?

'My friend . . .' he heard his name mangled as they managed it in this town, and turned to look down at a man in scholar's robes who, once or twice, had invited him into his home. Amazingly enough, he had the three Mongol guardsmen in tow.

'Will you join me at my home, most worthy man of the West, for some refreshment?' asked the man.

There being nothing else to do, Peter accepted. Besides, he enjoyed the little man's company.

The Persian sipped sherbet, then smiled at his fellows. 'As happened the last time we were in Kashgar, this pearl of scholars will now prepare to plunder our minds. I ask you, of my brothers, is this the action of a scholar, or of a freebooter of books?'

'He is our host,' said Peter, obliquely rebuking the young Persian. 'If it pleases him to question us—'

'By the beard of the Prophet, my honoured brother from the West, it pleases me not at all that you are so melancholy. Is it not truth that a wise man of your race once wrote of the consolations of philosophy? You are not a foolish man: perhaps you might avail yourself of them. behold: here are friends who perhaps can guide you.'

'Already,' said Peter, 'you have been like rain in the Land of Fire: most welcome, most unexpected – and I thank you a thousand times. So I beg you, my masters, speak. I am eager to begin these consolations.'

MELISSA SCOTT

The King who was Summoned to Damascus

It is said as truth in the mountains that hold our Alexandria – Alexandria-the-Least, the Alexandria beyond Balkh – that our kings are immortal. It is true that they are very hard to kill. My lord's great-grandfather's grandfather, who was the first of his house to accept the word of the Prophet, took a spear through the body during the Long Siege and lived. My lord's father, Abdul Rahman, survived a dozen such blows, and if the assassin's knife had not unluckily pierced through the heart, Abdul Rahman being far from the citadel at the time, he would be living still. Or if he had brought his healer with him, as he had always done before ... But he is dead, and Harithah, who served him as healer and taught me that art, does not speak of his death. And I serve the king Isma'il.

It was in the fifth year of his reign that my lord was summoned to Damascus. This was a matter that had been brewing for some time. My lord, like his father and grandfather before him, exacted toll from the merchants who made their way through the passes below the city and, more to the point, did not share his profits with Damascus. But no one had expected it to come to a head so quickly. Hearing the order read, the nobles frowned and tugged at their beards, while the chief of the merchants and the masters of the scholars murmured uneasily to each other. My lord stopped that with a glance and looked again at the messenger. The messenger, himself an emir and a favourite of the sultan, stared back at my lord and lifted one eyebrow in arrogant question. In spite of my training, I looked up then, and saw my lord's face darken with anger. Still he did not speak. I looked away and saw the nobles hiding their smiles behind their hands.

'King Isma'il,' the Emir said at last, softly, barely disturbing the silence. 'The Sultan Saladin is waiting for your answer.'

There was a wealth of menace in those words, threats that did not have to be made explicit. I saw the chief of the merchants grow pale, and the scholars made distressed faces. The lord Jafar, my lord's half-brother and commander of the armies, gave a cry of protest.

'How dare he? Saladin is powerful, my lord, but he's very far away!' He jerked his head at the waiting emir. 'This one is here – and so is Karim.'

There was a growl of agreement from the other nobles. I glanced to my left and saw the lord Karim smile slowly, contemptuously. He stood among his own nobles, clustered against the painted walls: he was in no real danger, no matter what Jafar threatened, until he left the audience chamber. It was Karim who had brought the accusation against my lord, Karim who was Emir of the Bactrian lands to the west, the latest move in four years of manoeuvrings to drive my lord from his taxing of the merchants taking the long road to India and the East. It was not so much that Karim wished to increase the sultan's income, any more than did my lord, but if the caravans paid no toll at the fortress-pass below the city, they could pay more toll to Karim. It was whispered in the eunuchs' quarters that Karim had overreached himself in appealing to Saladin, despite the favour Saladin had shown him; that he had not expected to be called to Damascus with my lord to prove his charges. I hoped the tales were true.

'King Isma'il.' To give him his due, the sultan's messenger did not flinch, or turn his gaze from my lord's face.

'I remind you that the emir is also under the sultan's protection.'

There was another murmur at that, angry but uncertain. Jafar opened his mouth to protest.

'Be silent.' My lord lifted his hand and was reluctantly obeyed. He smiled then, as sweetly as a child, and I braced myself, still sitting at his feet, for what would follow. I could see the other eunuchs of the household doing the same – we are safer than men for demonstrating my lord's temper – but my lord surprised us all.

'My lord Humayd,' my lord said, quite calmly, 'and you, Karim. I will accept the Sultan Saladin's invitation –' he stressed the word gently, and Karim bit his lip. '– in order that I may clear myself of these unjustified accusations.'

Jafar opened his mouth to speak again and my lord frowned him down. 'My people, you know the reputation of the Sultan Saladin. I will trust in that as my shield against calumny.' My lord's voice changed subtly. 'And were that not enough, as God send it shall be, we are still armoured in the law of the Prophet, which protects the innocent, and in the powers God has granted to our people.'

That was threat for threat: even in Damascus they know of our kings' amazing longevity, and of the other powers wielded by the more daring of our scholars – though like Karim they prefer to attribute all of this to bargains with the jinn. The messenger paled in spite of himself and passed a hand across his mouth. Over his shoulder I saw the younger of the scholars whispering to his master. Around the fringes of the room the nobles nudged each other, grinning. I looked up again – the chamberlain who had taught me deportment rolled his eyes to heaven – and saw my lord was smiling too. It was his hunting smile, that said he had plans he had not yet revealed to anyone.

'Come, my lords,' he said, and clapped his hands to end the audience. 'We shall go to Damascus.'

At my lord's order, I attended him at the council

session that afternoon. Jafar, who as a soldier officially disapproves of all indulgences, looked down his nose at me and wondered aloud what my lord was thinking of. A few of the others, warriors all, laughed with him, and my lord's face darkened again. He laid a heavy hand on my head, twining his fingers in my hair; I blinked hard against the tears.

'Am I king here? This is my shadow. He goes where I say.' My lord smiled at me then and released his hold on my hair. 'Sit, Little Shadow, you're welcome here.'

I sank on to the cushions at his side, knowing my face to be red with shame: it is not my place to be a cause of argument. The vizier, who besides my lord and, of course, Harithah, is the only person at court who knows of the existence of the king's healer, gave me a sympathetic glance and then lifted both hands to gain my lord's attention.

'My king, and my lords, if my king wishes to go to Damascus, I may not oppose him, but I must in duty say I do not like it.'

I looked away, across the fretted shadows from the long windows, feeling the breeze that came off the sheer mountain snowfield above us, willing myself to be unnoticeable. The nobles' voices seemed to fade, and I became – not invisible, but insignificant. It is a simple thing, averting even the first glance: I was not cut to preserve any extraordinary beauty, though I'm considered pretty enough, but because our kings do not trust a whole man with a healer's power. This almost-invisibility was the first trick Harithah taught me when the soldiers brought me to the citadel. She had said then, bitterly, that God would have done better to give our healing powers to the dumb animals, who could be content to live as pets. I had not understood, until it was explained that our power was kept a secret, for fear that assassins would first attack the healer, and then the unprotected king. She had been thought the old king's concubine; I am considered nothing more.

Rising voices pierced the fragile shell of my concentration, drew my mind back to the council. I looked slowly back towards the circle and realized in an instant that there was no need for caution. The nobles were staring at my lord with a mix of fear and frustration in their eyes; Fath Abdul Hakim, the oldest of them all, had gone so far as to stretch out his hands to my lord in supplication.

'My king, I beg you to reconsider this—'

Jafar slammed his hand down flat on the stones in front of him. 'Isma'il, I speak as your brother. It is foolish to put yourself in the hands of Saladin, especially after you've disobeyed him.' His voice changed, became almost cajoling. 'The Franks have pressed him hard, even if he's beaten them back into their cities now. There's no guarantee this peace will last any longer than the others. He'll never be able to leave watching them long enough to come to us. We may remain here and snap our fingers at this sultan.'

My lord shook his head, the hunting smile on his lips again. 'Are we to cut ourselves off from the heirs of the Prophet? And if you're wrong and he does come east – well, you remember what happened the last time we were besieged. No, I must go to Damascus.'

'But, my king,' another of the nobles protested, and Jafar exploded, 'My king, you're guilty of what he says.'

My lord's smile widened and for the first time he glanced at me in council. It was a little movement, scarcely more than a flicker of his eyelids, but I was suddenly afraid. 'I have my own answers, ones he will not have heard.' Then the smile vanished from his lips. 'By God, I will go to Damascus, and you, Jafar, will go with me. And anyone else I say.'

There was a long silence then, the nobles glancing from one to the other, but no one dared to make any further protest. My lord's temper was never of the most even. At last the vizier cleared his throat. 'As my king will have it,' he said, 'but who will govern the city while he is gone?'

It was a fair question and a welcome distraction, though there was in truth only one answer. Too many of the nobles were of the royal blood, no matter how diluted; only the vizier himself, or the chief chamberlain, both eunuchs and royal slaves, could be so trusted. I barely listened to the discussion, wondering just what my lord had in mind for me. A healer's talents can do so much more than heal.

I did not find out until that night, when my lord at last retired to his quarters. He settled himself on his cushions beneath the spangled canopy, and the dumb slave who serves the inner chamber hastened to remove his shoes and his heavy woollen coat. I poured the wine and waited.

'Well, Little Shadow,' he said, 'do you think it's a mistake, going to Damascus?'

'My lord knows best,' I answered.

My lord laughed softly and drained his cup. At his gesture, I filled it again. 'Yes, I do,' he said. 'And I know my servants, too. These so-called scholars of mine may not be able to get their spells past Karim's sorcerers, but I still have you. The old woman told me, Little Shadow, that you know the art of shaping thoughts. I wish to leave Damascus acquitted of all wrongdoing, and with a charter from the sultan himself to tax these passes.'

My surprise must have shown on my face, because my lord laughed again. 'Come, Little Shadow, don't look so shocked. Can you do this, with your art?'

'My lord,' I said, 'I've never done it.'

He slammed his cup against the low table, spilling wine on to the pillows. The slave darted to mop up the mess, but my lord ignored him. 'Don't lie to me, Little Shadow,' he said. 'Harithah says you can.'

'My lord,' I said again, and stopped, looking for the right words. It was never easy to explain the workings of the power to my lord; he was one who had no patience with art or science, wishing only to be obeyed. 'My lord, I know how such things are done, and yes, I've done them, but it helps to know the person whose thoughts one wishes to influence. I do not know Saladin.'

My lord looked at me with a deepening frown. 'You will come to know him.' There was a note in his voice that chilled me.

I bowed my head, knowing better than to argue. One

does not argue with my lord when he speaks in that fashion. 'As my lord wishes, then.'

His look became, briefly, a caress. 'Excellent, Little Shadow.' He clapped his hands for the slave. 'Have the master of the household fetch my concubines.'

The slave bowed and backed away. I bowed also. 'With your permission, my lord, I'll retire.'

My lord waved his hand, his mind already on other things, and I slipped into the curtained alcove that contained my bed. My lord had taken heed of his father's fate and I was never far from him. Already my services had been needed once, when a bazaar-boy stabbed him; I slept only lightly now, a corner of my mind turned always to the inner chamber. I lay there in the dark, the blankets drawn up to my chin, listening with half an ear as the chief eunuch presented each of the concubines. There were only five, and the sixth who was with child, but a pilgrim scholar had said once that this was the ceremonial used in Damascus and in Cairo, and my lord had followed it ever since.

My lord made his choice, and the chief eunuch departed with the others. I wished I could be deaf in truth to what would inevitably follow. I whispered the spell Harithah had taught me for such nights, barely breathing the words. The darkness wrapped itself around me, leaving only a spark of myself to wait and watch by the curtained door. The woman was as safe as any of my lord's concubines could ever be: she had been the bond-slave of a bandit lord and was grateful to serve in my lord's household.

I could lie in the cocoon of my thoughts and consider Damascus and Saladin. I knew little of the great sultan beyond the tales brought by the pilgrim scholars, and what I did know did not bode well for my lord's plan. As a young man he had driven the infidel Franks out of Egypt, and after rising to the sultanate had harried them out of Palestine and Syria as well. The surviving Franks had signed a treaty only the winter before, and the coast was at peace for the first time in years.

Yet through all the wars, the storytellers said, Saladin

had never once neglected the affairs of the rest of the realm – was a builder as well as a conqueror. It would not be easy to influence such a man – I could shape the thoughts of a slave, used to obeying orders, with relative ease, but I had never yet been able to influence my lord, and Saladin by all accounts was a far greater king than he. There were drugs, of course, to smooth the way for my spells, drugs easy to procure and to prepare, but the great Saladin would surely have slaves set to prevent such poisonings . . . I slept before I'd thought of any means of obeying my lord's command.

We left for Damascus two weeks later, my lord's household and the nobles' households making a great jostling caravan that spread out for half a mile along the roads. My lord brought all his women and his finest belongings, not wanting to seem a pauper before the lords of Damascus; his nobles did the same. Even I had fine new clothes, and a coat embroidered at the throat in silk from the East. My lord ate only from dishes of silver, and the chief eunuch went in constant fear of robbers. I thought there could be nothing finer in the world.

Then we came to Damascus. At my lord's command we of the household put on our finest clothes, and dressed my lord himself in a robe of silk banded at the neck and sleeves with golden thread. His turban we pinned with the great red jewel taken a hundred years before from an Indian king, and we scented his beard with musk. We took down the plain travelling curtains that covered the women's wagons and replaced them with brightly woven carpets. The grooms polished the harness rings and the brass bells on each bridle until they shone like gold. There was even a peacock's feather tucked into my horse's headstall.

We were met at the city gates by a great array of notables in their finery, and slowed our pace to keep down the dust so they could see us too. They were a magnificent crowd, many wearing robes of silk as fine as anything my lord owned, one or two wearing robes so heavily embroidered in gold thread that they seemed bowed by its weight.

The sunlight glittered from the coloured stones that fastened their turbans and sparkled on their hands. I wondered which of these was Saladin.

Grooms came running to hold my lord's horse, and my lord let them take the bridle, his eyes flickering appreciatively across the crowd. The nobles halted too, clustering together. I kept close at my lord's side. Then the crowd parted and a figure rode from among them, a man riding a white horse with trappings of white leather studded with silver. His own robe seemed to have been made from beaten silver. I blinked, dazzled, and then recognized the emir Karim. He had left for Damascus before us, with Humayd, who'd brought the sultan's message.

'King Isma'il,' he said, with a bow that had more of irony than of respect. 'I am sent by the Sultan Saladin to welcome you to Damascus and to ask your indulgence on his behalf, as affairs of state have kept him from greeting you in person.' He gestured to the waiting crowd and the jewels on his hand flashed in the sunlight. 'The merchants of Damascus greet you also and beg for your patronage.'

I heard my lord give a little gasp of shock and I felt the envy flare behind me, like the heat of a fire against my back. If these were the common merchants of Damascus, some of whom were as richly dressed as was my lord, what would the court be like? My lord's face darkened, but he answered courteously enough.

'Thank you for your welcome, my lord, and you may assure the sultan we understand that affairs of state press hard on him.' He raised his voice, to be heard by the crowd as well. 'And we thank you also for your courtesy.'

'If you will follow me, King Isma'il,' Karim said, 'I myself will take you to the quarters prepared for you in the palace.'

My lord nodded, stiff-faced, and beckoned to the chief eunuch. I heard him murmur something about largesse, and knew a stab of fear. If the merchants were so wealthy, how much would the beggars expect from a king? My lord would not allow himself to be so shamed. The chief eunuch hesitated and my lord gave him such a look of anger that the chief eunuch was struck dumb. He bowed and handed my lord a bulging purse. As we rode into the first market at Karim's side, beggars appeared. My lord smiled, still stiffly, and tossed a handful of coin into the crowd. The coins showed gold as they fell. I barely heard the faint protest from Jafar: the coin my lord had brought to maintain his household during our stay in Damascus, thrown away on a pack of beggars.

My lord was allotted rooms in one wing of the citadel, with his own small harem quarter and a fountain court-yard filled with fruit trees. His nobles were given similar, but smaller, rooms to either side; at my lord's order, our soldiers stood guard along the corridors. When the sultan's chambermaids had left, I wandered through our new quarters, marvelling at the richness of the furnishings. Nothing that could be gilded or painted had been left plain; the floor was covered in blue and gold tiles that made a pleasing lattice-pattern. The cushions of the inner chamber were of silk damask, and the canopy above the bed was of woven gold. Next to all that splendour my lord's silver dishes looked old and tarnished, little more than bazaar trash.

'Little Shadow!'

I turned, to find my lord scowling at me. He tossed something in my direction and I caught it automatically. It was a gold coin, like the ones he had thrown to the beggars in the market. I turned it over in my hand, wondering why he had given it to me.

'Well? Can't you make me another sackful, wizard?'

I shook my head. 'I'm sorry, my lord, I'm not an alchemist.'

'I wish to God you were,' he said sourly, and held out his hand. I laid the coin carefully in his palm and he stared at it for a long time, as though it had some special message carved into its surface. At last he said, 'We go before the sultan tomorrow, Karim and I, and you'll go with me. Remember what I told you.'

I bowed. To attempt to shape the thoughts of someone

so powerful is a dangerous thing even to contemplate. At least this meeting, of necessity the first of many, would give me a chance to see the sultan, to get some idea of how his mind worked, so that I might influence him. 'I will, my lord.'

Again, the next morning, we dressed my lord in his finest robes and brought out the chest of jewels. There were pieces I did not recognize among the familiar stones; as we went about our duties the chief eunuch whispered that my lord had ordered each of the nobles to send the best jewels he owned. From the chamberlain's carefully downcast eyes, I guessed the nobles had given unwillingly and ungenerously.

We were not kept waiting in the antechamber for more than a few minutes, a courtesy even my lord was quick to recognize. The chamberlains escorted us in past audience-seekers from all parts of the empire, past scholars and merchants as well as nobles, even past a trio of Franks, tall, fair men I recognized too late to stare at. Karim was there before us, but my lord controlled himself and made his obeisance with some grace.

'My lord Saladin,' he said. 'I am here, as you commanded.'

'Rise.'

The sultan's voice was low and pleasant, touched with the power of a man who is always obeyed. I placed my lord's chair as I had been instructed, and waited with downcast eyes while he seated himself. I knelt beside him then, and only then dared to glance at Saladin. He was not a young man, though his hair and beard were still black as jet, and in that court of peacocks he alone wore white. He alone, of all of them, had no need of finery.

Behind him stood the jurists and the scholars and the reciters of traditions, ready to offer their opinions; to either side waited the great nobles of the realm. I glanced at them sidelong, and could read the curiosity behind their impassive faces.

'My lord Karim,' Saladin said, 'and you, King Isma'il. I have summoned you here so that this dispute between you may be settled according to the law, and without blood-shed. Will you begin, Karim, by stating your complaint?'

My lord frowned, and started to speak, but the sultan held up his hand. 'When he is finished, King Isma'il, you will have the same space of time to answer, and that time again to make your own complaint.'

My lord still seemed inclined to argue, but then thought better of it. 'As my lord commands,' he growled.

'Then, Karim, begin,' Saladin said, and gestured to a slave who sat at the edge of the dais. The man turned a golden hourglass, and Karim began to speak. The slave turned the glass once more before he'd finished. My lord spoke for a little less than the allotted time, leaving per-haps two fingers' width of sand in the glass, but I barely heard either of them, watching Saladin instead. The sultan listened well, never betraying his annoyance when Karim presumed upon the service he'd done the sultan during the Egyptian wars, or when my lord spoke too loudly of his traditional rights. I could feel the temper of the mind behind that quiet face, and feared to meddle with it.

'My lords,' Saladin said, at last. 'My lords, you've spoken very eloquently of your rights, but you've neglec-ted another right that operates here – my right. You speak of the privileges granted you for your good service, Karim, but none of those includes the right to set tolls on the roads. That I've granted you certain dispensations I don't deny, but whether those dispensations can extend so far as to allow this is at least a matter for the jurists to consider.' He gestured to the men behind him, and my lord smiled slowly. Then Saladin turned to him, and my lord's smile faded before the sultan's steady gaze.

'As for you, King Isma'il, these rights you claim are taken with your title from Iskandar's time, a time of legend. This is a question of law, and must be considered as such.' The sultan rose to his feet, ending the audience. 'I will consult with my legal scholars, my lords. Until I have heard their advice, I ask you to accept the freedom of my court. I hunt tomorrow; I trust you will both accom-pany me.'

'I thank my lord for the honour.' Karim bowed deeply, as graceful as any courtier. My lord murmured some answer, his face twisted in a scowl, but managed to depart with some dignity. As we left the audience chamber, he laid a heavy hand on my shoulder.

'So I hunt with Saladin tomorrow, Little Shadow. You will accompany me.'

'Yes, my lord,' I answered, and his fingers tightened slowly, until I gasped with pain.

'Do you understand me?' he asked, quietly, not looking at me.

'Yes, my lord,' I said again, suddenly dry-mouthed. I understood what he wanted, as clearly as if he'd spoken aloud. He wanted me to work my spells on Saladin, to bend the sultan's thoughts to my lord's purpose. I doubted I could do it, not without greater preparation, if ever I could, but I did not dare say that to my lord. 'I will do as you asked,' I said, and bent my head in submission.

My lord nodded. 'Tomorrow, Little Shadow.'

'My lord, I will try,' I said, 'but—'

'Tomorrow,' my lord said. He turned away, releasing me. I bowed to his retreating back. At least I had seen Saladin today; tomorrow perhaps I would be able to get close enough to begin my lord's work.

To my chagrin, however, and to my lord's great annoyance, the hunt was very large, so large that we could do little more than watch the sultan from afar. For this, I breathed a prayer of thanks: even my lord has been forced to learn enough of our arts to understand I cannot act across a distance.

Saladin greeted my lord quite courteously across the milling mass of dogs and handlers, but came no closer. I heard my lord curse softly, and braced myself for a bruising ride. There was little comment on my presence, for which I was grateful; in any case, there were other favourites riding with their masters.

For a time the hunt rode south, with much shouting and laughter, and then turned west, towards the mountains. The crowd had thinned and separated into a dozen different groups of riders, each one seeking the best path over the rising ground. The dogs vanished, voices fading over the hills. The sultan was nowhere in sight and 'I feared we had lost the hunt, but then to my left I saw the Emir Karim. He lifted his whip in salute to my lord.

'King Isma'il,' he called, 'I congratulate you on your horses.' There was a hint of mockery in his voice, but my lord smiled slowly. Even I understood: our horses were not as beautiful as the emir's, but they were stronger animals, and nimbler – faster across this broken land.

'I thank you, Emir,' my lord called back. 'Will you set a race?'

He could not keep the savage pleasure from his voice, but the emir did not seem to notice. 'As you wish, King Isma'il,' Karim answered, bowing easily over his horse's neck, 'but let's set stakes as well, like civilized men.'

That insult was a little too plain, and my lord's hand fell to his sword. He mastered himself with an effort and growled, 'A thousand pieces of gold, Emir, if that's not too high for you.'

Karim managed a haughty smile. 'Very well. Will you name your mark?'

My lord pointed ahead towards the slope of the mountain, where a single pine jutted from the far side of a ridge. The ground between was broken, rocky, but better than the ground around our city; our horses would have an easy time of it. 'To the tree, there.'

I saw the emir scowl, and knew my lord had chosen well. 'Agreed,' Karim answered. 'Shall the qadi call the start?'

'Certainly,' my lord said, 'and he can certify the wager, too.'

'Very well,' Karim said shortly, and gestured for the jurist to come forward.

'Stay close, Little Shadow,' my lord murmured, and rode forward to take his place beside Karim. They conferred briefly with the qadi, the horses blowing uneasily, then separated. An instant later, the qadi gave the signal, and they were off. With a roar, the rest of the hunters surged after them.

I remember little of the ride up the side of the mountain. One moment, it seemed, I was breathing the dust of twenty riders, and in the next my mount had outdistanced them all, and the pine tree loomed suddenly near, just over the top of the next ridge. Nearby a dog was barking hysterically, but I hardly noticed it. I had lost the hunt, the emir and my lord.

I reined in, looking warily about me, and saw, further down the slope, the emir and the rest of the hunt. Karim was dismounted with several others, studying his mare's foreleg. I smiled and let my horse pick its way across the ridge. My lord was waiting beneath the pine tree, his horse dancing angrily beneath him. There were sheep on the hill behind him, and a herder's mongrel darted back and forth between the sheep and the tree, yapping frantically. My lord glared at it and curbed his horse savagely.

'Well? And where is the respected emir?'

'My Lord, I think his horse is lamed.'

My lord smiled, and then forced himself to assume a suitable expression of sorrow. 'A pity for the horse, but that will teach Karim that our mountains breed some things better than the cities.'

The dog, emboldened by the horse's sudden stillness, darted for its ankles. The horse shied, nearly unseating my lord, who swore furiously. 'Damned mongrel, I'll have its hide.'

The dog scurried back a dozen paces and turned to bark again. My lord cursed and spurred his horse after it. The dog broke and ran, almost under the horse's feet. I heard it yelp as one hoof grazed it. It ran limping now, and my lord gave a shout of triumph, lifting his whip.

'No!' A boy, the herder's boy, came darting from the rocks where he'd hidden when my lord appeared. I think he meant only to put himself between my lord and the dog, perhaps to take the whip's blows himself, but his foot slipped on a piece of stone and he fell, almost beneath the horse's forefeet. The horse was battle-trained and struck twice before my lord hauled it away. The boy lay still, his face and chest a mass of blood.

I'd flung myself from my horse before I'd thought, and crouched beside the broken body. Life was gone, but not far; I raised my hands and caught it before it could flee for ever. I looked then at the smashed face, the crushed chest: such a small body, so clearly underfed, would not hold much strength for me to draw on, but I myself was strong enough. Slowly, still holding his spirit prisoned, I eased the bones back into their proper places with hand and mind. I coaxed the torn flesh together, feeling for the pattern of his body. As the wounds closed, I could feel his spirit struggling against me, not to flee, but to return to its proper place. I released it, letting exhaustion sweep through me like a chill.

Then I was aware of my lord's hand on my shoulder, shaking me. 'How dare you?' he hissed. I had never heard him so angry, and even in the daze that follows such a healing, I trembled in fear. On the slope above my lord I saw Karim, holding the bridle of a borrowed horse. He was smiling, and seeing the understanding in that smile, I grew colder still.

'He wouldn't have seen, my lord,' I whispered, but I doubted my own words. Beside me, the herder's boy scrambled to his feet and ran, scattering his sheep. The dog followed, running more easily. There was blood on the ground where he had lain; too late, I scraped dirt over the mark. My lord's face twisted.

'How dare you do this?' he said again, and brought his whip down across my shoulders. Even through the good cloth of my coat, the blow stung, and I choked back a cry of pain. My lord lifted the whip again.

'King Isma'il!' It was the sultan's voice, and I saw Karim and the others now lining the ridge bow low. My lord lowered his whip reluctantly and made his own obeisance. I turned, still on my knees, and prostrated myself in the dust.

'Is something wrong?' Saladin continued. He let his horse pick its own way around the end of the ridge, his eyes fixed on my lord.

'The boy displeased me,' my lord said, through clenched teeth.

Karim laughed softly. 'There was a shepherd's boy, my lord, who fell. The eunuch wished to aid him, but King Isma'il was – displeased.'

'That's –' my lord just stopped himself from giving Karim the lie, '– not what happened. It was a private matter.'

I did not dare lift my head, but I could hear the disapproval in the sultan's voice. 'Surely private matters should be settled privately, King Isma'il?'

'As the sultan pleases.' My lord touched me with the tip of his whip; I looked up into a face set and white with anger. 'Get on your horse, Shunnar,' he said. 'We will return to the palace.'

My lord had never beaten me before, beyond a blow or two when I was careless, but he did that night. I had betrayed a centuries-old secret, he said, and for nothing better than a common shepherd's brat, when a healer's service was the prerogative of kings. I had betrayed him in the city of his enemies. Afterwards, I lay on my stomach on the pallet at the foot of my lord's bed – there was no curtained alcove here – and counted the welted bruises. The cane bit hard; I wished it were in a healer's power to heal himself.

My lord was already asleep, lying alone for once, snoring softly. I lay awake in the darkness, feeling abused and guilty and afraid. Worse than the bruises was my new knowledge: haughty I had known my lord to be, but I had never known before that he was cruel – cruel even to me, who had served him all my days. I hadn't thought when I moved to help the herder's boy; I had known only that if I did not act at once, he would be beyond even the reach of my art. Harithah had trained me always to act quickly, without thinking. That drilled instinct had saved our kings before now, but Karim had seen, and if he understood what I had done . . . I shook myself, wincing as I jarred a healing cut. What could the emir know, even if he had seen? Only that I was a wizard, a healing wizard, and that if I were killed my lord would be defenceless. I shivered again, newly afraid.

I don't know how long I'd lain there, drifting in and out of dreams no different from my waking fears, when I heard the sound of stone on stone. It had come from the centre of the room. I sat up, not even certain if I'd really heard it, and saw a slab of stone rise silently from the floor at the foot of the bed. The faint light of a shuttered lantern spilled across the tiles. I cried out just as the slab wobbled and slid aside. My lord stirred, and suddenly black-robed men were hauling themselves up out of the hole.

'The boy first,' one said, not loudly, and a second man lifted his crossbow. I flung myself backward too late and the bolt took me in the belly. I barely felt it, frantic to reach my lord. He was on his feet now, naked, sword in hand to face his enemy. The second assassin was jerking at the handle of his bow; a knife gleamed in the first man's hand. Then something struck me in the ribs, and it was as though the lantern had been blown out.

When I knew myself again, I was lying on a steep hill of black glass. Above me was a cold sky and the sickle moon, their sickly light puddled on the glass around me. My skin was grey in that light. The scholars and reciters of traditions do not know this place, but Harithah had told me of it; the hill that leads to death. She had stood on its brink, she told me, and caught her lord's soul before it could slide beyond her reach. But there was no one to catch me. I shivered, expecting to fall, and realized then that my hands were hurting me, a stabbing pain like nothing I'd ever known before. I looked up and saw I clutched two tufts of grass, holding myself motionless against the hill. Each blade was like the blade of a knife, and blood ran like ink across my skin. Already the first threads of it had reached my elbows; I sobbed aloud with the pain of it, but I did not let go. If I could hold, if I could hold, I could somehow draw myself up again, back to the world of the living, away from death . . .

Shunnar! It was not a voice, properly, but words within my mind, and in the same instant there was a cold weight on my ankle. *My hands*, I screamed, and felt the knife blades against my very bones. The cold grip tightened and I felt a second chill hand brush past my other foot. With an effort I turned my head, and saw my lord lying further down the slope, struggling to grasp me more securely. Even as I recognized him I felt his hand slip a little; my lord felt it, too, and lay still.

Little Shadow, he called again, *help me*.

I cannot, I answered, and sobbed again at the agony in my hands.

You are a wizard, my lord said, and I felt him reach again for me. His hand slipped further and he stopped. *Save me, Little Shadow, and I'll help you*.

How? I cried . My own blood smeared my face, warm and sticky, my strength draining with it, running away down my arms.

Reach your foot to me, my lord said, *let me climb past you. When I reach the top, I'll pull you up*.

I hesitated, not quite believing in his promises, and my lord lunged for me again, as though he'd hoped to catch me off guard. I evaded his grasp by instinct alone. He was lying, I knew it then with a certainty colder than his touch. He would use my body, my power, as his ladder, and not turn back for me. I knew in the same instant I could not hold him and save myself. I had served him since I was a child, not with love perhaps, but with loyalty. Yet he had beaten me and now he would repay me with a lie. He was not worth even my death. With a final effort, I twisted myself free of his hold. He called my name as he fell.

I lay there for a long moment, gathering strength. I had betrayed my lord, though inadvertently, and caused his death when he would have betrayed me, and yet I was – not dead. With his weight gone, the pain in my hands was almost bearable; inch by inch, I drew myself up the gleaming hill.

I floated then in my lord's bedchamber, unseen by the four assassins crouched over the newly broken strongbox. A body – *my* body – lay sprawled across the foot of the bed, a crossbow's bolts buried in its chest and stomach. Automatically I reached to touch those wounds, to heal them, and felt the barrier, cold as iron, that warned me away. A healer cannot heal himself.

That left me only one choice, and had I been able I would have laughed at the irony of it all. My lord – my lord's body lay beside the bed, knife wounds in his chest and throat. Expertly, easily, I reached for them, brought the flesh together as it should be. I had no pattern this time, but I knew that body too well to make any foolish errors. The gaping wounds closed. I took a deep breath and let my self slide into the empty shell. For an instant it was like putting on a stranger's clothes, ill-fitting, loose in places, and too tight, binding in others, and then he – I – lived.

I opened my eyes very slowly, aware for the first time of a rhythmic pounding at the door and Jafar's voice shouting hoarsely for his brother to let him in. The assassins heard it too, to judge by their glances at the door, but the bar was strong, and held. They went back to their looting of my lord's treasures.

Silently, obeying what this body already knew, I let my hand slide across the tiles until it curled around the hilt of my lord's sword. I braced myself, and then, with a shout, leaped to the attack. The assassins were not unnaturally surprised to see the body of a man they'd slain attacking them, and my lord was a noted soldier. I had gutted two before they really knew what had happened; I killed the third and fourth almost as easily. I stood for a long moment, staring at the bodies, and then at my hands – his hands, broader than mine, the wrists marked with coarse hairs – before I could bring myself to unbar the door.

Jafar was at the head of the crowd. He cried out when he saw me, and sagged against the doorframe. Behind him

I could see more of our nobles, and the pale face of
Karim. Beneath the careful mask of shock, I could feel his
furious disappointment. Then the crowd parted and the
sultan himself strode through. I was suddenly aware of my
nakedness, and dropped my hand to hide it. Hastily, Jafar
handed me his outer robe, and I wrapped it around
myself.

'What is this?' the sultan asked.

I could hear, in his voice, the thought that my lord –
that *I* was dangerous; I could feel in my lord's body an
animal strength I had not known before. Perhaps it was
just the ease with which my lord's body had killed the
assassins that made me bold, but I reached out to catch
the sultan in the web of my power. The look in his eyes,
calm, appraising, even curious, made me stop. That was
my lord's way; it need not be my own.

'I have been attacked while under your protection,' I
said instead. 'I ask for justice.'

Saladin nodded slowly, his eyes sweeping across the
room. 'You shall have justice,' he agreed, then bent his
gaze on me. He suspected, I realized suddenly, and fought
back the urge to use my power to conceal what had
happened. 'I will send for you, King Isma'il, to tell me
what transpired here.'

I bowed, and tried to make the gesture my lord's. 'As
the sultan wishes.'

Slaves and servants and my lord's soldiers crowded into
the room, and Jafar with them. The chief eunuch, still
murmuring broken words of fear and relief, brought my
my lord's clothes. He had been my superior in the
household; it was all I could do not to bow to him in
thanks. I saw his eyes flicker towards the soldiers bundling
my body in one of the assassin's cloaks, and realized with
a shock that he grieved for me. I fumbled into the clothes,
finer than any I had worn, and turned to face Jafar. My
lord would have killed him for his carelessness, and he
knew it.

'Isma'il, I—' He stopped abruptly, mastering his fear. 'I
do not understand how they passed my guards.'

I pointed to the centre of the room and the displaced stone.

Jafar's breath hissed between his teeth. 'A tunnel ... Isma'il, I swear, I knew nothing of this—'

'Be silent, Jafar!' The harsh shout startled me: I had underestimated my lord's body's strength. I mastered myself hastily and went on. 'I know who is responsible for this, and I will see him punished.'

Jafar bowed shakily, not knowing certainly whether he'd been spared. I watched him from under my lashes, wondering if I should say more.

'King Isma'il.'

I turned almost without hesitation, to face a bowing stranger, a eunuch of the sultan's household. 'Well?'

'The sultan will see you now.'

Despite the silken courtesy, it was an order. I barely stopped myself from bowing to him. 'Very well.'

The eunuch brought me to a section of the palace I had not visited before, to an antechamber hung with tapestries of green and gold, verses from the Qur'an. Guards waited beside the far door, ceremonial spears in their left hands, right hands on the hilts of their swords. Their eyes flickered over me, looking for the sword I had not even missed. They saw I was unarmed, and relaxed slightly.

'The king Isma'il,' the eunuch said, and gestured, bowing, for me to enter.

Saladin sat alone in the centre of the room, very straight-backed among the gold-embroidered cushions. Half a dozen lamps were lit, filling the room with light, but the sultan's face was half in shadow. I bowed as I had seen my lord bow. At the sultan's nod, the eunuch placed a cushion on the floor behind me, and withdrew.

'Sit, my lord,' Saladin said softly.

I did as I was told, the sultan watching me with hooded eyes. I could not read his thoughts in his face, and did not dare try more.

'You've demanded justice,' Saladin said at last. 'For whom?'

'For myself,' I answered, and some impulse made me add, 'and for Shunnar.'

'For the boy?' Saladin said, still softly. 'What was he to you?'

I choked on my answer. I knew I should speak as my lord would have spoken, shrug and say I had been nothing, a catamite, but it was still myself that was under discussion. For my own pride's sake, I would not say it. 'A servant,' I said, finally, 'and a good one.'

The sultan nodded twice, thoughtfully, as though I had been far more eloquent. He knew what had happened, or at least he guessed much of it, I thought, and felt myself grow cold, I tensed, and felt my power gathering within me, fed by my lord's great strength. If he speaks again, I thought, if he censures or accuses, I will have to strike.

Saladin smiled. 'And who was behind this attack?'

My mouth fell open; after an instant I closed it, lifting my hand to my lips to conceal an incredulous smile. My fingers touched hair instead, and I tugged at my lord's beard to hide my surprise. 'Karim, my lord,' I answered. 'It was Karim.'

'Do you have proof of this?' Saladin asked, still smiling faintly. Whatever he knew, or suspected, I realized then, he would not accuse me.

'No, my lord,' I answered, 'but you will find it.'

The sultan clapped his hands sharply, twice, and the eunuch returned, bowing. Saladin murmured to him, speaking too softly for me to hear the words; the eunuch bowed again and vanished.

'If there is proof,' Saladin said, 'it will be found.' He was silent for a moment, staring at me as though he would weigh my very soul. 'And you,' he said at last, 'what do you wish from all of this?'

I hesitated, choosing my words with care. 'I ask no more than an alliance with you, my lord. I would wish for the right to levy toll at the fortress-pass, as has traditionally been the right of the kings of Alexandria.'

The sultan nodded slowly. 'These things can be done.'

In the end, it was as Saladin had promised. The proof

against Karim was overwhelming – he had made no effort to hide it, so sure had he been of his agents' success. I saw him die, and took a certain pleasure in it. A week later I swore to an alliance with the sultan, receiving in return his charter to tax the passes – I could do no less for my lord, having failed him in more important things – and we set out on the long journey home. Shunnar, the Little Shadow, I buried in Damascus. I am Isma'il – the king who came back from Damascus.

WILLIAM R. FORSTCHEN

The Truthsayer

Know that I, Ali, was the truthsayer of my lord
Muhammad, Shah of Shahs, ruler of Khwarazm, greatest
of all the realms of Islam. Khwarazm, which stretched
from the Indus to the Tigris, from the turquoise blue of
the ocean to the frozen north, was a realm of a thousand
cities, with bejewelled wonders such as Bokhara, Merv
and Samarkand. All are gone now, and are but dust and
tear-stained memories. You, who are blessed by the
Prophet, doubt not my words, for they are truth.

I lived through the fall of an empire, and fled with my
lord Muhammad Shah across the endless stretch of the
burning sand, in search of refuge where no refuge could
be found.

And it is I alone who met my lord Subotai, commander
of the tumans of the guard, first among first, Orkhon and
eagle to Ghenghis Kha Khan, shaker of the world. Listen
now as I tell how I met Subotai of the twenty thousand
hunters and thus lost the truth for ever, and did gain my
revenge as well . . .

The envoy had come in the morning, before the scarlet of
the sun had washed the curtain of darkness aside and
brought the mullahs to cry from the thousand minarets of
Samarkand. And I was thus summoned out of my hidden
chambers to perform my appointed task.

'Ali,' my lord Muhammad cried, even before I had
pressed my forehead to the turquoise floor of his audience
chamber, 'is what this man speaks the truth?'

Since that terrible first day of the war my lord Muhammad had not summoned me, for he knew what was hidden behind my eyes. But his fear at last had driven him to use my powers once again.

Still short of breath from having run from the far end of the palace in answer to Muhammad's summons, I rose to my feet. I turned to the corner of the room where he pointed, and thus for the first time beheld one of the warriors who had come out of hell to destroy the heart of Islam. A Mongol, swordless but still in fighting armour, stood before me.

'Ask him,' my lord cried.

'Draw away from us,' I said softly. And the warriors who surrounded the Mongol looked to Maluk, commander of the bodyguard, who nodded in agreement. The men drew back and some whispered darkly about magicians and consort of the jinn and turned their faces away from me in fear. Though I was young, and short of stature from stunted growth, they feared me far more than the foul-smelling warrior who looked down at me with contempt.

'The truthsayer will tell us,' I heard them whisper, but their words I ignored, for already I had turned my thoughts in preparation.

The Mongol smelled of sweat, horse and leather – but there was no smell of fear. His dark, oval features were calm, and his almond-coloured eyes regarded me with contempt.

'Do you speak our tongue?' I asked softly, while opening my inner self to the task appointed unto me. A task that I was born to; a task that, since my birth eighteen years before, I had been trained to. For I was a truthsayer, and the last of my kind.

Born in the high Pamirs, I am a truthsayer, as was my sire and his sire before him unto fifty generations. It is said by some that the power of delving for the truth in men was given to our family by Allah as a blessing to the founder of our line. Others say that it was the curse of a jinni that did this thing to my clan. Be it blessing or curse we had the power always to see the truth in other men.

For know you that when a man speaks, his soul shines forth in all the colours of the rainbow. And I who was trained like my grandsires before me can see the light within, and know if the man speaks the truth or not.

And those of us who truly hold the power could as well project our truth into the hearts of others, so that they might believe our every word and then act upon it as if it were their own thought. But there was a price to this gift, this magic, if you should call it that. For I was for ever bound to tell the truth – or for ever after would I be one condemned.

And I am the last of my kind, for all of my people are gone now. But as the setting of the sun comes after the rising, so that must be told in its own time and not before.

I gazed upon the Mongol, and as our eyes locked, I knew that he somehow sensed the power given unto me. Then he spoke.

'I come as an envoy from my mighty chief, Ghenghis Kha Khan,' the Mongol said, his voice echoing in the audience chamber. 'For it is his wish that you submit to him. For it is his command that you,' and he looked away from me and turned his gaze upon my lord, 'Muhammad Shah shall come to the tent of Ghenghis and there pass between the fires of purification to lay your sword on the ground. If you do so, your life and the lives of your people shall be spared.'

'That I shall never do. He'll kill me!' my lord Muhammad shrieked.

The Mongol smiled as if he had heard the voice of a child.

'Last year my lord Ghenghis sent unto you envoys to seek a treaty of trade. And you insulted them, calling them barbarians out of the east, then burned their beards and slew their leader.

'Then my lord Ghenghis sent yet another envoy, and you slew him as well, claiming that to hunt us would be easy sport if we ever dared to confront you.

'Then know this, Muhammad Shah, for we have come

to seek judgement; and who now is hunting whom? We have invaded your realm from three directions, and you have not stopped us. Know that we have defeated your armies and even your mightest of generals, in revenge for your crimes. And like a coward, you fled behind the walls of Samarkand. But all this we have done only for a beginning.'

He stopped for a moment and gazed around the court, which listened in fearful silence as if the angel of death had come to announce who was to be chosen.

'Know that this is only a beginning,' the Mongol continued. 'For if you refuse us, oh Shah, then every man, every woman, every child, shall be condemned. We shall fight without mercy, we shall level your cities, we shall make your mosques into stables for our horses, we shall turn your fields back to deserts, and your homes to dust.

'To you, oh Shah of this accursed race, my lord Ghenghis, master of the world, has turned his special hate, his special contempt.

'If you refuse to submit here and now, my lord Ghenghis shall call upon Subotai and the tumans of his most precious guard.'

Many of the court whispered this new name fearfully, and thus I heard it spoken for the first time.

'My lord Subotai is the most exalted of the Orkhons, the hunting eagles of Ghenghis. Know that Subotai commands the two tumans of the guard, the twenty thousand of Ghenghis which are the first among first. And those twenty thousand shall be assigned a single task. They shall have the honour of the Hunt of Emperors.

'They shall turn aside from all other tasks, they shall not return until either they are dead or you are dead, for they shall live for nothing else but your extinction. Once Subotai is loosened to kill a king, nothing else exists for him. And the warrior who comes to the tent of my lord Subotai carrying your head shall receive his weight in gold. Twice in our wars has my lord Ghenghis declared a Hunt of Emperors. Twice has the gold been measured out. And a third time it shall be measured, if you do not submit.

'And now I ask you do you submit, oh Shah, to the will, the wrath of Ghenghis Kha Khan? If you refuse, sleep not, oh Shah, for the guard by your bed could be of us. Lie not with a woman, for 'neath her pillow could be a blade, for she might be of us. Walk not by the moonlight, or 'neath the blaze of the midday sun, for always there shall be death at your side. Look always to the horizon, for there you shall see the horsetail standard of Subotai, for ever hunting you until your headless corpse is laid in its grave.'

Before I could speak, my lord cried out with incoherent rage.

'Slay him!' he cried.

The Mongol did not flinch but merely smiled with contempt as the guards pushed me aside and spilled the scarlet life of the warrior upon the cool turquoise of the palace floor.

Trembling, I went to the throne and knelt by the feet of my lord.

As a truthsayer I had watched the Mongol, and even as he spoke I had probed within. I had seen the crystalline light of his truth, had watched it shimmer through his every word. For to the eyes of a truthsayer, words take upon them not just a sound, but a colour as well. Truth stands pure, like polished silver, while lies shine forth with the colouring of brass. And in each word, as well, there is shaped within it the colours of love, of hate, of greed and of joy.

Not only had the warrior spoken the truth, but he had spoken it with conviction and firm belief, in the same way you or I would claim that the sun would appear in the east at its appointed hour.

'It was the truth, my lord,' I whispered. 'This was not bravado, nor idle boast. Even as he spoke I could see the confidence in him, as if such things had been done before with ease. That man spoke the truth, on that I swear.'

Muhammad sank back upon the throne and was silent. I rose to stand by his side, and as I looked into his eyes I could see his fear.

His eyes met mine and my knowledge of his fear was revealed. With a backhanded blow, he knocked me to the ground, and rising, he swept out of the room.

Soon all were gone except for Maluk, who came to my side, helped me to my feet, and wiped the blood from my face.

'You have sworn upon your sword to serve him,' I whispered, 'and I upon the lives of my family. I shall serve him faithfully, for a truthsayer cannot break his word or lie.'

'And yet,' Maluk observed, 'did he keep his bond to you and your family?'

'That is not for me to discuss,' I whispered.

Thus started the long ride of Muhammad, famed in the chronicles as the Hunt of a Thousand Leagues. Before the light of the sun had yet kissed the tallest minaret, Muhammad fled Samarkand, and we of his court followed him into the desert. From the first prayer of morning until the high heat of noonday we rode hard, and then took shelter until the waning of the sun. Then, if there was moonlight, we rode through the cool of night, until again we stopped for but a brief rest before the hour of dawn and yet another day.

Muhammad claimed that he was bent on visiting his cities to rally their garrisons. He also claimed that by moving his ruse would deceive the Mongols as to our plans, for he believed that through sorcery Ghenghis knew where he was at all times. Thus by separating himself from his main army, he would confuse the Mongols, who would know not where our true strength was hidden.

No one made comment to this even as we drew further to the south, away from the seat of war. One did not need to be a truthsayer to see the truth behind his lies.

Whenever Muhammad saw me looking at him he would turn away, for he knew that I would see the fear in his heart and the lie that he lived. But I did not reveal such things to others, for I had sworn to serve him, in spite of what he had done unto me.

But he did use me nevertheless to interrogate each of his courtiers as to their loyalty – and here was another of his great failings in the use of a truthsayer. For I and those before me had served in many of the great courts, from the land of the Franks to the distant people of Ch'in. But our power was in our very secrecy.

The Greeks keep their secret of the fire that burns on water. Legend has it that only two men in the entire realm of the Byzantines know the true workings of the alchemy. So too a wise ruler never revealed that he had a truthsayer in his ranks, but kept him well hidden in the background of court, and then would consult him in private as to the truth or lies of what those around him said. Thus in most lands, not one in ten thousand knew of our existence.

But Muhammad had paraded me as he would a prize captive, showing me off to his courtiers, and in the showing implying that they lied and I was needed. Foolish man, so foolish, but I had made vow to serve him. And when word was known that I was to question those in our party, more than one slipped away in the night.

On the twelfth day of our journey a courier on a lathered horse came up to us, swaying with exhaustion, and handed a dispatch to Muhammad.

Stopping, he read the message, then let it drop to the dust of the road.

Turning, Muhammad rode on. And as the courier passed through the ranks, we soon knew.

Samarkand had fallen to the storm of the Mongols and all were dead or slave. The mightiest citadel of our empire had collapsed in less than a week.

And there was darker news, as well. The courier had outraced a column of horsemen earlier in the day in order to reach us. The column was led by a horsetail standard. The Mongols were less than the turning of an hourglass behind.

A guard trailing to our rear saw them first, and came galloping across the open fields of waist-high grass, waving his scimitar in the afternoon sun.

Maluk, sensing what was the report, detailed his men even as the guard came within shouting distance.

'The Mongols,' he cried against the rising wind, 'the Mongols are riding over the ridge behind us!'

Maluk swung out a line of fifty horsemen in open formation to form a screen to the rear. My lord Muhammad, who was riding at the front of our column, slowed his horse and then stopped. That which he had feared since the confrontation with the Mongol envoy was now reaching out, and like many who have death at their shoulder, Muhammad's curiosity about the darkness made him stop to look.

Turning his horse, he cantered back down the line, and we as his court were compelled to follow.

An arrow's flight ahead of us, the advance guard moved back up the road from which we came, acting as a screen, while behind us our main body of half a thousand men swung out into battle formation.

My lord reached the ridge and stopped, his hands hanging limp by his side. Riding on a small gelding, I came up behind my lord and watched in silence.

Across the far side of the valley, a league away, we saw them – each detachment moving in slow, deliberate fashion.

'Two units of a hundred,' Maluk said softly.

'Is that them? Is that Subotai?' Muhammad asked.

'I cannot say. See, there is a standard to the fore, but from here I cannot see if it is the seven horsetails, the insignia of Subotai.'

'Let us slay them,' Muhammad said grimly.

'My lord, they want us to see them, and to come back and attack them. Beyond that next ridge there may be a thousand, ten thousand, already ranging out of our flank.'

Muhammad looked not at Maluk but kept his gaze upon the Mongols; and like a hare that gazes into the eyes of the cobra, he was already lost to the venomous jaws.

'Allah is great!' Muhammad cried. And unsheathing

his scimitar he started down the slope towards the enemy formations, which were deploying as if to receive an attack.

'Stay to the rear with me,' Maluk roared, looking in my direction. 'In a few moments that is where we will be needed.'

My lord, with most of his guards swinging out to either side, soon reached the bottom of the valley and started up the other slope. And it was at that moment that He Who is Inscrutable decreed that the drama would not end here, for my lord's horse stumbled into a hidden ditch and fell. The charge went forward around him, pursuing the Mongols who had broken and were now running away.

The handful of guards that Maluk had held back along with the courtiers came to our lord's side even as he crawled out of the ditch, shaken but unhurt.

And suddenly there was a high-pitched whistling that rumbled across the sky. From beyond the ridge, a shadow rose up to the heavens.

The flight of whistling arrows darkened the heavens, converged, and then fell into the midst of our attacking line with a deathlike rattle that swept hundreds out of their saddles and into the hands of Allah. Along the ridge above us Mongols by the thousand appeared, sweeping outward like a crashing wave, with a roar that shook the heavens.

'It is a full tuman,' Maluk cried. 'There, there is the standard of Subotai!' and he pointed to the centre of the line which loomed above us.

With a cry, he galloped up to Muhammad's side. Jumping from his mount, he pushed my lord into the saddle and slapped the horse across the flank to send the Lion of Islam galloping away.

The courtiers were already fleeing, with the few remaining guards swinging in behind them. I saw Maluk draw out his scimitar and face towards the advancing host.

Kicking my horse forward, I came up to Maluk's side.

Leaping on to my mount, he wrapped one arm around me and away we dashed, racing before the gaping jaws of doom.

Looking back on that stricken field, I saw what was left of our men waver and then start to fall back, but already the pincers of death were descending from either side of the ridge. There was another rushing roar as thousands of bows snapped as one. The swarm of arrows arched up, paused, and then rushed down; our men disappeared 'neath the avalanche of steel-tipped shafts.

'It is but a few leagues to the next post station and fresh mounts,' Mulak cried. 'Pray that they have not posted flankers far out to forward, or we are indeed lost.'

Without concern for the rest of us Muhammad was already far ahead. As Mulak and I crested the ridge which Muhammad had charged down but moments before, we paused for a moment to let our horse regain its wind.

The five hundred guards were dead, and already the tuman was sweeping to the bottom of the valley. They rolled forward like an irresistible storm which stretched from horizon to horizon.

A column of fire suddenly blazed upward from where the standard of Subotai stood and then burst in the sky with a roll of thunder. I had once seen such a thing when a magician from Ch'in had performed at my lord's court, but it still struck me with terror.

'They use such sky thunder as signals,' Maluk cried. 'They must know that they have met the guard of the Shah.' Even as he spoke, ten thousand voices gave an exalted cry that made me cower as if struck by the force of the northern wind.

The host surged forward and we turned to race in front of them.

Our horses were full bodied and swifter in the short run than the small but sturdy ponies of the Mongols. We reached the royal post station just behind our lord, who was already remounting as the rest of his court came galloping in.

Within minutes I was upon a fresh horse riding by

Maluk's side; and falling in with our lord, we galloped out of the post station, trailed by a dozen guards and those few others who had found remounts.

From horizon to horizon behind us, we could see the rolling dust of the Mongol's unstoppable advance.

By day we marked them on the far horizon by the clouds of dust. By night, their campfires reddened the sky behind us.

Ever southward we ran, day after relentless day, as the sun rose yet higher in the sky.

There was no stop, no rest for us, only a world of fear – fear as we wondered where the second tuman hid, and why it had not yet revealed itself. Fear as each of us worried that our mount might fail and thus leave us to fall behind into the open jaws of death.

And that fear marked my lord Muhammad so that his hair was soon streaked with grey and his red-rimmed eyes retreated into a skull-like face of terror. And all of this I marked in my heart.

Muhammad spoke of going into the mountains to rally our defence, and then a courier came down from those mountains and told us that Merv had been taken. A million prisoners had surrendered when six tumans gained the walls. That million had been driven out into the plains beyond the city and commanded to bind each other, then stand in rows of a hundred. A single tuman had then done the work of slaughter, one man to each hundred.

The courier cried that a pyramid of a million skulls had then been built as a monument to victory.

We turned from the mountains of death and moved instead to the high plateau of ancient Persia. Through Isfahan we rode, and there an army awaited my lord. Some thought that he would stand here and fight, but instead he commanded the army to ride back east and meet Subotai while he continued on to Baghdad.

To Baghdad, which was a city outside our realm, but Muhammad, Shah of Shahs, Lion of Islam and Emperor did not speak of that, and said instead that he was going to rally new armies that would come to the aid of Khwarazm.

It was a hot evening of sullen heavy air as we approached the river that marked the end of Muhammad's realm. For months we had been hunted, but now he felt arrogant and spoke loudly of raising a new army in the realm of the caliph which he would lead back to smite the unbelievers, but his boast was cut in mid-sentence by the flight of an arrow, which tore out the throat of a guard who had stopped.

The air hummed with feathered death as half a hundred Mongols charged out from a ravine to our left, while a column of fire rose up behind them and burst with a thunderclap roar.

'It must be the second tuman,' Maluk cried, galloping his horse forward to come up to Muhammad's side.

'So close to safety,' Muhammad shrieked, 'so close.'

And he was right, but it was useless to lament. The second tuman which the envoy had promised us had swept to the north and finally arrived in front of us. We were in the net.

Muhammed turned away and fled back into the cauldron of death, and the arrows of our tormentors whistled in our ears.

Hard we rode, harder than I ever imagined human flesh could bear. Learning from the Mongols, we had fresh remounts travelling with us, so that as soon as a horse faltered he was cast aside and a fresh mount was taken. Gradually we outdistanced them, but this was merely a physical thing, for in my lord's mind they were always an arrow's flight behind.

We crossed back through the high gates of Asia and came down into the Caspian plain. To the front of us would soon be the inland sea. My lord considered going back east, but we were met by reports that there was nothing to go back to. What had once been cities were now desert. What had once been thriving realms were now graveyards, for Ghenghis Kha Khan hunted without mercy. Khwarazm was dead, and the hunting of us had now crossed a thousand leagues of death. The stench of corruption hovered in the air; Khwarazm was a charnel house with tens of millions dead. Dead because my lord had once slain an ambassador for sport, and would not then face the truth of his actions.

The dead followed us, hovered over us, I could sense the millions who watched and waited. And the oppression of their presence carved into the soul of Muhammad who knew that not even death now would be a release.

The war was now far away by the Indus but still the twenty thousand huntsmen followed us whichever way we turned, and gradually they closed in the circle for the kill.

We came at last to a small fortress a day's ride from that inland sea, called by some the Caspian. The fortress had been bypassed in the first sweep and thus its walls were still intact.

My lord came to the gate, and announcing his presence, was shown in by the garrison commander who looked at us with barely concealed terror. All knew that Muhammad Shah had death riding upon his cape and Subotai, who was the bringer of that death, was galloping at our heels.

My lord, as was his right, led the people of the town in their prayers. Then, calling Mulak, he retired to a small room by the fortress gate.

I waited outside with the few loyal guards while the sky darkened to indigo and star-studded splendour. Finally, as the crescent moon sank in the west, Mulak stepped out of the shadows.

'I leave, my friend,' he whispered, crouching by my side.

'Then I had best get my horse to ride with you.'

'No,' and he laughed softly, but the laugh was grim, distant, as if he was a man who had seen his fate, which is called by some their kismet.

'I am to take the guards and leave at once, wearing the cloak of the Shah. Hide yourself, for Subotai shall be here

259

at dawn. Hide yourself and let the storm pass, for it is rumoured that even the Mongols are relenting and suffering some to live again.'

'Why do you wear the Shah's cloak?' I asked.

'For it is his wish that the people of this doomed town believe that I am the Shah. As I leave with fanfare though the eastern gate, Muhammad shall slip over the opposite wall and make for the sea. I am the decoy to lead Subotai astray.'

'Then I shall go with you. For surely he commands it of me as well.'

'He did,' Mulak whispered. 'His words were that I should take the accursed one who stares at him with truth in his eyes and make sure that he falls. Those were his words.'

And I could tell they were true and I knew why. For a man who leads a nation to doom cannot bear to know the truth of what he is and what he has let happen. He knew that I understood the real reason for everything that he had done. He had need of me in our long ride, but he came to hate me more and more with each passing day, for I alone knew all the truth.

'But I must go,' I announced and started to rise to my feet.

'Forgive me, my little friend,' Mulak whispered, and I never saw the mailed fist that struck me, or felt the gentle hands that carried me to a back alley and hid me away.

I awoke to the braying of trumpets and cries of fear. It was already dawn and all around me there was madness.

Gaining my feet I wandered out of the alley to be nearly trampled by a rush of men moving towards the city wall.

'Down!'

Men dived into doorways and flattened against walls. It was as if a shadow had passed over us. Then there came the familiar rattling hail of arm-length shafts. Anyone in the open was swept away.

'Forward!'

I followed the men in their rush and mounted the stairs to the battlement.

There was another cry; another volley swept over us. Continuing on, I pressed to the wall above the gate and there I saw what we had feared for so long.

The seven-horsetail standard was before me, while drawn up in serried ranks were ten thousand, while yet ten thousand more rode behind them encircling the city to the north. A deep rolling thunder echoed from the hills as the great drums which signalled the attack beat out their tempo of death.

Still on horseback, the massed archers raised up their bows yet again and unleashed another flight that darkened the sky.

Some of the guards looked at me and, not knowing who I was, mumbled suspiciously. Then one who had served in the court at Samarkand told them that I was the truthsayer of Muhammad. Many of them now cursed me and my master for bringing death to them, but their attention was turned back to outside the wall, for a host of a thousand had started its advance. The Mongols would not wait for siege; they had come to storm a city. I, and many who stood by me, knew that once started, such a host could not be stopped. Some of the soldiers fell to their knees and, facing towards the south-west, called out their submission to the will of Allah.

As the Mongols advanced, four units of a thousand came in on the flanks and swept the walls with roaring volleys of fire arrows. Any who dared to show himself was doomed, and the dead toppled from the wall like gnats caught in an open flame. Never had there been such precision to war, never such grim certainty of success and it filled all of us with dread. For men such as these had destroyed an empire, and we were but an annoying speck to be pushed aside and crushed.

The advancing thousand broke into a charge and swept forward. The first rank coming neath the wall reined in under its shelter. The next rank, dragging ladders, swung in as well and raised their ladders up. Rank after rank now swept forward, leaping from their mounts to scurry up the wall, while overhead the sky was blackened with arrows that blotted out the sun.

As the first wave swept over the wall, there came from them a terrible shriek of triumph that roared like thunder and tore into one's heart like icy steel. The city behind me was already in flames, while before me came death.

But Allah had not yet willed it so, and even as I drew my small scimitar and rushed blindly forward to die, an arrow struck me, knocking me from the wall. And as I fell, I prayed that this was but my first step towards Paradise.

'Truthsayer.'

The voice was harsh, guttural, and I feared that having been judged wanting, a demon had been sent to fetch me into damnation.

'Truthsayer,' and I was roughly shaken.

My eyes focused and all that I could see at first was a tall standard, from which hung seven horsetails.

A face came into view and my head cleared.

'Are you Muhammad's truthsayer?' And, shaken again, I was dragged to my feet.

Knocked out twice in less than a day, my thoughts were clouded, and I could but mumble.

'Drink!'

Someone forced open my mouth and a hot scalding fluid seared my throat. Coughing, I came fully awake. My side was numb and, looking at my right shoulder, I saw a broken shaft sticking out of it – I thought for a moment that I would faint.

'Don't look at it,' the voice commanded. 'Now answer me, are you the truthsayer of Muhammad?'

I nodded in reply.

'Spare him,' the voice commanded. 'Treat him and bring him to me when he is ready.'

Firm but gentle hands rested on my shoulders. Looking up, I saw the face of a man from Ch'in gazing down at me.

'I am the healer to Subotai,' the man said softly. 'You are safe with me now.'

I looked back at the one who had questioned me, but already the man had remounted and was riding away.

'Yes, that was he. And you are now his prisoner.'

It had hurt, but I bore the pain without complaint as the healer drew the barbed point from my flesh. Fate had slowed the shaft so that it had not penetrated far, nor did it nick a bone and thus cripple me. The physician bound my wound, and in less than the turning of an hourglass I was led through the burning city, blackened with smoke and choked with the dead and dying.

The horsetail standard was planted on a low hill outside the gate, and Subotai sat mounted by its side. He was hard, harder than any man I have ever seen. At his command twenty thousand would rush to their death, and such a command he would not hesitate to give. At the flicker of his finger a city of a million could be razed, and he had done such a thing without a moment of remorse.

'You are the truthsayer?' he asked, speaking haltingly as he searched for the right words in my tongue.

'Yes,' I replied, struggling to mask my fear.

'We have not found the body of Muhammad within these walls. Did he die here or did he flee?'

'I do not know if he is dead within this city.'

Subotai looked to the chieftains that ringed him and there was a brief murmur of comments.

'As I understand such things, you as a truthsayer are sworn to speak clearly. Is that not so?' the physician asked in a kind voice that nevertheless spun out a web of entrapment.

'Yes, that is the truth.'

'Then it should be easy to surmise where your lord Muhammad is,' Subotai replied coldly.

'I can refuse to speak,' I cried defiantly.

'Little man,' the physician replied, 'by the very command for you to speak the truth, we can compel you to speak. I need but simply ask a question and say that if it is

263

true you should speak, if it is not true you should be silent. I have heard of truthsayers and I have often thought of the challenge it would be to entrap one.'

His words cut me, for I knew that in such logic there was no escape for me.

Subotai gazed at me in silence, as if appraising a horse, or a weapon which he was about to grasp.

'It is strange,' he said quietly. 'A man who can speak but the truth, and can find the truth in the hearts of others. Did your lord love you for your truth?'

I could not lie.

'No, he hated me, as do most men when they face one who will not lie and can see the lie in their own hearts.'

Subotai nodded and smiled.

'I know the fault in my own heart and thus I can look at you without fear. Can you look into your own heart without that fear?'

Such a statement from the commander of the infidel host took me aback, but I answered not.

'Did you know what Muhammad planned to do?'

'I did not hear my lord give his plans,' I replied, and Subotai's gaze followed me as if he was the cat and I his prey.

'Then did you hear another speak of what your lord planned?'

I answered not.

'If you heard nothing, then answer not,' the healer whispered.

I groaned and the words escaped.

'I know where he planned to go.'

'We have heard a report,' Subotai replied, 'that your lord was seen to flee in the middle of the night, going out the eastern gate. I thought that might be a ruse, and that he remained hidden in the town, or went some other way.

'Therefore, truthsayer, do you know if it was the Shah who fled eastward with his guards?'

I had sworn, I had sworn oath to Muhammad never to betray him. The men who surrounded me were my enemies. They had slaughtered my people by the millions, had laid waste to our entire world, and now their hunt was at its climax. There was only the revenge now, only the revenge, and I started to weave my spell, raising its power so that when next I spoke I would project full belief into another man's heart, so that he would not for one instant doubt my words, even as I condemned myself and my trust.

'Was that the Shah who rode to the east?' Subotai demanded.

I was silent, gathering my strength for the moment of my own sacrifice and fulfilment.

'Answer me, truthsayer!' Subotai shouted.

'Yes!' I screamed. 'Yes, it was the Shah who rode to the east!' And even as I cried out my lie, I turned all my powers of magic to Subotai's mind, making him to believe my words. And believe them he did, even as I condemned myself for ever, and lost the true power of the truthsayer in the lying. But I had my revenge, as well.

Turning, I staggered away, and the physician put his arms about me.

'You have your answer, my lord,' the physician cried. 'Now let him live, he can be of use. I shall tend to him.'

I heard a mounting thunder and thought it was the blood rushing in my ears, but it was instead the tumans moving to the east in pursuit.

I placed my hands over my eyes to shield them from the light, and I felt as if my head was about to burst asunder. I, who was once a truthsayer, had broken covenant to keep a covenant. I had lied.

They came back that evening and his visage was grim. He knew what I had done. I expected death by his sword; I had prayed to Allah for my release, but now I was accursed, a truthsayer who had lied – Allah would not release me.

Commanded to ride by Subotai's side, I galloped with him westward through the moonlit night. Each step of the horse was an agony to me, but I did not cry out in the presence of my enemies.

Finally, with the coming of dawn, we could smell the damp breeze of the sea and came to the crest of a hill. With one voice the Mongols cried out, and as they drew scimitars their roar of triumph was like thunder tearing across the skies. Even as they galloped into the village, the single remaining boat in the town put out to sea. The horsemen drove through the village. Some in their fury plunged into the sea, driving their horses forward until both beast and man disappeared beneath the waves.

I could see him. I could see for one last time my lord Muhammad, Shah of Shahs, the Lion of Islam, Emperor of Khwarazm. He huddled on the foredeck of the vessel, cowering in fear. And thus he stayed until the ship receded away, its hull disappearing beyond the horizon; and for the first time since the beginning of the war and the hunt, I smiled.

At last Subotai turned to me.

'You lied,' he said coldly. 'And from that lie, the coward who was your lord escaped on to the sea. But know that even into the sea we shall follow him. We might not kill his body, but already we have killed his mind with fear of us. And for the moment that is enough. Know, little man, that fear of death is oftentimes worse punishment than death itself.

'I found the false shah who had tried to mislead us, and I slew him with my own hand. He was a worthy opponent, and seemed far more a man than your king.'

'The man you killed was my friend,' I whispered sadly.

By my breaking oath, I had given life to Muhammad, who did not deserve it, and death to my friend.

'You were once a truthsayer. My lord Ghenghis had heard rumour of such as you. It is indeed a rare thing, a truthsayer. We had thought perhaps it was merely legend.'

'But I was the last, and we are no more in this dark age.'

'Why? Where did you come from?'

'Already no one knows its name. For I was the last. In the first battle of the war, my valley was destroyed, my people put to the sword by order of the Shah so that no one ever again would have a truthsayer who could speak of my lord's defeat or serve as truthsayer to the Mongols. For my lord was the type of man who could not allow such a thing to be owned by others, for as he used me, he also feared me.'

'So why then did you save him?' Subotai demanded. 'For he destroyed your people as well. You are a madman to me. You have broken your law to save one who killed your family.'

I smiled a sad distant smile, for at least now I could speak the truth.

'My lord Muhammad I was sworn to serve, and once a truthsayer makes a covenant such as that he can not break it.

'I know that there are two ways to kill a man. To kill him through his body, and thus release him from this world of strife. But there is another way, as well,' I said, then fell silent.

'Speak, truthsayer, for I have no patience with riddles.'

I smiled at Subotai.

'The other way is to kill his soul with fear. Muhammad slaughtered my father, my mother, my entire race, so that once I am gone, truthsayers will disappear from this world for ever. But I have had my revenge.

'I could see the fear that you created in him, and the fear I created in him, as well, for he could not stand to see the truth, either about others or himself. For months I weaved my spell about him, so that with every passing moment he became consumed with the truth – the truth of his own cowardice and the responsibility of leading his people to slaughter. If you had but looked into his eyes, you would have seen what the truth had done to him. I drove him mad with my spell of making him always aware of the truth.'

Subotai gazed upon me, and weak as I was, I could not judge what he thought or felt. But I cared not, for at that moment I wanted death.

'If I had told the truth,' I whispered, 'he would now be

dead, and in the hands of Allah. But now he lives instead, tormented by fear.

'Through his stupidity which started this war, and through his cowardice which caused him to flee rather than to come to terms with his deeds, tens of millions have died. I made him to realize by my powers that he will be haunted by their ghosts in this world and the next, never to outrun them.

'And he must suspect and will soon know that I, a truthsayer, broke covenant and condemned myself for ever so that he might live out his unworthy life. That is why I lied. Better that he live in a fear of his own creating than die a worthy death such as my friend Mulak, who would have died anyhow before he surrendered.'

I looked away from Subotai.

'I lied, but in so doing, I have had my revenge for all that he has done to me, to my people, and to Islam. But, strangely, in so doing I kept my faith to him as well, for after all, did I not swear an oath to serve him, and to prevent death from ever touching him?

'My revenge,' I said sadly, 'was also my sworn duty, and my loyalty to him as well.'

So saying, I knelt to the ground and prepared to meet my fate.

The blade did not come from the scabbard. Subotai turned and started away. Suddenly he stopped and looked back at me.

'I have served my Khan – the hunt is ended, for surely Muhammad is already dead . . . dead in the spirit if not yet the flesh. Now you, who were once a truthsayer, hear *my* truth. Serve me now instead and live, for you, Ali the truthsayer, are truly a fearful weapon.'

So saying, my lord Subotai turned and galloped away.

Thus did I meet and come to serve my lord Subotai. From the western plains of Poland to the distant seas of Ch'in, I served him as he conquered all the known world to the honour of his lord Ghenghis and the son of Ghenghis, called Ogadai. But those are other tales for another time.

And now Subotai is gone as well, and I write this tale even as my life spins out its last days in service to my lord Kubalai Khan.

What I have said was truth, for I was once a truthsayer, the last of all the truthsayers. O world, which I fear shall slip further and yet further into iniquity, you shall not see such as we again. For we could find that which was best in the hearts of men, and we could wage, if need be, war with but the power of truth.

And of Muhammad, know that Subotai had spoken truth as well, when he said that he was already dead of spirit. For Muhammad reached an island of holy men in the middle of the sea. The sword of Subotai never found him, yet he raved for the rest of his days about a wind-blown standard and the unforgiving eyes of a stunted man . . . and then, old and forgotten, he died.

May Allah forgive me my sins, and bring me safe passage to Paradise so that I might one day stand before His presence, where only the truth shall be spoken for ever.

HARRY TURTLEDOVE

The Banner of Kaviyan

The troop of horsemen rode slowly back towards the citadel. Chainmail jingled on their shoulders, gleamed in the boiling sun. A sentry spied the glitter before he could recognize the men who caused it. As any good soldier would, he must have shouted a warning, for Shahin saw the battlements suddenly bristle with men and spears.

That was as it should be, the young Persian noble thought. Had the lizard-eaters bested his men, Gomishan might have had to stand siege.

He shook his head like a horse. Sweat sprayed in all directions. It gave him little relief. In the sweltering humidity of Tabaristan, more instantly oozed from his pores.

Soon the sentry's challenge floated through the still air. Next to Shahin, the standard-bearer unfurled Gomishan's black-striped orange banner and waved it above his head. The warriors on the walls cheered, but made no move to open the gates of the fortress until they saw faces and knew the returning band was no Arab ruse. Then they came rushing out to greet their comrades.

Thick, sweet wine had already begun to go to Shahin's head when he met his father in the courtyard. He was still on his horse, and grinned down at the older man. 'We won,' he said foolishly.

'So I gathered,' murmured Pakor, *dihqan* of Gomishan. He also smiled, but thinly. 'Come inside; tell me how it went.' He saw Shahin's face fall, and the thin smile became a grin wide as the one his son had worn a moment

270

before, yet still sharp and clever. 'Not all the maidens will be gone when we are finished, I assure you.'

Shahin laughed and dismounted. A groom hurried up to lead his horse back to the stables. Pakor took his son by the elbow and steered him towards the forbidding grey-brown stone pile of the keep.

They paused a moment in the entry hall to let their eyes adjust to the gloom of the interior. Shahin's glance went to the polished bronze mirror that hung on the wall. As always when he saw himself and his father together, he was struck by the thought that they shared the same face, the only difference being that Pakor had used it longer. In both of them, deep-set dark eyes peered from under heavy black brows and broad, swarthy foreheads. They both had proud noses and thin, wide mouths; the beards of both climbed high on their rather hollow cheeks.

But Shahin's beard was still thin in a couple of places, and soft with the softness of youth. Pakor's was heavy and curling and streaked with grey, as if the first snows had fallen on the peaks of the Elburz mountains to the south. The lines of worry and command that Shahin had to shout or scowl to bring out were branded ineradicably on his father's forehead, between his eyes, and at the corners of his mouth.

A figure detached itself from the shadows the *dihqan*'s high seat cast at the far end of the great hall, and hobbled towards them. Pakor raised a hand in salute, as he would have to no other man in his dominions. 'Hail, Grandfather,' he said, and then, louder, to make sure the old man heard: 'Hail.'

Pakor the elder nodded stiffly. Just back from the first battle he had led, Shahin seemed to see his great-grandfather through new eyes. He suddenly realized that the elder Pakor's features, like the younger's, were also his, but had been ruined, not strengthened, by time. That proud nose stood forth, a beak, like a boulder of hard stone still not worn down by a stream which has eroded away everything nearby.

He was used to thinking of his great-grandfather as the

oldest man he had ever seen; he had never before imagined the young man trapped inside that wrinkled, mottled skin, that sparse white beard. Fear touched him, as it had not in combat. Would he look like that in some distant year? He doubted he would live so long. Few men did.

Walking slowly to accommodate the elder Pakor, Pakor the *dihqan* led him and Shahin to an antechamber off the great hall. They sank down on mounds of cushions. Shahin, as he had done countless times, helped his great-grandfather lower himself. 'Thank you, lad,' the old man said in his creaking voice.

A servant appeared in the doorway. 'Fetch us wine,' the *dihqan* told him, 'and roast meat, if any is left, and then leave us to ourselves and see that others do the same.' The man smiled, bowed, and trotted away. He returned shortly with a wineskin and with enough slices of lamb, Shahin thought, to feed most of the troop he had led.

When the platter was empty, the *dihqan* Pakor wiped his mouth on his sleeve. He turned to Shahin. 'Tell us how it was, son. Where did you meet them? How did you fight?'

'We came on them by the river, Father, not far from where the man-eating tiger slew the rice farmer last year. The banner of Gomishan being what it is, I took that for a good omen.'

'As I would have done,' the *dihqan* agreed. His grandfather also nodded.

'The good god Ahura Mazda smiled upon us with his sun, and with his fortune,' Shahin went on. 'The Arabs were still finishing their breakfasts when we burst upon them from the undergrowth. We plied them with arrows, then rushed among them with sword and spear. It was more slaughter than battle: we slew close to forty, and sent the rest fleeing westward toward Lahijan. We lost but three ourselves, and one other lost his hand, poor fellow. Never has the Persian race won a grander victory,' he boasted, feeling young and strong and full of triumph.

'Well done, my son,' cried Pakor the *dihqan*. He leaned

forward to kiss Shahin, first on the right cheek then on the left.

And, 'Aye, well done,' echoed the elder Pakor, yet his voice was less joyful than his grandson's. A cataract dimmed one of his eyes; the other speared and held Shahin. 'But speak not of famous victories, not for what in my time would have been hardly a cattle raid.'

'Yes, sir,' Shahin said resignedly; his father assumed a patient look. They had both heard, countless times, of how things were in the elder Pakor's youth, when the Persian King of Kings' dominions stretched from India to Mesopotamia; when Pakor, in the army of the great marshal Shah Baraz, campaigned in Palestine and Egypt and through Asia Minor and saw, across the Bosphorus, the Christian churches of Constantinople. For one brief moment, victory in the age-old struggle against the empire of Rome seemed close enough to reach out and touch.

But the Persians had fallen instead, first against the Romans, then into civil war, then to the Arabs. The elder Pakor had lived through it all; he was but in early middle age when he fought at Qadisiya, in the battle that sealed Persia's doom. Shahin had trouble imagining the armies of thousands and tens of thousands of which his great-grandfather always spoke. Next to them, he supposed, his fight might look small. But no such armies existed today, not here in Tabaristan, the only land whose proud Persian *dihqans* still held out against the Arab tide. How, though, could he tell the old man he had lived out the worth of his memories?

Besides, today the elder Pakor's reminiscences were taking a tack different from the usual. Instead of talking of his comrades of old – young men then, now almost surely dead – he was saying, 'This tigerskin rag under which we fight is well enough, I suppose, but it is no sure harbinger of victory, as the banner of Kaviyan was, long ago.'

Pakor the *dihqan* interrupted, a privilege his grandfather granted him as a man grown but would have denied to Shahin. 'I've heard you speak of his banner before. How then has the line of the Kings of Kings failed, and

273

how have the lizard-eaters from the desert come to infest our land if it was as powerful as you claim?'

'By Ahura Mazda, it was!' The elder Pakor's voice cracked in anger. 'I marched under it, when Shah Baraz took Jerusalem and then Alexandria from the Romans. For years I fought under it, and never tasted defeat. The magi had set victory in that banner, with spells the wizards nowadays are too stupid and too puny to imagine, let alone try. There was only the one banner of Kaviyan, and never will its like come again.'

The quick tears of old age filled his eyes. 'And it was lovely, too: of silk of a blue whose secret the dyers hereabouts would slay themselves to learn. Set on it, in gold and silver thread, were the sun and moon our army reverenced. The slightest breeze would set it rippling, huge though it was. That too was a spell, or so the soldiers said, and I believe it.'

The elder Pakor was looking towards Shahin, but plainly saw only the banner of Kaviyan. The longing on his face was so great that Shahin could almost see it too, hear it snapping in the wind, feel the spirit flowing from it to the men who followed it.

More quietly than he had expected to, he echoed his father's question: 'Then what, sir, happened to this standard?'

Rage darkened his great-grandfather's seamed cheeks. 'Khusro the King of Kings happened to it, may Ahriman curse him with fire for ever! To him it was but another treasure, no more. The fool took it from his army and stored it away with his gold and jewels. No one ever learned where for certain, whether at his summer palace at Dastigerd or in Ctesiphon, the capital.'

'Such a talisman!' Shahin exclaimed, excited in spite of himself by the elder Pakor's tale. 'Why did he not fetch it out when the Romans turned the tables on us? Why did not the later Kings of Kings, to use against the Arabs when they burst upon us?'

'I have thought much on that,' the elder Pakor said, 'the good god Ahura Mazda having granted me these long years in which to do so. My guess is that the banner was kept somewhere in Ctesiphon. Khusro shunned the city, and had for a quarter of a century: sorcerers and astrologers had predicted he would be destroyed if he entered it. But when, as you say, the Romans bore down on Dastigerd, Khusro fled to Ctesiphon. Why else would he have dared, but to seek out the banner of Kaviyan?'

'It did not help him then,' Pakor the *dihqan* observed.

'He did not find it,' his grandfather replied. 'Not many could have been trusted with the secret of its hiding-place – who would not have been tempted to rebel, knowing triumph rode in his standard? Perhaps all who knew where it was had died; remember, a decade had gone by since Khusro stole it from the soldiers who needed it. So he fled out of Ctesiphon again, to be overthrown and put to death by his son. He died slowly and vilely, yet not, I think, half so much as he deserved, for bringing our great land to ruin.'

'Then what became of the banner?' Shahin asked.

'Ah, lad, that no one knows. Maybe the Arabs took it away as booty when they sacked Ctesiphon, though I own I never heard of its reappearing. Likelier, I would say, it lies there still, hidden for ever in the rubble.'

'For ever? No, it must not!' cried Shahin. 'It should be brought forth to the world again, to give back to us Persians our freedom and our glory once again!'

'Spoken like a prince,' younger and elder Pakor said at the same time. They looked at each other, surprised, then smiled. Shahin's great-grandfather went on sadly, 'But who shall search it out?'

'By the good god, I shall!' Shahin declared. In his mind's eye the young man saw an army gather behind him; saw it follow him to drive the Arabs back to their burning sands; saw himself, under the banner of Kaviyan, crowned with the crown of the Kings of Kings, a crown so heavy with gold and jewels that when the King of Kings sat on his throne a gold chain hanging down from the ceiling helped bear its weight.

The *dihqan* Pakor said no, then, and with increasing

frequency as the days went by. His years let him see all too clearly the obstacles that lay in his son's path, and how tiny was Shahin's chance for success. The elder Pakor said never a word. His years let him see how many things were possible.

Within a fortnight, Shahin set out.

In his head, Shahin had known his entire life that the Arabs ruled all of Persia outside the backwater that was Tabaristan; they had, after all, encroached even there. His heart, though, was not prepared for what he found when he traversed the passes of the Elburz range and came into lands that had been under the invaders' control since his father was born.

First to strike him was the state of the *ateshkade*. He knew the Arabs cared nothing about fire-temples themselves. They had their own new and foolish religion (how a single god could be all-powerful and yet tolerate evil was beyond him). But he had never expected his own people to neglect them as well. Yet he rode past several obviously in need of repair and cleansing. Because they were open to the elements, being but domes supported on four pillars, they showed the result of negligence more quickly than solider structures would have.

That was bad. What happened when he begged shelter at a *dihqan*'s castle south of the mountains was worse. The fault did not lie in his reception; his father could not have treated a guest with more courtesy. But the lord of the castle was a hawk-nosed, lean-faced Arab in flowing robes. Watching and listening to him order about his Persian servants filled Shahin with impotent fury.

He could not even soothe his feelings with the wine cup. The Arab, whose name was Yaqut, drank only sweetened fruit juice and permitted nothing stronger in his household. Shahin had heard this of the Arabs, but had not believed it. Surely no race could be so stupid as to deprive itself of wine!

Yaqut, Shahin soon learned, was not stupid in the least, no matter what he drank. 'What sets you on the road, my master?' he asked. His tone was lazy, but his eyes bored into Shahin's as he waited for him to reply. Again the young Persian thought he resembled a hawk; the reflected firelight lent his gaze the opaque ferocity of a falcon's.

'Nothing but a longing to see more than I can out of my window,' Shahin said.

'Ah,' Yaqut said politely. One of his arched eyebrows rose. 'Doubtless your father Pakor would have preferred that you merely chose another window to look out of instead.' He smiled at Shahin's stricken expression. 'Oh, yes, my master, I know of Pakor: a brave man, and a good one, for an infidel. Now let me ask you again' – suddenly his voice was whipcrack sharp; he knew how to question men – 'what sets you on the road?'

Shahin thought furiously fast. 'My father and I quarrelled, and I am no longer welcome at Gomishan.' Inspiration struck; he added, 'You will gain no ransom for holding me.'

'By Allah, such was never my intent: you have eaten my bread and salt.' Shahin put little confidence in the oath to the god he did not follow, but his folk also recognized the bond of bread and salt. He dipped his head, acknowledging Yaqut's civility.

After that, their talk was less sharp-edged, though the Arab continued to probe delicately. Shahin told as much truth as he could, that seeming the best way to fend him off without rousing what were plainly – and deservedly, the young Persian had to admit to himself – ever-ready suspicions. Of the banner of Kaviyan, though, Shahin had the sense to say nothing. As the son of a *dihqan*, he was unimportant enough to be forgotten tomorrow, or the day after; as would-be leader against the Arabs, he would never leave this castle alive.

He came to be grateful for his host's abstemiousness. Wine might have loosened his tongue.

He yawned. 'Your pardon,' he said to Yaqut. 'I have been on the road several days now.'

'Of course.' The Arab flicked a long-fingered hand, waving away the apology. He called to a serving-girl, a pretty young Persian maid: 'Come here, Shiren. Take this fellow up to the guest chamber and keep him warm tonight.' Yaqut turned, smiling, to Shahin. 'I trained her myself. She is lively. You will enjoy her.'

He might have been speaking of a dog or a horse. Shahin had to hide his rage at the thought as he followed the Persian girl upstairs. Yaqut was one of the conquerors. He did as he pleased.

Shahin found the girl to be all Yaqut had claimed. Afterwards, delight and shame warred in him. He leaned up on an elbow to ask her, 'Would you not sooner be free of your foreign master?'

Steeped in Persian poetry, as he lay with her he had thought of her eyes as bottomless black pools filled with mystery. Now they were filled only with puzzlement. 'Free to do what?' she asked. 'I eat well enough here – better than I would in the peasant's hut where I was born. I sleep under fleeces, not sackcloth. Yaqut is no crueller than most men, or so I gather.'

'But—' Shahin paused, scratched his head. Being the son of a *dihqan*, he had never had to look at life in such basic terms. He tried again: 'All else being equal, would you not prefer a Persian overlord in this castle?'

She shrugged. 'If everything else were the same, what difference would that make?'

The shrug bared her tawny breasts and brown nipples. She pulled sheepskins back over herself. Modesty had nothing to do with it, nor did lust when she snuggled against him. The night was chilly. If anything, Shahin felt that more than the girl did. In the narrow jungle strip between the Caspian Sea and the Elburz range, cold nights were only distant rumours.

Shahin wondered if Yaqut had called the serving-maid a bedwarmer in the most literal sense of the word. That too, he decided sleepily. He put an arm around her to make sure she would not roll away, then turned his head and blew out the lamp.

In the days that followed, Shahin came more and more to

appreciate the Persian girl's point of view. Once he could no longer take a full belly or a snug bed for granted, they became much more attractive when he did have them. He acquired a spare sword – and a scar on his forearm – from a meeting with a fellow to whom even the little he had as a traveller seemed a good deal.

He made his way south and west across the Iranian plateau. Peasants and herders laboured as they always had, but some *dihqans'* castles were burnt-out shells, others in the hands of the Arabs. The further he drew from his homeland, the easier he became about taking shelter with the men out of the southern desert. Comfort mattered more to him now that he had seen what life was like without it. Moreover, the further he was from Gomishan, the less the danger of being recognized as a man out of the last free corner of Persia.

And indeed, after Yaqut – who after all lived close enough to the border to know of Shahin's father – the Arabs showed little concern for him. He seemed just another traveller, and they guested him without suspicion. The irony of that appealed to him.

Yet he did not go unnoted after all. That he found out one night at a keep not far from the town of Shahpur Khwast. The local lord, an Arab named ibn Kathir, was open-handed in his hospitality. In return for his bounty (or rather, Shahin thought, the bounty he stole from his Persian subjects), though, he insisted on tracing his genealogy back generation upon generation for Shahin. 'Is that not wonderful?' he said when at last he was through.

'Most wonderful, my master,' Shahin murmured. He had heard such chains before, although never at such stupefying length – genealogy was an Arab passion. Shahin never understood why. At the base of each family tree stood a lizard-eating desert rat, and below him probably a lizard. Where lay the pride in that?

A quiet scratching at Shahin's door eventually woke him from a sound sleep (after ibn Kathir's performance, that, at least, was assured). He approached the door, sword in hand, and suddenly threw it wide.

Ibn Kathir's steward, a round-faced, elderly Persian, recoiled in fright, almost dropping the tiny lamp he held. His voice, however, did not rise above a whisper: 'By the good god, young sir, clothe yourself and follow me. There is someone who would have speech with you.'

Shahin lowered his blade; no foe would summon him in Ahura Mazda's name. He threw on tunic and trousers, stepped out into the hall. The steward closed the door after him. 'You must not be missed,' he said softly, 'or you will never leave here alive.' He padded down the hallway in soft, silent sandals; after a moment, Shahin, barefoot, went along.

He was soon hopelessly lost, and a little while later found himself scuffing through thick dust. No one, he thought, had come into this part of the castle for years. He wondered whether ibn Kathir even knew of these dark passageways. He also wondered what the steward wanted of him. His hand tightened on his sword hilt as suspicion returned. What place could be better for a quiet murder?

But that made no sense either. Both ibn Kathir and his steward had more straightforward ways of ridding themselves of an unwanted guest than this sort of game.

The steward stopped. He waved Shahin on. 'In that chamber ahead is the one of whom I spoke.' He turned his back. 'Go ahead. I may truthfully take oath now, should ibn Kathir require it, that I have not seen you enter.'

Whatever was in the wind, then, was not to the advantage of the Arab lord. That decided Shahin. He stepped forward. The dim little pool of light around the steward showed footprints already in the dust.

In the gloom, Shahin fumbled with the door latch. When at last the door opened, it did so on oiled hinges, with no creak or groan to betray anything out of the ordinary in this long-abandoned hall. Whoever waited inside for Shahin had a lamp, a brighter one than the steward carried. It gave him a better look at the prints he had followed here.

He had just realized how small they were when the person with the lamp whispered, 'Come in, and close the door behind you.' Even whispering, that voice could never have belonged to a man. Beginning now to understand, Shahin did as he was bid.

'I am Mirud,' she said, 'wife to ibn Kathir. You know our fate if we are discovered here together?'

'Yes,' he said, and did not elaborate. He had never seen the wife of any of the lords at whose keeps he had stayed, nor thought to, any more than a visitor to Pakor's hall at Gomishan was likely to meet the *dihqan*'s lady.

Mirud's speech told Shahin at once she was as Persian as he; it held none of the guttural Arab accent. Her looks confirmed the flavour of her words. She was a classic Persian beauty, swarthy, wide-mouthed, with bold cheekbones, flashing dark eyes, and wavy hair spilling over her shoulders like a fountain of midnight. She was just enough older than Shahin to be able to intimidate him because of this as well.

She said, 'You are the one who would raise the banner of Kaviyan once more?' It was framed as a question, but was not; Shahin heard the certainty in Mirud's voice.

'How do you know that?' he blurted. Then he began to think. 'Did ibn Kathir tell you?' If the Arab knew, as seemed only too likely, his journey would come to an ignominious end here.

But Mirud was shaking her head. 'He knows *nothing* of this,' she said, hissing in contempt: 'Nothing, by Ahura Mazda! We Persians may lie under the fist of the desert-dwellers, but we have our *qanats* through which word passes without their notice.' The underground irrigation channels were rare in Tabaristan, which had water in plenty, but Shahin grasped the image and nodded at its aptness.

'What then?' he asked. 'Why do you risk both of us with this meeting?'

'To help you take the revenge on the Arabs I cannot secure for myself. I was a girl when my father gave me to ibn Kathir, trading his daughter's body for what he hoped would be influence with the new master hereabouts. Influence!'

281

She made the word a curse. Tears stood in her eyes – tears of fury. Shahin thought uneasily. She went on, 'He treats me in but two ways: as a piece of furniture most times, and as a piece of meat when he hopes to get another son on me. I would slay him, did I not know what would befall the Persians around this holding afterwards. Aiding you will bring him and all those like him low without revealing my hand. I think that will only make my pleasure sweeter at his fall.'

Shahin slowly nodded. At best, a woman's life was harsher than a man's. Given young to a man who cared nothing for her past his own pleasure ... He shivered, thanking the good god he had been spared Mirud's fate. But he was cautious as he asked, 'How is it you can help me?' Rage was not enough.

She recognized his doubts. 'What would it mean to you if I told you my grandfather's brother was one of the treasure-keepers of Khusro, miscalled the Victorious?'

Shahin was suddenly very alert.

'Yes,' she said, 'Do you know of the three empty seats before the throne of the King of Kings?'

He nodded again. Minstrels sang of those seats, and his great-grandfather had spoken of them. They were for the three lords the Kings of Kings dreamed of making their vassals: the emperor of China, the emperor of the Romans, and the great khagan of the steppe nomads to the north. For two generations the seats, the throne and the palace had been ruins.

'Good,' she said. 'Look under the middle seat, the one reserved for the Roman emperor. Khusro had won such victories against the Romans, I suppose, that he thought he would not need the banner of Kaviyan again. When he found he did—'

'—it was too late,' Shahin finished for her. He had to remind himself that a shout of joy would be fatally dangerous. Whispering, 'I thank you; from the bottom of my heart I thank you, my lady,' seemed a substitute too thin-blooded to be borne. He took a step toward Mirud.

She stooped to set down the lamp. For a moment she

stood in his arms, her lips eager against his. Then she drew away, and waved him back when he tried to embrace her again. 'I am ibn Kathir's wife,' she told him. 'If the day comes when that is no longer so, if the day should come when he falls fighting in vain against Persia's reborn freedom, then gladly will I give myself to you. Till that day, you may not have me.'

'Had I no inducement before to go on to Ctesiphon, you would have given me one,' he said.

Mirud smiled. 'Spoken like a warrior prince in a ballad. Do as such warriors would, and you will have your reward. For now, though, let Kartir take you back to your chamber, and I will return to the women's quarters. You have never seen me – I am but a dream.'

'A sweet one, my lady,' Shahin said.

'A courtier as well as a warrior. Now go.'

Riding down early in the morning from the foothills of the Zagros mountains into the Mesopotamian plain, Shahin briefly thought he was returning to a warm, humid climate like that of Tabaristan. The dryness and chill nights of the Iranian plateau had never stopped oppressing him. He thanked Ahura Mazda that he had not tried to traverse it in winter. He had never seen snow, save at a distance, and had no interest in striking up a closer acquaintance with it.

The sun rose higher, and hotter, in the sky. Before noon, Shahin had abandoned his nostalgic thoughts of home. Instead, he began to wonder if he was travelling through the fiery hell where Ahriman punished sinners. He could not imagine how, in this furnace of a country, some of the land ahead was so green.

As he rode on, he learned the answer: wherever canals brought the waters of the Tigris, crops would grow, and grow abundantly. Where the canals did not reach, only sere brown desert remained, here and there dotted with nomads' black tents. To such land as that, the Arabs were welcome, Shahin thought.

The farmers who tilled and weeded the muddy farmlands were stocky brown men who had no Persian. Nor could Shahin fathom the Syriac they spoke, though a word here and there reminded him of Arabic. He had a smattering of that tongue, from a lifetime of helping his father scheme against the men who used it. Finally he came upon a Christian priest who also spoke it after a fashion.

'Ctesiphon?' The priest pointed downstream. 'Three days' ride, I think it is, if you care to visit a pile of rubble.'

'I care.' Shahin saw the priest's threadbare robe, his bare feet. He remarked, 'The Arabs have not left you much.'

The priest shrugged. 'I need little. So long as I pay the land tax for my church, I am left in peace. Better that than the persecutions my flock endured under the Persians.' He drew the sign of the cross on his breast, frowned when Shahin did not follow suit. 'God go with you,' he said, but the warmth was gone from his voice.

Shahin was also scowling as he rode south-east. He had never thought anyone could prefer Arab rule to Persian. He had never thought memory of the King of Kings could fade so fast, either, but in Mesopotamia it had. But the priest – fool of a Christian, he thought irritably – had not even recognized him as a member of the one-time ruling race of this land.

That will change, he thought, when the banner of Kaviyan flies at my back. And if the Kings of Kings had persecuted Christians, they doubtless knew what they were doing.

On the fourth day, Shahin rode past a little village called Baghdad in the morning, then, as the sun was lowering behind him, drew near the ruins of Ctesiphon. Tears came to his eyes when he compared the ruined grandeur to the squalour that endured. Baghdad, when the Arabs came, had had nothing worth plundering, and so remained intact. Ctesiphon was less lucky.

Even after half a century he could see scorch marks on the tumbled, polished stones. What had been the walls of shops and palaces, fire-temples and mansions, were now gap-toothed piles of wreckage. The sack of Ctesiphon had not ended its plundering, Shahin realized. In Baghdad he had seen stones to match these, plastered with mud into the sides of hovels. The vultures still found meat on these old bones.

He rode through the ruins. They extended for almost a mile. His travels in the past weeks had greatly broadened his horizons, but he had never imagined a city, even a dead city, could be so vast. He wondered how, among so many buildings, he would ever find the remains of Khusro's palace.

He was no – what did the Romans call them? – philosopher, to spend all his time thinking, but he could use his wits well enough at need. No one, he reasoned, would have been allowed to build higher than the King of Kings. He urged his horse up a hillock of debris, peered around. There! he thought – that brick- and stone-work was more battered than most, but once it had been the grandest of any he could see.

By then night was falling. Shahin dismounted and led his horse down the shaky slope; better that than risking a fall that might injure it – or him. He spread his blankets in the partial shelter of a shattered building that once must have been home to a great lord. He had thought excitement would keep him up for hours. The next thing he knew, the morning sun was shining in his face.

He gnawed on hard bread, drank blood-warm water from his supply. He let his horse graze a little in a weed-filled courtyard that in happier days had surely been a *paradise* – a formal garden. Then he vaulted on to the beast and made for the residence of the King of Kings.

The journey took three times as long as he had expected, for every way towards his destination was choked with debris. At last he realized he was struggling through barricades thrown up in a last desperate defence of the palace. Too late then for the banner of Kaviyan; but now its hour was come round again.

More than once, he rode over men's bones. He raised a hand in salute to the fallen warriors, and prayed they had reached heaven. At least they had gone to their last rest in proper fashion, polluting neither earth nor water nor fire, but feeding carrion birds and scavengers that went on four legs.

The closer he drew, the more ruinous the palace appeared. The hope that had burned so high in him wavered – how could anything have survived unplundered through such a sack as this? Every wall was broken, every chamber in the building broken into. The Arabs, Ahriman take them all, must have raped every copper.

At last he found the throne room. His horse's hooves echoed on stone. The only other sound was the harsh screech of a crow in the distance.

The dais on which the King of Kings' throne had stood was empty. That came as no surprise to Shahin. The throne had been of gold and jewels and ivory. He hoped Arabs had killed each other, fighting over its remains.

But that was merely the thought of a moment, for before the dais he saw the three seats made for the humiliation of the other great rulers of the world. Those seats were carved from plain grey stone, to mark their insignificance when set before the grandeur of the throne. And because they were so plain, they had not suffered much in the sack. The one on the left, intended for the emperor of China, had a chunk broken from its back. The one on the right, intended for the great khagan, was overturned but unbroken. And the central seat, intended for the Roman emperor, might have been made yesterday.

Shahin examined the floor where it sat. He saw nothing out of the ordinary: it looked like the rest of the once-polished marble. If anything was under there, how could he hope to find it? He tried to shove aside the seat. It would not budge. He kicked it, and accomplished nothing more than hurting his foot. He hopped about and swore.

When at last the pain subsided he sat down heavily, and full of frustration, by the seat that was to have been the great khagan's. He leaned against it and sighed in brief animal pleasure; the stone was cool against his back. Then the seat shifted, and he had to scramble to keep from falling over backwards and cracking his head on it.

Shahin frowned. He got to his feet and looked from the overturned seat to the one that still stood. To the eye, they were identical. 'And yet,' he said aloud, trying to clarify his thoughts, 'the one moves under my weight, while I cannot budge the other with all my strength. That is not as it should be.'

He tried to push the Roman emperor's seat again, with no better luck than before. Breathing hard – more from anger than exertion – he stooped to examine the way the seat's legs met the floor.

At first he thought, as he was meant to think, that the seat simply sat in place, as did its neighbours to the left and right. But he was no longer willing to believe that. He peered more closely. Excitement flowered in him. The legs of the Roman emperor's seat did not rest on the floor – they went into it. So perfectly did they fit the sockets cut into the marble that only someone already suspicious (desperate, Shahin thought, was probably the truer word) would have noticed the cunning deception.

He rose, went round to the front of the seat. He set his hands where (sadly, he thought) the fundament of no Roman ruler had ever rested, lifted with all his might. When he felt the seat stir, he redoubled his efforts. The seat went over backwards with a crash that boomed like thunder in the silent throne room and made his horse snort and sidestep with fright.

Shahin smiled, thinking how proud his great-grandfather would be: here single-handed he had overturned the Romans against whom the elder Pakor fought so long. Then he became serious again, going to his knees to study in turn each of the four dark, rectangular hollows he had found.

Three were only hollows. The fourth – Shahin's breath came short, almost as if in the act of love. A circular hole, a bit wider than his finger, had been drilled in the marble. He reached blindly down into it. His finger touched a spring. He felt the click as well as hearing it.

Even after so many years, the mechanism Khusro's artisans had built functioned perfectly. A cubit-square section of the floor, one Shahin would have sworn to be no different from the rest, tilted on silent hinges. The banner of Kaviyan, carefully folded, nested in the cavity revealed.

Shahin murmured a prayer of thanksgiving as he gently lifted the banner into the world once more. Its long seclusion had done it no harm. The fine silk felt softer, smoother to his fingers than any woman's skin. Lacking a standard on which to raise the banner, Shahin spread it on the throne-room floor.

It was as though a section of the bright noon sky had come to rest there. The sun and moon glittered in gold and silver. Staring in awe at them, Shahin understood how the armies of the Kings of Kings felt themselves invincible when they marched and fought under this standard. Its magic pulled at him, made him want to draw his sword and drive the Arab savages and their lying faith out of Persia and back to the wastelands that had spawned them.

He took a deep slow breath, mastered himself. Even with the banner of Kaviyan, one man would not do that alone. He wondered how many leagues lay between him and the nearest Persian. More than he could count on one hand, he guessed.

The sooner he returned to his homeland, then, the sooner his people's vengeance for half a century of torments could begin. He folded the banner, put it in his saddlebag. Then he prostrated himself before the empty dais, just as if a Khusro or Hormizd still sat on the throne.

'That day shall come again,' he declared. His horse snorted, as if it knew the burden it was carrying.

Shahin was not sorry to put Ctesiphon behind him. The reminders of Persia's grandeur and how it had fallen oppressed him, the more so as the banner of Kaviyan worked its spell, showing him images of the empire as it was in its days of glory.

He slept under the stars that night, spreading his blanket over soft grass. On the blanket he reverently set the folded banner of Kaviyan, as a pillow for his head. The moon on the banner gleamed with a sweet silver glow that had nothing to do with the fading firelight falling on it.

The dreams that filled Shahin's head! He saw the great Shapur storm Roman Antioch, saw the Roman emperor Valerian in bonds at his feet. He saw the first Khusro sack Antioch again, and then turn east to crush the power of the White Huns. He watched three hundred years of glory in a night, always from a lofty angle of view: from the perspective of the upraised banner of Kaviyan, he realized at last.

Sunrise brought the visions to an end. Opening his eyes to the world around him made him wonder which was real and which the dream: what he had seen seemed more substantial, surely more satisfying, than the flat, hot Mesopotamian countryside to which he woke.

A fly bit him on the cheek. He swatted, swore, laughed ruefully. 'This is the world that is,' he said. 'The banner of Kaviyan is too exalted to notice vermin.'

He pushed the pace hard that day, and by sunset was beyond cultivated land. Off in the distance he saw once more the black tents of Arab nomads, and around them, antlike, veiled women in black tending cookfires. He frowned. It seemed to him they should have sensed the revived majesty of the Persians that he carried, and fled from it in terror. But they remained oblivious. Not for long, he thought, not for long.

When he camped, he made no fire, not wanting to draw thieves – and no nomads were anything but. He watched the stars come out, one by one. Then he took out the banner of Kaviyan once more, and marvelled again at the magic glow the magi had imparted to the sun and moon upon it. He set it gently on his blanket, lay his head upon it, and gladly sank into sleep.

As he had hoped, the wonderful dreams returned. This time he seemed to march with the second Khusro's armies, and saw in his visions the triumphs his great-grandfather had known in person. He saw the Christian patriarch of Jerusalem carried off into captivity, saw Persian armies returned to the Nile and take up rule again after an absence of nine hundred years. He rejoiced, viewing Khusro re-create the ancient empire of Darayavahush and Khshayarsha.

Then the vision darkened. Instead of joining Shah Baraz on his campaign against Constantinople, the campaign that should have slain the Roman empire once and for all, the banner of Kaviyan was taken from the army. Its mourning reminded Shahin of the mourning of brother for absent brother, or of wife for husband.

It showed him little of the lonely journey to Ctesiphon; he thought it did not care to recall that time. But he saw very clearly its being set into the stone prison from which he had rescued it, and saw the marble panel swing shut on it, enclosing it in darkness.

Such anguish filled Shahin at its imprisonment that he awoke. He gasped in surprise and dismay – a shadowy figure bent over him, arm outstretched to snatch the banner of Kaviyan from beneath his head. Its sorcerous glow must have drawn the robber, who also gasped. He clouted Shahin with a cudgel.

Stars exploded in his head, brighter than the ones in the sky. The robber seized the banner. But the blow that should have stretched Shahin senseless in the dirt failed in its purpose, so great was his fury. He grappled with the thief. The fellow struck him again, then broke free and ran for his horse. He vaulted aboard, galloped off into the night.

Shahin turned towards his own mount. But he was swaying like a man in the last stages of drunkenness. He took a couple of tottering steps in the direction of the beast, then fell on his face.

He groaned when he woke. All the hangovers he had ever known were as nothing beside the lethal ache in his head. There was dried blood in his hair, and more on his temple. When the sun rose, an hour or so later, it drove knives of pain through his eyes.

Climbing to his feet was fresh torment. He had to try

three times before he managed to scramble on to his horse; the second resulted in a fall that left him briefly unconscious again. When at last he was mounted, he went slowly after the robber. Of itself, his hand kept sliding to his sword hilt. Now personal, not Persian, vengeance was uppermost in his mind.

Luckily, his assailant had left a track a blind man could follow. Shahin rode on, swaying now and then in the saddle but always keeping his eyes to the ground, as a hound does while following a scent.

He only raised his head when the pain in it became too much for him to bear. As well for him that he did: he saw in the distance the ragtag flock of Arab tents he had passed the day before. The trail led straight for them.

'I might have known,' Shahin muttered, and winced at the sound of his own voice. 'Filthy Arab thief.'

He dismounted, tethered his horse in the shade of a tall thornbush. However much he might want to, he could not storm a camp by himself. Stealth would have to serve instead. Quiver at his belt, bow in his right hand, he began working his way towards the black tents.

He had played this deadly game before. It was harder, he found, in the desert than through the lush, concealing foliage of Tabaristan. The sun blazing down on his battered head helped not at all. Still, he made progress, drifting like a shadow from a bush to a stone to a tiny hillock that concealed him while he plotted his route to the next stone.

At last he had advanced almost to within bow-shot of the nearest tent. There he stayed, in the shelter of a bush sadly less leafy than the one that shaded his mount. The Arabs had three sentries out, placed so he could not hope to pick them all off from the same spot. Bandits, he thought resentfully, learned some of the same tricks as soldiers.

No help for it but to wait till nightfall, he decided. In the darkness chaos might work for him – a single man could make himself seem an army. He drank from his canteen. The water was hot and stale, but replaced some of what he had sweated away. He dozed a little.

Mostly, though, he watched the tents. The sentries – Ahriman smite them with boils – stayed disgustingly alert. He only saw a couple of other men. The rest were likely out with the flocks.

Women kept going from tent to tent, as women will. Sometimes children tagged at their heels, more often not. As he had seen before, the women wore coarse wool dyed black as their tents (black as their hearts, he thought). They displayed their wealth with bracelets and anklets and strings of gold and silver coins round their necks: when the sun struck right, he could see the glitter.

Save for their jewellery, the only splashes of colour on their robes were their veils. Some were dyed red with henna, others the rich yellow of saffron. Shahin scratched his head in puzzlement as the sun crawled across the sky. He had been telling the women apart by their veils, but what was he to think when a red and two yellows came into a tent and, not much later, three blues came out? A little later, a red and a green went in, and two more blues came out.

That blue was particularly rich and vibrant, too. It drew Shahin's eye to it, much as . . .

'No,' he whispered. He could not even shriek, not without drawing the sentries down on him. His nails dug into his palms until they pierced flesh. Tears ran down his face. He pounded his head into the sand. A rock cut his cheek, but the pain was as nothing next to the pain in his heart.

For this, he thought wildly, for this he had rescued the banner of Kaviyan? To have it cut to pieces as nomad booty? Then he saw that, though he raised the question in despair, its answer had to be yes. For if Persia's glory was embodied in the banner, was not the banner in turn tied up with Persia? And what was Persia in these sorry days? Only a captive of the Arabs: if his travels had shown him anything, it was that.

'Not all of Persia, though,' he said out loud. Gomishan, by the good god, still was free. With or without the banner of Kaviyan, he could help it hold. Swallowing a last agonized curse, he crawled backwards out from under the shade of the thornbush, began the slow, cautious journey back to his horse – and back to his home.

On the way, though, he made sure he took a wide detour around the town of Shahpur Khwast.

SUSAN SHWARTZ

The
Consolations of Philosophy

By the time that the Persian noble turned guard had
finished the tale of the banner of Kaviyan, the sun's own
banners had dipped quite low behind the mountains in
the west that Peter would never again see. Then all the
men in the room started, for into the room rushed a
servant from the master of caravans, and he threw himself down upon the carpets before the scholar who was
the host. So quickly had he run from his master's house
that he had broken into an unseemly sweat, and his eyes
were wide.

Peter of Wraysbury forced himself to sink back against
his cushions and feign unconcern. The Mongol laid aside
his blade. But he felt himself begin to sweat, as had the
servant, and his heart pounded until he felt as if his
temples might burst and the blood gush from his mouth
and ears as if he had taken his death wound. For a
moment, hope that his messenger had returned sang in
his heart and veins.

'Oh my masters,' said the servant when he had
recovered his breath, 'my lord commands me to tell you
that the storytellers have returned to Khotan, as they
promised three Ramadans ago, to keep the holy fast
here.'

The scholar and his guests murmured gravely, as was
proper, that they had heard of the fame of these storytellers.

'My master bids you to a feast that he will give at sunset, the first night of Ramadan.'

They made the ritual protests, but Peter knew that the others would come. As for himself, what was his choice? If the news was not of his messenger, well enough that it was of the storytellers, who had been kind to him and drawn his life story from him.

More confident and at ease now, the servant cocked his head to one side and actually grinned. 'One final thing my master bid me to say. He knows the delight that his guest . . .' like all Kashgari, he made a slaughter of Peter's name . . . 'takes in the telling of tales, and he also knows that when the storytellers departed Kashgar the time before, that they wished him to tell a tale. My master would beseech his thrice-esteemed guest from the west to favour his other guests with that story.'

'You are trapped, my friend!' laughed the scholar.

Trapped? Aye, that was the word for it. There being nothing else to do but submit, Peter protested his inadequacy, then informed the servant he would obey, tossed him a coin, and dismissed him. Shortly after, the call to prayers freed him to leave the scholar's house and walk back to the caravan master's.

They had spoken – healer, scholar, warrior and noble of a conquered race – of loyalty and truth. *What* is *truth*? Peter mused. Pilate had asked that, and not paused for a reply. Well, Peter would. He had learned much that was false, much of tears and laughter, and – this learning came hard – that the caravan master's charity had redeemed him not just from bodily death but from the more subtle death of ignorance.

For years he had wandered in the East, spoken with people, and yet had he not always held himself aloof, felt himself to be a trifle better than his acquaintances because he was a Christian and a knight? That was truth. And there was truth in another memory – he had pledged his word: a thousand days, and if no ransom came, he would submit to be sold as a slave.

He wandered through the square, emptied now, and

past a mosque from which came the sound of chanted prayers. *Islam*, he knew now, meant submission to God's will which might be harsh, might be inexplicable, but – in the end – simply *was*.

How was that any different than *fiat voluntas tuas* – let thy will be done?

Thy will. God's will, never mine, thought Peter. He had given his word and pledged his honour under God, and he would honour his pledge even if it led him to the block or to death. He had pined for the consolations of philosophy. And through his friends' tales, he had learned how a man might be a slave, stunted, tormented of heart, or no man at all, yet remain serene of bearing. Well, he had no choice but to endure. Perhaps, he thought, one day I too will meet a jinna. Perhaps she will look like that dancer in Khotan.

But it was time to turn from such fancies to matters of the spirit.

Outside the mosque where the men of Kashgar and their guests welcomed the holy month of Ramadan, Peter of Wraysbury bent the knee. 'Thy will be done,' he whispered, and returned to the caravan master's house.

The feast had started, and it was the most lavish that the caravan master had held since the last Ramadan or, perhaps, for three Ramadans in a row. Assembled were merchants of all types, many of them men who had feasted and told tales here before: Peter saw faces that he recognized, faces that smiled at him with warmth rather than mere courtesy. That warmed him. Perhaps if he were a slave, they would still smile at him kindly.

The storytellers looked down the huge room, spied Peter, and gestured a welcome.

For a time, all were content merely to sit and eat. But when their first hunger had been sated, the youngest of the storytellers sat up, begged pardon of his elders for speaking first and held up a hand.

'Do you recall, man of the West,' he addressed Peter, 'that when we last met, you were told that we wished to hear a story from you when we returned, as we promised to do. Well, now we are here. We have kept our part of the bargain. Now, do you keep yours too.'

The caravan master interrupted Peter's instinctive and mannerly protest of his incompetence, his illiteracy, and his total coarseness and haltness in Arabic, coupled with his unwillingness to insult such an assembly.

'Nevertheless . . .' he said, and Peter bowed.

'Nevertheless,' he took up the word and drew it out until the guests all smiled, 'I shall do my poor best to entertain you, or, at the very least, not to bore you past endurance.'

Drawing into his conscious mind the legends he had read since he was a child and the stories he had learned while captive in Kashgar, Peter sat up straighter, in conscious imitation of the storytellers, drew a deep breath, and began his tale.

M. J. ENGH

The Lovesick Simurgh

There was a Persia, you know, a dozen centuries before Mohammed came out of his desert to talk of the One God. And long before he was born, prophets had made known to Persians the workings of the universe. Some would say that Zarathustra, who listened to Darkness as well as to Light, was in a better position to give a balanced picture than Mohammed, whose only information came from angels. Mani, too, who visited the Seventh Heaven long before Mohammed arrived there, was well aware that the One Good God does not have everything his own way.

Nowadays, of course, it would be imprudent to do or say anything of which Mohammed could not approve. But thoughts are free, and a thought can fly like a simurgh.

When the Roman emperor Valerian was captured at the battle of Edessa and made to serve King Shapur as his undergroom, offering his back as a step when the king mounted his horse, one of the bronze eagles that topped the Roman standards was brought home to the king's bedroom in Ctesiphon as a decoration for the foot of the king's bed. In that position, it faced the golden and enamelled simurgh that watched over the head of the bed. The eagle was deeply mortified, and heaved a brazen sigh.

'My emperor,' it said, 'will avenge these outrages.'

'Your emperor,' replied the simurgh, 'is much too busy. He is downstairs mucking out the stables. If he proves himself adept at handling horse shit, he may in time be allowed to try his hand with a currycomb.'

'The empire,' said the eagle, drawing itself up, 'is never without a head. At this moment, the emperor's son, Gallienus, a tried and proven soldier, is emperor at home. He will be preparing an expedition to rescue his father.'

'What empire is that?' enquired the simurgh. 'Oh, you're still talking about those whippersnappers the Romans. No, I don't think your Gallienus is preparing an expedition.'

The eagle, which was accustomed to gaze unblinking at the noonday sun, stared fiercely at the simurgh. 'Why should I listen,' it demanded, 'to a barbarous creature like you? You seem to have the muzzle of a dog, and the manners to go with it, though your tail is a peacock's.'

'I am a simurgh,' the simurgh answered, 'and for that reason alone you should listen to me – since, far from being a barbarous creature, I was a guardian of kings when your emperors' ancestors were small-time pig farmers trying to steal their neighbour's acorns. More to the point, perhaps, you cannot help listening to me while nothing separates us but the length of the royal bed. And on my Oriental side,' it added, preening its multicoloured feathers, 'I am akin to the Chinese dragon, as you may note by my scales and hind talons.'

The eagle gave a snort of disdain.

The simurgh wrinkled its lip, half showing its teeth. 'Surely even Roman eagles,' it said, 'have heard of the silk of China, since it is in hopes of controlling the Silk Road that you make war so often and so fruitlessly against Persia.'

The eagle's eyes flashed scorn. 'What can you know,' it cried, 'of Roman policy or Roman warfare? I travel with the legions and share their dangers, while you perch in an overheated bedroom. When you see the Emperor Gallienus come marching into Ctesiphon, you'll change your tune.'

'Wrong on all points,' said the simurgh. 'But I like your spirit. Indeed, I find you uncommonly attractive.'

At that moment King Shapur entered in state, for it was the royal bedtime, and lamps and candles and torches made such a blaze of light that the simurgh's tail coruscated like molten jewels. The eagle kept its head proudly upright; and for some time after the guards and servants had withdrawn, leaving only two or three women with the king in bed, it did not deign to lower its eyes beneath the horizon of its beak. But bit by bit the noises from the bed overcame its stern reserve, until presently it was watching as avidly as the simurgh.

At last the simurgh cleared its throat. 'You were saying?' it remarked.

The eagle, which had not been saying anything when their conversation had been broken off, took this as a sign of weakness on the simurgh's part. 'Everything I've heard about the lascivious depravity of Persia,' it said, 'seems to have been understated.'

'Morality, like politics, is essentially local,' the simurgh rejoined. 'The homosexual excesses to which so many Romans are addicted would be considered bizarre in Persia. But some things are universal.' Its golden eyes half closed, and the tip of its forked tongue touched its lips. 'For a Roman,' it purred, 'you are exquisitely appealing.'

The eagle flexed its talons. 'I am, of course, a she-eagle,' it said.

'That is of no concern to me,' said the simurgh, 'since I, like all perfect beings, am hermaphroditic.'

The eagle shuddered. 'I have always heard,' it said, 'that Persia is the land of monsters. What a relief it will be when the Emperor Gallienus arrives!'

'Forget your Emperor Gallienus!' the simurgh exclaimed impatiently. 'He is in Milan, attempting to negotiate a truce with the successful rebels in Gaul. But you are here with me.' And its tongue flickered.

'You know nothing of the Emperor Gallienus,' the eagle said stiffly.

'I have powers,' said the simurgh, 'beyond the comprehension of mere birds. At this very instant, I could bring the Emperor Gallienus, or at least a spiritual copy of him, to this very bedroom.'

At these words, the eagle quivered with excitement,

and its eyes grew very large and piercing. The simurgh licked its chops, quivering with an excitement of its own. 'Do you doubt me, beautiful and primitive creature?' it cried. 'See, and marvel!'

No sooner had it spoken than the Emperor Gallienus appeared at the bedside. He was unshaven, he looked tired though not particularly grief-stricken, and he peered around him at the half-dark bedroom with considerable interest. 'Am I in Persia?' he asked.

'You are in the bedroom of the King of Kings, Shapur the Conqueror,' announced the simurgh.'

Gallienus had not expected an answer to his question, which had been inspired by the unfamiliar furnishings, and he was especially surprised to be answered by a mythological creature made of gold and enamel. But he was an emperor, and knew how to accept the unexpected. 'I suppose, then,' he said, 'that these people sleeping in the bed are King Shapur and some of his friends, wives or servants; and that that eagle at the bed's foot is from one of the standards captured with my father. Is the old gentleman still alive?'

The eagle, which was holding itself rigidly at attention, uttered a shrill warcry. 'O glorious commander-in-chief,' it cried, 'your imperial father is alive and unhurt, and only awaits your coming with another army to set him free.'

'I am relieved,' said Gallienus. 'And I am glad to see that the Roman military spirit still lives in you. But my father is an emperor, and will understand that I have other things to do than rush around the world repairing the damage caused by his foreign adventurism.'

The eagle's cry had wakened King Shapur, but he lay silent and motionless, only opening his eyelids a crack. The women still slept, for they were not royal, and so had not heard the eagle. The simurgh laughed, making the colours of its peacock tail flash and wink. 'You are wise,' it told Gallienus. 'Although I suspect that the wisdom of Romans is usually accidental.'

'I am a student of war, politics and philosophy,' said Gallienus. 'Moreover, I have a wife.'

'So do most men,' said the simurgh. 'But that does not seem to have increased the prevalence of wisdom.'

'Ah, but those men,' said Gallienus, 'are not married to Salonina.'

At that, the Lady Salonina appeared beside him, a very regal woman with her hair let down for bed. She looked closely at King Shapur. 'This man is only pretending to be asleep,' she observed.

The King opened his eyes and sat up, wrapping a sheet around himself for modesty. 'Madam,' he said, 'when I wake to find strangers at my bedside in the middle of the night, prudence outweighs hospitality. But I see that you and your husband, although my deadliest enemies, are merely spirits, phantoms or dreams, and there is no need for me to call in my guards.'

Solonina and Gallienus exchanged glances. 'Nothing is further from my mind,' said Gallienus, 'than a war with Persia.'

'Then why do you mention it?' asked Shapur.

'Because it was in *your* mind, King Shapur,' said Salonina, and all three of them laughed, to the bewilderment of the eagle.

'You are new to this business of ruling, Gallienus,' Shapur began, with the air of one preparing to give advice.

'No, I am not,' said Gallienus. 'I have worked side by side with my father since before he came to power, and I have been co-emperor with him for seven years. I am forty years old, which is said to be the time when a man's powers are at their height, and I am reliably informed that I have the blessing of heaven. No doubt I could punish Persia immediately and bring my father home in triumph; but I have business in the West which interests me more just now.'

'You and I,' said Shapur, 'are very nearly of an age, but I have been sole monarch and King of Kings for almost two decades. From my spies and your deserters I know that the Roman dominions have been incessantly racked by civil wars and torn by revolts for many years. I know that at this moment you are trying to retrieve the western half of your so-called empire from the hands of a rebel. Why should I not press home my victories and smash the power of Rome for ever?'

'Your father, like mine,' said Gallienus, 'came to his throne by force of arms. My father, like yours, has worked hard to ensure the succession to his sons and grandsons – or at least to give them a fighting chance at it. Did you know that I am the first legitimate heir to ascend the throne in a quarter century that has seen a dozen emperors? I mean for my son to be the second.'

'And if my father-in-law's seven years seems short to you,' said Salonina, 'consider that his predecessors' reigns were measured in months.'

'Both your father-in-law and your husband have been unusually lucky,' said Shapur, 'as Roman luck goes.'

'We like to think that more than luck is involved,' said Gallienus.

King Shapur laughed. 'The blessing of heaven? I doubt that. The blessing of heaven is reserved for those who understand the workings of the universe. To you Romans, who worship a veritable chaos of squabbling deities, the universe must appear chaotic indeed. Small wonder that your dominions are so ungovernable. But Persians know that the tension between the two great powers of Light and Dark keeps the fabric of the universe stretched taut and strong, and what sometimes seems like chaos is only an ornamental design embroidered upon it.'

'The empire is like a sea,' said Salonina. 'The storms that sweep its surface are scarcely noticed in the serene depths. And even at the surface, those storms are only temporary aberrations of the unbroken level from which all altitudes are measured.'

'Your simile is pretty but not apt,' said Shapur. 'I think rather that your empire is a raft afloat on the stormy sea, and rapidly breaking up. And (to dispense with all figures of speech) now that I have seen you, if only in astral form, I am determined to crush your armies, kill your husband, and demonstrate to you that a Persian ruler is a better lover than a Roman. I can do all this because I have, in a very powerful and material form, that blessing of heaven about which your present husband prates.' And he gestured towards the simurgh above his head.

The simurgh, finding all eyes but the king's (and the sleeping women's) upon it, made itself exceedingly beautiful. The eagle stared at it with repugnance and fascination. The simurgh stretched its lionlike forepaws complacently, making the gold claws go in and out.

Salonina took Gallienus' hand. 'Anyone foolish enough to put it to the test,' she said, 'would find it extremely difficult to kill my husband without first killing me. And I wonder what you can know of heaven, you who have not studied it experimentally.'

'We are planning,' said Gallienus, 'to build a new city, founded and administered on the principles of philosophy, and directed by that young but brilliant Egyptian called Porphyry.'

'Who is the greatest philosopher since Plato,' Salonina added.

'Bird of Heaven, what do you say to that?' asked Shapur, casting his eyes upward to the simurgh.

'I say that Plato was a greedy child,' said the simurgh, 'who thought that whatever he fancied must be real, and whatever he disliked unreal. But Zarathustra the Wise knew that desire and revulsion, light and dark, are equally balanced, and for good reason.'

'There are always extremists,' said Shapur, 'like the followers of Mani, whom I have recently had to ban from my kingdom, who insist on shifting the balance all one way. They think that since light is good, then light without darkness must be better.'

'Or like the Christians whom my father forbade to practise their intolerant cult,' said Gallienus.

'And yet the balance must be shifted a little,' said Salonina, 'or that tension you spoke of would be as sterile as total darkness or unrelieved light. Without a little imbalance there would be nothing to keep the universe running and we would have a perfectly balanced death, or

304

rather nothingness. Porphyry understands this.'

'That is true,' said Gallienus. 'And that is why, now that my father is otherwise occupied, I am considering revoking his edicts against the Christians. I too know the Manichaeans, and fear them. They condemn the whole physical universe as evil, and consider it a sin to reproduce. A Manichaean state would be depopulated in one generation. But the Christians are less absolute and therefore less dangerous.'

'It makes little difference what you decide,' said Shapur, 'since your laws will soon be replaced by mine. And in the interest of getting an early start on our war, I want a good night's sleep. Excuse me – until we meet, more efficaciously, in the flesh.' And he lay down and pulled the silken coverlet to his chin.

Gallienus and Salonina exchanged smiles that looked a little troubled. King Shapur began to snore.

'Don't worry,' said the simurgh. 'This was only a dream for the king, and he will remember nothing of it when he wakes. For that matter, you will remember nothing when I send you back to your bodies, which I am about to do.'

'Wait,' said Gallienus. 'While I am here, in some sense, let me see my father.'

'Why?' demanded the simurgh. 'Until this moment, you have seemed profoundly unconcerned by his captivity.'

'If I have seemed unconcerned,' said Gallienus, 'it is because he is in no more danger here than in his own dominions. If he manages to achieve a natural death, he will be the first emperor in decades not to have been either murdered or killed in civil war. I am content to leave him in captivity, both for that reason and because I want a free hand to pursue my own policies, which are better than his. But we have worked together for a long time, we have been as good friends as is possible for a father and son who are both emperors, and – even if neither of us will remember it an hour from now – I would like to see the old gentleman one more time and tell him the things I have forgotten to say in forty years. He is a tough old bird, and can probably handle anything the Persians may do to him; but I would like to see him nonetheless.'

'No,' said the simurgh. And before Gallienus could speak again, both he and Salonina vanished.

The eagle gave a shriek of indignation and beat its bronze wings thunderously, but the sleepers barely stirred. 'Can even a barbarous monstrosity be so cruel?' it cried. 'Why did you deny his request?'

'A matter of simple justice,' said the simurgh impatiently. 'Every day, millions of sons and daughters are denied that very request by the accidents of circumstance. Why should your emperor be excepted from the laws of life? Besides, and more urgently, I wanted to be alone with you.'

The eagle stiffened. 'We are not alone,' it observed formally.

The simurgh made a vulgar noise. It spread its glittering tail, showed its fangs, and made clutching motions with its paws and talons. Then, to the eagle's surprise, it uttered a heartrending groan. 'Beautiful and primitive creature,' it exclaimed, 'I adore you, I am sick with love for you, I yearn to embrace you. But we are separated for ever by the length of this bed. If only you could fly!'

'Of course I can fly,' said the eagle, and spread its wings. In fact it had never flown before, being only the bronze top-piece of a standard, but then it had never before conversed with a simurgh, a king, an empress, or an emperor, and it felt that on this night it could do anything. It was surprised, therefore, to find that it could not budge from its place at the bed's foot.

The simurgh laughed hollowly. There was a fevered gleam in its golden eyes. 'Would you have come to me, my pretty nestling?' it cried.

'Certainly not,' said the eagle. 'I would have flown back to my legion, or what is left of it.'

'Ah, faithless one!' cried the simurgh. 'Or rather, too faithful! My only comfort is that you cannot fly away from me.'

'And mine,' said the eagle, 'is that if I cannot fly, apparently neither can you.'

The simurgh lifted its muzzle and gave forth a desolate howl that raised the hackles on the eagle's neck. 'Do you imagine that I am so powerless?' it said, when it had collected itself a little. 'Like a thought, I can fly in an instant to any spot in the universe. If I could believe that you might share my passion, I think that – But no, I will stay at my post.'

At this, a chill ran through the eagle. 'What do you mean?' it asked faintly.

The simurgh groaned. 'I mean that night after night I perch, as you so prettily put it, in this overheated bedroom, watching and listening to the satisfaction of amorous passions, while my own are only aroused. And when now at last I am presented with an object worthy of my desire, I find it an added torture. I cannot fly to you, my love, because I must not leave the head of this bed. Here, beneath my sheltering wings, are conceived the thoughts, dreams, plans by which Persia is governed. Left to himself, without my equilibrating influence, this king would plunge into all-out war with Rome. It is to prevent that, my darling, that I deny myself the enjoyment of your beautiful person.'

'But you are contemptible in every way!' exclaimed the eagle. 'I had supposed that at least you were loyal to Persia.'

'I am the very spirit of Persia, the wisdom of Persia, heaven's blessing upon Persia,' said the simurgh. 'There is no Persia and no loyalty without me.'

'Then why,' said the eagle, 'do you try to prevent your king from continuing a war in which he has so far been victorious?'

'Do you remember nothing of what has been said here tonight?' the simurgh answered. 'The civilization of this world hangs upon two great poles, the strength of Persia and the strength of Rome, and is sustained by the tension between them. For centuries, the occasional war has served to keep the tension screwed tight and to redress temporary imbalances. But King Shapur, potent as he is in battle, is too headstrong. If he were to push forward his war now, it is just possible that he might succeed in breaking the power of Rome for ever, and civilization would topple into ruin.'

The eagle shuddered. 'So it would,' it agreed devoutly.

'Far more likely,' the simurgh went on, 'such a war would only provoke the retaliation that your emperor and empress are so wisely reluctant to make, and it would be the power of Persia that was for ever broken.' This time the simurgh itself shuddered, and the enamels of its tail grew dull for a moment.

But the eagle's eyes gleamed suddenly in the light of the dying lamps. 'Far more likely?' it murmured. 'I believe you are as wise as you are handsome.' And it began to preen the feathers of its throat and breast.

'Does it matter through which door ruin enters, once we have issued it an invitation?' cried the simurgh. 'Whether Persians dance on the grave of Rome, or Romans on the grave of Persia, the result will be the same – the collapse of commerce and learning, of philosophy and wealth.'

'How beautiful you are when you are excited,' said the eagle, which had passed all its days in military camps and barracks, and had no great opinion of civilization. And it fluffed its feathers and spread its tail provocatively.

The simurgh laughed a feverish laugh. 'So even the Roman bird of war is not immune to the effects of an overheated royal bedroom! And after all, what does the civilization of mere mortals matter, compared to the desires of such beings as you and I? Why should we care if the balance holds or not? Let the world plunge into the whirlpool of the absolute, where there is only one direction, for ever down, around and down!'

As it raved, the simurgh had begun a curious seesaw motion, rocking from side to side and kneading the bedstead with its leonine paws, while rainbows of iridescence scintillated along its scales. The eagle blinked and settled its feathers discreetly. The last lamp burned out, but an unearthly half-light still radiated from the head of the bed.

The simurgh, for the first time, had begun to spread its wings. 'What is it to us,' it pursued, 'whether that doomed and gallant city of philosophers is ever built among the battlefields? What is it to us if the marbles of Rome are burnt to make lime, and the holy scriptures of Zarathustra to heat cooking pots? But why do you shrink from me, my exquisite fledgling?'

'I do not shrink,' said the eagle grimly, and making every effort to look forbidding. 'No doubt some residual scrap of honour in you still shrinks from desertion of duty.'

Under the eagle's fierce glare the simurgh faded slightly, and settled back into a less amorous posture. 'You chide me all too properly,' it said, with a hollow laugh. 'But when you thought more of Roman victory than of human civilization, you were too seductive for me to resist. Are we to be trapped for ever, then, at opposite poles of the royal bed, racked between duty and desire, between Persia and Rome, between civilization and ruin?'

'My emperors,' said the eagle, 'are wise, and know what is best. I only follow orders.'

Here King Shapur awoke, and began looking under the bed for the royal chamberpot. 'Civilization, I suppose,' the eagle said to itself, 'is greater than Rome. And yet,' it added musingly, 'a dog's muzzle, a lion's paws, the tail of a peacock, and something like a dragon in between. There was nothing like that in the barracks.' And it tucked its head under its wing and began to dream.

SUSAN SHWARTZ

Ramadan, Again

Once Peter of Wraysbury finished his tale, he rose from his cushions, stripped off his robe, and knelt before the master of caravans whose men had saved his life.

'Oh my master,' he began, 'suffer me to speak. When your servants found me in the desert and took me up, giving me life where I had expected only death, I asked for grace to send a messenger to the lords of the West. You graciously allowed me the space of a thousand days – as in the old tales – for such a messenger to return with gold. Well, the time has come, and the messenger has not. Whether or not he yet lives is in the hands of God, and no matter for mere men. What is certain, however, is this: the time has come and I must fulfil my bond to you.'

At that moment he became aware that he knelt on but one knee, as was proper for vassals before their lords, not slaves before their masters. At the thought, he cast himself down upon both knees. Pulling off his headcloth, he bent his head until his bright hair swept against the rugs and the cool blue tiles.

The eldest storyteller turned to the master of caravans and to the old scholar who had entertained Peter just that day. 'It is even as you said, oh prince among merchants and venerable sage. So, tell me, how is this tale to end?'

The scholar merely smiled. From the bosom of his robe he produced a small bundle wrapped in heavy silk, and held it out to the master of caravans. 'This, most noble host, is a copy of the Qur'an I have had since my pilgrimage to Mecca. It has been precious to me for its truth, not for the beauty of its calligraphy and the richness of its gilding. Yet I offer it to you as part of my friend's ransom.'

The rug merchant clapped his hands. His eldest apprentice entered the room, a rolled carpet across his left shoulder, its fringes dropping down on either side almost to his knees. He unrolled the carpet with a flourish, and the Tree of Paradise depicted thereon shone with such splendour that the lamplight itself appeared diminished and tawdry. 'This carpet,' said the rug merchant, 'may not possess the history – or the designs – of which I once, in a lewder moment, spoke, but it is well woven, the prize of last season's trading. And I offer it gladly for my friend.'

From sashes and sleeves, the jewel merchant and the goldsmith produced glistening treasure and cast it upon the jewel-like carpet. 'That,' declared the jewel merchant, 'is a diamond, the fabled gem of adamant.'

'And that,' said the goldsmith, 'is a necklace fit for the dowry of any empress.'

Yet you offer this for me, for my freedom? Peter asked, too moved to protest. He was glad that his suppliant's posture allowed him to hide his face – and his tears.

The Ch'in physician brought out a lacquer box filled with rare medicinal herbs. The silk merchant cast a roll of gauzy saffron veiling upon the rug. With an apology for having brought a weapon to a feast, the Mongol warrior drew his sword and, lifting a corner of the delicate silk, allowed it to drift down upon the blade, which instantly severed it. He grinned and drew his breath in satisfaction at the temper of the fine steel, then laid it at the caravan master's feet. The horsetrader rose and offered to take the caravan master to his stables, there to choose whatever horse he would, though the horsetrader himself would suggest a noble bay mare and her colt. All of the guests offered some treasure as part of the ransom.

'You do not wish, it appears,' said the eldest story-teller, 'that this stranger be sold as a slave.'

'He is no stranger,' said the scholar. 'He is our friend.'

'Then, my brothers,' said the storyteller, 'can we be less

311

than they?' He pulled a turquoise ring from his finger and cast it on to the heaps of treasure. His companions added a necklace and, from a turban, a brooch heavy with dark rubies.

Then all turned to face the master of the caravans.

'I cannot accept this treasure,' said he. 'For the western man Peter' – for a wonder, he got the name almost right – 'is no slave, but a guest of my house. But if it is treasure that you offer, then I ask that you offer it to him. Thus you enable your friend to support himself, and not live upon another man's bread. For though he is welcome in my house as a guest until the end of his days, I know that this galls him.'

'I vowed that I would be a slave if no ransom came,' said the knight, raising his head and dashing away his tears. He trembled as he rose again to his knees and supported himself with one chilled hand against the cool tiles of the floor. 'The ransom did not come, though the thousand days are come and gone. I am prepared to honour my pledge.'

'Here is your ransom, man!' cried the youngest story-teller. 'Here! And with it you have made such a tale as to win the hearts and the gold of sultans, khans, soldiers – and slaves. You may not refuse such a gift . . .'

As Peter of Wraysbury turned to the men who had become his friends and brothers, there came a great clamour outside the caravan master's house. That worthy rose from his brocade cushions. 'What broil is this in the street?' he demanded. 'Who is so unmannerly that he would break into a feast during Ramadan?'

That question was answered in the instant, as the carved wood doors flung apart and four men strode into the room. They were tall and their robes were frayed and stained with much travel. They made no bows nor gestures of courtesy, and when they spoke, their Arabic was faulty, harsh and more blunt than that tongue is wont to be.

Their hair was shaggy, and beneath the masks of dust and grime their faces seemed pale and their eyes light –

grey, or blue, or amber. Light eyes, Peter realized. Light eyes like his own. And, just like his own, their hair was fair.

They glanced about as if looking for a man they did not see. *How can they not know me?* Peter thought, then realized, *for that first instant, I did not know them.*

His astonishment faded and his manners returned. Quickly he rose to his feet. It felt strange to stride forward and bow to the newcomers, knight to knight. Judging from their looks of surprise, he seemed as strange to them as they to him.

'My lords,' said Peter, 'I bid you welcome to Kashgar, and to my master's house.' Sweet God, it had been years since he had spoken French. It felt strange in his mouth after the rolling compliments of Arabic.

'You *are* Peter of Wraysbury?.'

Again, he bowed, stifling a sly smile.

'Then we bring you this gold to buy you back from the heathen.'

As he had done earlier that evening, Peter of Wraysbury dropped to one knee. 'My lords,' he said, his voice husky, 'with all my heart I thank you. When you return to the West, commend me to your lords, and to my most noble lord, Edward of England, and pray tell them that I shall honour them and pray for them all the days of my life.'

'Take the gold, for God's sake, Wraysbury,' said the foremost knight. 'And then make your preparations to come back west with us. For surely – my God, Wraysbury, you cannot be planning to *stay* with these people!'

'They are not 'these people', sir,' said Peter. 'They are my brothers, as are you yourself. And I beseech you, speak in Arabic so that all my brothers, not just the scholars, may understand.'

He turned back to the master of caravans, the gold in his hands. 'My master,' he said, 'here is the gold for which I hoped. I pray you to accept it, and to grant me my freedom.'

'Oh my guest, honoured in my house,' began the

merchant, 'how may I grant you that which is already yours?' The master of caravans smiled. 'I had no dream, now or ever, of selling you as a slave. Rather, though, I delighted to see how a man of the West faced hardship. You have been cheerful in adversity, as all the tales commend unto us. You have been as faithful as the healer, as truthful as the truthsayer, and as wise as many a greybeard. Thus, it is fitting that honour – and this treasure – be yours. As for your freedom, you were born with it.'

'Then, my brothers and my friends,' asked Peter, 'may I beg that you will accept this gold, not as payment for your treasures, for since they are your gifts, they are beyond price, but as the gift of one friendly heart to others?'

The assembled men all shook their heads. Peter had heard polite refusals before. This one looked as though it was sincere.

The assembled knights grimaced. 'God's wounds, Wraysbury,' interrupted one of them. 'Can you not understand? Accept the fact that you are a rich man and come home with us.'

Peter of Wraysbury smiled. For the first time since the bandits had sacked the caravan in which he rode, he felt warm, not from heat, but from satisfaction and joy. 'Indeed, my lord, I may not do that, for I am still sworn to a quest. Have you forgotten that before God and man, I swore to seek out John, priest and king, where he holds court in Asia? That vow still holds.'

The knights broke ranks, and Peter saw that behind them stood the priests, crosses in hands, horror on their faces. One fumbled in his scrip to produce a much-folded document.

'By God, Wraysbury, that story is an old fraud. You know that some man or other – but not a fabulous priest–king – sent an embassy to Edward of England.'

'I was there,' said Peter of Wraysbury. 'Aye, he asked him for aid for the Holy Land.'

'Well, since then His Holiness Innocent IV has sent messengers to one of these khans, and the messengers were lucky to have escaped with their whole skins.'

The priest stepped forward and handed Peter the document he had produced.

'Read this,' he said.

Peter bent over the letter. The ink was very faint, but still readable.

'By order of the Supreme Khan, Bachu Noyon send these words – Pope, dost thou know that thine envoys have come to us with thy letters? Thine envoys have uttered big words. We know not whether they did so by thine order. So, we sent thee this message. If thou desirest to reign over the land and water, thy patrimony, thou must come thyself, Pope, to us, and present thyself before him who reigns over the surface of all the earth. And if thou comest not, we know not what will happen. God knows. Only, it would be well to send messengers to say whether thou wilt come or not, and whether thou wilt come in friendship or no.'

'God knows?' asked the Mongol officer. 'That is not a question, it is a warning. Your Pope's envoys have put him in double danger by their big words.'

The priests blenched. 'The hordes once again? God spare us!'

Peter looked about, but there was, of course, no wine to offer them.

'Wait,' he said. 'It is hardly for me to order things in my master's – very well then, lord, in my host's house. But if I may speak, then I would ask those haughty knights and priests to sit and to wash the dust of their journey from them, and feast with us. And then, perhaps, they might be permitted to rest before they return to the West and bear to my lord my decisions.

'I have sworn a vow to find Prester John. Yet my lord has sent gold and, it seems, is eager for me to resume my service to him. If, as seems true, the khan is wroth with the West, how better may I serve my lord than by serving as a messenger myself and trying to set things right? And that is what I have decided to do.

'My friend,' he turned to the caravan master, 'you have

refused treasures and gold, both from my hands and from the hands of my friends simply because the greatest treasure of all – a man's freedom – is not yours to sell. But will you accept this gold from me, not as ransom, but as one partner to another? When your caravan next leaves Kashgar to cross the desert, I would join it, not as a slave, nor yet as a driver, but as one of its masters. For I must go to Ch'in and seek out Prester John. And though I myself am but a poor storyteller, I would tell the khan this wondrous tale of a thousand nights and a ransom.'

Ramadan ended, and from the gates of Kashgar departed the caravans. To the west plodded men of the West. And to the east, accompanied by soldiers, merchants and tale-tellers, rode Peter of Wraysbury. New silver spurs gleamed at his heels. He rode the spirited bay mare that had been the horsetrader's gift, and wore the Mongol officer's sword, and he was dressed (and jewelled) as finely as a merchant prince. He saluted his partner. Then, from the eastward gate of Kashgar he rode, bound for Ch'in and to seek out Prester John.

To learn more about
the world of the *Arabian Nights*
compiled by Sandra Miesel

Versions of the Arabian Nights

Arabian Nights: Unexpurgated Edition. trans. Sir Richard Burton. New York, in press (reprinted from the edition of 1885–88)

Tales from The Thousand and One Nights. trans. N. J. Dawood. Penguin Classics, 1973

The Thousand and One Nights. trans. Edward William Lane, ed. Stanley Lane-Poole. 4 vols. New York, 1926 (reprinted from the edition of 1839–41)

Michaud, Roland and Michaud, Sabrina. *India of One Thousand and One Nights*. Thames & Hudson, 1986

Historical-cultural surveys

Holt, P. M., etc. *The Cambridge History of Islam*. 4 vols. Cambridge, 1978

The Genius of Arab Civilization, Source of Renaissance. ed. John R. Hayes. Kegan Paul International, 1983

Hodgson, Marshall G. *The Venture of Islam*. 3 vols. Chicago, 1977

Islam and the Arab World. ed. Bernard Lewis. New York, 1976

Peters, F. E. *Allah's Commonwealth: A History of Islam in the Near East 600–1100 A.D.* New York, 1973

Von Grünebaum, Gustave E. *Medieval Islam: A Study in Cultural Orientation*. 2nd edn. Chicago, 1953

Watt, W. Montgomery. *The Majesty That Was Islam*.
Sidgwick & Jackson, 1974

Religion

Arberry, A. J. *The Koran Interpreted*. New York, 1970 Allen
& Unwin, 1981
The Koran. trans. N. J. Dawood. Baltimore, 1956 Penguin
Classics, 1970
Nicholson, Reynold A. *Studies in Islamic Mysticism*.
Cambridge University Press, 1979 (reprinted from the edition
of 1921)
Rauf, Mohammed Abdul. *Islam, Creed and Worship*.
Washington, 1974
Schimmel, Annemarie. *Mystical Dimensions of Islam*. Univ.
N. Carolina, 1975

Literary culture

Arberry, A. J. *Aspects of Islamic Civilization as Depicted in
the Original Texts*. Ann Arbor, 1967
Knappert, J. *Islamic Legends: Histories of the Heroes, Saints,
and Prophets of Islam*. 2 vols. London, 1985
Nicholson, Reynold A. *A Literary History of the Arabs*.
Cambridge University Press, 1969 (reprinted from the edition
of 1907)
Schimmel, Annemarie. *As Through a Veil: Mystical Poetry in
Islam*. New York, 1982

Literature in translation

Attar, Farid ud-Din. *The Conference of the Birds*. trans.
Afkhan Darbandi and Dick Davis, Penguin Classics, 1984
Chelkowski, Peter J. *Mirror of the Invisible World: Tales
from the* Kamseh *of Nizami*. New York, 1975
Firdausi of Tus. *The Epic of the Kings: Shah-nama*. trans.
Reuben Levy, revised Amin Banani. Routledge, 1985
Kritzeck, J. *Anthology of Islamic Literature*. New York, 1964
Translations of Eastern Poetry and Prose. Reynold A.
Nicholson. C. E. Bosworth, Curzon (reprint of 1922 edition),
1987

Arts and architecture

Blunt, Wilfred. *The Splendors of Islam*. New York, 1976
Burckhardt, Titus. *Art of Islam: Language and Meaning*.
Trans. P. Hobson. World of Islam Festival Publishing Co.,
1976
Du Ry, Carel J. *Art of Islam*. trans. Alexis Brown, New
York, 1970
The Treasures of Islam. ed. Toby Falk. New York, 1985
Kühnel, Ernst. *The Minor Arts of Islam*. trans. Katherine
Watson. Ithaca, 1971
Lings, Martin. *The Koranic Arts of Calligraphy and
Illumination*. World of Islam Festival Pub. Co., 1976
Moynihan, Elizabeth B. *Paradise as a Garden: In Persia and
Mughal India*. New York, 1979
Schimmel, Annemarie. *Calligraphy and Islamic Culture*.
New York, 1984

Facsimiles of illuminated books

Schimmel, Annemarie and Welch, Stuart Cary. *Anvari's
Divan: A Pocketbook for Akbar*. New York, 1983
Séguy, Marie-Rose. *The Miraculous Journey of Mahomet*.
New York, 1977
Welch, Stuart Cary. *A King's Book of Kings*. Thames &
Hudson, 1972

Society

Ahsan, M. M. *Social Life Under the Abbasids*. Longman,
1979
Lane, Edward William. *Arabian Society in the Middle Ages:
Studies from the Thousand and One Nights*. ed. Stanley
Lane-Poole. C. E., Bosworth, Curzon, 1987 (reprint
edition)
Lapidus, Ira. *Muslim Cities in the Later Middle Ages*.
Cambridge Univ. Press, 1984, 1967
Levy, Reuben. *The Social Structure of Islam*. Cambridge
University Press, 1957

Natural and occult sciences

Nasr, Seyyed Hossein. *An Introduction to Islamic*

Cosmological Doctrines. Thames & Hudson, 1981
——. *Islamic Science: An Illustrated Study*. Luzac, 1976
——. *Science and Civilization in Islam*. Cambridge, Mass., 1966

Military Life

Mayer, L. A. *Islamic Armourers and Their Work*. Geneva, 1962
——. *Saracenic Heraldry*. Oxford, 1933
Parry, V. J. and Yapp, M. E. eds. *War, Technology and Society in the Middle East*. OUP, 1975

About the authors

M. J. Engh, also known as Mary Jane Engh, former librarian, is author of the novels *Arslan* and *Wheel of the Winds*. She has travelled in Italy, France, Yugoslavia and Turkey, stalking the noble Roman lady Galla Placidia whose life story she is currently writing.

William Forstchen, a finalist from Maine for the Teacher in Space Program, is a writer, lecturer and space activist. Author of the Ice Prophet series, as well as a recent comic space opera, Bill is a Central Asia specialist who is plotting a four-book series on the Mongol Conquests. His most recent books are concerned with gaming; one involves Alexander the Great

Esther Friesner is the witty and prolific author of the Twelve Kingdoms series, and the award-winning *Harlot's Ruse*, as well as the modern fantasy *New York by Knight*, a trilogy to be published by Ace Books, and a number of short stories. She earned her PhD from Yale University and is currently researching a novel set during the fourteenth century.

Tanith Lee, winner of the World Fantasy Award, the August Derleth Award, and many others, is one of the most versatile writers working in the fields of fantasy and science fiction. Equally adept at writing fantasy or SF, short stories or novels, she is known for tales of werewolves, vampires, amorous robots, and the Arabian Nights-like stories of a melancholy Death and his attendant demons.

Sandra Miesel is the author of *Dreamrider*, a novel of alternative timelines, and of studies of J. R. R. Tolkien, Poul Anderson and Gordon Dickson, as well as numerous articles in newspapers, magazines and encyclopaedias, and a short story which appeared in *Moonsinger's Friends*. A paleographer, columnist, and editorial consultant both for Tor and for Baen Books, she is currently working on a doctorate in medieval history at Indiana University.

Larry Niven has won the 1971 Hugo and Nebula awards for *Ringworld*, the culmination of his Tales of Known Space series, as well as the 1976 Hugo for best novella, and the 1966, 1971 and 1974 awards. Though he is known especially for his high-tech science fiction and for his collaborations with Jerry Pournelle – most recently *Footfall*, a Hugo nominee – he is also the author of some fine fantasies, among them *Inferno, The Magic Goes Away,* and *The Magic May Return.*

Andre Norton, winner of the Gandalf and the Balrog, is also a Grand Master of the Science Fiction Writers of America. One of the most popular writers in the field, Andre Norton has written fantasy and SF for both adults and children. Among the series for which she is best known are the Witch World series (soon to be increased by four anthologies written by other writers), the Time Traveller series, and the books about the Solar Queen. With Robert Adams, she is editor of the four volumes of *Magic in Ithkar*.

Elizabeth Scarborough is one of the brightest and funniest of the newer fantasy writers. A former army nurse in Vietnam, she is now a full-time writer. Among her books are the series introduced by *Song of Sorcery*, and followed by *Bronwyn's Bane*, and *The Christening Quest, The Drastic Dragon of Draco, Texas* and, derived from the Arabian Nights themselves, *The Harem of Aman Akbar.*

Melissa Scott was the 1986 winner of the John Campbell Award for best new writer. Among her books are *The Game Beyond, Five-Twelfths of Heaven, Silence in Solitude, the Empress of Earth, The Kindly Ones* and *A Choice of Destinies*, the story of an alternative Earth in which Alexander the Great went *west* and took on Rome. This is her first published short story. She is currently completing her dissertation on military history at Brandeis University.

Susan Shwartz is also editor of *Hecate's Cauldron, Habitats* and *Moonsinger's Friends*. She is author of numerous short stories and novelets, the Heirs to Byzantium trilogy, *Silk Roads and Shadows*, as well as many articles and reviews that have been published in *Vogue, the New York Times, the Washington Post* and *Connoisseur*. An Arthurian specialist who earned her PhD at Harvard, she is currently working on a novel of Han-dynasty China with Andre Norton. Her story *Temple to a Minor Goddess* was a Nebula nominee.

Nancy Springer is author of the Isle trilogy (*The White Hart, The Silver Swan* and *The Sable Moon*). In addition to a young adult novel, her most recent publications are *Chains of Gold* and *Wings of Flame*, set in a fantasy kingdom reminiscent of Persia, and in which horses are sacred. She is an accomplished horsewoman. Her story *The Boy Who Plaited Manes* was a Nebula and Hugo nominee.

Judith Tarr is author of the Hound and the Falcon trilogy (*Isle of Glass, The Golden Horn* and *Hounds of God*) as well as of the Avaryan Rising trilogy, plus a handful of extremely well-received short stories, among them 'Defender of the Faith' and 'Piece de Résistance'. Writing and Schooling an Arabian horse are her passions. In 1988, she completed her dissertation on Medieval Latin at Yale University. She has won the Crawford Award for fantasy.

Harry Turtledove earned a PhD in Byzantine studies at UCLA, then took a job as technical writer for the Board of Education in California, and – some time in between working and helping to raise two children – sold a tetralogy to Del Rey, a novel set in an alternative Byzantium to Davis Publications, and numerous short stories, especially to *Analog*.

Gene Wolfe, a former mechanical engineer, is best known as the author of the Book of the New Sun series. Winner of the Nebula, the World Fantasy, and the Campbell awards (to name but a few), he is also author of *Soldier of* *the Mist, The Isle of Doctor Death* and *Free Live Free*, as well as almost a hundred short stories.

Jane Yolen, author of many short stories and more than one hundred books for wise children and adults of all ages, is also a poet, a ballad-singer, and a noted lecturer. She is very probably America's answer to Hans Christian Andersen. Among her books are *The Girl Who Cried Flowers*, nominated for the National Book Award, the comical Commander Toad series, the adult SF novel *Cards of Grief*, and the collections *Merlin's Booke*, *Neptune Rising*, and *Dragonfields*.